THE DEATH OF THE HEART

Elizabeth Bowen was born in Dublin in 1899, the only child of an Irish lawyer and landowner. She was educated at Downe House School in Kent. Her book *Bowen's Court* (1942) is the history of her family and their house in County Cork, and *Seven Winters* (1943) contains reminiscences of her Dublin childhood. In 1923 she married Alan Cameron, who held an appointment with the BBC and who died in 1952. She travelled a good deal, dividing most of her time between London and Bowen's Court, which she inherited.

She is considered by many to be one of the most distinguished novelists of the present age. She saw the object of a novel as 'the non-poetic statement of a poetic truth' and said that 'no statement of it can be final'. Her first book, a collection of short stories, *Encounters*, appeared in 1923, followed by another, *Ann Lee's*, in 1926. *The Hotel* (1927) was her first novel, and was followed by *The Last September* (1929), *Joining Charles* (1929), another book of short stories, *Friends and Relations* (1931), *To the North* (1932), *The Cat Jumps* (short stories, 1934), *The House in Paris* (1935), *The Death of the Heart* (1938), *Look at All Those Roses* (short stories, 1941), *The Demon Lover* (short stories, 1945), *The Heat of the Day* (1949), *Collected Impressions* (essays, 1950), *The Shelbourne* (1951), *A World of Love* (1955), *A Time in Rome* (1960), *After-Thought* (essays, 1962), *The Little Girls* (1964), *A Day in the Dark* (1965) and her last book *Eva Trout* (1969).

She was awarded the CBE in 1948, and received the honorary degree of Doctor of Letters from Trinity College, Dublin, in 1949 and from Oxford University in 1956. In the same year she was appointed Lacy Martin Donnelly Fellow at Bryn Mawr College in the United States. In 1965 she was made a Companion of Literature by the Royal Society of Literature. Elizabeth Bowen died in 1973.

THE
DEATH OF THE HEART

Elizabeth Bowen

PENGUIN BOOKS

Penguin Books Ltd, Harmondsworth, Middlesex, England
Viking Penguin Inc., 40 West 23rd Street, New York, New York 10010, U.S.A.
Penguin Books Australia Ltd, Ringwood, Victoria, Australia
Penguin Books Canada Limited, 2801 John Street, Markham, Ontario, Canada L3R 1B4
Penguin Books (N.Z.) Ltd, 182–190 Wairau Road, Auckland 10, New Zealand

—

First published in Great Britain by Jonathan Cape 1938
Published in Penguin Books 1962
Reprinted 1979, 1981, 1984 (twice), 1986

—

—

First published in the United States of America by
Alfred A. Knopf, Inc., 1939

—

—

Printed and bound in Great Britain by
Cox & Wyman Ltd, Reading

Contents

Part One

THE WORLD

I

THAT morning's ice, no more than a brittle film, had cracked and was now floating in segments. These tapped together or, parting, left channels of dark water, down which swans in slow indignation swam. The islands stood in frozen woody brown dusk: it was now between three and four in the afternoon. A sort of breath from the clay, from the city outside the park, condensing, made the air unclear; through this, the trees round the lake soared frigidly up. Bronze cold of January bound the sky and the landscape; the sky was shut to the sun – but the swans, the rims of the ice, the pallid withdrawn Regency terraces had an unnatural burnish, as though cold were light. There is something momentous about the height of winter. Steps rang on the bridges, and along the black walks. This weather had set in; it would freeze harder tonight.

On a footbridge between an island and the mainland a man and woman stood talking, leaning on the rail. In the intense cold, which made everyone hurry, they had chosen to make this long summerlike pause. Their oblivious stillness made them look like lovers – actually, their elbows were some inches apart; they were riveted not to each other but to what she said. Their thick coats made their figures sexless and stiff as chessmen: they were well-to-do, inside bulwarks of fur and cloth their bodies generated a steady warmth; they could only see the cold – or, if they felt it, they only felt it at their extremities. Now and then he stamped on the bridge, or she brought her muff up to her face. Ice pushed down the channel under the bridge, so that while they talked their reflections were constantly broken up.

He said: 'You were mad ever to touch the thing.'

7

'All the same, I feel sure you would have, St Quentin.'

'No, I doubt that. I never do want to know, really, what anyone thinks.'

'If I'd had the slightest idea –'

'However, you did.'

'And I've seldom been more upset.'

'Poor Anna ! . . . How did you find it, though?'

'Oh, I wasn't looking for it,' said Anna quickly. 'I should far rather not know that the thing existed, and till then, you see, I'd had no idea that it did. Her white dress came back with one of mine from the cleaners; I unpacked mine because I wanted to put it on, then, as Matchett was out that day, I took hers up to hang it up in her room. Portia was out at lessons, of course. Her room looked, as I've learnt to expect, shocking: she has all sorts of arrangements Matchett will never touch. You know what some servants are – how they ride one down, and at the same time make all sorts of allowance for temperament in children or animals.'

'You would call her a child?'

'In ways, she's more like an animal. I made that room so pretty before she came. I had no idea how blindly she was going to live. Now I hardly ever go in there; it's simply discouraging.'

St Quentin said rather vaguely: 'How annoying for you!' He had screwed round his head inside the folds of his scarf, to consider Anna with abstract attentiveness. For she had this little way of travestying herself and her self-pities, till the view she took of herself, when she was with him, seemed to concert exactly with the view he took of her sex. She wrote herself down like this, obligingly, to suit him, with a touch of friendly insolence. He saw in this over-acting a kind of bluffing, which made him like Anna, whom he liked much more. Her smoothness of contour, her placid derisive smile, her way of drawing her chin in when she did smile, often made him think of a sardonic bland white duck. But there seemed no doubt at this moment that, beyond acting, she was really put out: her chin was tucked inside her big fur collar, and under the fur cap she wore peaked forward her forehead was wrinkled up. She was looking down unhappily at her muff, with her fine blonde lashes cast on her cheek; now and then a hand came out of her muff and she dabbed at the tip of her nose with a handkerchief. She could feel St Quentin looking, but took no notice: she detected the touch of malice in his pity for women.

'All I did,' she went on, 'when I had hung her dress up, was to take one look round, rather feeling I ought. As usual, my heart sank; I really did feel it was time I took a line. But she and I are on such curious terms – when I ever do take a line, she never knows what it is. She is so unnaturally callous about *objects* – she treats any hat, for instance, like an old envelope. Nothing that's hers ever seems, if you know what I mean, to belong to her: which makes it meaningless to give her any present, unless it's something to eat, and she doesn't always like that. It may be because they always lived in hotels. Well, one thing I had thought she'd like was a little *escritoire* thing that came from Thomas's mother's – her father may well have used it. I'd had that put in her room. It has drawers that lock and quite a big flap to write on. The flap locks too: I hoped that would make her see that I quite meant her to have a life of her own. You know, though it may seem rash, we even give her a latchkey. But she seems to have lost the keys – nothing was locked, and there was no sign of them.'

'How annoying!' said St Quentin again.

'It was indeed. Because if only – However ... Well, that wretched little *escritoire* caught my eye. She had crammed it, but really, stuffed it, as though it were a bin. She seems to like hoarding paper; she gets almost no letters, but she'd been keeping all sorts of things Thomas and I throw away – begging letters, for instance, or quack talks about health. As Matchett would say, it gave me rather a turn.'

'When you opened the desk?'

'Well, it looked so awful, you see. The flap would not shut – papers gushed out all round it and even stuck through the hinge. Which made me shake with anger – I really can't tell you why. So I scooped the papers all out and dropped them into the arm-chair – I intended to leave them there, then tell her she must be tidy. Under the papers were some exercise books with notes she had taken at her lessons, and under the exercise books this

9

diary, which, as I say, I read. One of those wretchèd black books one buys for about a shilling with *moiré* outsides ... After *that*, of course I had to put everything back the way it was.'

'Exactly as it had been?'

'Exactly, I'm quite certain. One may never reproduce the same muddle exactly, but she would never know.'

There was a pause, and St Quentin looked at a seagull. Then he said: 'How inconvenient it all is!'

Inside her muff, Anna drove her hands together; raising her eyes she looked angrily down the lake. 'She's made nothing but trouble since before she was born.'

'You mean, it's a pity she ever was?'

'Well, naturally, I feel that at the moment. Though I would rather, of course, that you didn't say so – she is Thomas's sister after all.'

'But don't you think perhaps you exaggerate? The agitation of seeing something quite unexpected often makes one think it worse than it is.'

'That diary could not be worse than it is. That is to say, it couldn't be worse for me. At the time, it only made me super-ficially angry – but I've had time since then to think it over in. And I haven't quite finished yet – I keep remembering more things.'

'Was it very ... unkind?'

'No, not meant to be that. No, she'd like to help us, I'm sure.'

'Then, mawkish, you mean?'

'I mean, more, completely distorted and distorting. As I read I thought, either this girl or I are mad. And I don't think I am, do you?'

'Surely not. But why should you be so upset if it simply shows what is the matter with her? Was it affected?'

'Deeply hysterical.'

'You've got to allow for style, though. Nothing arrives on paper as it started, and so much arrives that never started at all. To write is always to rave a little – even if one did once know what one meant, which at her age seems unlikely. There are ways and ways of trumping a thing up: one gets more dis-

'I see,' said St Quentin shortly. Drumming with stiff, gloved fingers on the bridge rail, he frowned down at a swan till it vanished under the bridge. His eyes, like the swan's, were set rather near in. He broke out: 'Fancy her watching me! What a little monster she must be. And she looks so aloof. Does she think I try to be clever?'

'She said more about your being always polite. She does not seem to think you are a snake in the grass, though she sees a good deal of grass for a snake to be in. There does not seem to be a single thing that she misses, and there's certainly not a thing that she does not misconstruct. In fact, you would wonder, really – How you do stamp, St Quentin! Are your feet so cold? You make the bridge shake.'

St Quentin, abstracted and forbidding, suggested: 'We might walk on.'

'I suppose we ought to go in,' Anna admitted, sighing. 'Though you see, *now*, why I'd rather not be at home?'

St Quentin, stepping out smartly, showed one of his quick distastes for more of the lake scene. The cold was beginning to nip their features, and to strike up through the soles of their feet. Anna looked back at the bridge regretfully: she had not yet done saying what she began there. Leaving the lake behind them, they made for the trees just inside the park fence. The circle of traffic tightens at this hour round Regent's Park; cars hummed past without a break; it was just before lighting-up time – quite soon the All Out whistles would sound. At the far side of the road, dusk set the Regency buildings back at a false distance: against the sky they were colourless silhouettes, insipidly ornate, brittle, and cold. The blackness of windows not yet lit or curtained made the houses look hollow inside ... St Quentin and Anna kept inside the park railings, making towards the corner where she lived. Interrupted in what she had been saying, she swung disconsolately her black muff, walking not quite in step with him.

St Quentin always walked rather too fast – sometimes as though he did not like where he was, sometimes as though resolved to out-distance any attraction of the hour or scene. His erect, rather forbidding carriage made him look old-fashioned, criminating, not necessarily more honest. *I* should know, after all.'

'I am sure you do, St Quentin. But this was not a bit like your beautiful books. In fact it was not like *writing* at all.' She paused and added: 'She was so odd about me.'

St Quentin, looking frustrated, started feeling about for his handkerchief. He blew his nose and went on, with iron determination: 'Style is the thing that's always a bit phony, and at the same time you cannot write without style. Look how much goes to addressing an envelope – for, after all, it's a matter of set-out. And a diary, after all, is written to please oneself – therefore it's bound to be enormously written up. The obligation to write it is all in one's own eye, and look how one is when it's almost always written – upstairs, late, overwrought, alone … All the same, Anna, it must have interested you.'

'It opened at my name.'

'So you read straight on from there?'

'No, it opened at the last entry; I read that, then went back and started from the beginning. The latest entry was about dinner the evening before.'

'Let's see: had you a party?'

'No, no: much worse than that. It had been simply her and me and Thomas. She must have bolted upstairs and written everything down. Naturally, when I'd read that I went back to the beginning, to see what had got her into that state of mind. I still don't see why she wrote the thing at all.'

'Perhaps', said St Quentin mildly, 'she's interested in experience for its own sake.'

'How could she be, yet? At her age, look how little she's got. Experience isn't interesting till it begins to repeat itself – in fact, till it does that, it hardly *is* experience.'

'Tell me, do you remember the first sentence of all?'

'Indeed I do,' Anna said. ' "*So I am with them, in London*".'

'With a comma after the "them"? … The comma is good; that's style … I should like to have seen it, I must say.'

'Still, I'm glad you didn't, St Quentin. It might make you not come to our house again. Or, if you did still come, it might make you not talk.'

even military – but this was misleading. He was tall, wore his dark, rather furry hair *en brosse*, and had a small Gallic moustache. He entered rooms with the air of a man who, because his name is well known, may find himself involved in some situation from which his nature revolts – for writers find themselves constantly face to face with persons who expect to make free with them, and St Quentin, apart from the slackish kindness he used with Anna and one or two other friends, detested intimacy, which, so far, had brought him nothing but pain. From this dread of exposure came his tendencies to hurry on, to be insultingly facile, to misunderstand perversely. Even Anna never knew when St Quentin might feel he was being presumed upon – but he and she were on the whole on such easy terms that she had given up caring. St Quentin liked her husband, Thomas Quayne, too, and frequented the Quaynes like a ghost who had once understood what married good feeling was. In so far as the Quaynes were a family, St Quentin was the family friend. Today, unnerved by having said too much, breathless from the desire to say more, Anna wished that St Quentin did not walk so fast. Her best chance to speak had been in keeping him still.

'How very unlike Thomas!' St Quentin said suddenly.

'What is?'

'She must be, I mean.'

'Very. But look what different mothers they had. And poor Mr Quayne, quite likely, never counted for much.'

St Quentin repeated: ' "So I am with them, in London". *That's* what is so impossible,' he said.

'Her being with us?'

'Could it not have been helped?'

'Not when she had been left to us in a will – or in a dying request, which is not legal, and so worse. Dying put poor Mr Quayne in a strong position for the first time in his life – or, at least, for the first time since Irene. Thomas felt very strongly about his father's letter, and even I felt bound to behave well.'

'I do doubt, all the same, whether those accesses of proper feeling ever do much good. You were bound to regret this one. Did you really imagine the girl would enjoy herself?'

'If Mr Quayne had had anything besides Portia to leave us,

the situation might not have been so tricky. But anything that he died with went, of course, to Irene, then, after *her* death, to Portia – a few hundreds a year. With only that will to make, he could not make any conditions: he simply implored us to have his daughter in what seemed (when he was dead like that, when we got the letter) the most quavering voice. It was Thomas's *mother*, you know, who had most of the money – I don't think poor Mr Quayne had ever made much – and when Thomas's mother died *her* money came straight to us. Thomas's mother, as no doubt you remember, died four or five years ago. I think, in some curious way, that it was her death, in the distance, that finished poor Mr Quayne, though I daresay life with Irene helped. He and Irene and Portia, all more and more piano, trailed up and down the cold parts of the Riviera, till he caught a chill and died in a nursing home. A few days before he died, he dictated that letter to us about Portia to Irene, but Irene, detesting us – and I must say with some reason – put it away in her glove-box till she died herself. Of course, he had only meant it to come into effect in case of anything happening to Irene: he didn't mean us to take the kitten from the cat. But he had foreseen, I suppose, that Irene would be too incompetent to go on living for long, and of course he turned out to be right. After Irene's death, in Switzerland, her sister found the letter and posted it on to us.'

'What a number of deaths in Thomas's family!'

'Irene's, of course, was a frank relief – till we got the letter and realized what it would mean. My heavens, what an awful woman she was!'

'It embarrassed Thomas, having a stepmother?'

'Irene, you know, was not what anybody would want at all. We tried to overlook that for Thomas's father's sake. He felt so much in the wrong, poor old man, that one had to be more than naturally nice to him. Not that we saw him much: I don't think he felt it right to see very much of Thomas – because he so wanted to. He said something one day when we all had lunch at Folkestone about not casting a shadow over our lives. If we had made him feel that it didn't matter, we should have sunk in his estimation, I'm sure. When we met – which I must confess was only two or three times – he did not behave at all like Thomas's father, but like an off-the-map, seedy old family friend who doubts if he has done right in showing up. To punish himself by not seeing us became second nature with him : I don't think he *wanted* to meet us, by the end. We came to think, in his own way he must be happy. We had no idea, till we got that letter of his, that he'd been breaking his heart, all those years abroad, about what Portia was missing – or, what he thought she was missing. He had felt, he said in the letter, that, because of being his daughter (and from becoming his daughter in the way that she had) Portia had grown up exiled not only from her own country but from *normal, cheerful* family life. So he asked us to give her a taste of that for a year.' Anna paused, and looked at St Quentin sideways. 'He idealized us rather, you see,' she said.

'Would a year do much – however normal you were?'

'No doubt he hoped in his heart that we'd keep her on – or else, perhaps, that she'd marry from our house. If neither should happen, she is to go on to some aunt, Irene's sister, abroad ... He only *spoke* of a year, and Thomas and I, so far, have not liked to look beyond that. There are years and years – some can be wonderfully long.'

'You are finding this one is?'

'Well, it seems so since yesterday. But of course I could never say so to Thomas – Yes, yes, I know : that *is* my front door, down there. But must we really go in just yet?'

'As you feel, of course. But you'll have to some time. At present, it's five to four : shall we cross by that other bridge and walk once more round the lake? – Though you know, Anna, it's getting distinctly colder – After that, perhaps we might have our tea? Does your objection to tea (which I do frightfully want) mean that we're unlikely to be alone?'

'She just might go to tea with Lilian.'

'Lilian?'

'Oh, Lilian's her friend. But she hardly ever does,' said Anna, despondent.

'But look here, Anna, really – you must not let this get the better of you.'

'That's all very well, but you didn't see all she said. Also you know, you do always seem to think there must be some obvious way for other people to live. In this case there is really not, I'm afraid.'

Beside the criss-cross diagonal iron bridge, three poplars stood up like frozen brooms. St Quentin stopped on the bridge to tighten his scarf and shake himself down deeper into his overcoat – he threw a homesick glance up at Anna's drawing-room window: inside, he saw firelight making cheerful play. 'It all certainly does seem very complex,' he said, and with fatalistic briskness went on crossing the bridge. Ahead lay the knolls, the empty cold clay silence of inner Regent's Park beneath a darkening sky. St Quentin, not in an elemental mood, did not happily turn his back on a drawing-room as agreeable as Anna's.

'Not even complex,' said Anna. 'Stupid from the beginning. It was one of those muddles without a scrap of dignity. Mr Quayne stayed quite devoted to his first wife – Thomas's mother – and showed not the slightest wish to leave her whatever happened. Irene or no Irene, the first Mrs Quayne always had him in the palm of her hand. She was one of those implacably nice women whose niceness you can't get past, and whose understanding gets into every crack of your temperament. While he was with her he always felt simply fine – he had to. When he retired from business they went to live in Dorset, in a charming place she had bought for him to retire to. It was after some years of life in Dorset that poor Mr Quayne started skidding about. He and she had married so young – though Thomas, for some reason, was not born for quite a number of years – that he had had almost no time to be silly in. Also, I think, she must have hypnotized him into being a good deal steadier than he felt. At the same time she was a woman who thought all men are great boys at heart, and she took every care to keep him one. But this turned out to have its disadvantages. In the photographs taken just before the crisis, he looks a full-blooded idealistic old buffer. He looks impressive, silly, intensely moral, and as though he would like to denounce himself. She would never let him denounce himself, and this was rather like taking somebody's toys away. He used to say her belief in him meant everything, but probably it frustrated him a good deal. It *was* rather slighting, wasn't it?'

'Yes,' said St Quentin. 'Possibly.'

'Have I told you all this before?'

'Not as a story. Of course, I've inferred some things from what you've said.'

'As a story it really is rather long, and in a way it makes me rather depressed ... Well, what happened, happened when Mr Quayne was about fifty-seven, and Thomas at Oxford in his second year. They'd already been living in Dorset for some time, and Mr Quayne seemed to be settled for the rest of his life. He played golf, tennis, bridge, ran the Boy Scouts, and sat on several committees. In addition to that he had paved most of the garden, and when he'd done that she let him divert a stream. Much of his own company put him into a panic, so he was always dangling round after her. People in Dorset said it was good to see them together, because they were just like lovers. She had never cared very much for London, which was why she'd put pressure on him to retire young – I don't think the business had amounted to much, but it was the one thing he'd had that was apart from her. But once she got him to Dorset, she was so nice that she was constantly packing him off to London – that is to say, about every two months – to stay at his club for a few days, see old friends, or watch cricket or something. He felt pretty flat in London and always shot home again, which was very gratifying for her. Till one time, when for a reason that did not appear till later, he sent her a wire to say, might he stay on in London for a few days more? What had happened was that he had just met Irene, at a dinner party at Wimbledon. She was a scrap of a widow, ever so plucky, just back from China, with damp little hands, a husky voice, and defective tear-ducts that gave her eyes always rather a swimmy look. She had a prostrated way of looking up at you, and that fluffy, bird's-nesty hair that hairpins get lost in. At that time, she must have been about twenty-nine. She knew almost nobody, but because she was so plucky, someone had got her a job in a flower shop. She lived in a flatlet in Notting Hill Gate, and was a *protégée* of his Wimbledon friend's wife's. Mr Quayne was put beside her at dinner. At the end of the party Mr Quayne, all in a daze already, saw her back in a taxi to Notting Hill Gate, and was asked in for some Horlicks. No one knows what happened – still less, of course, why it did. But from that evening on, Thomas's father lost his head completely. He didn't go back to Dorset for ten days, and by the end of that time – as it came out later – he and Irene had already been very wicked. I often think of those dawns in Notting Hill Gate, with Irene leaking tears and looking for hairpins, and Mr Quayne sitting up denouncing himself. His wife was much too nice to have pretty ways, but I daresay Irene had plenty – if that is how you like them. I've no doubt she made the most fussy capitulations; she would make him feel she had never fallen before – and I should think it's likely she never had. She would not be everyone's money. You may be sure that she let Mr Quayne know that her little life was from now on entirely in his hands. By the end of those ten days he cannot have known, himself, whether he was a big brute or St George.

'At all events, he arrived back in Dorset at once pensive and bouncing. He started in digging a lily pond but at the end of a fortnight said something about a tailor, and went dashing off back to London again. This went on, apparently, all through that summer – he and Irene had met in May. When Thomas got back in June he noticed at once, he remembers, that his home was not what it was, but his mother never said anything. Thomas went abroad with a friend; when he got back in September his father was black depressed – it stood out a mile. He didn't once go to London while Thomas was home, but the little person had started writing him letters.

'Just before poor Thomas went back to Oxford, the bomb went off. Mr Quayne woke Thomas's mother up at two in the morning and told her the whole thing. What had happened I'm quite sure you can guess – Irene had started Portia. She had done nothing more about this, beyond letting him know; she had gone on sitting in Notting Hill Gate, wondering what was going to happen next. Mrs Quayne was quite as splendid as ever: she stopped Mr Quayne crying, then went straight down to the kitchen and made tea. Thomas, who slept on the same landing, woke to feel something abnormal – he opened his door, found the landing lights on then saw his mother go past with a tray of tea, in her dressing-gown, looking, he says, just like a hospital nurse. She gave Thomas a smile and did not say anything: it occurred to him that his father might be sick, but not that he had been committing adultery. Mr Quayne, apparently, made a night of it: he stood knocking his knuckles on the end of the big bed, repeating: "She is such a staunch little thing!" Then he routed out Irene's letters and three photographs of her, and passed Mrs Quayne the lot. When she had done with the letters and been nice about the photos, she told him that now he would have to marry Irene. When he took that in, and realized that it meant the sack, he burst into tears again.

'From the first, he did not like the idea at all. To get anywhere near the root of the matter, one has got to see just how dumb Mr Quayne was. He had not got a mind that joins one thing and another up. He had got knit up with Irene in a sort of a dream wood, but the last thing he wanted was to stay in that wood for ever. In his waking life he liked to be plain and solid; to be plain and solid was to be married to Mrs Quayne. I don't suppose he knew, in his own feeling, where sentimentality stopped and want began – and who *could* tell, with an old buffer like that? In any event, he had not foreseen ever having to put his shirt on either. He loved his home like a child. That night, he sat on the edge of the big bed, wrapped up in the eiderdown, and cried till he had no breath left to denounce himself. But Mrs Quayne was, of course, implacable: in fact by next day she had got quite ecstatic. She might have been saving up for this moment for years – in fact, I daresay she had been, without knowing. Mr Quayne's last hope was that if he curled up and went to sleep now, in the morning he might find that nothing had really happened. So at last he curled up and went to sleep. She probably didn't – Does this bore you, St Quentin?'

'Anything but, Anna; in fact, it curdles my blood.'

'Mrs Quayne came down to breakfast worn but shining, and Mr Quayne making every effort to please. Thomas, of course, saw that something awful had happened, and his one idea was to stave everything off. After breakfast, his mother said that he was a man now, walked him round the garden and told him the whole story in the most idealistic way. Thomas saw his father watching them round the smoking-room curtain. She made Thomas agree that he and she must do everything possible to help his father, Irene, and the poor little coming child. The idea of the baby embarrassed Thomas intensely on his father's behalf. Words still fail him for how discreditably ridiculous the whole thing appeared. But he was sorry about his father having to go, and asked Mrs Quayne if this *was* really necessary: she said it was. She had got the whole thing sorted out in the night, even down to the train he was to catch. She seemed to be quite taken with her idea of Irene: Irene's letters had gone down better with her than with Mr Quayne, who did not like things in writing. In fact, I'm afraid Mrs Quayne always liked Irene a good deal better than, later, she liked me. Mr Quayne's faint hope that the whole thing might be dropped, or that his wife might find some way to make it all right, must have been dispelled as he watched them walk round the garden. *He* was not allowed a say for one single minute – to begin with, he strongly disapproved of divorce.

'During the two days before his departure (during which he stayed in the smoking-room and had his meals sent in to him on a tray) Mrs Quayne's idealism spread round the house like flu. It very strongly affected poor Mr Quayne. All the kick having gone from the affair with Irene, he fell *morally* in love with his wife all over again. She had got him that way when he was twenty-two, and she got him again like that at fifty-seven. He blubbered and told Thomas that his mother was a living saint. At the end of the two days, Mrs Quayne had him packed for and sent him up to Irene by the afternoon train. Thomas was told off to drive him to the station: all the way, and while they waited on the platform, Mr Quayne said not a word. Just before the train started, he leaned out and beckoned as though he had something to say. But all he said was: "Bad luck to watch a train out." After that he bumped back into his seat. Thomas did watch the train out, and he said its blank end looked quite wretchedly futureless.

'Mrs Quayne went up to London the following day, and put the divorce proceedings on foot at once. It is even said that she called and had a kind word with Irene. She sailed back to Dorset all heroic reserve, kept the house on, and stayed there through it all. Mr Quayne, who detested being abroad, went straight to the south of France, which seemed to him the right place, and months later Irene joined him, just in time for the wedding. Portia was then born, in Mentone. Well, they stayed round about there, and almost never came home. Thomas was sent by his mother to visit them three or four times, but I think they all found it terribly lowering. Mr Quayne and Irene and Portia always had the back rooms in hotels, or dark flats in villas with no view. Mr Quayne never got used to the chill at sunset. Thomas saw he would die of this, and he did. A few years before he did die, he and Irene came back for a four months' visit to Bournemouth – I suppose Bournemouth because he knew no one there. Thomas and I went to see them two or three times, but as they had left Portia behind in France, I never met *her* till she came to live with us here.'

'Live? I thought she was only staying.'

'Whatever it's called, it comes to the same thing.'

'But why was she called Portia?'

Anna, surprised, said: 'I don't think we ever asked.'

Mr Quayne's love life had taken them round the lake. Already, the All Out whistles were blowing: an inch of park gate was kept open for them alone, and a keeper waited by it with such impatience that St Quentin broke into a stately trot. Cars slid lights all round the Outer Circle; lamps blurred the frosty mist from here to the Quaynes' door. Anna swung her muff more light-heartedly; she was less unwilling to go in to tea now.

2

THE front door of 2 Windsor Terrace brushed heavily over the mat and clicked shut. The breath of raw air that had come in with Portia perished on the steady warmth of the hall. Warmth stood up the shaft of staircase, behind the twin white arches. She slid books from under her elbow on to the console table, dropped her latchkey back into her pocket, and went to the radiator, tugging off her gloves. She just saw her reflection cross the mirror, but the hall was a well of dusk – not a light on yet, either upstairs or down. Everywhere, she heard an unliving echo: she entered one of those pauses in the life of a house that before tea time seem to go on and on. This was a house without any life above-stairs, a house to which nobody had returned yet, which, through the big windows, darkness and silence had naturally stolen in on and begun to inhabit. Reassured, she stood warming her hands.

Down there in the basement a door opened: there was an intent pause, then steps began to come up. They were cautious – the steps of a servant pleasing herself. Whitish, Matchett's long face and tablet of apron soared steadily up the dark of an arch. She said: 'Ah, so you're in?'

'This minute.'

'I heard you all right. You were very quick with that door. Likely you left that key outside in the lock again?'

'No, it's here, truly.' Portia scooped the key from her pocket.

'You didn't ought to carry that key in your pocket. Not loose like that – and with your money too. One of these days you'll go losing the lot. She gave you a bag, didn't she?'

'I feel such a goat with a bag. I feel so silly.'

Matchett said sharply: 'All girls your age carry bags.'

Vexed ambition for Portia made Matchett click her teeth; her belt creaked as she gave an irate sigh. The dusk seemed to baulk her; they could barely see each other – her hand went up decidedly to the switch between the arches. Immediately, Anna's cut-glass lamp sprang alight over their heads, dropping its complex shadow on the white stone floor. Portia, her hat pushed back from her forehead, stood askance under the light; she and Matchett blinked; there followed one of those pauses in which animals, face to face, appear to communicate.

Matchett stayed with her hand propped on the pillar. She had an austere, ironical, straight face, flesh padded smoothly over the strong structure of bone. Her strong, springy, lustreless hair was centre parted and drawn severely back; she wore no cap. Habitually, she walked with her eyes down, and her vein-marbled eyelids were unconciliating. Her mouth, at this moment stubbornly inexpressive, still had a crease at each end from her last unwilling smile. Her expression, her attitude were held-in and watchful. The monklike impassivity of her features made her big bust curious, out of place; it seemed some sort of structure for the bib of her apron to be fastened up to with gold pins. To her unconscious sense of inner drama, only her hands gave play: one hand seemed to support the fragile Regency pillar, the other was spread fanwise, like a hand in a portrait, over her aproned hip. While she thought, or rather, calculated, her eyes would move slowly under her dropped lids.

It was five to four. The cook, whose night out it was, lay in her afternoon bath: in front of the pantry mirror the parlour-maid, Phyllis, was trying on a new cap. These two girls in their twenties had been engaged by Anna, and formed, as it were, Anna's party below stairs. Matchett, on the other hand, had been not a matter of choice: she had been years in service in Dorset with Thomas Quayne's mother, and after Mrs Quayne's death had come on to 2 Windsor Terrace with the furniture that had always been her charge. A charwoman, Mrs Wayes, now came in to clean and polish, ostensibly leaving Matchett freer to maid Anna and Portia and valet Thomas. But Mrs Wayes's area was, in fact, jealously limited by Matchett – accordingly, Matchett kept longer hours than anyone in the house. She slept alone, next the box-room: across the same top landing the cook and Phyllis shared an airy attic with a view of Park Road.

By day, she exacted an equal privacy. The front of the basement had been divided into Phyllis's pantry and a slit of a sitting-room, which, by an arrangement Anna did not question,

Matchett occupied in her spare time. Boiling her own kettles
on her gas ring, she joined the kitchen party only for dinner: if
the basement door happened to be left open, you could hear the
fun break out when she had withdrawn again. Her superior
status was further underlined by the fact of her not wearing a
cap: the two girls took orders from Anna, Matchett suggestions
only. The two young servants did not resent Matchett – she
might be repressive, but kept herself to herself – they had learnt
that no situation is ever perfect, and Anna was as a mistress
amiable, even lax. No one knew where Matchett went on her
afternoons off: she was a countrywoman, with few friends here.
She never showed fatigue, except fatigue of the eyes: in her
sitting-room, she would sometimes take off the glasses she wore
for reading or sewing, and sit with one hand shading her forehead stiffly, like someone looking into the distance – but with
her eyes shut. Also, as though wishing to remain conscious of
nothing, she would at the same time often unbutton the tight
shoe-straps that cut into the arches of her feet. But mostly she
sat bolt upright, sewing, under the pulled-down electric light.

On the middle floors of the house, where she worked and
the Quaynes lived, her step on the parquet or on the staircase
was at the same time ominous and discreet.

It was five to four, not quite tea time yet. Portia, turning away
inconsequently and seriously, faced round once more to the
radiator and spread her fingers a few inches above it, so that the
hot vibration travelled up between. Her hands were still mottled
from the outdoor cold; her fingers had bloodless tips. Matchett
looked on in silence, then said: 'That's the way to give yourself chilblains. Those want rubbing – here, give me!' She came
over, took Portia's hands and chafed them, her big bones
grinding on Portia's painfully. 'Quiet,' she said. 'Don't keep
pulling away like that. I never saw a girl so tender to cold.'

Portia stopped wincing and said: 'Where's Anna?'

'That Mr Miller called, and they went out.'

'Then can I have tea with you?'

'She left word they'd be in at half past four.'

'O-oh,' said Portia. 'That's no good, then. Do you think she'll
ever be out?'

Matchett, impassively not replying, stooped to pick up one of Portia's woolly gloves. 'Mind and take these up,' she said. 'And those books too. Mrs Thomas spoke about those exercise books. Nothing does down here that isn't here for the look.'

'Has anything else been wrong?'

'She's been on about your bedroom.'

'Oh golly! Has she been in there?'

'Yes, she seemed quite put out,' said Matchett monotonously. 'She said to me this morning, did I not find dusting difficult with all that mess about? Your bears' party, she meant, and one and another thing. "Difficult, madam?" I said. "If I made difficulties, I should not be where I am." Then I asked if she had any complaint. She was putting her hat on – up in her room, it was. "Oh dear no," she said, "I was thinking of you, Matchett. If Miss Portia would put some of those things away –" I made no remark, so she asked for her gloves. She went half out of the door, then she gave me a sort of look. "Those arrangements are Miss Portia's hobbies, madam," I said. She said: "Oh, of course," and went out of the house. No more was said at the time. It isn't that she's so tidy, but she thinks how things look.'

Matchett's voice was flat and dispassionate: when she had done she folded her lips exactly. Letting her hair fall forward to hide her face from Matchett, Portia stooped over the table, getting her books together. Books under her arm, she stood waiting to go up.

'All I mean is', went on Matchett, 'don't give her more to pick on. Not for a day or two, till it passes off.'

'But what was she doing in my room?'

'I suppose she just took the fancy. It's her house, like it or not.'

'But she always says it's my room ... Has she touched things?'

'How would I know? What if she did? You didn't ought to have secrets, at your age.'

'I noticed some toothpowder had come off the top of one of my bears' cakes, but I thought that was the draught. I suppose I ought to have known. Birds know if you have been at their eggs: they desert.'

'And, pray, where would you desert to? – You'd better go on

25

up, if you don't want her and Mr Miller right in on top of you. They'll be in early, likely, with this cold.'

Portia, sighing, started up to her room. The solid stone staircase was so deep in carpet that her feet made no sound. Sometimes her elbow, sometimes her school-girlish overcoat, unbuttoned, brushed on the white wall. When she got to the first landing, she leaned down. 'Will Mr St Quentin Miller be having tea?'

'Why not?'

'He talks so much.'

'Well, then, he won't eat you. Don't you be so silly.'

Portia went on up, up the next flight. When the bedroom door had been heard shutting, Matchett returned to the basement. Phyllis was darting about in her saucy new cap, getting ready the tray for drawing-room tea.

When Anna, with St Quentin on her heels, came into the drawing-room it appeared to be empty – then by the light of one distant lamp and the fire they perceived Portia, sitting on a stool. Her dark dress almost blotted her out against a dark lacquer screen – but now she rose up politely, to shake hands with St Quentin. 'So here you are,' said Anna. 'When did you get back?'

'Just now. I've been washing.'

St Quentin said: 'How dirty lessons must be!'

Anna went on, with keyed-up vivacity: 'Had a nice day?'

'We've been doing constitutional history, musical appreciation, and French.'

'Goodness!' said Anna, glancing at the tea-tray set inexorably with three cups. She switched on all the other lamps, dropped her muff in a chair, came out of her fur coat, and peeled off the two *tricots* she had worn under it. Then she looked round with these garments hanging over her arm. Portia said: 'Shall I put those away for you?'

'If you would be angelic – look, take my cap as well.'

'How obliging ...' St Quentin said, while Portia was out of earshot. But Anna, propping her elbow on the mantelpiece, looked at him with implacable melancholy. In the pretty air-tight room with its drawn aquamarine curtains, scrolled sofa, and half-circle of yellow chairs, silk-shaded lamps cast light into the mirrors and on to Samarkand rugs. There was a smell of freesias and sandalwood: it was nice to be in from the cold park. 'Well,' St Quentin said, 'we shall all be glad of our tea.' Loudly sighing with gratification, he arranged himself in an armchair – crossed his legs, tipped up his chin, looked down his nose at the fire. By sitting like this, he exaggerated the tension they had found in the room, outside which he consciously placed himself. Everything so nearly was so pleasant – Anna rapped on the marble with her finger-nails.

He said: 'My dear Anna, this is only one of what will be many teas.'

Portia came back again; she said: 'I put your things on your bed: was that right?' For tea, she returned to her stool by the fire; here she sat with her plate on her knees, her cup and saucer on the parquet beside her – when she drank she stooped half way to meet her cup. Sideways on to the hearth she commanded an equal view of Anna on the sofa, pouring out tea and smoking, of St Quentin constantly wiping buttered toast from his fingers on to his handkerchief. Her look, steady, level, and unassuming, missed nothing the other two did. Once the telephone rang: Anna crossly reached round the end of the sofa to answer it.

'Yes, it is,' she replied. 'But I'm not here at tea time; I never am; I told you. I thought this was when you were so busy? Surely you ought to be? ... Yes, of course I have ... Must you really? ... Well six, then, or half past.'

'A quarter past,' put in St Quentin, 'I'm going at six.'

'A quarter past,' Anna said, and hung up with no change of face. She sat back again on the sofa. 'Such affectation. ...'

'Oh, no?' said St Quentin. They just glanced at each other.

'St Quentin, your handkerchief's terribly buttery.'

'Your excellent toast. ...'

'You wave it about so much – Portia, do you really like a stool without any back?'

'I like this particular stool – I walked all the way home, Anna.'

Anna did not reply; she had forgotten to listen. St Quentin said: 'Did you really? We just walked in the park. The lake's frozen,' he added, cutting himself some cake.

'Well, it can't be *quite*: I saw swans swimming about.'

'You are quite right: it's not frozen completely. Anna, what *is* the matter?'

'I'm sorry, I was just thinking. I hate my lax character. I hate it when people take advantage of it.'

'I'm afraid we can't do much about your character now. It must have set – I know mine has. Portia's so lucky; hers is still being formed.'

Portia fixed St Quentin with her blank dark eyes. An alarming vague little smile, already not quite childish, altered her face, then died. She went on saying nothing – St Quentin rather sharply recrossed his legs. Anna bit off a yawn and said: 'She may become anything ... Portia, what hundreds of bears you've got on your mantelpiece. Do they come from Switzerland?'

'Yes, I'm afraid they collect dust.'

'I didn't notice the dust; I just thought what hundreds there were. All hand-carved, I suppose, by the Swiss peasants ... I went in there to hang up your white dress.'

'If you'd rather, Anna, I could put them away.'

'Oh no, why? They seemed to be having tea.'

The Quaynes had a room-to-room telephone, which, instead of ringing, let out a piercing buzz. It buzzed now, and Anna put out a hand, saying: 'That must be Thomas.' She unhooked. 'Hullo? ... Yes, St Quentin is, at the moment. Very well, darling, soon.' She hung up the receiver. 'Thomas is back,' she said.

'You might have told him that I am just going. Does he want anything special?'

'Just to say he is in.' Anna folded her arms, leaned her head back, looked at the ceiling. Then: 'Portia,' she said, 'why don't you go down to Thomas in the study?'

Portia lit up. 'Did he say for me to?' she said.

'He may not know you are in. He'd be ever so pleased, I'm sure ... Tell him I'm well and will come down as soon as St Quentin goes.'

'And give Thomas my love.'

Getting up from the stool carefully, Portia returned her cup and plate to the tray. Then, holding herself so erect that she quivered, taking long soft steps on the balls of her feet, and at the same time with an orphaned unostentation, she started making towards the door. She moved crabwise, as though the others were royalty, never quite turning her back on them – and they, waiting for her to be quite gone, watched. She wore a dark wool dress, in Anna's excellent taste, buttoned from throat to hem and belted with heavy leather. The belt slid down her thin hips, and she nervously gripped at it, pulling it up. Short sleeves showed her very thin arms and big delicate elbow joints. Her body was all concave and jerkily fluid lines; it moved with sensitive looseness, loosely threaded together: each movement had a touch of exaggeration, as though some secret power kept springing out. At the same time she looked cautious, aware of the world in which she had to live. She was sixteen, losing her childish majesty. The pointed attention of St Quentin and Anna reached her like a quick tide, or an attack: the ordeal of getting out of the drawing-room tightened her mouth up and made her fingers curl – her wrists were pressed to her thighs. She got to the door, threw it ceremonially open, then turned with one hand on it, proudly ready to show she could speak again. But at once, Anna poured out another cup of cold tea, St Quentin flattened a wrinkle out of the rug with his heel. She heard their silence till she had shut the door.

When the door shut, St Quentin said: 'Well, we might do better than that. *You* did not do well, Anna – raving about those bears.'

'You know what made me.'

'And how silly you were on the telephone.'

Anna put down her cup and giggled. 'Well, it is something', she said, 'to be written up. It's something that she should find us so interesting. If you come to think of it, we are pretty boring, St Quentin.'

'No, I don't think I'm boring.'

'No, I don't either. I mean, I don't think I am. But she does, if you know what I mean, rather bring us up to a mark. She insists on our being something or other – what, I'm not quite sure.'

'A couple of cads – What a high forehead she's got.'

'All the better to think about you with, my dear.'

'All the same I wonder where she got that distinction. From what you say, her mother was quite a mess.'

'Oh, the Quaynes have it: one sees it in Thomas, really,' Anna said – then, palpably losing interest, curled up at her end of the sofa. Raising her arms, she shook her sleeves back and admired her own wrists. On one she wore a small soundless diamond watch. St Quentin, not noticing being not noticed, went on: 'High foreheads suggest violence to me ... Was that Eddie, just now?'

'On the telephone? Yes. Why?'

'We know Eddie is silly, but why must you talk to him in such a silly way? Even if Portia *were* here. "I'm not here; I never am here." *Tcha!*' said St Quentin. 'Not that it's my affair.'

'No,' Anna said. 'I suppose it isn't, is it?' She would have said more, had not the door opened and Phyllis sailed in to take away the tea. St Quentin looked at his handkerchief, frowned at the butter on it, and put it away again. They did not pretend to talk. When tea had gone, Anna said: 'I really ought to go down and talk to Thomas. Why don't you come too?'

'No, if he'd felt like me,' said St Quentin, without resentment, 'he'd have come up here. I shall go very soon.'

'Oh, I wanted to ask you – how is your book going?'

'Very nicely indeed, thank you very much,' said he promptly, extremely repressively. He added with some return of interest: 'What happens when you go down? Do you turn Portia out?'

'Out of her brother's study? How ever could I?'

Thomas Quayne had been standing near the electric fire, holding a tumbler, frowning, trying to shake the day off, when his half-sister came round the study door. Her face – hair back in a snood from the high temples, wide-apart unfocusing dark eyes – seemed to swim towards him over the reading lamp. To come in here at all was an act of intimacy, for this was Thomas's own room. He never studied down here, except in so far as his relaxation was studied, but the room had been called the study to suggest importance and quiet. It had matt grey walls, Picasso-blue curtains, armchairs and a sofa covered in striped ticking, tables for books, book-shelves, and a desk as large as a dinner-table. Having heard a step that was not Anna's, Thomas ground his feet pettishly into the goat's-hair rug.

'Oh, hullo, Portia,' he said. 'How are you?'

'Anna said you might like me to come down.'

'What's Anna doing?'

'Mr Miller is there. They're not doing anything special, I don't think.'

Shaking what was left of the drink round in his glass, Thomas said: 'I seem to be back early.'

'Are you tired?'

'No. No, I just got home.'

Portia stood with her hand on the back of an armchair; she ran one finger along a dark red stripe, then a grey stripe, looking down at the finger attentively. Then, as Thomas said nothing more, she came round the chair and sat down – drew up her knees, nursed her elbows, and stared forward into the red con-cavity of the electric fire. At the other end of the hearth-rug Thomas sat down also, and remained also staring, but staring at nothing, with a concentration of boredom and lassitude. Anyone other than Anna being near him, anyone other than Anna ex-pecting something gave Thomas, at this time of the evening, a sense of pressure he could hardly endure. He liked best, at this time of the evening, to allow his face to drop into blank lines. Someone there made him feel bound to give some account of himself, to put on some expression or other. Actually, between six and seven o'clock he thought or felt very little.

'It's freezing,' he unwillingly said at last. 'It bites your face off, out there.'

'Yes, it nearly bit mine off – and my hands too. I walked all the way home.'

'Do you know if Anna went out?'

'I think she walked in the park.'

'Mad,' said Thomas, with an intimate pleasure. He brought out his cigarette case and looked into it flatly: it was empty.

'Would you mind', he said, 'passing that cigarette box – No, just there by your elbow – What did you do today?'

'Would you like me to fill your case?'

'Oh, thank you so much: thanks – What did you say you'd been doing?'

'Constitutional history, musical appreciation, French.'

'Liking it? I mean, how are you getting on?'

'I do think history is sad.'

'More, shady,' said Thomas. 'Bunk, misfires, and graft from the very start. I can't think why we make such a fuss now: we've got no reason to expect anything better.'

'But at one time, weren't people braver?'

'Tougher, and they didn't go round in rings. And also there was a future then. You can't get up any pace when you feel you're right at the edge.'

Portia looked blank, then said: 'I know some French. I know more French than some of the other girls.'

'Oh well, that is always something,' said Thomas. His voice trailed off – slumped in his chair, across the fire from Portia, he sat slowly turning his head with an uneasy baited look, like an animal being offered something it does not like. Thomas had very dark hair, always brushed very flat, and decidedly drawn eyebrows, like his father's and Portia's. Like his father's, his expression was obstinate, but with a hint of deep indecision behind. His head and forehead were rather grandly constructed, but at thirty-six his amiable, mobile face hung already loosish over the bony frame. His mouth and eyes expressed something, but not the whole, of him; they seemed to be cut off from the central part of himself. He had the cloudy, at some moments imperious look of someone conscious of fulfilling his destiny imperfectly; he looked not unlike one of the lesser Emperors. Now, one hand balanced his tumbler on the arm of his chair, the other hung to the floor, as though rather vaguely groping for something lost. There was clearly, at this moment, nothing that Thomas was at all moved to say. The vibration of London was heard through the shuttered and muffled window as though one were half deaf; lamplight bound the room in rather unreal circles; the fire threw its hard glow on the rug. The house held such tense, positive quiet that he and she might have been all alone in it. Portia raised her head, as though listening to this.

She said: 'A house *is* quiet, after a hotel. In a way, I am not used to it yet. In hotels, you keep hearing other people, and in flats you had to be quiet for fear they should hear you. Perhaps that is not so in flats with a big rent, but in our flats we had to be very quiet, or else the landlord jumped out.'

'I didn't think the French minded.'

'When we took flats, they were in people's villas. Mother liked that, in case something should happen. But lately, we lived in hotels.'

'Pretty awful,' said Thomas, making an effort.

'It might be if you *had* ever lived in a house. But mother and I got fond of it, in some ways. We used to make up stories about the people at dinner, and it was fun to watch people come and go. Sometimes, we got to know some of the other people.'

Thomas absently said: 'I expect you quite miss all that.'

At that, she looked away in such overcome silence that he beat a tattoo on the floor with his hanging-down hand. He said: 'I realize much more than that, of course. It was rotten about your mother – things like that shouldn't happen.'

She said with quite surprising control: 'It's nice being here with you, though, Thomas.'

'I wish we could give you a better time. We could if you were grown-up.'

'But by that time perhaps I –'

She stopped, for Thomas was frowning into his empty tumbler, wondering whether to get another drink. Deferring the question, he turned to look doubtfully at the books stacked beside him at elbow-level, at the reviews and magazines balancing on their top. He rejected these after a glance, put his glass down and reached the *Evening Standard* from the edge of his desk. 'Do you mind', he said, 'if I just have a look at this?' He frowned at one or two headlines, stopped, put down the paper, went across to his desk, and defiantly jabbed a button of the house telephone.

'I say,' he said into the receiver, 'is St Quentin living here? ... Well, as soon as he does, then ... No, don't do that ... Yes, I suppose I am, rather.' He hung up the receiver and looked at Portia. 'I suppose I *am* back rather early,' he said.

But she only looked through him, and Thomas felt the force of not being seen ... What she did see was the *pension* on the crag in Switzerland, that had been wrapped in rain the whole afternoon. Swiss summer rain is dark, and makes a tent for the mind. At the foot of the precipice, beyond the paling, the lake made black wounds in the white mist. Precarious high-upness had been an element in their life up there, which had been the end of their life together. That night they came back from Lucerne on the late steamer, they had looked up, seen the village lights at star-level through the rain, and felt that that was their dear home. They went up, arm-in-arm in the dark, up the steep zigzag, pressing each others' elbows, hearing the night rain sough down through the pines: they were not frightened at all. They always stayed in places before the season, when the funicular was not working yet. All the other people in that *pension* had been German or Swiss: it was a wooden building with fretwork balconies. Their room, though it was a back room facing into the pinewoods, had a balcony; they would run away from the salon and spend the long wet afternoons there. They would lie down covered with coats, leaving the window open, smelling the wet woodwork, hearing the gutters run. Turn abouts, they would read aloud to each other the Tauchnitz novels they had bought in Lucerne. Things for tea, the little stove, and a bottle of violet methylated spirits stood on the wobbly commode between their beds, and at four o'clock Portia would make tea. They ate, in alternate mouthfuls, block chocolate and *brioches*. Postcards they liked, and Irene's and Portia's sketches were pinned to the pine walls; stockings they had just washed would be exposed to dry on the radiator, although the heating was off. Sometimes they heard a cow bell in the thick distance, or people talking German in the room next door. Between five and six the rain quite often stopped, wet light crept down the trunks of the pines. Then they rolled off their beds, put their shoes on, and walked down the village street to the viewpoint over the lake. Through torn mist they would watch the six o'clock steamer chuff round the cliff and pull in at the pier. Or they would attempt to read the names on the big still shut hotels on the heights opposite. They looked at the high chalets stuck on brackets of grass – they often used to wish they had field-glasses, but Mr Quayne's field-glasses had been sent home to Thomas. On the way home they met the cows being driven down through the village – kind cows, damp, stumbling, plagued by their own bells. Or the Angelus coming muffled across the plateau would make Irene sigh, for once she had loved church. To the little Catholic church they had sometimes guiltily been, afraid of doing the wrong thing, feeling they stole grace. When they left that high-up village, when they left for ever, the big hotels were just being thrown open, the funicular would begin in another day. They drove down in a fly, down the familiar zigzag, Irene moaning and clutching Portia's hand. Portia could not weep at leaving the village, because her mother was in such pain. But she used to think of it while she waited at the Lucerne clinic, where Irene had the operation and died: she died at six in the evening, which had always been their happiest hour.

A whir from Thomas's clock – it was just going to strike six. Six, but not six in June. At this hour, the plateau must be in snow, and but for the snow dark, with lights behind shutters, perhaps a light in the church. Thomas sits so fallen-in, waiting for Anna, that his clock makes the only sound in his room. But our street must be completely silent with snow, and there must be snow on our balcony.

'The lake was frozen this morning,' she said to him.

'Yes, so I saw.'

'But it broke up this afternoon; there were swans on it ... I suppose it will freeze again.'

St Quentin could be heard saying good-bye to Anna, outside in the hall. Thomas quickly picked up the *Evening Standard* and played at reading it. Portia pressed the palms of her hands to her eyes, got quickly up, and went to turn over books at a far table, so that she could keep her back to the room. The table toppled with books that had no place: Anna wanted this room to look cheerfully casual, Thomas made it formlessly untidy. When St Quentin had slammed the hall door on his own last remark, Anna came smiling into the study. Thomas seemed to

wait while he counted three, then he looked at her over the
Evening Standard.

'Well, darling,' said Anna, 'poor St Quentin has gone.'

'I hope you didn't turn him out?'

'Oh no,' said Anna vaguely, 'he just shot out in his usual way.'
She found Thomas's glass on the floor, and said: 'Have you
and Portia been having a drink?'

'No, that's only mine.'

'How I wish you'd put them on the table.' She raised her
voice: 'Oh, Portia, I hate to worry, but if they have given you
any homework, don't you think you ought to do it now? We
might all go to a movie later on.'

'I've got an essay to write.'

'My dear, you sound very snuffly. Did you catch cold today?'

Portia turned, at the table, and faced Anna – who stopped,
though with something further on the tip of her tongue. Lips
drawn in, clutching her belt, Portia, with stricken determination, walked straight past Anna out at the study door. Anna
went to the door to make sure it was shut, then exclaimed:
'Thomas, you've been making her cry.'

'Oh, was she? I think she's missing her mother.'

'Goodness!' said Anna, stricken. 'But what started her off?
Why is she missing her mother *now*?'

'You say I have no idea what people feel – how can I know
when they are going to?'

'In some way, you must have unsettled her.'

Thomas, who had been looking hard at Anna, said: 'If it
comes to that, you unsettle me.'

'No, but listen,' said Anna, catching hold of his hand but
holding it at a distance away from her, 'is she really missing
Irene? Because, if so, how awful. It's like having someone very
ill in the house. Oh yes, I can easily pity her. I wish I could
manage to like her better.'

'Or love her, even.'

'My dear Thomas, that's not a thing one can *mean* to do.
Besides, would you really like me to love her? To get wrapped
up in her, to wait for her to come in? No, you'd only like me

to seem to love her. But I'm not good at seeming – I was horrid to her at tea. But I had my reasons, I must say.'

'You don't have to remind me that you don't like this.'

'After all, she's in some way yours, and I married you, didn't I? Most people have something in their family. For God's sake don't get worked up.'

'Did I hear you say we'd got to go to a movie?'

'Yes, you did.'

'Why – now, Anna, why? We haven't stayed still for weeks.'

Anna, touching her pearls with an undecided hand, said: 'We can't all just sit around.'

'I don't see why not.'

'We can't all *three* sit around. It gets me down. You don't seem to know what it's like.'

'But she goes to bed at ten.'

'Well, it never *is* ten, as you know. I cannot stand being watched. She watches us.'

'I cannot see why she should.'

'I partly see. Anyhow, she makes us not alone.'

'We could be tonight,' said Thomas. 'I mean after ten.' With an attempt at calmness, he once more put his hand out – but she, one mass of nervosity, stepped clear. She posted herself at the far side of the fire, in her close-fitting black dress, with her folded arms locked, wrapped up in tense thought. For those minutes of silence, Thomas fixed on her his considering eyes. Then he got up, took her by one elbow, and angrily kissed her. 'I'm never with you,' he said.

'Well, look how we live.'

'The way we live is hopeless.'

Anna said, much more kindly: 'Darling, don't be neurotic. I have had such a day.'

He left her and looked round for his glass again. Meanwhile, he said to himself in a quoting voice: 'We are minor in everything but our passions.'

'Wherever did you read that?'

'Nowhere: I woke up and heard myself saying it, one night.'

'How pompous you were in the night. I'm so glad I was asleep.'

3

THOMAS QUAYNE had married Anna eight years ago. She used to visit friends near his mother's house in Dorset, so they had met down there. She was then an accomplished, on the whole idle girl, with various gifts, who tried a little of everything and had even made money. She posed as being more indolent than she felt, for fear of finding herself less able than she could wish. For a short time, she had practised as an interior decorator, but this only in a very small way – she had feared to commit herself, in case she could not succeed. She had been wise, for she had not really succeeded, even in that small way. She did not get many clients, and almost at once drew in, chagrined by the rebuff. She drew satirical drawings, played the piano sometimes, had read, though she no longer did, and talked a good deal. She did not play outdoor games, for she did nothing she did not happen to do casually and well. When she and Thomas first met, she was reticent and unhappy: she had not only failed in a half chosen profession but failed in a love affair. The love affair, which had been of several years' duration, had, when Thomas and she met, just come to a silent and – one might guess from her manner – an ignominious end. She was twenty-six when she married Thomas, and had been living with her father at Richmond, in an uphill house with an extensive view.

Thomas liked from the first her smiling, offhand melancholy, her good head, her good nature, an energy he detected under her indolence. Though ash blonde she had, in some way, the personality more of a dark woman. She was, in fact, the first blonde woman who had attracted Thomas: for one thing, he had always detested pinkness, but Anna had an opaque magnolia skin. Her well-built not very slender body moved with deliberation, well in her control. He was affected by the smoothness and unity of her manner, which just was not hard. Her clothes, as part of her style, also pleased and affected him.

Before they met, his few loves had been married women, and the suspicion, later the certainty, that Anna had already had a lover only made her seem kinder, less far from himself. He did not do well with young girls; he was put off by their candid expectancy. He dreaded (to be exact, he dreaded at that time) to be loved with any great gush of the heart. There was some nerve in his feeling he did not want touched: he protected it without knowing where it was. Already, when he met Anna, he had been thinking of marriage; his means would by now allow it; he did not like the stresses of an affair. Back in London from Dorset, he and Anna met often, alone or at the houses of mutual friends: they dropped into an idiom of sentimental teasing or of intimate sharpness with one another. When they agreed to marry, Thomas was happy enough, and Anna perfectly willing. Then they married: Thomas discovered himself the prey of a passion for her, inside marriage, that nothing in their language could be allowed to express, that nothing could satisfy.

Using capital transferred to him by his mother, Thomas had bought himself into, and now controlled with his partner, an advertising agency, Quayne and Merrett. The business did very well. Anything opportunist or flashy about the venture (of which old Mrs Quayne had not liked the idea, at first) was discounted by Thomas's solid, sub-imperial presence at his official desk. He got back the confidence of his father's associates – this business with no past soon took on, for the old men, an almost dusty prestige. Flair might be suspect, but they saluted ability: Thomas was a chip of better quality than the old block had been. Quayne and Merrett held their ground, then got more ground; Thomas showed weight, his partner, Merrett, acumen. The vivacious young men they needed were recruited by Merrett. From the business, and from interest on the residue of his mother's capital, Thomas derived, at present, an income of about two thousand five hundred a year. Anna, upon the death of her father, had succeeded to five hundred a year.

The Quaynes had expected to have two or three children: in the early years of their marriage Anna had two miscarriages. These exposures to false hopes, then to her friends' pity, had turned her back on herself: she did not want children now. She pursued what had been her interests before marriage in a leisurely, rather defended way. As for Thomas, the longer he lived, the less he cared for the world. He turned his face away from it, in on Anna. Now he was thirty-six, he could think of nothing with which he could have wished to endow a child.

When his father died, and then finally when Irene died, Thomas had felt himself disembarrassed. His mother had made a point of keeping Mr Quayne's photographs where they had always been, all over the Dorset house, as though the old gentleman were no more than away on some rather silly holiday. She spoke constantly, naturally, of 'Your father'. When *she* died, he discontinued his visits to the couple abroad, telling himself (and no doubt rightly) that these visits were not less embarrassing to Mr Quayne and Irene than they were to him. In those sunless hotel rooms, those chilly flats, his father's disintegration, his laugh so anxious or sheepish, his uneasiness with Irene in Thomas's presence, had filled Thomas with an obscure shame – on behalf of his father, himself, and society. From the grotesqueries of that marriage he had felt a revulsion. Portia, with her suggestion – during those visits – of sacred lurking, had stared at him like a kitten that expects to be drowned. Unavowed relief at the snuffing-out of two ignominious people, who had caused so much chagrin, who seemed to have lived with so little pleasure, had gone far to make Thomas accord with his father's wish. It was fair, it was only proper (he said when the letter came) that Portia should come to London. With obsessed firmness, he had stood out against Anna's objections. 'For one year,' he said. '*He* only said for a year.'

So they had done what was proper. Matchett, when she was told, said: 'We could hardly do less, madam. Mrs Quayne would have felt it was only right.'

Matchett had helped Anna get ready Portia's room – a room with a high barred window, that could have been the nursery. Standing up to look out of the window, you saw the park, with its map of lawns and walks, the narrow part of the lake, the diagonal iron bridge. From the bed – Anna tried for a moment with her head on the pillow – you saw, as though in the country, nothing but tops of trees. Anna had, at this moment before they met, the closest feeling for Portia she ever had. Later, she stood on a chair to re-set the cuckoo clock that had been hers as a child. She had new sprigged curtains made, but did not re-paper the room – Portia would only be in it for a year. Stuff from the two cupboards (which had made useful store-places) was moved to the box-room; and Matchett, who was as strong as a nigger, carried the little desk from another floor. Anna, fitting a pleated shade on the bed lamp, could not help remarking: 'This would please Mrs Quayne.'

Matchett let this pass with no comment of any kind: she was kneeling, tacking a valance round the bed. She never took up a remark made into the air – thus barring herself against those offhand, meaning approaches from which other people hope so much. She gave, in return for hire, her discretion and her un-stinted energy, but made none of those small concessions to whim or self-admiration that servants are unadmittedly paid to make. There were moments when this correctness, behind her apron, cut both ways: she only was not hostile from allowing herself no feeling at all. Having done the valance she got up and, with a creak of her poplin dress at the armpits, reached up and hung a wreathed Dresden mirror Anna had got from some-where on a nail above a stain on the wall. This was not where Anna meant the mirror to hang – when Matchett's back was turned she unostentatiously moved it. But Matchett's having for once exceeded her duties put Anna less in the wrong. When the room was ready, it looked (as she told St Quentin) very pretty indeed: it ought to be dear to Portia after endless hotels. There was something homely, even, about the faded paper – and also they added, at the last minute, a white rug by the bed, for the girl's bare feet. If Anna had fought against Portia's coming, she knew how to give her defeat style . . . Portia arrived as black as a little crow, in heavy Swiss mourning chosen by her aunt – back from the East in time to take charge of things. Anna ex-plained at once that mourning not only did not bring the dead back but did nobody good. She got a cheque from Thomas, took Portia shopping round London and bought her frocks, hats, coats, blue, grey, red, jaunty, and trim. Matchett, unpacking these when they came home, said: 'You have put her in colours, madam?'

'She need not look like an orphan: it's bad for her.'

Matchett only folded her lips.

'Well, what, Matchett?' Anna said touchily.

'Young people like to wear what is usual.'

Anna had been askance. The forecast shadow of Portia, even, had started altering things – that incident of the mirror had marked an unheard-of tendency in Matchett, to put in her own oar. She said, more defensively than she intended to: 'I've got her a dead white evening dress, and a black velvet one.'

'Oh, then Miss Portia is to dine downstairs?'

'Surely. She's got to learn to. Besides, where else could she eat?'

Matchett's ideas must date from the family house, where the young ladies, with bows on flowing horsetails of hair, supped upstairs with their governess, making toast, telling stories, telling each other's fortunes with apple peel. In the home of today there is no place for the miss: she has got to sink or swim. But Matchett, upstairs and down with her solid impassive tread, did not recognize that some tracts no longer exist. She seemed, instead, to detect some lack of life in the house, some organic failure in its propriety. Lack in the Quaynes' life of family custom seemed not only to disorientate Matchett but to rouse her contempt – family custom, partly kind, partly cruel, that has long been rationalized away. In this airy vivacious house, all mirrors and polish, there was no place where shadows lodged, no point where feeling could thicken. The rooms were set for strangers' intimacy, or else for exhausted solitary retreat.

The Marx Brothers, that evening at the Empire, had no success with Portia. The screen threw its tricky light on her unrelaxed profile: she sat almost appalled. Anna took her eyes from the screen to complain once or twice to Thomas: 'She doesn't think this is funny.' Thomas, who had been giving unwilling snorts, relapsed into gloom, and said: 'Well, they are a lowering lot.' Anna leaned across him: 'You liked Sandy Macpherson, didn't you, Portia? – Thomas, do kick her and ask if she liked Sandy Macpherson?' The organist still loudly and firmly playing had gone down with his organ, through floodlit mimosa, into a bottomless pit, from which *Parlez-Moi d'Amour* kept on faintly coming up till someone down there shut a lid on him. Portia had no right to say that people were less brave now ... Now the Marx Brothers were over, the three Quaynes dived for their belongings and filed silently out – they missed the News in order to miss the Rush.

Anna and Portia, glum for opposing reasons, waited in the foyer while Thomas went for a taxi. For those minutes, in the mirror-refracted glare, they looked like workers with tomorrow ahead. Then someone looked hard at Anna, looked back, looked again, registered indecision, raised his hat, and returned, extending a large anxious delighted hand. 'Miss *Fellowes*!'

'Major Brutt! How extraordinary this is!'

'To think of my running into *you*. It's extraordinary!'

'Especially as I am not even Miss Fellowes, now – I mean, I am Mrs Quayne.'

'Do excuse me –'

'How could you possibly know? ... I'm so glad we've met again.'

'It must be nine years plus. What a great evening we had – you and Pidgeon and I –' He stopped quickly: a look of doubt came into his eyes.

Portia stood by, meanwhile. 'You must meet my sister-in-law,' said Anna at once: 'Major Brutt – Miss Quayne.' She went on, not with quite so much assurance: 'I hope you enjoyed the Marx Brothers?'

'Well, to tell you the truth – I knew this place in the old days; I'd never heard of these chaps, but I thought I would drop in. I can't say I –'

'Oh, you find them lowering, too?'

'I daresay they're up to date, but they're not what I call funny.'

'Yes,' Anna said, 'they are up to date for a bit.' Major Brutt's eyes travelled from Anna's smiling and talking mouth, via the camellia fastened under her chin, to the upturned brim of Portia's hat – where it stayed. 'I hope', he said to Portia, '*you* have enjoyed yourself.'

Anna said: 'No, I don't think she did, much – Oh, look, my husband has got a taxi. Do come back with us: we must all

43

have a drink ... Oh, Thomas, this is Major Brutt' ... As they walked out two-and-two to the taxi, Anna said to Thomas out of the side of her mouth: 'Friend of Pidgeon's – we once had an evening with him.'

'*Did* we? I don't – When?'

'Not you and I, silly: I and Pidgeon. Years ago. But one really must have a drink.'

'Naturally,' said Thomas. Putting on no expression, he steered her by one elbow through the crowd at the door – for whenever you come out, you never avoid the Rush. In the taxi, infected by Major Brutt, Thomas sat bolt upright, looking hard at everything through the window in a military way. Whereas, Major Brutt, beside him, kept glancing most timidly at the ladies' faces flowering on fur collars in the dark of the cab. He remarked once or twice: 'I must say, this is an amazing coincidence.' Portia sat twisted sideways, so that her knees should not annoy Thomas. Oh, the charm of this accident, this meeting in a sumptuous place – this was one of those polished encounters she and Irene spied on when they had peeped into a Palace Hotel. As the taxi crawled into Windsor Terrace, she exclaimed, all lit up: 'Oh, thank you for taking me!'

Thomas only said: 'Pity you didn't like it.'

'Oh, but I did like being there.'

Major Brutt said firmly: 'Those four chaps were a blot – This where we stop? Good.'

'Yes, we stop here,' Anna said, resignedly getting out.

The afternoon mist had frozen away to nothing: their house, footlit by terrace lamps, ran its pilasters up into glassy black night air. Portia shivered all down and put up her hands to her collar; Major Brutt's smart clatter struck a ring from the pavement; he slapped his coat, saying: 'Freezing like billy-o.'

'We can slide tomorrow,' said Thomas. 'That will be jolly.' He scooped out a handful of silver, stared at it, paid the taxi, and felt round for his key. As though he heard himself challenged, or heard an echo, he looked sharply over his shoulder down the terrace – empty, stagy, E-shaped, with frigid pillars cut out on black shadow; a façade with no back. 'We're wonderfully quiet up here,' he told Major Brutt.

'Really more like the country.'

'For God's sake, let us in!' Anna exclaimed – Major Brutt looked at her with solicitude.

It was admirably hot and bright in the study – all the same, indoors the thing became too far-fetched. Major Brutt looked about unassumingly, as though he would like to say 'What a nice place you've got here,' but was not sure if he knew them well enough. Anna switched lamps on and off with a strung-up air, while Thomas, having said: 'Scotch, Irish, or brandy?' filled up the glasses on the tray. Anna could not speak – she thought of her closed years: seeing Robert Pidgeon, now, as a big fly in the amber of this decent man's memory. Her own memory was all blurs and seams. She started dreading the voice in which she could only say: 'Do you hear anything of him? How much do you see him, these days?' Or else, 'Where is he now, do you know?' Magnetism to that long-ago evening – on which Robert and she must have been perfect lovers – had made her bring back this man, this born third, to her home. Now Thomas, by removing himself to a different plane, made her feel she had done a thoroughly awkward thing. The pause was too long: it smote her to see Major Brutt look, uncertain, into his whisky, clearly feeling ought he not, then, to drink this? Ought he not to be here?

Otherwise, he could wish for nothing better. The Quaynes had both seen how happy he was to come. He was the man from back somewhere, out of touch with London, dying to go on somewhere after a show. He would be glad to go on almost anywhere. But London, these nights, has a provincial meanness bright lights only expose. After dark, she is like a governess gone to the bad, in a Woolworth tiara, tarted up all wrong. But a glamour she may have had lives on in exiles' imaginations. Major Brutt was the sort of man who, like a ghost with no beat, hesitates round the West End about midnight – not wanting to buy a girl, not wanting to drink alone, not wanting to go back to Kensington, hoping something may happen. It grows less likely to happen – sooner or later he must be getting back. If he misses the last tube, he will have to run to a taxi; the taxi lightens his pocket and torments him, smelling of someone else's woman's scent. Like an empty room with no blinds his imagination gapes on the scene, and reflects what was never there. If this *is* to be all, he may as well catch the last tube. He may touch the hotel porter for a drink in the lounge – lights half out, empty, with all the old women gone to bed. There is vice now, but you cannot be simply naughty.

'Well, here's luck,' Major Brutt said, pulling himself together, raising his glass boldly. He looked round at their three interesting faces. Portia replied with her glass of mild-and-soda: he bowed to her, she bowed to him, and they drank. 'You live here, too?' he said.

'I'm staying here for a year.'

'That's a nice long visit. Can your people spare you?'

'Yes,' Portia said. 'They – I –'

Anna looked at Thomas as much as to say, check this, but Thomas was looking for the cigars. She saw Portia, kneeling down by the fire, look up at Major Brutt with a perfectly open face – her hands were tucked up the elbows of her short-sleeved dress. The picture upset Anna, who thought how much innocence she herself had corrupted in other people – yes, even in Robert: in him perhaps most of all. Meetings that ended with their most annihilating and bitter quarrels had begun with Robert unguarded, eager – like that. Watching Portia she thought, is she a snake, or a rabbit? At all events, she thought, hardening, she has her own fun.

'Thanks very much, no: no, I never smoke them,' Major Brutt said, when Thomas at last found the cigars, Having lit his own, Thomas looked at the box suspiciously. 'These *are* going,' he said. 'I told you they were.'

'Then why don't you lock them up? It's Mrs Wayes, I expect; she has got a man friend and she's ever so good to him.'

'Has she been taking your cigarettes?'

'No, not lately: Matchett once caught her at it. Besides, she is far too busy reading my letters.'

'Why on earth not sack her?'

'Matchett says she is thorough. And thorough chars don't grow on every bush.'

Portia excitedly said: 'How funny bushes would look!'

'Ha-ha,' said Major Brutt. 'Did you ever hear the one about the shoe-tree?'

Anna swung her feet up on the sofa, a little back from the others, and looked removed and tired – she kept touching her hair back. Thomas squinted through his glass of drink at the light: now and then his face went lockjawed with a suppressed yawn. Major Brutt, having drunk two-thirds of his whisky, in his quiet way started dominating the scene. Portia's first animation was in the room somewhere, bobbing up near the ceiling like an escaped balloon. Thomas suddenly said: 'You knew Robert Pidgeon, I hear?'

'I should say so! An exceptional chap.'

'I never knew him, alas.'

'Oh, is he dead?' said Portia.

'*Dead?*' Major Brutt said. 'Oh, Lord, no – at least, I should think that is most unlikely. He had nine lives. I was with him most of the War.'

'No, I'm sure he wouldn't be dead,' Anna agreed. 'But do you know where he is?'

'I last had actual news of him in Colombo, last April – missed him there by about a week, which was bad. We are neither of us much of a hand at letters, but we keep in touch, on the whole, in the most astonishing way. Of course, Pidgeon is full of brain: the man could do anything. At the same time, he is one of those clever fellows who can get on with almost anyone. He is not a chap, of course, that I should ever have met if it hadn't been for the War. We both took it on the Somme, and I got to know him best after that, when we were on leave together.'

'Was he badly wounded?' said Portia.

'In the shoulder,' said Anna, seeing the pitted scar.

'Now Pidgeon was what you could call versatile. He could play the piano better than a professional – with more go, if you know what I mean. In France, he once smoked a plate and did a portrait of me on it – exactly like me, too; it really was. And then, of course, he wrote a whole lot of stuff. But there was absolutely no sort of side about him. I've never seen a man with so little side.'

47

'Yes,' Anna said, 'and what I always remember is that he could balance an orange on the rim of a plate.'

'Did he do that often?' said Portia.

'Very often indeed.'

Major Brutt, who had been given another drink, looked straight at Anna. 'You haven't seen him lately?'

'No, not very lately. No.'

Major Brutt quickly said: 'He was always a rare bird. You seldom hear of him twice in the same place. And I've been rolling round myself a good bit, since I left the Army, trying one thing and another.'

'That must have been interesting.'

'Yes, it is and it's not. It's a bit uncertain. I commuted my pension, then didn't do too well out in Malay. I'm back here for a bit, now, having a look round. I don't know, of course, that a great deal will come of it.'

'Oh, I don't see why not.'

Major Brutt, a good deal encouraged, said: 'Well, I've got two or three irons in the fire. Which means I shall have to stick around for a bit.'

Anna failed to reply, so it was Thomas who said: 'Yes, I'm sure you're right to do that.'

'I'll be seeing Pidgeon sometime, I dare say. One never knows where he may or may not turn up. And I often run into people – well, look at tonight.'

'Well, do give him my love.'

'He'll be glad to hear how you are.'

'Tell him I'm very well.'

'Yes, tell him that,' Thomas said. 'That is, when you do see him again.'

'If you always live in hotels,' said Portia to Major Brutt, 'you get used to people always coming and going. They look as though they'd be always there, and then the next moment you've no idea where they've gone, and they've gone for ever. It's funny, all the same.'

Anna looked at her watch. 'Portia,' she said, 'I don't want to spoil the party, but it's half past twelve.'

Portia, when Anna looked straight at her, immediately looked away. This was, as a matter of fact, the first moment since they came in that there had been any question of looking straight at each other. But during the conversation about Pidgeon, Anna had felt those dark eyes with a determined innocence steal back again and again to her face. Anna, on the sofa in a Récamier attitude, had acted, among all she had had to act, a hardy imperviousness to this. Had the agitation she felt throughout her body sent out an aura with a quivering edge, Portia's eyes might be said to explore this line of quiver, round and along Anna's reclining form. Anna felt bound up with her fear, with her secret, by that enwrapping look of Portia's: she felt mummified. So she raised her voice when she said what time it was.

Portia had learnt one dare never look for long. She had those eyes that seem to be welcome nowhere, that learn shyness from the alarm they precipitate. Such eyes are always turning away or being humbly lowered – they dare come to rest nowhere but on a point in space; their homeless intentness makes them appear fanatical. They may move, they may affront, but they cannot communicate. You most often meet or, rather, avoid meeting such eyes in a child's face – what becomes of the child later you do not know.

At the same time, Portia had been enjoying what could be called a high time with Major Brutt. It is heady – when you are so young that there is no talk yet of the convention of love – to be singled out: you feel you enjoy human status. Major Brutt had met her eyes kindly, without a qualm. He remained standing: his two great feet were planted like rocks by her as she knelt on the rug, and from up there he kept bellowing down. When Anna looked at her watch, Portia's heart sank – she referred to the clock, but found this was too true. 'Half past *twelve*,' she said. 'Golly!'

When she had said good night and gone, dropping a glove, Major Brutt said: 'That little kid must be great fun for you.'

4

MOST mornings, Lilian waited for Portia in the old cemetery off Paddington Street: they liked to take this short cut on the way to lessons. The cemetery, overlooked by windows, has been out of touch with death for some time: it is at once a retreat and a thoroughfare not yet too well known. One or two weeping willows and tombs like stone pavilions give it a prettily solemn character, but the gravestones are all ranged round the walls like chairs before a dance, and half way across the lawn a circular shelter looks like a bandstand. Paths run from gate to gate, and shrubs inside the paling seclude the place from the street – it is not sad, just cosily melancholic. Lilian enjoyed the melancholy; Portia felt that what was here was her secret every time she turned in at the gate. So they often went this way on their way to lessons.

They had to go to Cavendish Square. Miss Paullie, at her imposing address, organized classes for girls – delicate girls, girls who did not do well at school, girls putting in time before they went abroad, girls who were not to go abroad at all. She had room for about a dozen pupils like this. In the mornings, professors visited her house; in the afternoon there were expeditions to galleries, exhibitions, museums, concerts, or classical *matinées*. A girl, by special arrangement, could even take lunch at Miss Paullie's house – this was the least of many special arrangements: her secretary lived on the telephone. All her arrangements, which were enterprising, worked out very well – accordingly Miss Paullie's fees were high. Though Thomas had rather jibbed at the expense, Anna convinced him of Miss Paullie's excellent value – she solved the problem of Portia during the day; what Portia learned might give her something to talk about, and there was always a chance she might make friends. So far, she had made only this one friend, Lilian, who lived not far away, in Nottingham Place.

Anna did not think Lilian very desirable, but this could not be helped. Lilian wore her hair forward over her shoulders in two long loose braids, like the Lily Maid. She wore a removed and mysterious expression; her rather big pretty developed figure already caught the eye of men in the street. She had had to be taken away from her boarding school because of falling in love with the cello mistress, which had made her quite unable to eat. Portia thought the world of the things Lilian could do – she was said, for instance, to dance and skate very well, and had one time fenced. Otherwise, Lilian claimed to have few pleasures: she was at home as seldom as possible, and when at home was always washing her hair. She walked about with the rather fated expression you see in photographs of girls who have subsequently been murdered, but nothing had so far happened to her ... This morning, when she saw Portia coming, she signalled dreamily with a scarlet glove.

Portia came up with a rush. 'Oh dear, I'm afraid I have made us late. Come on, Lilian, we shall have to fly.'

'I don't want to run: I am not very well today.'

'Then we'd better take a 153.'

'If there is one,' said Lilian. (These buses are very rare.) 'Have I got blue rings under my eyes?'

'No. What did you do yesterday evening?'

'Oh, I had an awful evening. Did you?'

'No,' said Portia, rather apologetic. 'Because we went to the Empire. And imagine, quite by chance we met a man who knew someone Anna used once to know. Major Brutt, his name was – not the person she knew, the man.'

'Was your sister-in-law upset?'

'She was surprised, because he did not even know she was married.'

'I am often upset when I meet a person again.'

'Have you seen a person make an orange balance on the rim of a plate?'

'Oh, anyone could: you just need a steady hand.'

'All the people Anna always knows are clever.'

'Oh, you've brought your handbag with you today?'

'Matchett said I was such a silly not to.'

'You carry it in rather a queer way, if you don't mind my saying. I suppose you will get more used to it.'

'If I got too used, I might forget I had it, then I might forget and leave it somewhere. Show me, though, Lilian, how you carry yours.'

They had come out into Marylebone High Street, where they stood for a minute, patiently stamping, on chance of there being a 153 bus. The morning was colder than yesterday morning; there was a black frost that drove in. But they did not comment upon the weather, which seemed to them part of their private fate – brought on them by the act of waking up, like grown-up people's varying tempers, or the state, from day to day, of their own insides. A 153 did come lurching round the corner, but showed every sign of ignoring them, till Lilian, like a young offended goddess, stepped into its path, holding up a scarlet glove. When they were inside the bus, and had settled themselves, Lilian said reproachfully to Portia: 'You do look pleased today.'

She said, in some confusion: 'I do like things to happen.'

Miss Paullie's father was a successful doctor; her classes were held in a first-floor annexe, built for a billiard-room, at the back of his large house. In order that they might not incommode the patients, the pupils came and went by a basement door. Passers-by were surprised to see the trim little creatures, some of whom hopped out of limousines, disappear down the basement like so many cats. Once down there, they rang Miss Paullie's special bell, and were admitted to a fibre-carpeted passage. At the top of a flight of crooked staircase they hung their hats and coats in the annexe cloakroom, and queued up for the mirror, which was very small. Buff-and-blue tiles, marble, gilt embossed wallpaper, and a Turkey carpet were the note of the annexe. The cloakroom, which had a stained-glass window, smelt of fog and Vinolia, the billiard- (or school-) room of carpet, radiators, and fog – this room had no windows: a big domed skylight told the state of the weather, went leaden with fog, crepitated when it was raining, or dropped a great square glare on to the table when the sun shone. At the end of the afternoon, in winter, a blue-black glazed blind was run across from a roller to cover the skylight, when the electric lights had been turned on. Ventilation was not the room's strong point – which may have been why Portia drooped like a plant the moment she got in. She was not a success here, for she failed to concentrate, or even to seem to concentrate like the other girls. She could not keep her thoughts at face-and-table level; they would go soaring up through the glass dome. One professor would stop, glare, and drum the edge of the table; another would say: 'Miss Quayne, please, *please*. Are we here to look at the sky?' For sometimes her inattention reached the point of bad manners, or, which was worse, began to distract the others.

She was unused to learning, she had not learnt that one must learn: she seemed to have no place in which to house the most interesting fact. Anxious not to attract attention, not to annoy the professors, she *had* learned, however, after some weeks here, how to rivet, even to hypnotize the most angry professor by an unmoving regard – of his lips while he spoke, of the air over his head ... This morning's lecture on economics she received with an air of steady amazement. She brought her bag in to lessons, and sat with it on her knee. At the end of the hour, the professor said good morning; the girls divided – some were to be taken round somebody's private gallery. The rest prepared to study; some got their fine pens out to draw maps; they hitched their heels up on the rungs of their chairs, looking glad they had not had to go out. Some distance away from the big table, Miss Paullie sat going through essays, in a gothic chair, at a table of her own. Because the day was dark, a swan-necked reading lamp bent light on to what Miss Paullie read. She kept turning pages, the girls fidgeted cautiously, now and then a gurgle came from a hot pipe – the tissue of small sounds that they called silence filled the room to the dome. Lilian stopped now and then to examine her mapping nib, or to brood over her delicate state. Portia pressed her diaphragm to the edge of the table, and kept feeling at her bag against her stomach. Everybody's attention to what they were doing hardened – optimistically, Portia now felt safe.

She leant back, looked round, bent forward, and, as softly as possible, clicked open her bag. She took out a blue letter: this she spread on her knee below the table and started to read for the second time.

Dear Portia: What you did the other night was so sweet, I feel I must write and tell you how it cheered me up. I hope you won't mind – you won't, you will understand: I feel we are friends already. I was sad, going away, for various reasons, but one was that I thought you must have gone to bed by then, and that I should not see you again. So I cannot tell you what a surprise it was finding you there in the hall, holding my hat. I saw then that you must have been seeing how depressed I was, and that you wanted, you darling, to cheer me up. I cannot tell you what your suddenly being there like that in the hall, and giving me my hat as I went away, meant. I know I didn't behave well, up there in the drawing-room, and I'm afraid I behaved even worse after you went away, but that was not altogether my fault. You know how I love Anna, as I'm sure you do too, but when she starts to say to me 'Really, Eddie', I feel like a wild animal, and behave accordingly. I am much too influenced by people's manner towards me – especially Anna's, I suppose. Directly people attack me, I think they are right, and hate myself, and then I hate them – the more I like them this is so. So I went downstairs for my hat that night (Monday night, wasn't it?) feeling perfectly black. When you appeared in the hall and so sweetly gave me my hat, everything calmed down. Not only your being there, but the thought (is this presumptuous of me?) that perhaps you had actually been waiting, made me feel quite in heaven. I could not say so then, I thought you might not like it, but I cannot help writing to say so now.

Also, I once heard you say, in the natural way you say things, that you did not very often get letters, so I thought perhaps you might like to get this. You and I are two rather alone people – with you that is just chance, with me, I expect, it is partly my bad nature. I am so difficult, you are so good and sweet. I feel particularly alone tonight (I am in my flat, which I do not like very much) because I tried just now to telephone to Anna about something and she was rather short, so I did not try any more. I expect she gets bored with me, or finds me too difficult. Oh Portia, I do wish you and I could be friends. Perhaps we could sometimes go for walks in the park? I sit here and think how nice it would be if –

'*Portia!*' said Miss Paullie.

Portia leaped as though she had been struck.

'My dear child, don't sit hunched like that. Don't work under the table. Put your work *on* the table. What have you got there? Don't keep things on your knee.'

As Portia still did nothing, Miss Paullie pushed her own small table from in front of her chair, got up, and came swiftly round to where Portia sat. All the girls stared.

Miss Paullie said: 'Surely that is not a letter? This is not the place or the time to read your letters, is it? I think you must notice that the other girls don't do that. And, wherever one is, one never does read a letter under the table: have you never been told? What else is that you have on your knee? Your bag? Why did you not leave your bag in the cloakroom? Nobody will take it here, you know. Now, put your letter away in your bag again, and leave them both in the cloakroom. To carry your bag about with you indoors is a hotel habit, you know.'

Miss Paullie may not have known what she was saying, but one or two of the girls, including Lilian, smiled. Portia got up, looking unsteady, went to the cloakroom, and lodged her bag on a ledge under her coat – a ledge along which, as she saw now, all the other girls' bags had been put. But Eddie's letter, after a desperate moment, she slipped up inside her woollen directoire knickers. It stayed just inside the elastic band, under one knee.

Back in the billiard-room, the girls' brush-glossed heads were bent steadily over their books again. These silent sessions in Miss Paullie's presence were, in point of fact (and well most of them knew it), lessons in the deportment of staying still, of feeling yourself watched without turning a hair. Only Portia could have imagined for a moment that Miss Paullie's eye was off what any girl did. A little raised in her gothic chair, like a bishop, Miss Paullie's own rigid stillness quelled every young body, its nervous itches, its cooped-up pleasures in being itself, its awareness of the young body next door. Even Lilian, prone to finger her own plaits or to look at the voluptuous white insides of her arms, sat, during those hours with Miss Paullie, as though Lilian did not exist. Portia, still burning under her pale skin, pulled her book on the theory of architecture towards her and stared at a plate of a Palladian façade.

But a sense of Portia's not being quite what was what had seeped, meanwhile, into the billiard-room. She almost felt something sniffing at the hem of her dress. For the most fatal thing about what Miss Paullie had said had been her manner of saying it – as though she did not say half of what she felt, as though she were mortified on Portia's behalf, in front of these better girls. No one had ever read a letter under this table; no one had even heard of such a thing being done. Miss Paullie was very particular what class of girl she took. *Sins* cut boldly up through every class in society, but mere misdemeanours show a certain level in life. So now, not only diligence, or caution, kept the girls' smooth heads bent, and made them not glance again at Irene's child. Irene herself – knowing that nine out of ten things you do direct from the heart are the wrong thing, and that she was not capable of doing anything better – would not have dared to cross the threshold of this room. For a moment, Portia felt herself stand with her mother in the doorway, looking at all this in here with a wild askance shrinking eye. The gilt-scrolled paper, the dome, the bishop's chair, the girls' smooth heads must have been fixed here always, where they safely belonged – while she and Irene, shady, had been skidding about in an out-of-season nowhere of railway stations and rocks, filing off wet third-class decks of lake steamers, choking over the bones of *loups de mer*, giggling into eiderdowns that smelled of the person-before-last. Untaught, they had walked arm-in-arm along city pavements, and at nights had pulled their beds closer together or slept in the same bed – overcoming, as far as might be, the separation of birth. Seldom had they faced up to society – when they did, Irene did the wrong thing, then cried. How sweet, how sweetly exalted by her wrong act was Irene, when, stopping crying, she blew her nose and asked for a cup of tea ... Portia, relaxing a very little, moved on her chair: at once she felt Eddie's letter crackle under her knee. What would Eddie think of all this?

Miss Paullie, who had thought well of Anna, was sorry about Portia, and sorry for Anna. She was sorry Portia should have made no friend here but the more than doubtful Lilian, but she quite saw why this was, and it really could not be helped. She regretted that Mrs Quayne had not seen her way to go on sending someone to fetch Portia, as she had done for the first weeks. She had a strong feeling that Portia and Lilian loitered in the streets on the way home. Miss Paullie knew one must not be old-fashioned, but it gave better tone if the girls were fetched.

Any girls who stayed to lunch at Miss Paullie's lunched in a morning-room in the annexe basement: down here the light was almost always on. The proper dining-room of the house was a waiting-room, with sideboards like catafalques: where Dr Paullie himself lunched no one asked or knew.

The lunch given the girls was sufficient, simple, and far from excellent – Lilian, sent to lunch here because of the servant shortage, always messed about at it with her fork. Miss Paullie, at the head of the table, encouraged the girls to talk to her about art. This Wednesday, this Wednesday of the letter, Portia seated herself as far away from Miss Paullie as she possibly could, whereupon Lilian seized the place next to Portia's with unusual zest.

'It really was awful for you,' Lilian said, 'I didn't know where to look. Why didn't you tell me you'd had a letter? I did think you were looking very mysterious. Why didn't you read it when you had your breakfast? Or is it the kind of letter one reads again and again? Excuse my asking, but who is it from?'

'It's from a friend of Anna's. Because I got him his hat.'

'Had he lost his hat?'

'No. I heard him coming downstairs, and his hat was there, so I gave it to him.'

'That doesn't seem a thing to write a letter about. Is he not a nice man, or is he very polite? What on earth were you doing in the hall?'

'I was in Thomas's study.'

'Well, that comes to the same thing. It comes to the same thing with the door open. You had been listening for him, I suppose?'

'I just was down there. You see, Anna was in the drawing-room.'

'You are extraordinary. What does he do?'

'He is in Thomas's office.'

'Could you really feel all that for a man? I'm never sure that I could.'

'He's quite different from St Quentin. Even Major Brutt is not at all like him.'

'Well, I do think you ought to be more careful, really. After all, you and I are only sixteen. Do you want red-currant jelly with this awful mutton? I do. Do get it away from that pig.'

Portia slipped the dish of red-currant jelly away from Lucia Ames – who would soon be a débutante. 'I hope you are feeling better, Lilian?' she said.

'Well, I am, but I get a nervous craving for things.'

When the afternoon classes were over – at four o'clock today – Lilian invited Portia back to tea. 'I don't know,' said Portia. 'You see, Anna is out.'

'Well, my mother is out which is far better.'

'Matchett did say that I could have tea with her.'

'My goodness,' Lilian said, 'but couldn't you do that any day? And we don't often have my whole house to ourselves. We can take the gramophone up to the bathroom while I wash my hair; I've got three Stravinsky records. And you can show me your letter.'

Portia gulped, and looked wildly into a point in space. 'No, I can't do that, because I have torn it up.'

'No, you can't have done that,' said Lilian firmly, 'because I should have seen you. Unless you did when you were in the lavatory, and you didn't stay in there long enough. You do hurt my feelings : *I* don't want to intrude. But whatever Miss Paullie says, don't you leave your bag about.'

'It isn't in my bag,' said Portia unwarily.

So Portia went home to tea with Lilian and, in spite of a qualm, enjoyed herself very much. They ate crumpets on the rug in front of the drawing-room fire. Their cheeks scorched, but a draught crept under the door. Lilian, heaping coals of fire, brought down, untied from a ribbon, three letters the cello mistress had written to her during the holidays. She also told Portia how, one day at school when she had a headache, Miss

Heber had rubbed with magnetic fingers Lilian's temples and the nape of her neck. 'When I have a headache I always think of her still.'

'If you've got a headache today, then ought you to wash your hair?'

'I ought not to, but I want it nice for tomorrow.'

'Tomorrow. What are you doing then?'

'Confidentially, Portia, I don't know what may happen.'

Lilian had all those mysterious tomorrows: yesterdays made her sigh, but were never accounted for. She belonged to a junior branch of emotional society, in which there is always a crisis due. Preoccupation with life was not, clearly, peculiar to Lilian: Portia could see it going on everywhere. She had watched life, since she came to London, with a sort of despair – motivated and busy always, always progressing: even people pausing on bridges seemed to pause with a purpose; no bird seemed to pursue a quite aimless flight. The spring of the works seemed unfound only by her: she could not doubt people knew what they were doing – everywhere she met alert cognisant eyes. She could not believe there was not a plan of the whole set-up in every head but her own. Accordingly, so anxious was her research that every look, every movement, every object had a quite political seriousness for her: nothing was not weighed down by significance. In her home life (her new home life) with its puzzles, she saw dissimulation always on guard; she asked herself humbly for what reason people said what they did not mean, and did not say what they meant? She felt most certain to find the clue when she felt the frenzy behind the clever remark.

Outdoors, the pattern was less involuted, very much simplified. She enjoyed being in the streets – unguarded smiles from strangers, the permitted frown of someone walking alone, lovers' looks, as though they had solved something, and the unsolitary air with which the old or the wretched seemed to carry sorrow made her feel that people at least knew each other, if they did not yet know her, if she did not yet know them. The closeness she felt to Eddie, since this morning (that closeness one most often feels in a dream) was a closeness to life she had only felt, so far, when she got a smile from a stranger across a bus. It seemed to her that while people were very happy, individual persons were surely damned. So, she shrank from that specious mystery the individual throws about himself, from Anna's smiles, from Lilian's tomorrows, from the shut-in room, the turned-in heart.

Portia turned over records and re-wound the gramophone on the shut seat, and Stravinsky filled the bathroom while Lilian shampooed her hair. Lilian turbaned herself in a bath towel, and Portia carried the gramophone back to the fire again. Before Lilian's cascade of hair, turned inside out and scented in the heat, was quite dry, it had struck seven; Portia said she would have to be going home.

'Oh, they won't bother. You rang up Matchett, didn't you?'

'You said I could, but somehow I never did.'

As Portia let herself into Windsor Terrace, she heard Anna's voice in the study, explaining something to Thomas. There came a pause while they listened to her step, then the voices went on. She stole over that white stone floor, with the chill always off, and made for the basement staircase. 'Matchett?' she called down, in a tense low voice. The door at the foot of the stairs was open: Matchett came out of the little room by the pantry and stood looking up at Portia, shading her eyes. She said: 'Oh, it's you!'

'I hope you didn't wonder.'

'I had your tea for you.'

'Lilian made me go back with her.'

'Well, that was nice for you,' said Matchett didactically. 'You haven't had your tea there for some time.'

'But part of the time I was miserable. I might have been having tea with you.'

' "Miserable" !' Matchett echoed, with her hardest inflection. 'That Lilian is someone your own age. However, you did ought to have telephoned. She's that one with the head of hair?'

'Yes. She was washing it.'

'I like to see a head of hair, these days.'

'But what I wanted was, to make toast with you.'

'Well, you can't do everything, can you?'

'Are they out for dinner? Could you talk to me while I have my supper, Matchett?'

'I shall have to see.'

Portia turned and went up. A little later, she heard Anna's bath running, and smelled bath essence coming upstairs. After Portia had shut her door, she heard the reluctant step of Thomas turn, across the landing, into his dressing-room: he had got to put on a white tie.

5

EDDIE's present position, in Quayne and Merrett's, made his frequentation of Anna less possible. She saw this clearly - when Thomas, more or less at her instance, got Merrett to agree to take Eddie on, she had put it to Eddie, as nicely as possible, that in future they would be seeing less of each other. For one thing – and leave it at that, why not? – Eddie would be quite busy: the firm expected work. However, this did not dispose of him. He felt grateful (at first) to Thomas, but not to Anna. No doubt she was kind, and no doubt he needed a job – badly needed a job: he had been on his beam ends – but in popping him like this into Quayne and Merrett's, was she using the firm as an *oubliette*? Suspiciousness made him send her frequent bunches of flowers, and post her, during his first few weeks at work, a series of little letters that seemed blameless, but at the same time parodied what he ought to feel. He wrote that this new start had made a new man of him, that no one would ever know how down he had been, that no one would ever know how he now felt, etc.

For some years, a number of people had known how Eddie felt. Before Anna had ever met him (he had been a friend of a cousin of hers, at Oxford) she had been told about his cosmic black moods, which were the things he was principally noted for. Her cousin knew no one else who went on like that, and did not believe that anyone else did, either. Denis, her cousin, and Eddie belonged about that time to a circle in which it was important to be unique. Everyone seemed to get a kick out of their relations with Eddie; he was like a bright little cracker that, pulled hard enough, goes off with a loud bang. He had been the brilliant child of an obscure home, and came up to Oxford ready to have his head turned. There he was taken up, played up, played about with, taken down, let down, finally sent down for one idiotic act. His appearance was charming: he had a proletarian, animal, quick grace. His manner, after a year of trying to get the pitch, had become bold, vivid, and intimate. He became a quite frank *arriviste* – at the same time, the one thing no one, so far, knew about Eddie was quite how he *felt* about selling himself. His apparent rushes of Russian frankness proved, when you came to look back at them later, to have been more carefully edited than you had known at the time. All Anna's cousin's friends, who found Eddie as clever as a monkey, regarded his furies, his denunciations (sometimes) of the whole pack of them as Eddie's most striking turn – at the same time, something abstract and lasting about the residue of his anger had been known, once or twice, to command respect.

When he left Oxford, he had a good many buddies, few responsible friends: he had grown apart from his family who, obscure and living in an obscure province, were not, anyhow, in a position to do anything for him. He came to London and got a job on a paper; in his spare time he worked off his sense of insult in a satirical novel which, when published, did him no good at all. Its readers, who were not many, were divided into those who saw no point in the book whatever, and those who did see the point, were profoundly offended, and made up their minds to take it out of Eddie. What security he had rested so much on favour that he could not really afford to annoy anyone: he had shown himself, not for the first time, as one of those natures in which underground passion is, at a crisis, stronger than policy. Some weeks after the appearance of the novel, Eddie found himself unstuck from his position on the paper, whose editor, though an apparently dim man, was related to someone Eddie had put in his book. Eddie's disillusionment, his indignation knew almost no bounds: he disappeared, saying something about enlisting. Just when people were beginning to notice, partly with relief, partly with disappointment, that he was not there, he reappeared, very cheerful, every sign of resentment polished away, staying indefinitely with a couple called the Monkshoods, in Bayswater.

Where he had got the Monkshoods nobody knew: they were said to have all been up Cader Idris together. They were a very nice couple, middle-aged, serious, childless, idealistic, and full of belief in youth. They were well off, and seemed disposed to make Eddie their son – with Mrs Monkshood, possibly, there was just a touch of something more than this. During the Monkshood period, Eddie helped his patrons with some research, went to useful parties, did a little reviewing, and wrote some pamphlets, which were printed by a girl who had a press in a loft. Arts and crafts had succeeded *Sturm und Drang*. It was at this time, when he looked like being less of a trouble, that Eddie was first brought to Anna's house by Denis: he found his way there again with kitten-like trustfulness. All seemed to be going almost too well when a friend whose girl Eddie had taken – or had, rather, picked up and put down again – got the Monkshood's ear and began to make bad blood. Eddie – unconscious, though perhaps a little affected by some threat of dissolution in the air – galloped towards his doom: he brought the girl back to his room in the Monkshoods' flat: the flat was too small for this, and the Monkshoods, already uneasy, heard more than they liked. Seeing no way to get rid of Eddie, they gave up their flat and went to live abroad. This made a deep wound in Eddie – he had been good to the Monkshoods, filial, attentive, cheerful. Quite at a loss to understand their very cruel behaviour, he began to see in his patrons perverse cravings he must all the time have flouted unconsciously. There appeared, now, to be no one he might trust.

Anna declared to whoever was interested that the Monkshoods had treated Eddie badly: she had shared his impression that they proposed to adopt him. Up to now, he had been a pleasure at Windsor Terrace, not in any way a charge on the nerves. The morning Denis had told her, not without pleasure, the bad news, Anna sent Eddie an impulsive message. He came round and stood in her drawing-room: she had been prepared to find him looking the toy of fate. His manner was, in fact, not much more than muted, and rather abstract – it showed, at the same time, a touch of savage reticence. She found he did not know, and did not apparently care, where he would eat next, or where he would sleep tonight. His young debauched face – with the high forehead, springy bronze hair, energetic eyebrows, and rather too mobile mouth – looked strikingly innocent. While he and Anna talked he did not sit down but stood at a distance, as though he felt disaster set him apart. He said he expected that he would go away.

'But away where?'

'Oh, somewhere,' said Eddie, dropping his eyes. He added, in a matter-of-fact voice: 'I suppose there really is something against me, Anna.'

'Nonsense,' she said fondly. 'What about your people? Why not go home for a bit?'

'No, I couldn't do that. You see, they're quite proud of me.'

'Yes,' she said (and thought of that simple home), 'I should think they were ever so proud of you.'

Eddie looked at her with just a touch of contempt.

She went on – making a little emphatic gesture. 'But, I mean, you know, you will have to live. Don't you want to get some sort of work?'

'That's quite an idea,' said Eddie, with a little start – of which the irony was quite lost on Anna. 'But look here,' he went on, 'I do hate *you* to worry. I really shouldn't have come here.'

'But I asked you to.'

'Yes, I know. You were so sweet.'

'I'm so worried about all this; I feel the Monkshoods are monsters. But perhaps it wouldn't have worked, in the long run. I mean, your position is so much freer, now. You can make your own way – after all, you are very clever.'

'So they all say,' said Eddie, grinning at her.

'Well, we'll just have to think. We've got to be realistic.'

'You're so right,' said Eddie, glancing into a mirror.

'And listen: do keep your head, do be more conciliating.

Don't go off at the deep end and have one of your moods – you really haven't got time. I've heard all about those.'

'My moods?' said Eddie, raising his eyebrows. He seemed not just taken aback, but truly surprised. Did he not know he had them? Perhaps they were really fits.

For the rest of that day, Anna had felt deeply concerned: she could not get Eddie out of her mind. Then at about six o'clock, Denis rang up to report that Eddie had just moved into his, Denis's, flat, and was in excellent spirits. He had just had a series of articles commissioned: they were the sort of articles he could do on his head. On the strength of this, he had borrowed two pounds from Denis and gone off in a taxi to the Piccadilly tube station left luggage office to bail out his things; he had promised, also, to bring back with him several bottles of drink.

Anna, considerably put out, said: 'But there's not room for two of you in that flat.'

'Oh, that will be all right, because I'm going to Turkey.'

'What on earth do you want to go to Turkey for?' said Anna, still more crossly.

'Oh, various reasons. Eddie can stay on here while I'm away. I think he'll be all right; he seems to have sloughed that girl off.'

'What girl?'

'Oh, that girl, you know, that he had at the Monkshoods's. He didn't like her a bit; she was a dull little tart.'

'I do think all you college boys are vulgar and dull.'

'Well, Anna darling, do see that Eddie isn't lonely. Eddie's such a dear, isn't he?' said Denis. 'He's what I always call so volatile.' He hung up before Anna could reply.

After two days, in which Anna's annoyance subsided, Denis really did go to Turkey, and Eddie sounded lonely in the flat. Anna, feeling he ought to be someone's responsibility, made him more or less free of Windsor Terrace. She hoped very much to keep him out of mischief. At first, these visits worked very well: Anna had never cared to be the romantic woman, but now Eddie became her first troubadour. He lent himself, gladly and quickly, or appeared to lend himself, to Anna's illusions about living. He did more: by his poetic appreciation he created a small world of art round her. The vanities of which she was too conscious, the honesties to which she compelled herself, even the secrets she had never told him existed inside a crystal they both looked at – not only existed but were beautified. On Anna, he had the inverse of the effect that Portia's diary was to produce later. He appeared to marvel at Anna – and probably did. If he went into black thoughts, he came out again, for her only, with a quick sweet smile. He showed with her, at its best, his farouche grace; the almost unwilling sweetness he had for her used to make her like hearing people, other people, call Eddie cold or recalcitrant ... This phase of sublime flattery, flattery kept delicate by their ironic smiles, lasted about six weeks. Then Eddie made a false move – he attempted to kiss Anna.

He not only attempted to kiss her, but made the still worse blunder of showing he thought this was what she would really like. When she was very angry (because he gave that impression) Eddie, feeling once more betrayed, misled, and insulted, lost his grip on the situation at once. Having lost his grip, he then lost his head. Though he did not love Anna, he had honestly tried to repay some of her niceness in a way he thought she could but like. It had been his experience that everyone did. If, in fact, in these last years he had found himself rather ruthlessly knocked about, it was because people *had* wanted only that: their differing interests in him, however diverse, seemed in the end to lead to that one point. Another thing that had led him to kiss Anna, or try to, was that he took an underlying practical view of life, and had no time for relations that came to nothing or for indefinitely polite play. When Anna made this fuss, he thought her a silly woman. He did not know about Pidgeon, or how badly she had come out of all that – if, in fact, she *had* ever come out of it. He suspected her of making all this fuss for some rather shady reason of her own.

They were both nonplussed, chagrined, but unhappily neither of them was prepared to cut their losses. Up to now, their alliance had been founded on hopes of pleasure: from now on they set out to annoy each other, and could not help playing each other up. Eddie began to dart devouring looks in company, to steal uneasy touches when they were alone. Anna would have been less annoyed by all this had she felt herself completely unmoved by Eddie; as it was, aware of the lack of the slightest passion behind it, she was offended by the pantomime. She countered his acting up with insulting pieces of irony. Her one thought was, to put him back in his place – a place she had never quite clearly defined. The more she tried to do this, the worse Eddie behaved.

There were times when Anna almost hated Eddie, for she was conscious of the vacuum inside him. As for him, he found her one mass of pretence, and detested the feeling she showed for power. Through all this, they did still again and again discover reaches of real feeling in one another. Anna did ask herself what they were both doing, but Eddie apparently never did. Could she be injuring genius? Once, in a fit of penitence, she rang up Denis's flat and heard Eddie in tears. The extreme pity she felt brought her, for some reason, to snapping point: she went straight downstairs and complained to Thomas that Eddie tired her more than she could bear.

This was a moment Thomas had seen coming, and he had awaited it philosophically. He had looked on at other declines and falls. He did not at that time dislike Eddie, whose efforts to please him pleased by their very transparency. He had watched, not without pleasure, Eddie annoy St Quentin and others of their friends. He had also read Eddie's novel with a good deal of pleasure, and more sympathy than Anna had brought to it: Eddie was still free to say a good deal about life that he, Thomas, was too deeply involved to say. So Thomas had read the novel with an appeased smile, almost with a sense of complicity. He passed on the book to Merrett, who, liking its savage glitter, pigeon-holed Eddie for possible future use. This was well, for the time came when Anna announced to Thomas that what Eddie needed was straight, regular work, that need not quite waste his wits – in fact, could they not use Eddie in Quayne and Merrett's? The moment happening to be propitious, Eddie was sent for for an interview.

The day Anna heard that Quayne and Merrett were prepared to give Eddie three months' trial, she rang Eddie up and asked him to come round. Their relation from now on, promised to be ideal: she was his patroness.

That morning Eddie was wearing a sober tie, and already seemed to belong to another world. His manner was civil, and extremely remote. He said how kind they had been at Quayne and Merrett's, and what fun it would no doubt be to write funny advertisements. 'How can I thank you?' he said.

'Why should you? I wanted to help.'

Eddie met her smile with an equally pious look.

She went on: 'I have been worried about you: that's what may have made me seem unsympathetic. I felt sure you needed a more regular life. Thomas thinks I am bad for you,' she added, rather unwisely.

'I don't think that's possible, darling,' said Eddie blithely. Then he bit off that manner. 'You've both been so good,' he said. 'I do hope I haven't been difficult? When I'm worried I seem to get everything on my nerves. And all the jobs I've been after turned me down flat. I really did begin to think there was something against me – which was stupid, of course.'

'But *have* you been looking for jobs?'

'What did you think I'd been doing, all this time? I didn't tell you about it, partly because it depressed me, partly because I thought you'd think it was sordid. All my friends seem to be rather out with me at the moment, so I didn't like to go round to them for backing. And of course, I owe a good deal of money – apart from everything else, I owe thirty-five shillings to Denis's charwoman.'

'Denis should not have left you with an expensive charwoman,' Anna angrily said. 'He never thinks. But surely you've had *some* money?'

'Well, I had till I spent it.'

'What have you been eating?'

'Oh, one thing and another. I must say, I was grateful for your very nice lunches and dinners. I do hope I wasn't snappy at meals? But being anxious gives me indigestion. I'm not like St Quentin and Denis and all those other people that you see – I'm afraid I haven't got very much detachment, darling, and getting nothing to do made me feel in disgrace.'

'You might have known we would help you. How silly you were!'

'Yes, I thought you probably might,' said Eddie, with perfect candour. 'But in a sort of way I rather hated to ask, and while you had it on me, it made it more difficult. However, look how lucky I am now!'

Anna collected herself. 'I'm so glad to know', she said, 'that what has been the matter was simply money. I was afraid, you know, it was really you and me.'

'Unfortunately', said Eddie, 'it was a good deal more.'

'I should rather call it a good deal less. To be right or wrong with people is the important thing.'

'I expect it would be if you had got money. However, Anna, you've got beautiful thoughts. It must have done me good to know you. But I'm not really interesting, darling: I'm all stomach.'

'Well, I'm so pleased that everything is all right,' Anna said with a slightly remote smile. She got up from the sofa and went to lean on the mantelpiece, where she tinkled a lustre. She could stay so still, and she so greatly disliked other people to fidget, that to fidget herself was almost an act of passion – and Eddie, aware of this, stared round in surprise. 'All the same,' she said, 'leaving aside money – which I do see is very, very important – what *has* been making you quite so impossible?'

'Well, darling, for one thing I wanted to make you happy, and for another I thought you might get bored if we kept on and on and nothing ever happened. You see, people have some-times got bored with me. And while everything round me was such a nightmare, I wanted something with you that wasn't such an effort, something to stop me from going quite mad.' Anna tinkled the lustre harder. 'Have no more nightmares,' she said.

'Oh no, darling: Quayne and Merrett's will be like a lovely dream.'

Anna frowned. Eddie turned away and stood looking out of the window at the park. Shoulders squared, hands thrust in his pockets, he took the pose of a chap making a new start. Her aquamarine curtains, looped high up over his head with cords and tassels, fell in stately folds each side of him to the floor, theatrically framing his back view. He saw the world at its most sheltered and gay: it was, then, the spring of the year before; the chestnuts opposite her window were in bud; through the branches glittered the lake, with swans and one running dark pink sail; the whole scene was varnished with spring light. Eddie brought one hand out of his pocket and pinched a heavy *moiré* fold of the curtain by which he stood. This half-conscious act was hostile: Anna heard the *moiré* creak between his finger and thumb.

She did not for a moment doubt that in his own mind Eddie was travestying the scene. Yes, and he showed her he felt he was bought goods, with 'Quayne and Merrett' pasted across his back. She said in a light little voice: 'I'm glad you're pleased about this.'

'Five pounds a week, just for being good and clever! How could I not be pleased!'

'I'm afraid they may want just a little more than that. You really will work, I hope?'

'To do you credit?'

Then, because she did not reply, there was a pause. Eddie swung round at her with his most persuasive, most meaningless smile. 'Do come and look at the lake! I don't suppose I shall ever look at it with you in the morning again: I shall be much too busy.' To show how immaterial this was, Anna good-temperedly came to join him. They stood side by side in the window and she folded her arms. But Eddie, with the affectionate nonchalance of someone whose nearness does not matter, put a hand on her elbow. 'How much I owe you!'

'I never know what you mean.'

Eddie's eyes ran over her doubtful face – the light seemed to concentrate in their brilliant shallows; his pupils showed their pin-points of vacuum. 'Marvellous,' he said, 'to have a firm in your pocket.'

'When did you first think I might fix this up for you?'

'Of course it occurred to me. But the idea of advertising was so repellent, and to tell you the truth, Anna, I'm so vain, I kept hoping I might get something better. You're not angry, are you, darling? You shouldn't judge people by how they have to behave.'

'Your friends say you always fall on your feet.'

The remark was another thing that he would never forgive her. After a stonelike minute he said: 'If I have to know people who ruin me, I mean to get something out of it.'

'I don't understand. Ruin you? Who does?'

'You do, and your whole lot. You make a monkey of me, and God knows what else worse. I'm ashamed to go back home.'

'I don't think we can have done you much harm, Eddie. You must still be quite rugged, while you can be so rude.'

'Oh, I can be rude all right.'

'Then what is upsetting you?'

'Oh, I don't know, Anna,' he said, in a burst of childishness. 'We seem to be on an absurd track. Please forgive me – I always stay too long. I came round to thank you for my lovely job; I came here intending to be so normal – Oh, look, there's a gull sitting on a deck chair!'

'Yes, it must be spring,' she said automatically. 'They've put the deck chairs out.' She opened her case and lighted a cigarette with a rather uncertain hand. Sun shone on the white gull on the green deck chair; a striped sail blew after the pink sail down the lake; smiling people walking and children running between the harp-shaped lawns composed a pattern of play. The carillon played a tune, then the clock struck.

'Is this the last time I shall call you darling, darling?'

It possibly was, she said. This gave her the chance to put it to him, as nicely as possible, that in future they would be seeing less of each other. 'But I know,' he insisted. 'That is what I was saying. That's exactly why I have come to say good-bye.'

'Only good-bye in a way. You exaggerate everything.'

'Well, good-bye in a way.'

'This won't really make any difference.'

'I quite understand, darling. But it will have to appear to.'

It turned out to have been hardly good-bye at all. But it was,

71

as Anna said to herself, the start of a third, and their most harmonious, phase. That evening, half a dozen camellias came, and three days later, when he had started work, a letter – the first of a series on the imposing office notepaper. In his open writing, so childish as to be sinister, he wrote how nice they all were in the office. In fact, his resentment against her kind act lasted for some weeks. The letter in which he said that this new start had made quite a man of him Anna tore up: she left the scraps in the grate. She asked Thomas how Eddie was really getting on, and Thomas said he was still showing off rather, but that there seemed no reason why he should not shape up.

Eddie came round to report six evenings later, bearing three sprays of flowering cherry in a blue paper sheath. After that, perspicacity, money to spend, or new friends elsewhere made him not repeat the visit for some time. He settled down to a routine of weekly tulips, cosy telephone calls, equivocally nice letters, and after the tulips, roses. Thomas, questioned further, reported that Eddie was doing well, though not so well as Eddie himself thought. When Denis came back from Turkey and wanted his flat, Anna wrote and said the flowers must stop: Eddie would have to begin to pay rent now. The flowers stopped, but Eddie, as though he felt communication imperilled, started coming round more often again. Office or no office, he was once more a familiar feature of Windsor Terrace when Portia arrived to join the family.

6

IT was half past ten at night. Matchett, opening Portia's door an inch, breathed cautiously through the crack: a line of light from the landing ran across the darkness into the room. Portia, without stirring on her pillow, whispered: 'I'm awake.' The entire top of the house was, in fact, empty: Thomas and Anna had gone to the theatre, but Matchett never let their going or coming temper her manner in any way. She was equally cautious if they were out or in. But only when they were not out did she not come up to say good night.

If, after ten o'clock, Matchett sank her voice and spoke still more shortly, this seemed to be in awe of approaching sleep. She awaited the silent tide coming in. About now, she served the idea of sleep with a series of little ceremonials – laying out night clothes, levelling fallen pillows, hospitably opening up the beds. Kneeling to turn on bedroom fires, stooping to slip bottles between sheets, she seemed to abase herself to the overcoming night. The impassive solemnity of her preparations made a sort of an altar of each bed: in big houses in which things are done properly, there is always the religious element. The diurnal cycle is observed with more feeling when there are servants to do the work.

Portia instinctively spoke low after dark: she was accustomed to thin walls. She watched the door shut, saw the bend of light cut off, and heard Matchett crossing the floor with voluminous quietness. As always, Matchett went to the window and drew the curtains open – a false faint day began again, tawny as though London were burning. Now and then cars curved past. The silence of a shut park does not sound like country silence: it is tense and confined. In the intricate half darkness inside Portia's room the furniture could be seen, and Matchett's apron – phosphorescent, close up as she sat down on the bed.

'I thought you were never coming.'

'I had mending to see to. Mr Thomas burnt the top of a sheet.'

'But does he smoke in bed?'

'He did last week, while she was away. His ash-tray was full of stumps.'

'Do you think he would always like to, but doesn't because she's there?'

'He smokes when he doesn't sleep. He's like his father; he doesn't like to be left.'

'I didn't think anyone left father. Mother never did – used *she* to, ever? I mean, did Mrs Quayne? – Oh Matchett, listen:

if she was alive now – I mean, if Thomas's mother was – what would I call her? There wouldn't be any name.'

'Well, what matter? She's gone: you don't have to speak to her.'

'Yes, she's dead. Do you think she is the reason Thomas and I are so unlike?'

'No, Mr Thomas always favoured his father more than he did her. You unlike Mr Thomas? How much liker are you wanting to be?'

'I don't know – Listen, Matchett, *was* Mrs Quayne sorry? I mean, did she mind being alone?'

'Alone? She kept Mr Thomas.'

'She'd made such a sacrifice.'

'Sacrificers', said Matchett, 'are not the ones to pity. The ones to pity are those that they sacrifice. Oh, the sacrificers, they get it both ways. A person knows themselves what they're able to do without. Yes. Mrs Quayne would give the clothes off her back, but in the long run she would never lose a thing. The day we heard you'd been born out there in France, she went on like a lady who'd got her first grandchild. She came after me to the linen room to tell me. "The sweet little thing," she said. "Oh, Matchett!" she said, "he always wanted a girl!" Then she went down in the hall to telephone Mr Thomas. "Oh Thomas, good news," I heard her say.'

Fascinated as ever by the topic, Portia turned over on to her side, drawing up her knees so that she lay in a bend round Matchett's sitting rump. The bed creaked as Matchett, bolt upright, shifted her weight. Sliding a hand under her pillow, Portia stared up through the dark and asked: 'What was that day like?'

'Where we were? Oh, it was quite a bright day, spring-like for February. That garden was very sheltered; it was the sunny side of that hill. I saw her go down the lawn without her hat, and across the stream Mr Quayne made: she started picking herself snowdrops down there the other side of the stream.'

'How could he *make* a stream?'

'Well, there was a brook, but not where Mrs Quayne wanted,

so he dug a new ditch and got it to flow in. He was at it all that summer before he went – how he did sweat: I could have wrung his clothes out.'

'But that day I was born – what did *you* say, Matchett?'

'When she said you were born? I said, "To think of that, madam", or something to that effect. I've no doubt she expected to hear more. But I felt it, the way I felt it quite went to my throat, and I couldn't say more than that. Besides, why should I? – not to her, I mean. Of course, we had all known you were to be coming: the others were all eyes to see how Mrs Quayne took it, and you may be sure she knew they were all eyes. I went back to putting away the linen, and what I said to myself was "The poor little soul!" She saw that, and she never forgave me for it – though that was more than she knew herself.'

'Why did you think me poor?'

'At that time I had my reasons. Well, she kept picking snowdrops, and now and then she'd keep stopping and looking up. She felt the Almighty watching, I daresay. None of that garden was out of sight of the windows – you could always see Mr Quayne, while he was working, just as if he had been a little boy. Then she came back in and she did the snowdrops, in a Chinese bowl she set store by – oh, she did set store by that bowl, till one of the girls broke it. (She came to me with the bits of it in her hand, smiling away she was. "Another little bit of life gone, Matchett," she said. But she never spoke a cross word to the girl – oh no, she liked herself far too well.) Then, that afternoon, Mr Thomas came back by a train from Oxford: he felt he ought to see, I daresay, how his mother really *was* taking it. I made up his room for him, and he stayed that night. He went about looking quite taken aback, with three snowdrops she gave him stuck in his buttonhole. He stopped and looked at me once, by the swing door, as though he felt he ought to say something. "Well, Matchett," he said to me, rather loud, "so I've got a sister." "Yes, indeed, sir," I said.'

'Was that all Thomas said?'

'I daresay the house felt funny that day for a young fellow like him, quite as though there had been a birth there. It did to us all, really. Then later on, Mrs Quayne sat down and played the piano to Mr Thomas.'

'*Did* they look at all pleased?'

'How should I know? They kept on at the piano till it was time for dinner.'

'Matchett, if Thomas does like a piano, why haven't they got a piano here?'

'He sold the piano when she died. Oh, she was fair to me, the fifteen years I was with her. You couldn't have had a better employer, as far as the work went: the one thing that put her out was if you made her feel she wasn't considerate. She liked me to feel that she thought the world of me. "I leave everything in safe charge with you, Matchett," she'd say to me on the doorstep, times when she went away. I thought of that as I saw her coffin go out. No, she'd never lift her voice and she always had a kind word. But I couldn't care for her: she had no nature. I've often felt her give me a funny look. She liked what I did, but she never liked how I did it. I couldn't count how often I've heard her say to her friends, "Treat servants nicely, take an interest in them, and they'll do anything for you." That was the way she saw it. Well, I liked the work in that house, I liked that work from the first: what she couldn't forgive me was that I liked the work for its own sake. When I had been the morning polishing in my drawing-room, or getting my marbles nice with a brush and soft soap, she would come to me and she'd say, "Oh, it does all look nice! I am so pleased, I am really." Oh, she meant well, in her own way. But with work it's not what you show, it's what you put into it. You'd never get right work from a girl who worked to please you: she'd only work to show. But *she* would never see that. Now, when Mr Quayne would come on me working in his smoking-room, or working in any place that he wanted to be, though he was so sweet-tempered, he'd give me a black look as though to say "You get out!" He'd know well I was against him, working in his smoking-room where he wanted to be. If he found a thing left different he used to bellow, because my having my way had put him out. But then, Mr Quayne was all nature. He left you to go your own way, except when it started to put him out.

But she couldn't allow a thing that she hadn't her part or share in. All those snowdrops and that piano playing – to make out she'd had her share in your being born.

'The day she died, though I wasn't up in her room, I could feel her watching how I'd take it. "Well," I said to myself, "it's no good – *I* can't play the piano." Oh, I did feel upset, with death in the house and all that change coming. But that was the most I felt. I didn't feel a thing here.' With a dry unflinching movement, Matchett pressed a cuffed hand under her bust.

She sat sideways on to the bed, her knees towards Portia's pillow, her dark skirts flowing into the dark round, only her apron showing. Her top part loomed against the tawny square of sky in uncertain silhouette; her face, eroded by darkness like a statue's face by the weather, shone out now and then when a car fanned light on it. Up to now, she had sat erect, partly judicial, partly as though her body were a vaseful of memory that must not be spilt; but now, as though to shift the weight of the past, she put a hand on the bed, the far side of Portia's body, and leant heavily on it so that she made an arch.

Through this living arch, the foot of the bed in fluctuations of half-darkness was seen. Musky warmth from her armpit came to the pillow, and a creak from the stays under her belt as she breathed in the strain of this leaning attitude. She felt as near, now, as anyone can be without touching one. At the same time, as though to re-create distance, her voice pitched itself further away.

'Oh, I felt bad,' she said, 'because I couldn't forgive her. Not about Mr Quayne – I could never forgive her that. When the nurse sent down word Mrs Quayne was going, cook said maybe we should go up. She said, having sent word they'd expect us to do something. (Cook meant, *she'd* expect us to do something.) So Cook and I went up and stood on the landing: the others were too nervous; they stayed below. Cook was a Catholic, so started saying her prayers. Mr and Mrs Thomas were there in the room with her. We knew it was over when Mrs Thomas came out, quite white, and said to me, "Oh Matchett." But Mr Thomas went by without a word. I had had his whisky put out in the dining-room and quite soon I heard them both in there.

Mr and Mrs Thomas were different to Mrs Quayne: they had their own ways of passing a thing off.'

'But Matchett, she meant to do good.'

'No, she meant to do right.'

Tentatively sighing and turning over, Portia put on Matchett's knee, in the dark, fingers that by being urgently living tried to plead for the dead. But the very feel of the apron, of the starch over that solid warm big knee, told her that Matchett was still inexorable.

'You know what she did, but how can you know what she felt? Fancy being left with somebody gone. Perhaps what was right was all she had left to do. To have to stay alone might be worse than dying.'

'She stayed there where she wanted, go who might. No, he had done her wrong, and she had to do herself right. Oh, she was like iron. Worse than dying? For your father, going away was that. He loved his home like a child. Go? – He was sent. He liked his place in the world; he liked using his hands. That stream wasn't the only thing he'd made. For a gentleman like him, abroad was no proper place. I don't know how she dared look at that garden after what she had done.'

'But if I had to be born?'

'He was sent away, as cook or I might have been – but oh no, we suited her too well. She stood by while Mr Thomas put him into the car and drove him off as if he had been a child. What a thing to make Mr Thomas do to his own father! And then look at the way your father and mother lived, with no place in the world and nobody to respect them. He had been respected wherever he was. Who put him down to that?'

'But mother explained to me that she and father had once done what was cruel to Mrs Quayne.'

'And what did she do to them! Look how they lived, without a stick of their own. You were not born to know better, but he did.'

'But he liked keeping moving on. It was mother wanted a house, but father never would.'

'You don't break a person's nature for nothing.'

Portia said in a panic: 'But we were happy, Matchett. We

had each other; he had mother and me – Oh, don't be so angry: you make me feel it was my fault for having had to be born.'

'And who had the right to quarrel with you for that? If you had to be, then you had to be. I thought that day you were born, as I went on with my linen. Well, that's one more thing happened: no doubt it is for a purpose.'

'That's what they all feel; that's why they're all always watching. They would forgive me if I were something special. But I don't know what I was meant to be.'

'Now then,' said Matchett sharply, 'don't *you* get upset.'

Portia had unconsciously pushed, while she spoke, at the knee under Matchett's apron, as though she were trying to push away a wall. Nothing, in fact, moved. Letting her hand fall back on to her face in the dark, she gave an instinctive shiver that shook the bed. She ground the back of her hand into her mouth – the abandoned movement was cautious, checked by awe at some monstrous approach. She began to weep, shedding tears humbly, without protest, without at all full feeling, like a child actress mesmerized for a part. She might have been miming sorrow – in fact, this immediate, this obedient prostration of her whole being was meant to hold off the worst, the full of grief, that might sweep her away. Now, by crossing her arms tightly across her chest, as though to weight herself down with them, she seemed to cling at least to her safe bed. Any intimations of Fate, like a step heard on the stairs, makes some natures want to crouch in the safe dark. Her tears were like a flag lowered at once: she felt herself to be undefendable.

The movement of her shoulders on the pillow could be heard; her shiver came through the bed to Matchett's body. Matchett's eyes pried down at her through the dark; inexorably listening to Portia's unhappy breaths she seemed to wait until her pity was glutted. Then – 'Why goodness,' she said softly. 'Why do *you* want to start breaking your heart? If that wasn't finished, I wouldn't go on about it. No doubt I'm wrong, but you do keep on at me, asking. You didn't ought to ask if you're going to work up so. Now you put it out of your head, like a good girl, and go right off to sleep.' She shifted her weight from her hand, groped over Portia, found her wet wrists, uncrossed them. 'Goodness,' she said, 'whatever good does *that* do?' All the same, the question was partly rhetorical: Matchett felt that something had been appeased. Having smoothed the top of the sheet, she arranged Portia's hands on it like a pair of ornaments: she stayed leaning low enough to keep guard on them. She made a long sibilant sound, somewhere right up in space, like swans flying across a high sky. Then this stopped and she suggested: 'Like me to turn your pillow?'

'No,' said Portia unexpectedly quickly, then added: 'But don't go.'

'You like it turned for you, don't you? However –'

'Ought we both to forget?'

'Oh, you'll forget when you've got more to remember. All the same, you'd better not to have asked.'

'I just asked about the day I was born.'

'Well, the one thing leads to the other. It all has to come back.'

'Except for you and me, nobody cares.'

'No, there's no past in this house.'

'Then what makes them so jumpy?'

'They'd rather no past – not have the past, that is to say. No wonder they don't rightly know what they're doing. Those without memories don't know what is what.'

'Is that why you tell me this?'

'I'd likely do better not to. I never was one to talk, and I'm not one to break a habit. What I see I see, but I keep myself to myself. I have my work to get on with. For all that, you can't but notice, and I'm not a forgetter. It all goes to make something, I daresay. But there's no end to what's been said, and I'll be a party to nothing. I was born with my mouth shut: those with their mouths open do nothing but start trouble and catch flies. What I am asked, I'll answer – that's always been sufficient.'

'Does no one but me ask you?'

'They know better,' said Matchett. Satisfied that the fold of Portia's upper sheet wanted no more attention, she drew back and once more propped herself on her hand. 'What's not said keeps,' she went on. 'And when it's been keeping some time it gets what not many would dare to hear. Oh, it wasn't quite welcome to Mr Thomas when I first came to this house after his mother dying, though he did speak civil and pass it off so well. "Why, Matchett," he said, "this feels like home again." Mrs Thomas took it quite easy; it was the work she wanted and she knew I was a worker. The things that came to them here from Mrs Quayne's were accustomed to the best care; Mrs Thomas knew they must have it. Oh, it is lovely furniture, and Mr and Mrs Thomas see the value of it. Valuables were the one thing Mrs Quayne and Mrs Thomas saw eye to eye about. You can see ten foot into my polish, and Mrs Thomas likes the look of a thing.'

'But what made you come here?'

'It seemed to me proper. I hadn't the heart, either, to let that furniture go: I wouldn't have known myself. It was that that kept me at Mrs Quayne's. I was sorry to leave those marbles I'd got so nice, but those had to stop and I put them out of my mind.'

'The furniture would have missed you?'

'Furniture's knowing all right. Not much gets past the things in a room, I daresay, and chairs and tables don't go to the grave so soon. Every time I take the soft cloth to that stuff in the drawing-room, I could say, "Well, you know a bit more." My goodness, when I got here and saw all Mrs Quayne's stuff where Mrs Thomas had put it – if I'd have been a silly, I should have said it gave me quite a look. Well, it didn't speak, and I didn't. If Mr and Mrs Thomas are what you say, nervous, no doubt they are nervous of what's not said. I would not be the one to blame them: they live the best way they can. Unnatural living runs in a family, and the furniture knows it, you be sure. Good furniture knows what's what. It knows it's made for a purpose, and it respects itself – when I say *you're* made for a purpose you start off crying. Oh, furniture like we've got is too much for some that would rather not have the past. If I just had to look at it and have it looking at me, I'd go jumpy, I daresay. But when it's your work it can't do anything to you. Why, that furniture – I've been at it years and years with the soft cloth: I know it like my own face ... Oh yes, I notice them all right.

But I'm not the one to speak: I've got no time. When they made a place for it, they made a place for me, and they soon saw nothing would come of *that*.'

'When I came, though, it was worse.'

'It was proper,' said Matchett quickly. 'The first mortal thing he had ever asked since he went –'

'Yes, this was the house my father talked about. He used to tell me how nice it was. Though he never came here, he did walk past it once. He told me it had a blue door and stood at a corner, and I expect he imagined the inside. "That's the part of London to live in," he used to say. "Those houses are leased direct from the King, and they have an outlook fit for Buckingham Palace." Once, in Nice, he bought a book about birds and showed me pictures of the water birds on this lake. He said he had watched them. He told me about the scarlet flowerbeds – I used to imagine them right down to the lake, not with that path between. He said this was the one gentleman's park left, and that Thomas would be wrong to live anywhere else. He used to tell me, and to tell people we met, how well Thomas got on in business, and how pretty Anna was – stylish, he used to call her – and how much they entertained, and what gay parties they had. He used to say, a young man getting on in the world is quite right to cut a bit of a dash. Whenever we spent a day in any smart place, he always used to notice the ladies' clothes, and say to me, "Now that would look well on Anna." Yes, he was ever so proud of Thomas and her. It always made him happy to talk about them. When I was little and stupid, I used to say, "Why can't we see them soon?" and he used to say, "Some day." He promised that some day I should be with them – and now, of course, I am.'

Matchett said triumphantly: 'Ah, he got his way – in the end.'

'I liked them for making father proud. But when I was with mother, I had to forget them – you see, they were a sort of trouble to her. She thought Anna laughed at how we lived.'

'Oh, Mrs Thomas didn't trouble to laugh. She'd let live and let die – so long as she wasn't trespassed upon. And she wasn't trespassed upon.'

'She had to have me here.'

'She had this room empty, waiting,' said Matchett sharply. '*She* never filled it, for all she is so clever. And she knows how to make a diversion of anything – dolling this room up with clocks and desks and frills. (Not but what it's pretty, and you like it, I should hope.) No, she's got her taste, and she dearly likes to use it. Past that she'll never go.'

'You mean, she'll never be fond of me?'

'So that's what you want?' Matchett said, so jealously pouncing that Portia drew back in her bed.

'She had a right, of course, to be where I am this minute,' Matchett went on in a cold, dispassionate voice. 'I've no call to be dawdling up here, not with all that sewing.' Her weight stiffened on the bed; drawing herself up straight she folded her arms sternly, as though locking love for ever from her breast. Portia saw her outline against the window and knew this was not pique but arrogant rectitude – which sent her voice into distance two tones away. 'I have my duties,' she said, 'and you should look for your fond-ofs where it is more proper. I'd be glad you should get them. Oh, I was glad somehow, that day she came and said you had been born. I might have done better to wish you out of it.'

'Don't be angry – oh, don't be! You're quite enough, Matchett!'

'Now don't you work yourself up again!'

'But don't, don't keep going off –' began Portia, desperate. Stopping, she put both arms out, with a rustle of sheet falling away. Matchett, reluctantly softening, inch by inch, unlocked her arms, leaned across the bed again, leaned right down – in the mysterious darkness over the pillow their faces approached, their eyes met but could not see. Something steadily stood between them: they never kissed – so that now there followed a pause at once pressing and null. Matchett, after the moment, released herself and drew a judicial breath. 'Well, I'm hasty, I daresay.' But Portia's hand, with its charge of nervous emotion, still crept on the firm broad neck, the strong spine. Matchett's embrace had made felt a sort of measured resistance, as though she were determined to will, not simply to suffer, the power of the dividing wall. Darkness hid any change her face might allow itself. She said finally: 'I'll turn your pillow now.'

Portia at once stiffened. 'No,, don't. I like it this way – No, don't.'

'Why ever not?'

'Because I like it this way.'

But Matchett's hand pushed underneath the pillow, to turn it. Under there, going wooden, her hand stopped. 'What's this you've got under here? *Now*, what have you got?'

'That's only just a letter.'

'What have you got it here for?'

'I must just have put it there.'

'Or maybe it walked,' said Matchett. 'And who's been writing *you* letters, may I ask?'

As gently as possible, Portia tried saying nothing. She let Matchett turn the pillow, then settled with her cheek on the new, cool side. For nearly a minute, propitiatingly, she acted someone grateful going to sleep. Then, with infinite stealth, she felt round under the pillow – to find the letter gone. 'Oh, *please,* Matchett!' she cried.

'The proper place for your letters is in your desk. What else did Mrs Thomas give you a desk for?'

'I like having a letter here when it's just come.'

'That's no place for letters at your age – it's not nice. You didn't ought to be getting letters like that.'

'It's not a letter like that.'

'And who wrote it, may I ask?' said Matchett, her voice rising.

'Only that friend of Anna's – only Eddie.'

'Ah! So he did?'

'Only because I got him his hat.'

'Wasn't he civil?'

'Yes,' Portia said firmly. 'He knows I like getting letters. I haven't had any letters for three weeks.'

'Oh, he does, does he – he knows you like getting letters?'

'Well, Matchett, I do.'

'So he saw fit to thank you kindly for getting his hat? It's the first manners he's shown here, popping in and out like a weasel.

84

Manners? He's no class. Another time, you leave Phyllis get him his hat, else let him get it himself – he's here often enough to know where it should be ... Yes, you mind what I'm saying: I know what I say.'

Matchett's voice, so laden and unemphatic, clicked along like a slow tape, with a stop at the last word. Portia lay in a sort of coffin of silence, one hand under the pillow where the letter had been. Outside the room there sounded a vacuum of momentarily arrested London traffic: she turned her eyes to the window and looked at the glass-dark sky with its red sheen. Matchett's hand in the cuff darted out like an angry bird, knocked once against the pleated shade of the bed lamp, then got the light switched on. Immediately, Portia shut her eyes, set her mouth, and lay stiff on the pillow, as though so much light dug into a deep wound. She felt it must be very late, past midnight: that point where the river of night flows underneath time, that point at which occurs the mysterious birth of tomorrow. The very sudden, anaesthetic white light, striped by the pleats of the shade, created a sense of sick-room emergency. As though she lay in a sick-room, her spirit retreated to a seclusion of its own.

Matchett sat with the captured letter in the trough of her lap. Meanwhile, her spatulate fingers bent and injured, with unknowing sensuous cruelty, like a child's, the corners of the blue envelope. She pinched at the letter inside's fullness, but did not take it out. 'You'd be wrong to trust him,' she said.

Safe for the minute, sealed down under her eyelids, Portia lay and saw herself with Eddie. She saw a continent in the late sunset, in rolls and ridges of shadow like the sea. Light that was dark yellow lay on trees, and penetrated their dark hearts. Like a struck glass, the continent rang with silence. The country, with its slow tense dusk-drowned ripple, rose to their feet where they sat: she and Eddie sat in the door of a hut. She felt the hut, with its content of dark, behind them. The unearthly level light streamed in their faces; she saw it touch his cheekbones, the tips of his eyelashes, while he turned her way his eyeballs blind with gold. She saw his hands hanging down between his knees, and her hands hanging down peacefully beside him as they sat together on the step of the hut. She felt the touch of calmness and similarity: he and she were one without any touch but this. What was in the hut behind she did not know: this light was eternal; they would be here for ever.

Then she heard Matchett open the envelope. Her eyes sprang open; she cried: 'Don't touch that!'

'I'd not have thought this of you.'

'My father would understand.'

Matchett shook. 'You don't care what you say.'

'You're not fair, Matchett. You don't know.'

'I know that Eddie's never not up to something. And he makes free. *You* don't know.'

'I do know when I'm happy. I know that.'

7

MAJOR BRUTT found it simple to pay the call: everything seemed to point to his doing that. To begin with, he found that an excellent bus, a 74, took him from Cromwell Road the whole way to Regent's Park. He was not a man to ring up; he simply rang a door bell. To telephone first would have seemed to him self-important, but he knew how to enter a house unassumingly. He had lived in parts of the world where you drop in: there seemed to him nothing complex about that. His impression of Windsor Terrace had been a warm and bright one; he looked forward today to seeing the drawing-room floor. Almost unremitting solitude in his hotel had, since his last visit, made 2 Windsor Terrace the clearing-house for his dreams: these reverted to kind Anna and to that dear little kid with fervent, tender, quite sexless desire. A romantic man often feels more uplifted with two women than with one: his love seems to hit the ideal mark somewhere between two different faces. Today, he came to recover that visionary place, round which all the rest of London was a desert. That last night, the Quaynes, seeing him out, had smiled and said heartily: 'Come again.' He took it that people meant what they said – so here he was, coming again. Thomas's having added 'Ring up first' had made no impression on him whatever. They had given him *carte blanche*, so here he was, dropping in. He judged that Saturday should be a good day.

This Saturday afternoon Thomas, home from the office, sat at his study table, drawing cats on the blotter, waiting for Anna to come back from a lunch. He was disappointed with her for lunching out on a Saturday and for staying so late. When he heard the bell ring he looked up forbiddingly (though there was just a chance Anna might have forgotten her key), listened, frowned, put whiskers on to a cat, then looked up again. If it had been her, she would ring two or three times. The ring, how-ever, did not repeat itself – though it lingered on uneasily in the air. Saturday made it unlikely that this could be a parcel. Tele-grams were almost always telephoned through. That it could be a caller did not, at his worst moment, enter Thomas's head. Callers were unheard of at Windsor Terrace. They had been eliminated; they simply did not occur. The Quaynes' home life was as much their private life as though their marriage had been illicit. Their privacy was surrounded by an electric fence – friends who did not first telephone did not come.

This being so, even Phyllis, with all her aplomb, her ever-consciousness of a pretty cap, had forgotten how to cope with a plain call. She well knew the cut of 'expected' people, people who all but admitted themselves, who marched in past her without the interrogatory pause. Some smiled at her, some did not – but well did she know the look of someone who knew the house. And, except for a lunch party or a dinner, nobody ever came who did not.

So, directly she opened the door and saw Major Brutt, she knew it was in her power to oppress. She raised her eyebrows and simply looked at him. For him, that promising door had opened on something on which he had not reckoned. He knew, of course, that people have parlourmaids – but that last time the hall had been so full of light, of good-bye smiles, of heaps of women's fur coats. He faltered slightly at once: Phyllis saw the drop in his masculine confidence. Her contempt for humility made her put him down as an ex-officer travelling in vacuum cleaners, or those stockings that are too shiny to wear.

So it was with snappy triumph that she was able to say Mrs Quayne was not at home. Modifying his expectant manner, he then asked for Mr Quayne – which made Phyllis quite sure that this person must be wanting something. She was quite right: he was – he had come all this way to see a holy family.

'Mr Quayne? I couldn't say,' Phyllis replied pursily. She let her eye run down him and added, 'sir'. She said: 'I could inquire if you like to wait.' She looked again – he did not carry a bag, so she let him in to a certain point in the hall. Too sharp to give Thomas away by looking into the study, she started downstairs to ring through on the room-to-room telephone. As she unhooked the receiver at the foot of the basement stairs, intending to say, 'Please, sir, I think there is someone –' she heard Thomas burst open his door, come out, and make some remark. Now Mrs Quayne would not have allowed that.

In the seconds before Thomas came to his door, Major Brutt may have realized this was a better house to be brought back to in triumph than to make one's way into under one's own steam. While he looked up the draughtless stairs behind the white arches, some aspirations faded out of his mind. He glanced at the console table, but did not like to put down his hat yet: he stood sturdily, doubtfully. Then a step just inside that known door made him re-animate like a dog: his moustache broadened a little, ready for a smile.

'Oh, *you*: splendid!' said Thomas – he held his hand out, flat open, with galvanized heartiness. 'I thought I heard some-one's voice. Look here, I'm so sorry you –'

'Look here, I do hope I'm not –'

'Oh, good God, no! I was simply waiting for Anna. She's out at some sort of lunch – you know how long those things take.'

Major Brutt had no idea – it had seemed to him rather more near tea time. He said: 'They must be great places for talk,' as Thomas, incompletely resigned, got him into the study, with rather too much fuss. The room now held fumy heavy afternoon dusk – Thomas had been asleep in here for an hour before unscrewing his pen, opening the blotter, and sitting down with some of his papers out. 'Everyone talks,' said Thomas. 'I can't think, can you, how they keep it up.' He looked at his cats with nostalgia, shut the blotter, swept some papers in a drawer, and shut the drawer with a click. That was that, he seemed to say, I *was* busy, but never mind. Meanwhile, Major Brutt pulled his trousers up at the knees and lowered himself into an armchair.

Thomas, trying to concentrate, said: 'Brandy?'

'Thanks, no: not just now.'

Thomas took this with just a touch of rancour – it made the position less easy than ever. Major Brutt was clearly counting on tea, and the Quaynes would be likely to cut tea out; Anna, with whom large lunches did not agree, would be likely to come home claustrophobic and cross. She and Thomas had planned to walk once right round the park, after that, at perhaps about five, to go to a French film. At the cinema they felt loverlike; they often returned in a taxi arm-in-arm. Thomas had a notion that, for Major Brutt, the little kid Portia might do just as well – in fact, she might really be his object. But, annoyingly, Portia was not to be found either. Saturday was her free day, when she might have been expected to be about. But having come for her lunch, Thomas was told, she had gone out immediately – nobody knew where. Matchett was said to say that she might not be in for tea. Thomas found he had formed, with regard to Portia, just enough habit of mind to be cross that she was not about on Saturday afternoon.

This accumulating worry made Thomas ask himself what on earth had made him go to the door when he might have stayed playing possum. Had the sense of siege in here oppressed him, or had he, in fact, felt lonelier than he thought? The *worry* of sitting facing this patient man! Then he gave Major Brutt a quick, undecided, mean look. One had clearly got the idea this Brutt was out of a job: had he not said something about irons in the fire? That meant he was after something. That was why he had come. *Now*, no doubt, he had something soft in Quayne and Merrett's in view – he would not be the first old buffer who had.

Then, Thomas had a crisis of self-repugnance. Twitching his head away, with a shamefaced movement, from that block of integrity in the armchair, he saw how business had built him, Thomas, into a false position, a state of fortification odious, when he noticed it, to himself. He could only look out through slits at grotesque slits of faces, slits of the view. His vision became, from habit, narrow and falsified. Seeing anything move, even an animal, he thought: What is this meant to lead to? Or a gesture would set him off: Oh, so *that's* what he's after ... Oh, then what *does* he want? Society was self-interest given a pretty gloss. You felt the relentless pressure behind small-talk. Friendships were dotted with null pauses, when one eye in calculation sought the clock. Love seemed the one reprieve from the watchfulness: it annihilated this uneasy knowledge. He could love with regard to nothing else. Therefore he loved without any of that discretion known to more natural natures – which is why astute men are so often betrayed.

Whatever he's after, or not after, he thought, we certainly can't use him. Quayne and Merrett's only wanted flair, and one sort of distilled nervosity. They could use any number of Eddies, but not one Brutt. He felt Brutt ought to try for some sort of area travel in something or other – perhaps, however, he was trying for that already. All he seemed to have to put on the market was (query) experience, that stolid alertness, that pebble-grey direct look that Thomas was finding morally hypnotic. There was, of course, his courage – something now with no context, no function, no outlet, fumbled over, rejected, likely to fetch nothing. Makes of men date, like makes of cars; Major Brutt was a 1914–18 model: there was now no market for that make. In fact, only his steadfast persistence in living made it a pity that he could not be scrapped ... No, we cannot use him. Thomas once more twitched his head. Major Brutt's being (frankly) a discard put the final blot on a world Thomas did not like.

Major Brutt, offered Thomas's cigarette case with rather hostile abruptness, hesitated, then decided to smoke. This ought to steady him. (That he wanted steadying, Thomas had no idea.) The fact, the fact of Thomas, Thomas as Anna's hus-

band, was a lasting shock. Major Brutt remembered Anna as
Pidgeon's lover only. The picture of that great evening together
– Anna, himself, Pidgeon – was framed in his mind, and could
not be taken down – it was the dear possession of someone with
few possessions, carried from place to place. When he had come
on Anna in the Empire foyer, it could be no one but Pidgeon
that she was waiting for: his heart had gone up because he
would soon see Pidgeon. Then Thomas had come through the
foyer, spoken about the taxi, put his hand under Anna's elbow
with a possessing smile. That was the shock (though she had
first said she was married), and it was a shock still. That one
great evening – hers, Pidgeon's, his own – had made one continuous thread through his own uncertain days. He would recall
it at times when he felt low. Anna's marriage to Pidgeon had
been one great thing he had to look forward to. When Pidgeon
kept saying nothing, and still said nothing, Major Brutt only
thought they were waiting a long time. There is no fidelity like
the fidelity of the vicarious lover who has once seen a kiss. By
being married to Thomas, for having been married to Thomas
for eight London years, Anna annihilated a great part of Major
Brutt. He thought, from her unhappily calm smile in the Empire foyer, that she must see what she had done to him; he
had taken some of her kindness for penitence. When later, back
in her home, she with her woman's good manners had led him
to talk of Pidgeon, their sole mutual friend, she had laid waste
still more. He had not known how to bear it when she spoke of
Pidgeon and the plate and the orange. Only Portia's presence
made him bear it at all.

But a man must live. Not for nothing do we invest so much
of ourselves in other people's lives – or even in momentary pictures of people we do not know. It cuts both ways: the happy
group inside the lighted window, the figure in long grass in the
orchard seen from the train stay and support us in our dark
hours. Illusions are art, for the feeling person, and it is by art
that we live, if we do. It is the emotion to which we remain
faithful, after all: we are taught to recover it in some other
place. Major Brutt, brought that first night to Windsor Terrace
at the height of his inner anguish on Pidgeon's account, already

began to attach himself to that warm room. For hospitality, and that little girl on the rug, he began to abandon Pidgeon already. Even he had a ruthlessness in his sentiments – and he had been living alone in a Cromwell Road hotel. The glow on the rug, Anna on the sofa with her pretty feet up, Thomas nosing so kindly round for cigars, Portia nursing her elbows as though they had been a couple of loved cats – here was the focus of the necessary dream. All the same it was Thomas he, still, could not quite away with. He hoped, by taking Thomas's cigarette, by being a little further in debt to him, to feel more naturally to him, as man to man.

He looked on Thomas as someone who held the prize. But in this darkening light of Saturday afternoon, loneliness lay on his study like a cloud. The tumbled papers, the ash, the empty coffee-cup made Pidgeon's successor look untriumphant, as though he had never held any prize. Even the fire only grinned, like a fire in an advertisement. Major Brutt, whose thought could puzzle out nothing, had, in regard to people, a sort of sense of the weather. He was aware of the tension behind Thomas's manners, of the uneasy and driven turnings of his head. Without nerves, Major Brutt had those apprehensions that will make an animal suddenly leave, or refuse to enter, a room. Was Pidgeon in here with them, overtowering Thomas, while Thomas did the honours to Pidgeon's friend? He had decided to smoke, so he pulled at his cigarette, reflecting the fire in his fixed, pebble-grey eyes. He saw that he ought to go soon – but not yet.

Thomas, meanwhile, gave a finished representation of a man happily settling into a deep chair. He gave, inadvertently, one overstated yawn, then had to say, to excuse this: 'It's too bad, Anna's not in.'

'Oh well, of course, I chanced that. Just dropping in.'

'It's too bad Portia's not in. I've no idea where she's gone.'

'I daresay she goes about quite a bit?'

'No, not really. Not yet. She's a bit young.'

'There's something sweet about her, if I may say so,' said Major Brutt, lighting up.

'Yes, there is, rather ... She's my sister, you know.'

'That's awfully nice.'

'Or rather, my half-sister.'

'Comes to much the same thing.'

'Does it?' said Thomas. 'Yes, I suppose it does. In a way, it feels a bit funny though. For one thing, she and I are a half generation out. However, it seems to work out all right. We thought we might try it here for a year or so, see how she liked things with us, and so on. She's an orphan, you see – which is pretty tough on her. We had never seen as much as we'd have liked to of her, because my father liked living abroad. We rather felt she might find us a bit of a proposition. Having just lost her mother, and not being grown up yet, so not able to go about with Anna, we thought she might find London a bit ... well – However, it seems to work out all right. We found some quite good classes for her to go to, so she's been making friends with girls of her own age. ...'

Overcome by the dullness of what he had been saying, Thomas trailed off and slumped further back in his chair. But Major Brutt, having listened with close attention, evidently expected more to come. 'Nice to have a kid like that to keep one cheerful,' he said. 'How old did you say she was?'

'Sixteen.'

'She must be great company for – for Mrs Quayne.'

'For Anna? Oh yes. Funny you and Anna running into each other. She's slack about keeping up with her old friends, and at the same time she certainly misses them.'

'It was nice of her to remember my name, I thought. You see, we'd only met once.'

'Oh yes, with Robert Pidgeon. Sorry I never met him. But he seems to move round, and I'm rooted here.' Casting at Major Brutt one last uneasy flash of suspicion, Thomas added: 'I've got this business, you know.'

'Is that so?' said Major Brutt politely. He knocked off his ash into the heavy glass tray. 'Excellent, if you like living in town.'

'You'd rather get out somewhere?'

'Yes, I must say I would. But that all depends, at the moment, on what happens to come along. I've got a good many –'

'Irons in the fire? I'm sure you are absolutely right.'

'Yes, if one thing doesn't turn up, it's all the more likely that another will ... The only trouble is, I've got a bit out of touch.'

'Oh yes?'

'Yes, I've stuck out there abroad too long, it rather seems. I'd rather like, now, to be in touch for a bit; I'd rather like to stay for a bit in this country.'

'But in touch with what?' said Thomas. 'What do you think there is, then?'

Some obscure hesitation, some momentary doubt made Major Brutt frown, then look across at Thomas in a more personal manner than he had looked yet. But his look was less clear – the miasma thickening in the study had put a film over him. 'Well,' he said, 'there must be something going on. You know – in a general way, I mean. You know, something you all –'

'We all? We who?'

'Well, you, for instance,' Major Brutt said. 'There must be something – that's why I feel out of touch. I know there must be something all you people get together about.'

'There may be,' said Thomas, 'but I don't think there is. As a matter of fact, I don't think we get together. We none of us seem to feel very well, and I don't think we want each other to know it. I suppose there is nothing so disintegrating as competitiveness and funk, and that's what we all feel. The ironical thing is that everyone else gets their knives into us bourgeoisie on the assumption we're having a good time. At least, I suppose that's the assumption. They seem to have no idea that we don't much care for ourselves. We weren't nearly so much hated when we gave them more to hate. But it took guts to be even the fools our fathers were. We're just a lousy pack of little Christopher Robins. Oh, we've got to live, but I doubt if we see the necessity. The most we can hope is to go on getting away with it till the others get it away from us.'

'I say, don't you take a rather black view of things?'

'What you mean is, I ought to take more exercise? Or Eno's, or something? No, look here, my only point was that I really can't feel you are missing very much. I don't think much goes on – However, Anna might know – Cigarette?'

'No thanks: not at the moment.'

'What's that?' said Thomas sharply.

Major Brutt, sympathetic, also turned his head. They heard a key in the hall door.

'Anna,' Thomas said, with a show of indifference.

'Look here, I feel I probably ought –'

'Nonsense. She'll be delighted.'

'But she's got people with her.' There certainly were voices, low voices, in the hall.

Repeating 'No, stay, do stay,' with enormous concentration, Thomas heaved himself up and went to the study door. He opened the door sharply, as though to quell a riot. Then he exclaimed with extreme flatness: 'Oh ... Hullo, Portia ... oh, *hullo*; good afternoon.'

'Good afternoon,' returned Eddie, with the matey deference he now kept for Thomas out of office hours.

'I say, don't let us disturb you: we're just going out again.' Expertly reaching round Portia, he closed Thomas's hall door behind Thomas's sister. His nonchalance showed the good state of his nerves – for since when had old Thomas taken to popping out? Portia said nothing: close beside Eddie she stood smiling inordinately. To Thomas, these two appeared to be dreadful twins – they held up their heads with the same rather fragile pride; they included him in the same confiding smile. Clearly, they had hoped to creep in unheard – their over-responsiveness to Thomas only showed what a blow Thomas had been. They both glowed from having walked very fast.

Thomas showed what a blow they were by looking heavily past them. He explained: 'I thought you were Anna.'

Eddie said nicely: 'I'm so sorry we're not.'

'Isn't she in?' said Portia mechanically.

'But I'll tell you who *is* here,' said Thomas. 'Major Brutt. Portia, you'd better show up, just for a minute.'

'We – we were just going out.'

'Well, a minute won't hurt you, will it?'

The most stubbornly or darkly drawn-in man has moments when he likes to impose himself, to emerge and be a bully. The diversion of a raindrop from its course down the pane, the frustration of a pet animal's will in some small way all at once become imperative, if the nature is to fulfil itself. Thomas took pleasure in thrusting Portia into the study, away from Eddie, to talk to Major Brutt. A hand on her shoulder-blade, he pushed her ahead of him with colourless, unadmitted cruelty. Eddie, dogged, determined to be as much *de trop* as he could, followed along behind.

Major Brutt, during the colloquy in the hall, had sat with his knees parted, turning his wrists vaguely, making his cuff-links wink. What he may have heard he shook off, like a dog shaking its ears. The little kid was propelled round the door at him: Thomas then made a pause, then introduced Eddie. Portia and Eddie lined up shoulder to shoulder, smiling at Major Brutt with a captive deference. In their eyes he saw the complicity of a suspended joy.

'I've come crashing round here,' Major Brutt said to Portia. 'Disturbing your brother a good bit, I'm afraid. But your sister-in-law had very kindly said –'

'Oh, I'm sure she did really mean it,' said Portia.

'At all events,' he went on, going on smiling with agonized heartiness, 'she's been well out of it. I gather she's out at lunch. But I've been keeping your brother from forty winks.'

'Not at all,' said Thomas. 'It's been frightfully nice.' He sat down again in his own chair so firmly that Portia and Eddie had either to sit down somewhere also, or else, by going on standing (as they continued to do), to make their semi-absence, their wish to be elsewhere, marked. They stood a foot apart but virtually hand in hand. Portia looked past Eddie liquidly, into nowhere, as though she did not exist because she might not look at him. Eddie began to smoke, but smoked very consciously. This announcement of their attachment – in a way that showed complete indifference to the company – struck on Thomas coldly: one more domestic fatigue. He also wondered how Eddie had the nerve ... To Major Brutt, kinder to love than Thomas, this seemed a holy anomaly.

'And where have you been?' said Thomas – who had, after all, every right to ask.

'Oh, we've been to the Zoo.'

'Wasn't it very cold there?'

They looked at each other, not seeming to know. 'It's all draughts and stinks,' Eddie said. 'But we did think it was pretty, didn't we, Portia?'

Thomas marvelling, thought: He really *has* got a nerve. What happens when Anna comes in?

8

'WHO was that old bird?'

'Major Brutt. He was a friend of someone Anna knew.'

'Who that she knew?'

'His name was Pidgeon.'

Eddie tittered at this, then said: 'Is he dead?'

'Oh no. Major Brutt says he thinks he is very well.'

'I've never heard of Pidgeon,' said Eddie, frowning.

Without guile, she said: 'But do you know all her friends?'

'I said we'd run into someone, you little silly. I told you we would, if we went back.'

'But you did ask me to fetch it –'

'I suppose I did – I must say I think Brutt's a rather nasty old thing. He leers.'

'Oh no, Eddie – he *doesn't*.'

'No, I suppose he doesn't,' said Eddie, looking depressed. 'I suppose he's really much nicer than I am.'

Turning and anxiously eyeing Eddie's forehead, Portia said: 'Today he looked rather sad.'

'You bet he did,' said Eddie. 'He wanted an innings. He may be a great deal nicer than I am, darling, but I do feel I ought to tell you that that sort of person makes me perfectly sick. And look how he'd rattled Thomas – poor old Thomas was all over the place. No, Brutt is a brute. Do you realize, Portia darling, that it is because of there being people like him that there are people like me? How on earth did he get into the house?'

'He said Anna'd asked him to come again.'

'What a cynic Anna is!'

'I do think, Eddie, you are exaggerating.'

'I've got no sense of proportion, thank God. That man palpably loathed me.' Eddie stopped and blew out his lower lip. 'Oh dear,' said Portia, 'I quite wish we hadn't met him.'

'Well, I told you we would if we went back. You know that house is a perfect web.'

'But you said you wanted my diary.'

They were having tea, or rather their tea was ordered, at Madame Tussaud's. Portia, who had not been here before, had been disappointed to find all the waitresses real: there were no deceptions of any kind – all the waxworks were in some other part. He and she sat side by side at a long table intended for a party of four or six. Her diary, fetched from Windsor Terrace, lay still untouched between their elbows, with a strong indiarubber band round it. She said: 'How do you mean that Anna is a cynic?'

'She has depraved reasons for doing the nicest things. However, that doesn't matter to me.'

'If it really doesn't, why does it upset you?'

'After all, darling, she is a human soul. And her character did upset me, at one time. I'm several degrees worse since I started to know her. I wish I had met you sooner.'

'Worse how? Do you think you are wicked?'

Eddie, leaning a little back from the table, looked all round the restaurant, at the lights, at the other tables, at the mirrors, considering the question seriously, as though she had asked him whether he felt ill. Then he returned his eyes closely to Portia's face, and said with an almost radiant smile: 'Yes.'

'In what way?'

But a waitress came with a tray and put down the teapot, the hot-water jug, a dish of crumpets, a plate of fancy cakes. By the time she had done, the moment had gone by. Eddie raised a lid and stared at the crumpets. 'Why on earth', he said, 'didn't she bring salt?'

'Wave to her and ask her – Shall I really pour out? ... But, Eddie, I can't see you are wicked. Wicked in what way?'

'Well, what do you hate about me?'

'I don't think I –'

'Try the other way round – what do you like least?'

She thought for a moment, then said: 'The way you keep making faces for no particular reason.'

'I do that when I wish I had no face. I can't bear people getting a line on me.'

'But it attracts attention. Naturally people notice.'

'All the same, it throws them on the wrong track. My goodness, they think, he's going to have a nerve-storm; he may be really going to have a fit. That excites them, and they start to play up themselves. So then that gives me time to collect myself, till quite soon I feel like ice.'

'I see – but –'

'No, you see the fact is, darling, people do rattle me – You do see?'

'Yes, I do.'

'It's vitally important that you should. In a way, I believe I behave worse with other people, Anna for instance, when you're there, because I always feel you will know why, and to feel that rather gins me up. You must never make me feel you don't understand.'

'What would happen if I did make you feel I didn't?'

Eddie said: 'I should stay unreal for ever.' He rolled her gloves up into a tight ball, and squeezed them in the palm of one hand. Then he looked in horror past the brim of her hat. She turned her head to see what he saw, and they both saw themselves in a mirror.

'I feel I shall always understand what you feel. Does it matter if I don't sometimes understand what you *say*?'

'Not in the least, darling,' said Eddie briskly. 'You see, there is really nothing intellectual between us. In fact, I don't know why I talk to you at all. In many ways I should so much rather not.'

'But we have to do something.'

'I feel it is a waste of you. You puzzle so much, with your dear little goofy face. Is it simply you've never met anybody like me?'

'But you said there wasn't anybody like you.'

'But there are lots of people who imitate what I really am. I suppose you haven't met any of them, either – Look, darling, do pour out; the tea's getting cold.'

'I hope I shall do it well,' said Portia, grasping the metal tea-pot handle in her handkerchief.

'Oh Portia, has no one really taken you out to tea before?'

'Not by myself.'

'Nor to any other meal? You do make me feel happy!' He watched her slowly filling his cup with a gingerly, wobbling stream of tea. 'For one thing, I feel I can stay still. You're the only person I know I need do nothing *about*. All the other people I know make me feel I have got to sing for my supper. And I feel that you and I are the same: we are both rather wicked or rather innocent. You looked pleased when I said Anna was depraved.'

'Oh, you didn't; you said she was a cynic.'

'When I think of the money I've wasted sending Anna flowers!'

'Were they very expensive?'

'Well, they were for me. It just shows what a fool I've learnt to be. I haven't been out of debt now for three years, and I've got not a soul to back me – No, it's all right darling, I can pay for this tea – To lose my head is a thing I literally can't afford. You must hear of the way I keep on living on people? But what it *has* come to is: I've been bought up. They all think I want what they've got and I haven't, so they think if they get me that is a fair deal.'

'I suppose it is, in a way.'

'Oh, you don't understand, darling – Would you think I was vain if I said I was good-looking?'

'No. I think you are very good-looking, too.'

'Well, I am, you see, and I've got all this charm, and I can excite people. They don't really notice my brain – they are always insulting me. Everyone hates my brain, because I don't sell that. That's the underground reason why everyone hates me. I sometimes hate it myself. I wouldn't be with these pigs if I hadn't first been so clever. Last time I went home, do you know, Portia, my younger brother laughed at my soft hands.'

Portia had not for some time looked straight at Eddie, for fear her too close attention might make him stop. She had cut her crumpet up into little pieces; she nibbled abstractedly, dipping each piece in salt. When the first crumpet was eaten she paused, wiped her fingers on the paper napkin, then took a long drink of tea. Drinking, she looked at Eddie over her cup. She put down her cup and said: 'Life is always so complicated.'

'It's not merely life – It's me.'

'I expect it is you *and* people.'

'I expect you are right, you sweet beautiful angel. I have only had to do with people who liked me, and no one nice ever does.'

She looked at him with big eyes.

'Except you, of course – Look, if you ever stop you never will let me see you *have* stopped, will you?'

Portia glanced to see if Eddie's cup were empty. Then she cast her look down at her diary – keeping her eyes fixed on the black cover, she said: 'You said I was beautiful.'

'Did I? Turn round and let me look.'

She turned an at once proud and shrinking face. But he giggled: 'Darling, you've got salt stuck all over the butter on your chin, like real snow on one of those Christmas cards. Let me wipe it off – stay still.'

'But I had been going to eat another crumpet.'

'Oh, in that case it would be rather a waste – No, it's no good; I'd hate you to give me serious thoughts.'

'How often do you have them?'

'Often – I swear I do.'

'How old are you, Eddie?'

'Twenty-three.'

'Goodness,' she said gravely, taking another crumpet.

While she ate, Eddie studied her gleamingly. He said: 'You've got a goofy but an inspired face. Understanding just washes over it. Why am I ever with anybody but you? Whenever I talk to other people, they jeer in their minds and think I am being dramatic. Well, I am dramatic – why not? *I* am dramatic. The whole of Shakespeare is about me. All the others, of course, feel that too, which is why they are all dead nuts on Shakespeare. But because I show it when they haven't got the nerve to, they all jump on me. Blast their silly faces –'

While she ate, she kept her eyes on his forehead, at present tense with high feeling, but ventured to say nothing. Her meticulous observation of him made her like somebody at a play in a foreign language of which they know not one word – the action has to be followed as closely as one can. Just a shade unnerved by her look he broke off and said: 'Do I ever bore you, darling?'

'No – I was just thinking that, except for Lilian, this is the first conversation with anybody I've had. Since I came to London, I mean. It's much more the sort of conversation I have in my head.'

'It's a lot more cheerful than the conversations in *my* head. In those, reproaches are being showered on me. I don't get on at all well with myself – But I thought you said you talked to Matchett at nights?'

'Yes – but she's not in London, she's in the house. And lately, she's been more cold with me.'

Eddie's face darkened at once. 'Because of me, I suppose?'

Portia hesitated. 'She never much likes my friends.'

Annoyed by her fencing, he said: 'You haven't got any friends.'

'There's Lilian.'

He scowled this aside. 'No, the trouble with *her* is, she's a jealous old cow. And a snob, like all servants. You've been too nice to her.'

'She was so nice to my father.'

'I'm sorry, darling – But listen: for God's sake never talk about me. Never to anyone.'

'How could I, Eddie? I never possibly would.'

'I could kill people when I think what they would think.'

'Oh Eddie, mind – you've splashed tea on my diary! Matchett only knows you because she came on your letter.'

'You *must not* leave those about!'

'I didn't: she found it where it was put.'

'Where?'

'Under my pillow.'

'*Darling!*' said Eddie, melting for half a moment.

'I was there all the time, and she didn't do more than hold it. All she knows is, I've had a letter from you.'

'But she knows where it was.'

'I'm sure she would never tell. She likes knowing things they don't, about me.'

'I daresay you're right: she's got a mouth like a trap. And I've seen her looking at Anna. She'll keep this to use in her own way. Oh, do beware of old women – you've no notion how they batten on things. Lock everything up; hide everything! Don't bat an eyelid, ever.'

'As if this was a plot?'

'We are a plot. Keep plotting the whole time.'

She looked anxious and said: 'But then, shall you and I have any time left?'

'Left for what, do you mean?'

'I mean, for ourselves.'

He swept this aside and said: 'Plot – It's a revolution: it's our life. The whole pack are against us. So hide, hide everything.'

'*Why?*'

'You've no idea what people are like.'

Her mind went back. 'Major Brutt noticed, I think.'

'Idealistic old wart-hog! And Thomas caught us – I told you we should never have gone in.'

'But you did say you wanted my diary.'

'Well, we were mad. You only wait till Anna has had a word with Brutt. Shall I show you the talk I and Anna will have then?' Eddie posed himself, leaning sideways on one elbow with Anna's rather heavy nonchalant grace. He drew his fingers idly across his forehead, putting back an imaginary wave of hair. Seeming to let the words drop with a charming reluctance, he began: ' "Now Eddie, you mustn't be cross with me. This bores me just as much as it bores you. But I feel –" '

Portia cast an anxious look round the tea-room. 'Oh, ought you to imitate Anna here. . .?'

'I may not feel in the mood to do it again. As a rule, the thought of Anna makes me much too angry. I should like you to hear the things she would say to me if she got this unparalleled opening ... She would say, to remember you're quite a child. She would imply she wondered what I could see in you, and imply that of course I must be up to *something*, and that she only just wondered what it was. She would say that of course I could count on her not to say a word to you about what I am really like. She would say that of course she quite realized that she and Thomas were dull compared to me, because I was a genius, too superior to do any work that she did not come and offer me on a plate. She would say, of course, people who pay their bills *are* dull, Then she would say she quite saw it must be a strain on me, having to live up to my reputation, and that she saw I must have what stimulus I could get. Last of all, she would say, "And, of course, she *is* Thomas's sister." '

'Well, I don't see the point of any of that.'

'No, you wouldn't, darling. But I would. Anna'd be on the sofa; I should sit screwed round on one of her bloody little yellow chairs. When I tried to get up she would say: "You do make me so tired." She'd smoke. Like this' – Eddie opened his cigarette case, raked the contents over languidly with his finger-tips, his head on one side, as though playing the harp, selected one cigarette, looked at it cryptically, fastidiously lit it, and once more shook back an imaginary lock of hair. 'She would say,' he said, ' "You'd probably better go now – Portia's probably waiting down in the hall." '

'Oh Eddie – would she ever say that?'

'She'd say anything. The thing about Anna is, she loves making a tart of another person. She'd never dare be a proper tart herself.'

Portia looked puzzled. 'But I'm certain you like her.'

'Yes, I do in a way. That is why she annoys me so.'

'You once said she'd been very kind.'

'Indeed she has – that's her way of getting under my skin. Darling, didn't you think me being Anna was funny?'

'No, not really. I didn't think you enjoyed it.'

'Well, it was: it was very funny,' said Eddie defiantly.

Then he made several faces, pulling his features all ways, as though to flake off from them the last figments of Anna. The impersonation had (as Portia noticed) had fury behind it: each hypothetical arrow to him from Anna had been winged by a demoniac smile. Now he pulled his cup towards him and abruptly drank up some cold tea. He looked so threatening, Portia thought for a moment he might be going to spit the tea out – as though he were no more than rinsing his mouth with it. But he did swallow the tea, and after that smiled, though in a rather fagged-out way, like an actor coming off after a big scene. At the same time, he looked relieved, as though he had shot a weight off, and pious, as though a duty had been discharged. He seemed now to exist in a guiltless vacuum. At last he turned her way and sat filling his eyes with Portia, as though it were good to be home again.

After a pause he said: 'Yes, I really do quite like Anna. But we have got to have a villain of some sort.'

But Portia had a slower reaction time. During the villain's speech, while she ate crumpet, her brows had met in a rather uncertain line. While not really surprised, she had seemed to be hypnotized by this view of Anna. She was disturbed, and at the same time exhilarated, like a young tree tugged all ways in a vortex of wind. The force of Eddie's behaviour whirled her free of a hundred puzzling humiliations, of her hundred failures to take the ordinary cue. She could meet the demands he made with the natural genius of the friend and lover. The impetus under which he seemed to move made life fall, round him and her, into a new poetic order at once. Any kind of policy in the region of feeling would have been fatal in any lover of his – you had to yield to the wind. Portia's unpreparedness, her lack of policy – which had made Windsor Terrace, for her, the court of an incomprehensible law – with Eddie stood her in good stead. She had no point to stick to, nothing to unlearn. She had been born docile. The momentarily anxious glances she cast him had only zeal behind them, no crucial perplexity. By making herself so much his open piano that she felt her lips smile by reflex, as though they were his lips, she felt herself learn and gain him: this was Eddie. What he said, how he looked was becoming inevitable. From the first, he had not been unfamiliar to her. It might be said that, for the first time since Irene's death, she felt herself in the presence of someone ordinary.

Innocence so constantly finds itself in a false position that inwardly innocent people learn to be disingenuous. Finding no language in which to speak in their own terms they resign themselves to being translated imperfectly. They exist alone; when they try to enter into relations they compromise falsifyingly – through anxiety, through desire to impart and to feel warmth. The system of our affections is too corrupt for them. They are bound to blunder, then to be told they cheat. In love, the sweetness and violence they have to offer involves a thousand betrayals for the less innocent. Incurable strangers to the world, they never cease to exact a heroic happiness. Their singleness, their ruthlessness, their one continuous wish makes them bound to be cruel, and to suffer cruelty. The innocent are so few that two of them seldom meet – when they do meet, their victims lie strewn all round.

Portia and Eddie, side by side at the table, her diary between them under one of her hands, turned on each other eyes in which two relentless looks held apart for a moment, then became one. To generate that one look, their eyes seemed for the first time to be using their full power. The look held a sort of superb mutual greeting rather than any softness of love. You would have said that two accomplices had for the first time spoken aloud to each other of their part in the same crime, or that two children had just discovered their common royal birth. On the subject of love, there was nothing to say: they seemed to have no projects and no desires. Their talk today had been round an understood pact: at this moment, they saluted its significance.

Portia's life, up to now, had been all subtle gentle compliance, but she had been compliant without pity. Now she saw with pity, but without reproaching herself, all the sacrificed people – Major Brutt, Lilian, Matchett, even Anna – that she had stepped over to meet Eddie. And she knew that there would be more of this, for sacrifice is not in a single act. Windsor

Terrace would not do well at her hands, and in this there was no question of justice: no outside people deserve the bad deal they got from love. Even Anna had shown her a sort of immoral kindness, and, however much Matchett's love had been Matchett's unburdening, it had *been* love: one must desert that too.

For Eddie, Portia's love seemed to refute the accusations that had been brought against him for years, and the accusations he had brought against himself. He had not yet told her of half the indignation he felt. Older than she was, he had for longer suffered the guilty plausibility of the world. He had felt, not so much that he was in the right as that he was inevitable. He had gone wrong through dealing with other people in terms that he found later were not their own. However kind seemed the bosom he chose to lean his head on, he had found himself subject to preposterous rulings even there – and this had soon made the bosom vile for him. With love, a sort of maiden virtue of spirit stood outside his calamitous love affairs – the automatic quick touches he gave people (endearments, smiles to match smiles, the meaning-unmeaning use of his eyes) were his offensive-defensive, in defence of something they must not touch. His pretty ways had almost lost correspondence with appetite; his body was losing its naïvety. His real naïvety stayed in the withheld part of him, and hoped for honour and peace. Though he felt cut apart from his father and mother, in one sense he had never left home. He hated Anna, in so far as he did hate Anna, because he saw in her eyes a perpetual 'What next?' Himself, he saw no Next, but a continuous Now.

He looked down at Portia's hand and said: 'What a fat diary!'

Lifting her hand, she uncovered the black-backed book. 'It's more than half full', she said, 'already.'

'When that's done, you're going to start another?'

'Oh yes, I think so: things are always happening.'

'But suppose you stopped minding whether they did?'

'There would always be lunch and lessons and dinner. There have been days that were simply that already, but in that case I always leave a blank page.'

'Do you think they were worth a whole blank page?'

'Oh yes, because they were days, after all.'

Eddie picked the diary up and weighed it between his hands. 'And this is your thoughts, too?' he said.

'Some. But you make me wonder if I might stop thinking.'

'No, I like you to think. If you stopped, I should feel as though my watch had stopped in the night ... Which of your thoughts are these?'

'My more particular ones.'

'Darling, I love you to want me to take it home ... But supposing I went and left it in a bus?'

'It's got my name and address, inside: it would probably come back. But perhaps, though, you could put it in your pocket?' They squeezed the note-book into his overcoat pocket. 'As a matter of fact,' she said, 'now there is you, I may not want my diary so much.'

'But we shan't often meet.'

'I could keep what I think for you.'

'No, write it down, then show me. I like thoughts when they were thought.'

'But, in a way, that would not be quite the same thing. I mean, it would alter my diary. Up to now, it's been written just for itself. If I'm to keep on writing the same way, I shall have to imagine you do not exist.'

'*I* don't make you different.'

'You make me not alone. Being that was part of my diary. When I first came to London, I was the only person in the world.'

'Look – what will you write in while I've got this book? Shall we go to Smith's and buy you another?'

'Smith's near here is shut on Saturday afternoon. I don't think, anyhow, I shall write about today.'

'No, don't; you're perfectly right. I don't want you to *write* about you and me. In fact you must never write about me at all. Will you promise me you will never do that?'

'Why not?'

'I just don't like the idea. No, just write about what happens.

Write about lessons, and those sickening talks I'm certain you have with Lilian, and what there is for meals, and what the rest of them say. But *swear* you won't write down what you feel.'

'You don't know yet if I do.'

'I hate writing; I hate art – there's always something else there. I won't have you choosing words about me. If you ever start that, your diary will become a horrible trap, and I shan't feel safe with you any more. I like you to think, in a sort of way; I like to think of you going, like a watch. But between you and me there must never be any thoughts. And I detest after-thoughts. In fact, I'm just as glad to be taking this book right away from you, even for a few days. Now, I suppose, you don't understand what I'm saying?'

'No, but it doesn't really matter.'

'The chap *you* ought to talk to is Major Brutt ... Oh, heavens!'

'Why?'

'It's six. I ought to be somewhere else. I must go – Here, angel, take your gloves ... *Now*, what's the matter?'

'You won't forget it's in your overcoat pocket?'

9

THE DIARY

Monday

THIS diary has come back from Eddie by post. He did not write any letter as he did not have time. The parcel had the office label outside. I shall have to write hard now, as I will have missed nine days.

The white rug from by my bed has gone away to be cleaned where I upset the varnish for my bears. Matchett has put a red one that pricks my feet.

Today we did Umbrian Art History, Book Keeping, and German Composition.

Tuesday

Eddie has not said about the diary yet. Lilian was bilious in lessons and had to go out, she says when she has feelings it makes her bilious. Today when I got home Anna was out, so I could have tea down with Matchett. She was busy mending Anna's purple chiffon dress so did not ask me anything at all. When Anna came in she sent for me to come up and said she meant to take me to a concert this evening as she had a spare ticket. She looked put out.

Today we did English Essay, First Aid, and a Lecture on Racine. I must dress for the concert now.

Wednesday

Eddie has not said about the diary yet. This morning Lilian and I were late for the first class, her mother is putting her on a diet. Last night when I was in the taxi with Anna she said she hoped I had enjoyed Eddie's and my walk. I said yes, and she said, Eddie says he did. So I looked out of the window. She said she had a headache, and I said then didn't the concert make it worse, and she said yes, naturally it did. It was a disappointment having to take me.

Today we did Hygiene and French Composition about Racine, and were taken to look at pictures of Umbrian Art at the National Gallery.

Tonight Thomas and Anna are going out to dinner. I do wonder if Matchett will say good night. I do wish my white rug would come back.

Thursday

Today I have got a letter from Eddie, he still does not say about this diary. He says he had lunch with Anna and that she was nice. He says he did think of ringing me up, but did not. He does not say why. He says he feels he is starting a new life.

I do wonder who it was who did not go to that concert with Anna after all.

He says we must meet soon.

Today we did essays on our favourite Umbrian Art, and had to say what its characteristics were. We did Heine and were given our German Compositions back. We had a Lecture on Events of the Week.

Friday

I have written to Eddie but not about this diary.

I wrote to Eddie at half past four, when I got in, then went out again to buy a stamp to post it. Matchett did not hear the door either time, or at least she did not come up. Having tea with Anna were two new people who did not know if they ought to talk to me. Anna did not make any special impression on them, and they did not make any special impression on her. I did not stay there when I had had my tea.

It felt funny to come in twice, because once I am in I am generally in. When I came in after buying the stamp I felt still odder than I generally do, and the house was still more like always than usual. It always gets more so in the afternoon. When Thomas comes in he looks as though he was smelling something he thought he might not be let eat. This house makes a smell of feeling. Since I have known Eddie I ask myself what this smell is more.

Today we got our Essays on Racine back, and some of the girls discussed what they had put. We did Metternich and were taken out to a Lecture on the Appreciation of Bach.

Tomorrow will be another Saturday.

Saturday

I got a letter from Eddie, saying about Sunday. He said to ring him up if I could not go, but as I can I need not ring up. Before lunch Thomas and Anna drove away in the car, they are going off for the week-end. Anna said I could ask Lilian to tea, and Thomas gave me five shillings to go to the pictures with, he said he did hope I should be all right. Lilian cannot, so I am by the study fire. I like a day when there is some sort of tomorrow.

Sunday

I shall just put 'Sunday', Eddie prefers that.

Monday

Today we began Siennese Art, and did Book Keeping, and read a German play. Anna is having quite a big dinner party, she says I should not really enjoy myself.

Anyhow I should not mind, after yesterday.

Tuesday

Today I have had a sort of conversation with Thomas. When he came in he rang to ask if Anna was there, so I said no and said should I come down and he was not sure but said yes. He was leaning on his desk reading the evening paper, and when I came in he said it was warmer wasn't it? He said in fact he felt stuffy. As he had not seen me last night, because of the dinner party, he asked had I had a nice week-end? He said he hoped I had not been at all lonely, so I said oh no. He asked if I thought Eddie was nice. I said oh yes, and he said, he was round here yesterday, wasn't he? I said oh yes and said we had sat down here in the study, and that I did hope Thomas did not mind people sitting down here in his study. He said oh no, oh no in a sort of far-off voice. He said he supposed I and Eddie were rather friends, and I said yes we were. Then he went back to reading the evening paper as if there was something new in it.

He did half want me to go, and I did half want to go too, but I did not. This was the first time Thomas had asked me something he did seem to want to know. I was pleased to hear the name of Eddie and sat on the arm of the armchair. When he wanted a cigarette himself he started to offer me one by mistake. I could not help laughing. He said, I forgot, then said, no, don't start being grown-up. He said, you know mistakes run in our family. He said when my father started getting to know my mother, while my father still lived in Dorset with Mrs Quayne, my father started to smoke a lot more. He said my father got so ashamed of smoking so much that he started to save his cigarette stumps up in an envelope, then buried them in the garden. Because it was summer with no fires to burn them in, and he didn't want Matchett to count the stumps. I said, how did Thomas know, and he gave a sort of laugh and said, I once caught him at it. He said, my father did not like being caught, but to Thomas it only seemed a joke.

Thomas said he did not know what had put this into his head and after that he gave me a sort of look when he did not think I was looking. All Thomas's looks, except ones at Anna, are at people not looking. But he did not mind when he found I was looking. After all he and I have our father. Though he and Anna have got that thing together, there is not the same thing inside him and Anna, like that same thing inside him and me. He said in a sort of quick way that was near me, I hope Eddie is polite? I said, what did he mean? And he said, well, I don't know Eddie, does he try it on? He said, no you probably don't know what I mean, I said no, and he said in that case it was all right, he supposed. I said, we talked, and Thomas looked at the rug, as though he knew where we had sat, and said, oh did you, I see.

Then Thomas sort of rumpled the rug up with his heel, as if he did not like people to have sat there. That lamp makes Thomas's face all bags and lines, as if he was alone in his room. He said oh well, we shall see how you make out. He took a book up and said it was a mistake to love any person, I said it is all right if you are married, isn't it? And he said quickly, oh of course, *that* is all right. I heard a taxi stopping like one of Anna's, so I said I must go and I went up. I felt so like Thomas I had been quite glad to hear the taxi stop.

Wednesday

Today we did Hygiene and French Elocution, and were taken to the National Gallery to look at pictures of Siennese Art. On the way to the National Gallery, Lilian said, what ever was on my mind? I said nothing, but she said that I was not attending. After the National Gallery she asked me to come to Peter Jones's with her to help her choose a semi-evening dress. Lilian's mother lets her choose her clothes so as to let her form her taste. But Lilian has got taste. I said I must telephone to Matchett, and Lilian said that the day might come when it would be awkward for me having to do that. Lilian chose a beautiful blue dress that just goes on her figure and cost four guineas.

When I got back I heard Anna in the study. I have not seen Thomas since yesterday.

Thursday

I got a letter from Eddie to ask if anyone had asked about Sunday. He says he drew a picture for me, but he forgot to put that in. He says next week-end he has got to be away.

My white rug has come back, it is fluffier than it was, it is fluffy like the underneath of a cat. I hope I shall not upset something on it again.

Today we did Essays on Siennese Art, we were asked to say what characteristics it had got that Umbrian Art has not got. We had a Lecture on Events of the Week, and a lady to teach us to read out.

Lilian's mother says her blue dress is too clinging, but Lilian does not agree that it is.

Tonight there is quite a fog.

Friday

When I woke my window was like a brown stone, and I could hardly see the rest of the room. The whole house was just like that, it was not like night but like air being ill. While I was having breakfast, I could just see people holding our railings tight. Thomas has his breakfast after I have mine, but today he came and said, this must be your first fog. Then Anna sent down to say, would I rather not go to Miss Paullie's, but I said, oh no, I would rather go. She sent down another message to say Matchett had better go with me, then. Thomas said, she's quite right, you'll never see the traffic, you'll just have to push it back with your hand. And of course Matchett's hand is stronger than mine.

The walk there was just like an adventure. Outside the park gate there were fires burning, Matchett said they were flares. She made me wrap my mouth up and not speak, or I should swallow the fog. Half way there we took a taxi, and Matchett sat straight up as if she was driving the taxi herself. She still made me not speak. When we got to Miss Paullie's, half the girls had not got there at all. We had the lights on all day, and it felt more like a holiday. At the end of it there was not so much fog left, but all the same Matchett came to fetch me home.

We were to have had a lecture on the Appreciation of Mozart, but because of the fog we had a Debate on Consistency being the Hobgoblin of Small Minds. We also wrote essays on Metternich's policy.

Tonight Anna and Thomas stayed at home for dinner. She said that whenever there was a fog she always felt it was something that she had done, but she did not seem to mean this seriously. Thomas said he supposed most people felt the same and Anna said she was certain they did not. Then we sat in the drawing-room, and they wished I was not there.

Tomorrow is Saturday, but nothing will happen.

Saturday

I was quite right in saying nothing would happen, even the fog had gone, though it has left a brown stain. Thomas and Anna went away for the week-end, but this time by a train. I sat in the drawing-room and started *Great Expectations*. Matchett was busy with Anna's clothes. I went down to her for tea, she said, well, *you're* quite a ghost. But really it is this house that is like that. Phyllis invited me in to hear the kitchen gramophone. They can only play that when Anna is away.

Until I went out with Eddie I did not feel like this, unless I felt like this without knowing.

Sunday

This time this day last week.

This morning I went for a walk in the park. It was rather empty. Dogs kept running round till they got lost and people whistled, and everything smelt of clay. I looked at the places we liked best, but they were not the same. Some Sundays are very sad. In the afternoon Matchett took me on a bus to afternoon service at St Paul's Cathedral. They sang 'Abide With Me'. On the way home Matchett said, did I know Thomas and Anna were going away in April? She said, they're set on going abroad.

This was a surprise. She said, the way I was always one to notice, she wondered I hadn't picked anything up. She said, no doubt you'll be told in their good time. I said, shall I stay here? And she said, you can't do that, I'll be spring cleaning the house. I said, well I do wonder, but she just shut her mouth. The streets outside the bus looked much darker, because of all the shops being shut.

I wish someone liked me so much that they would come to the door when I was out and leave surprises for me on the hall table, to find when I came in.

When we got back from St Paul's, Matchett went in at the basement, but she made me go in at the front door with my key.

After supper, I sat on our rug in front of Thomas's fire. I thought some of the things that Eddie had told me on this rug.

His father is a builder.

When he was a child he knew pieces of the Bible straight off by heart.

He is quite afraid of the dark.

His two favourite foods are cheese straws and jellied *consommé*.

He would not really like to be very rich.

He says that when you love someone all your saved-up wishes start coming out.

He does not like being laughed at, so he pretends he wants people to laugh at him.

He has thirty-six ties.

Written down these look like the characteristics of things we have to write down at lessons. I do wonder if it would ever strike Eddie to leave a surprise for me on the table when I was out.

Monday

Eddie wrote to me while he was away. He says he is with people he does not like at all. He asks me to ring him up at the office and say what evening Anna will be out, but I do not know how to find out.

Today we did more about Siennese Art, Book Keeping, and

German Composition. Lilian was not waiting in the churchyard, in fact she got to lessons late. She has been upset by an actor, and asked me to tea with her tomorrow. When I got back Anna was quite pleased and told me about her week-end away as if I was St Quentin. Perhaps she is pleased about going to go abroad. She cannot tell me this till she thinks what to do with me.

Tuesday

Oh, it is just like an answer to a prayer, Major Brutt has sent me a jigsaw puzzle. I found it on the table when I came in. He says he would like to imagine me doing it.

Today we did English Essay and First Aid, and were taken to see *Le Cid* at a girls' school. Then I went to tea with Lilian for her to tell me about the actor. She was introduced to him somewhere, then wrote to him to say that she did admire his art, because she does admire it very much. The actor did not answer till she wrote the third time, then he invited Lilian to tea. She wore her blue dress with a coatee over it. There were other people at tea, but he asked her to stay on, and then he behaved in an awful way. She says he was passionate. Lilian was upset, and she says when she got home she wrote him two letters explaining the way she felt. But he did not answer either of the letters, and Lilian thinks now she must have hurt his feelings. This is making her quite bilious again.

No table in my room looks large enough to hold the whole of my jigsaw. I wonder if Matchett would mind if I did it on the floor.

Wednesday

Matchett is sending Anna's white velvet dress to the express cleaners, because Anna has to wear it tomorrow night. I said here, and Matchett said, no, out. So I ought to tell Eddie, I said I would.

Today we did Hygiene and French Elocution and were taken to look at historical dresses at the London Museum, which made a change. We also looked at a model of London burning, and

Miss Paullie said we must all do all that we could to prevent a future war.

I have telephoned to Eddie.

Thursday

Eddie says our lies are not our fault. So I am supposed to be going out with Lilian. They say that will be all right so long as I'm in by ten. I shall have to get to Lilian's house on the way back, because they might send Matchett to fetch me there. But where Eddie lives is quite somewhere else. What shall I do if I have not enough money?

Friday

Yesterday was all quite all right.

Saturday

This morning Anna took me out shopping. This afternoon, Thomas took me to the Zoo. She let me choose what we would have for lunch. Have they been saying things to each other, or have they got to tell me they are going away?

Sunday

They took me with them to lunch with people who live in Kent. So most of the day I have sat in the car and thought, except when we got out to have lunch. Anna and Thomas sat in front of the car, every now and then he said, how is she getting on? So Anna would turn round and have a look.

Since we got back, I have been getting on with my puzzle.

Last Thursday evening, when I first got to Eddie's, it was not like where I imagined he lived. He does not like his room and I'm sure it knows. He showed me all his books and said he was so glad I was not fond of reading at all. We had very nice cold foods off cardboard dishes, Eddie had thought of macaroons for me, and we then made coffee on his gas ring. He asked if I could cook, and I said my mother did when she lived in Notting Hill Gate. There were forks but he could only find one knife, fortunately the ham was in ready-made slices. He said he had never had a person to supper before, when he is alone he goes to a restaurant, and with people he goes to restaurants too. I said that must be lovely, and he said no it wasn't. I said, has no one been here before, then, and he said, oh, yes, I have people, to tea. I said who, and he said oh, ladies, you know. Then he did an imitation of a lady coming to tea with him. He pretended to throw his hat off on the divan and pat his hair up in front of the glass. Then he walked round the room, looking at things and sort of swaying himself. Then he did a lady curling up in his chair and smiling at him in a mysterious way. Then he showed me all sorts of things he does himself, like picking up the lady's fox fur and making a cat of it. I said, what else do you do, and he said, as little as I can get away with, darling. I said, why ever did he ask them to tea, and he said it was cheaper than giving them lunch out, but more tiring in the long run.

Then he picked the imaginary hat off the divan and pretended to jump hard on it with both feet. He said that I was such a weight off his mind. Then he gave me the last macaroon to finish, and put his head on my lap and pretended to go to sleep, but he said, don't drop crumbs in my eyes. When he woke up, he said that if he was a lady's fox fur and I was him, I would certainly stroke his head. While I did, he made himself look as if he had glass eyes, like a fur.

He said, what a pity we are too young to marry. Then he laughed and said, didn't that sound funny? I said, I don't see why Eddie, and he said, no, it doesn't sound funny, it sounds sweet. Then he shut his eyes again. At twenty minutes to ten I moved his head and said I must get a taxi.

I promised him I would not write down that. But Sundays make one have to think of the past.

Major Brutt will be disappointed if I don't get on with that puzzle more than I do.

Monday

When I got back from Miss Paullie's this afternoon I found Anna in my room doing my puzzle. She said she was sorry but she could not stop, so she and I went on doing the puzzle. She said where did I get the table it's on from, and I said it was a table Matchett had got from somewhere. She said, oh. She had got one whole corner done, a bit of sky with an aeroplane in it. She smiled away to herself and looked about for more pieces, and said well, how are all your beaux? She said she had better ask Major Brutt to dinner, and, then we could make him do the plainer part of the sky. Then she said, who else shall we ask, Eddie? She said, you say, it is your party you know. We went on with the puzzle till past the time for Anna to get dressed.

Today we started Tuscan Art, and did Book Keeping and German Grammar.

Tuesday

When I went down to breakfast past Anna's door it was a crack open, she was talking to Thomas. She was saying, well it's your something-or-other not mine. Thomas often sits on their bed while she drinks her morning coffee. Then she said, she's Irene's own child, you know.

Lilian has still heard nothing more from the actor.

Today we did First Aid and discussed our English Essays, and were taken to a lecture on Corneille.

Wednesday

I had a letter from Eddie, he does not say what he did at the week-end. He says not to say to Anna about those imitations, because once or twice she has been to tea there herself. What does he think I tell Anna? He does sometimes puzzle me.

Today it rained a great deal. We did Hygiene, and had a discussion on Corneille, and were taken to the National Gallery.

This afternoon, Anna took me to a grand afternoon party with gold chairs, but there were several girls of my age there. I wore my black velvet. Some lady came up and said to Anna, I hear you're just going abroad, too. Anna said, oh, I don't know, then gave me a sort of look.

Thursday

Today we had a lecture on Events of the Week, and a special lecture on Savonarola, and Elocution (in German).

Thomas and I were alone for dinner tonight, as Anna was

having dinner with somebody. He asked if I minded if we did not go out to anything, as he said he had had rather a day. He did not seem to want to talk about anything special. At the end of dinner he said I'm afraid this is rather dull, but it is family life. I said that when we lived in the South of France we often did not talk. He said, oh, talking of the South of France, I forget if I told you we are going to Capri. I said that would be very nice. He coughed and said, I mean Anna and I are going. He went quickly on to say, we have been wondering what would be the nicest plan for you. I said I thought London was very nice.

Friday

Last night, when I had just finished putting away this diary, Matchett came up to say good night. She clapped her hands at me for not being in bed yet. Then I told her I *had* been told that they were going abroad. She said, oh, you have? and sat down on my bed. She said, she's been on at him to tell you. I said, well they can't help it, I'm not their fault. She said no, but if they did right by you you wouldn't be always out after that Eddie. I said, well after all, they are married, and I'm not married to either of them. She said, it's one marriage and then another that's done harm all along. I said to Matchett that at any rate I'd got her. Then she leaned right on my bed and said, that's all very well, but are you a good girl? I said I didn't know what she meant, and she said no, that is just the trouble. She said, if Mr Thomas had been half of the man his father was, I'd have – I said, what, Matchett? And she said, never you mind.

She got up, stroking her apron, with her mouth tight shut. She said, he's a little actor, he is. She said, he had a right to leave you alone. Her good nights are never the same now.

Tomorrow will be Saturday.

Saturday

This morning Anna came with a quite ordinary smile and said, Eddie's wanting you on the telephone. It was quite a time since I'd heard the telephone ring, so Anna must have been having a talk first. He said, what about another walk in the park? He said, it's all right, I know, they are going out to Richmond. He said to meet on the bridge at three.

Matchett took no notice when we met on the stairs.

We did meet on the bridge at three.

Sunday

This morning they got up late, so I got on with my puzzle. When they were up they said they would do whatever I liked. I could not think what, so one of them said Epping. So we drove there to a place called The Robin Hood and had sausages for our lunch. Then Thomas and I went for a walk in the forest, Anna stayed in the car and read a detective story. The forest is full of blackish air like London, the trees do not look the same in it. He told me they had arranged for me to stay at the seaside at the time when Anna and he would be in Capri. I said oh, yes, that that would be fun. Thomas gave me a sort of look and said yes he thought it would.

When we got back to the car Thomas said, I've been talking plans with Portia. Anna said, oh, have you, I'm so glad. She was so interested in her detective story, she went on with it all the way home.

I told them how much I had enjoyed my day.

Anna said, it will be spring before we know where we are.

Part Two

THE FLESH

I

EARLY in March the crocuses crept alight, then blazed yellow and purple in the park. The whistle was blown later: it was possible to walk there after tea. In fact, it is about five o'clock in an evening that the first hour of spring strikes – autumn arrives in the early morning, but spring at the close of a winter day. The air, about to darken, quickens and is run through with mysterious white light; the curtain of darkness is suspended, as though for some unprecedented event. There is perhaps no sunset, the trees are not yet budding – but the senses receive an intimation, an intimation so fine, yet striking in so directly, that this appears a movement in one's own spirit. This exalts whatever feeling is in the heart.

No moment in human experience approaches in its intensity this experience of the solitary earth's. The later phases of spring, when her foot is in at the door, are met with a conventional gaiety. But her first unavowed presence is disconcerting; silences fall in company – the wish to be either alone or with a lover is avowed by some look or some spontaneous movement – the window being thrown open, the glance away up the street. In cities the traffic lightens and quickens; even buildings take such feeling of depth that the streets might be rides cut through a wood. What is happening is only acknowledged between strangers, by looks, or between lovers. Unwritten poetry twists the hearts of people in their thirties. To the person out walking that first evening of spring, nothing appears inanimate, nothing not sentient: darkening chimneys, viaducts, villas, glass-and-steel factories, chain stores seem to strike as deep as natural rocks, seem not only to exist but to dream. Atoms of light quiver between the branches of stretching-up black trees. It is in this unearthly first hour of spring twilight that earth's almost agonized livingness is most felt. This hour is so dreadful to some people that they hurry indoors and turn on the lights – they are pursued by the scent of violets sold on the kerb.

On that early March evening, Anna and Portia both, though not together, happened to be walking in Regent's Park. This was Portia's first spring in England: very young people are true but not resounding instruments. Their senses are tuned to the earth, like the senses of animals; they feel, but without conflict or pain. Portia was not like Anna, already half way through a woman's checked, puzzled life, a life to which the intelligence only gives a further distorted pattern. With Anna, feeling was by now unwilling, but she had more resonance. Memory enlarged and enlarged inside her an echoing, not often visited cave. Anna could remember being a child more easily and with more pleasure than she could remember being Portia's age: with her middle teens a cloudy phase had begun. She did not know half she remembered till a sensation touched her; she forgot to look back till these first evenings of spring.

At different moments, they both crossed different bridges over the lake, and saw swans folded, dark white ciphers on the white water, in an immortal dream. They both viewed the Cytherean twisting reaches at the ends of the lake, both looked up and saw pigeons cluttering the transparent trees. They saw crocuses staining the dusk purple or yellow, flames with no power. They heard silence, then horns, cries, an oar on the lake, silence striking again, the thrush fluting so beautifully. Anna kept pausing, then walking quickly past the couples against the railings: walking alone in her elegant black she drew glances; she went to watch the dogs coursing in the empty heart of the park. But Portia almost ran, with her joy in her own charge, like a child bowling a hoop.

You must be north of a line to feel the seasons so keenly. On the Riviera, Portia's notions of spring had been the mimosa, and then Irene unpacking from storage trunks her crushed cotton frocks. Spring had brought with it no new particular pleasures – for little girls in England spring means the Easter holidays: bicycle rides in blazers, ginger nuts in the pockets, blue violets in bleached grass, paper-chases, secrets, and mixed hockey. But Portia, thanks first to Irene, now to Anna, still knew nothing of this. She had come straight to London ... One Saturday, she and Lilian were allowed to take a bus into the country: they walked about in a wood near the bus stop. Then it thundered and they wanted to go home.

The day before Thomas and Anna were to start for Capri, Portia was to go to a Mrs Heccomb, living at Seale-on-Sea. Here Mrs Heccomb's late husband, a retired doctor, had been the secretary of the golf club. Mrs Heccomb, before her rather late marriage, had been a Miss Yardes, once Anna's governess. She had stayed on with Anna and her father at Richmond, keeping house and supporting the two of them gently, till Anna was nineteen. She had not been teaching Anna for several years before that: she had done no more than escort her to and from day school, see that she practised the piano, and make her feel her position as a motherless girl. But she had been quite a feature of Anna's home – that house uphill with a fine view of the river, an oval drawing-room, a terraced garden with almond trees. Anna used to call her Poor Miss Taylor: she had been as much pleased as surprised when Miss Yardes had followed Miss Taylor's pattern and, at the end of her annual holiday, announced her engagement to a widower. Anna and Miss Yardes had just at that time reached an uncomfortable phase of semi-confidence – for one thing, Robert Pidgeon had just appeared, and Miss Yardes was being too conscious of him. Though this loss had made a sad tear in daily habit, it had been on the whole a relief to see Miss Yardes go. Anna took on the housekeeping; the bills went up but meals became more amusing. Anna's father footed the bills without a quiver, and touched her by saying how much nicer this was. It turned out he had only kept Miss Yardes on all this time because he fancied a girl should have a woman about. During Miss Yardes's reign, Anna's father had felt free to form the habit of being self-protectively unobservant: this he did not discontinue after Miss Yardes had gone.

He continued, therefore, hardly to notice Robert or any of the less important young men.

Robert had celebrated Miss Yardes's wedding by bringing out to Richmond a package of fireworks; he and Anna went down the garden together and let the fireworks off on the wedding night. On their way back to the house, he kissed Anna for the first time. After that, he had gone abroad for two years, and she began to go about by herself. His subsequent irresponsible behaviour had been, she since understood, just as much her fault as his. This began after he came back from abroad. Late at nights, in fact in the small hours, they would rush in his car up Richmond Hill, to the house in which Anna's father slept soundly, where the thermos of milk no longer waited, where Miss Yardes no longer kept her door ajar. In the drawing-room, the embers of the fire would be coaxed alight again by the knowing Robert, then the Chinese cushion slipped under Anna's head ... They did not marry because they refused to trust each other.

On her marriage, then, Mrs Heccomb *née* Miss Yardes had gone to live at Seale, on the Kentish coast, about seventy miles from London. Here her husband had bought a strip of reclaimed beach, just inland from the esplanade. On this he built a house facing the Channel, with balconies, a sun porch, and Venetian shutters to batten against storms. For in winter storms flung shingle on to the lawns, and even, if the windows were left open, on to the carpets and pianos of these exposed houses along the esplanade. This house of his Dr Heccomb considered a good investment – and so it proved: in July, August, September he, his second wife, and the children of his first marriage moved out of Seale and took rooms at a farm inland, while the house was let for six guineas a week. During these summer exiles, Dr Heccomb drove himself daily to the Seale golf club in a small car. He was popular; all the members knew him well; he came in on every celebration there was. It was on the return from one of these parties that Dr Heccomb, driving home too gaily into the sunset, drove himself head-on into a charabanc. After this shocking affair, the hat went round at the golf club for Mrs Heccomb; and the widow received eighty-five pounds in token of sympathy. This did not seem worth investing, so she spent it on mourning for herself and the children, a secretarial training for Daphne Heccomb, and a fine cross for Dr Heccomb in Seale churchyard.

During her years at Richmond she not only had not had to worry about money but had formed rather luxurious ideas. As a widow after several years of marriage she was contented but incompetent. Her well-wishers were more worried about her than she was herself. She had not, it is true, been left with nothing, but she did not seem to know how little she had. Anna's father had insisted on adding a small pension, and on his death had left an annuity. Anna sent Mrs Heccomb clothes she no longer wore, as well as various perquisites. Mrs Heccomb rather enjoyed eking out her income: she gave piano lessons in Seale and Southstone, painted table mats, lamp shades, and other objects, and occasionally took paying guests – but her house's exposed position in bad weather, the roar of the sea on the shingle, and the ruthless manners of the two Heccomb children almost always drove these guests away after a short time.

The Heccomb children helped her by growing up and becoming self-supporting. Daphne worked in a library at Seale, Dickie in a bank at Southstone, four miles away. They continued to live at home, and could contribute their share to the house. Dr Heccomb's friends at the club or their mother's relations had found these positions for them, for Mrs Heccomb had not exerted herself. Inevitably, she had had rather grander ideas: she would have liked Dickie to go into the Army; she had tried to model Daphne on the lines of Anna. When she first took them on – and she had been married, as she may have realized, very largely in order *to* take them on – the young Heccombs had been rough little things, not at all the type of children she would have stayed with had she been their governess. And they grew up rough, in spite of all she had done. The fact was, though one did not refer to this, that her husband's first wife had not been quite-quite. But her affectionate nature resigned her to these young people, who continued to stay on because they were comfy with her, because all their friends lived around, because they had no desire to see the rest of the world. They tired soon of the sport of baiting her paying guests, so, when they could each contribute fifteen shillings a week, asked that the paying guests might be given up. This made a quieter home.

Daphne and Dickie Heccomb, when they were not working, were to be found with the rest of their gay set at rinks, in cafés, cinemas, and dance halls. On account of their popularity and high spirits, other people were glad to pay for them. Seaside society, even out of season, is ideal for young people, who grow up in it gay, contented, and tough. Seale, though itself quiet, is linked by very frequent buses to Southstone, which boasts, with reason, almost every resource.

Mrs Heccomb herself had a number of friends at Seale. The sea front is rather commercial and not very select: most of her friends lived in those pretty balconied villas or substantial gabled houses up on the hill. In fact, she had found her level. She did a few good works and attended the choral society. Had she not been so worried about her step-children growing up common, hers would have been a very serene life. She was glad to have achieved marriage, not sorry that it was over.

At Charing Cross, Matchett put Portia into the train, then narrowly watched the porter put in the suitcases. When the train began to draw out, she waved several times after it, in a mystic semaphore, her fabric-gloved hand. She had given Portia a bottle of boiled sweets, though with instructions not to make herself ill. Her manner, during the drive in the taxi, had threatened the afternoon like a cloud that covers the sky but is almost certain never to break. Her eyelids looked rigid – tear-bound, you would have said. By giving such a faultless impersonation of a trusted housemaid seeing a young lady into a train, she had made Portia feel that, because of Eddie, the door between them had been shut for ever. While she bought the sweets at the kiosk, her face went harder than ever, in case this action be misunderstood. She said: 'Mr Thomas would wish it. Those are thirst-quenchers, those lime drops are. You don't know when you'll get your tea.'

Portia could not but be glad when the train steamed out. She put a sweet in both cheeks and began to look at her book. She had not travelled all by herself before, and for some time dared not look at anyone else in the carriage for fear of not doing so unconcernedly.

As the train drew in Lymly, the junction for Seale, Mrs Heccomb waved two or three times – first at the engine, as though signalling it to stop, then in order that Portia should not overlook her. This was unlikely, for hers was the only figure on the platform stretching its dead length. This unfrequented junction, far from the village, at the mouth of a cutting, exists alone among woods. Ground ivy mats its lozenge-shaped flowerbeds, and a damp woody silence haunts it – except when boat trains, momentary apparitions, go rocking roaring through. Mrs Heccomb wore a fur coat that had been Anna's, that cut her a little across the back. She wore the collar turned up, because a draught always blows down a main line. Methodically, she began to search down the train, beginning with the first carriage after the engine. On seeing Portia alight from the far end she broke into a smooth trot, without any break in deportment. When she came up to Portia she looked at her small round hat, took a guess at her mental age, and kissed her. 'We won't try and talk', she said, 'till we're quite settled.' A porter took the luggage across the platform to another, waiting, train, very short, with only three coaches. Not for some minutes after they *were* settled did this train puff off down the single line through the woods.

Mrs Heccomb, sitting opposite Portia, balanced on her knee a coloured wicker shopping-basket, empty. She had a plump abstracted rather wondering face, and fluffy grey hair piled up under her hat. Portia noted scars in her fur coat where buttons had been cut off and moved out. 'So isn't this nice,' she said. 'You've come, just as Anna said. Now tell me, how is my dear Anna?'

'She told me to be sure and give you her love.'

'Fancy thinking of that, when she's just going abroad! She takes things so calmly. Are they all packed up?'

'Matchett's still got to finish.'

'And then she'll spring-clean the house,' said Mrs Heccomb,

viewing this vision of order. 'What a treasure Matchett is. How smoothly things can run.' Seeing Portia looking out at the woods, she said:

'And perhaps you'll quite enjoy a little time in the country?'

'I am sure I shall.'

'Where we live, I'm afraid, is not really the country, it is the sea. However –'

'I like the sea, too.'

'The sea in England, or rather the sea round England, will be quite new to you, won't it?' said Mrs Heccomb.

Portia saw Mrs Heccomb did not expect an answer, and guessed that Anna had told her the whole story – where they had lived, and why they never came home. Anna would not have gone on seeing Mrs Heccomb if this had meant her having to be discreet. Anna was truly fond of Mrs Heccomb, but there would have been nothing to say, when they were not at matinées, had Anna not made stories out of her passing worries and got sympathy for them. About three times a year, Anna sent Mrs Heccomb the price of a day ticket to London, then very warmly devoted the day to her. This was always a great success – it was never known, however, whether Mrs Heccomb's worries came up too. Did she talk to Anna about her step-children? 'I'm afraid they are pretty awful,' Anna had said.

'Do you skate?' Mrs Heccomb said suddenly.

'I'm afraid I don't know how to.'

Mrs Heccomb relieved, said: 'Perhaps that is just as well. You need not go to the rink. Are you fond of reading?'

'Sometimes.'

'You are quite right,' said Mrs Heccomb, 'there is plenty of time to read when you are older, like I am. At one time, Anna read too much. Fortunately she loved gaiety, too: she always had so many invitations. In fact, she still enjoys herself like a young girl. How old are you, Portia, if I may ask?'

'Sixteen.'

'That makes such a difference,' said Mrs Heccomb. 'I mean, it's not as though you were eighteen.'

'I do quite enjoy myself, even now.'

'Oh yes, I'm sure you do,' said Mrs Heccomb. 'I do hope

you'll enjoy the sea while you are with us. And there are some interesting places, ruins, for instance, round. Yes, I do hope . . .'

'I'm sure I shall enjoy myself very much.'

'At the same time,' said Mrs Heccomb, flushing under her hair, 'I don't want you to feel a *visitor* here. I want you to feel completely at home, just as you do with Anna. You must come to me about any little trouble, just as you would to her. Of course, I hope there may be no little troubles. But you must ask me for anything that you want.'

Portia chiefly wanted her tea: lime drops do leave you thirsty, and she still tasted the tunnels in her mouth. She feared they must still be far from the coast – then the train ran clear of the woods along a high curved ridge. Salt air blew in at the carriage window: down there, across flat land, she saw the sea. Seale station ran at them with no warning; the engine crawled up to buffers: this was a terminus. The door through from the booking-hall framed sky, for this was an uphill station, built high on a ramp. While Mrs Heccomb had her chat with the porter, Portia stood at the head of the flight of steps. She felt elated here, thinking: 'I shall be happy.' The view of sea, town, and plain, all glassy-grey March light, seemed to be tilted up to meet her eyes like a mirror. 'That is my house,' said Mrs Heccomb, pointing to the horizon. 'We're still rather far away, but this is the taxi. He always comes.'

Mrs Heccomb smiled at the taxi and she and Portia got in.

The taxi drove down a long curve into Seale, past white gates of villas with mysterious gardens in which an occasional thrush sang. 'That would be our way really,' said Mrs Heccomb, nodding left when they reached the foot of the hill. 'But today we must go the other, because I have to shop. I do not often have a taxi to shop from, and it is quite a temptation, I must say. Dear Anna begged me to have the taxi *up* to the station, but I said no, that the walk would be good for me. But I said I might take the taxi the rather longer way home, in order to do my shopping.'

The taxi, which felt narrow, closed everything in on them, and Portia now saw only shop windows – the High Street shop windows. But what shops! – though all were very small they all looked lively, expectant, tempting, crowded, gay. She saw numbers of cake shops, antique shops, gift shops, flower shops, fancy chemists, and fancy stationers. Mrs Heccomb, holding her basket ready, wore a keyed-up but entirely happy air.

The shopping basket was soon full, so one began to pile parcels on the taxi seats. Every time she came back to the taxi, Mrs Heccomb said to Portia: 'I do hope you are not wanting your tea?' By the Town Hall clock it was now twenty past five. A man carried out to them a roll of matting, which he propped upright opposite Portia's feet. 'I am so glad to have this,' said Mrs Heccomb. 'I ordered it last week, but it was not in till today ... Now I must just go to the end' – by the end she meant the post office, which was at the end of the High Street – 'and send Anna that telegram.'

'Oh?'

'To say you've arrived safely.'

'I'm sure she won't be worried.'

Mrs Heccomb looked distressed. 'But you have never been away from her before. One would not like her to go abroad with anything on her mind.' Her back view vanished through the post-office door. When she came out, she found that she had forgotten something right down the other end of the town. 'After all,' she said, 'that will bring us back where we started. So we can go back the shorter way, after all.'

Portia saw that all this must be in her honour. It made her sad to think how Matchett would despise Mrs Heccomb's diving and ducking ways, like a nesting water-fowl's. Matchett would ask why all this had not been seen to before. But Irene would have been happy with Mrs Heccomb, and would have entered into her hopes and fears. The taxi crossed a canal bridge, heading towards the sea across perfectly flat fields that cut off the sea-front from the town. The sea-line appeared between high battered rows of houses, with red bungalows dotted in the gaps. These were all raised above the inland level, along a dike that kept the sea in its place.

The taxi turned and crawled along the back of the dike; Mrs Heccomb brisked up and began to muster her parcels. From here, the chipped stucco backs of the terraces looked higher than anything seen in London. The unkempt lawns and tamarisks at their foot, the lonely whoosh of the sea away behind them made them more mysterious and forbidding. Gaunt rusted pipes ran down between their windows, most of which were blank with white cotton blinds. These fields on their north side were more grey than the sea. That terror of buildings falling that one loses in London returned to Portia. 'Who lives there?' she said, nodding up nervously.

'No one, dear; those are only lodging houses.'

Mrs Heccomb tapped on the glass, and the taxi, which already intended stopping, stopped dead with a satirical jerk. They got out; Portia carried the parcels Mrs Heccomb could not manage; the taximan followed with the suitcases. They all three scrabbled up a steep shingly incline and found themselves alongside the butt end of a terrace. Mrs Heccomb showed Portia the esplanade. The sea heaved; an oblique wind lifted her hat. Shingle rolled up in red waves to the brim of the asphalt; there was an energetic and briny smell. Two steamers moved slowly along the horizon, but there was not a soul on the esplanade. 'I do hope you will like it,' said Mrs Heccomb. 'I do hope you can manage those parcels: can you? There is no *road* to our gate – you see, we're right on the sea.'

Waikiki, Mrs Heccomb's house, was about one minute more down the esplanade. Numbers of windows at different levels looked out of the picturesque red roof – one window had blown open; a faded curtain was wildly blowing out. Below this, what with the sun porch, the glass entrance door, and a wide bow window, the house had an almost transparent front. Constructed largely of glass and blistered white paint, Waikiki faced the sea boldly, as though daring the elements to dash it to bits.

Portia saw firelight in the inside dusk. Mrs Heccomb rapped three times on the glass door – there was a bell, but it hung out of its socket on a long twisted umbilical wire – and a small maid, fixing her large cuffs, could be seen advancing across the living-room. She let them in with rather a hoity-toity air. 'I have *got* my latchkey,' said Mrs Heccomb, 'but I think this is practice for you, Doris ... I always latch this door when I'm out,' she, added to Portia. 'The seaside is not the country, you see ... Now, Doris, this is the young lady from London. Do you remember how to take her things to her room? And this is the matting that the man is just bringing. Do you remember where I told you to put it?'

While Mrs Heccomb thanked and paid off the driver, Portia looked politely round the living-room, with eyes that were now and again lowered so as not to seem to make free with what they saw. Though dusk already fell on the esplanade, the room held a light reflection from the sea. She located the smell of spring with a trough of blue hyacinths, just come into flower. Almost all one side of the room was made up of french windows, which gave on to the sun porch but were at present shut. The sun porch, into which she hastily looked, held some basket chairs and an empty aquarium. At one end of the room, an extravagant fire fluttered on brown glazed tiles; the wireless cabinet was the most glossy of all. Opposite the windows a glass-fronted book-case, full but with a remarkably locked look, chiefly served to reflect the marine view. A dark blue chenille curtain, faded in lighter streaks, muffled an arch that might lead to the stairs. In other parts of the room, Portia's humble glances discovered such objects as a scarlet portable gramophone, a tray with a painting outfit, a half-painted lamp shade, a mountain of maga-zines. Two armchairs and a settee, with crumpled bottoms, made a square round the fire, and there was a gate-legged table, already set for tea. It was set for tea, but the cake plates were still empty – Mrs Heccomb was tipping cakes out of paper bags.

Outside, the sea went on with its independent sighing, but still seemed an annexe of the living-room. Portia, laying her gloves on an armchair, got the feeling that there was room for everyone here. She learned later that Daphne called this the lounge.

'Would you like to go up, dear?'

'Not specially, thank you.'

'Not even to your room?'

'I don't really mind.'

Mrs Heccomb, for some reason, looked relieved. When Doris brought in tea she said in a low voice: 'Now, Doris, the mat-ting. . . .'

Mrs Heccomb took off her hat for tea, and Portia saw that her hair, like part of an artichoke, seemed to have an up-growing tendency: it was pinned down firmly to the top of her head in a flat bun. This, for some reason, added to Mrs Heccomb's expression of surprise. At the same time, her personality was most reassuring. She talked so freely to Portia, telling her so much that Portia, used to the tactics of Windsor Terrace, wondered whether this really were wise. And what would be left to say by the end of the first week? She had yet to learn how often intimacies between women go backwards, beginning with revelations and ending up in small talk without loss of esteem. Mrs Heccomb told stories of Anna's youth at Richmond, which she invested with a pathetic prettiness. Then she said how sad it would always be about those two little babies Anna had almost had. Portia ate doughnuts, shortbread, and Dundee cake and gazed past Mrs Heccomb at the vanishing sea. She thought how gay this room, with its lights on, must look from the esplanade, thought how dark it was out there, and came to envy herself.

But then Mrs Heccomb got up and drew the curtains. 'You never know,' she said. 'It does not quite do.' (She referred to being looked in at.) Then she gave Portia another cup of tea and told her how much she must miss her mother. But she said how very lucky she was to have Thomas and Anna. For years and years, as Miss Yardes, she had had to be tactful and optimistic, trying to make young people see things the right way. This may have exaggerated her feeling manner. Now independence gave her a slight authority: when she said a thing *was* so, it became so forthwith. She looked at the mahogany clock that ticked loudly over the fire and said how nice it was that Daphne would soon be home. This Portia could not, of course, dispute. But she said: 'I think I will go up and brush my hair, then.'

While she was up in her room combing her hair back, hearing the tissue paper in her suitcase rustle, watching draughts bulge the new matting strip, she heard the bang that meant Daphne was in. Waikiki, she was to learn, was a sounding box: you knew where everyone was, what everyone did – except when the noise they made was drowned by a loud wind. She heard Daphne loudly asking something, then Mrs Heccomb must have put up a warning hand, for the rest of Daphne's question got

bitten off. Portia thought, I do hope Daphne won't mind me ...
In her room, the electric light, from its porcelain shade, poured
down with a frankness unknown at Windsor Terrace. The light
swayed slightly in that seaside draught, and Portia felt a new
life had begun. Downstairs, Daphne switched the wireless on
full blast, then started bawling across it at Mrs Heccomb: 'I
say, when *is* Dickie going to mend that bell?'

2

WHEN Portia ventured to come down, she found Daphne pot-
tering round the tea table, biting pieces out of a macaroon, while
Mrs Heccomb, busy painting the lamp shade, shouted above the
music that she would spoil her supper. Mrs Heccomb's shouting
had acquired, after years of evenings with Daphne and the
music, the mild equability of her speaking voice: she could
shout without strain. There was, in fact, an air of unconscious
deportment about everything that she carried through, and as
she worked at the lamp shade, peering close at the detail then
leaning back to get the general effect, she looked like someone
painting a lamp shade in a play.

As Portia came round the curtain Daphne did not look at her,
but with unnerving politeness switched the wireless off. It
snapped off at the height of a roar, and Mrs Heccomb looked up.
Daphne popped the last piece of macaroon into her mouth,
wiped her fingers correctly on a *crêpe de Chine* handkerchief,
and shook hands, though still without saying anything. She
gave the impression that she would not speak till she had
thought of something striking to say. She was a fine upstanding
girl, rather tall; her close-fitting dark blue knitted dress showed
off her large limbs. She wore her hair in a mop, but the mop was
in an iron pattern of curls, burnished with brilliantine. She had
a high colour, and used tangerine lipstick. Pending having
something to say to Portia, she said over her shoulder to Mrs
Heccomb: 'None of them will be coming in tonight.'

'Oh, thank you, Daphne.'

'Oh, don't thank *me*.'

'Daphne has so many friends,' Mrs Heccomb explained to Portia. 'But she says that none of them will be coming in to-night.'

Daphne gave the rest of the cakes a rather scornful once-over, then bumped into an armchair. Portia, as unostentatiously as possible, edged round the room to stand beside Mrs Heccomb, who worked with her tray of painting materials drawn up under a special lamp. Though all this was alarming, she did not feel so alarmed as she did at Windsor Terrace, where St Quentin and all those other friends of Anna's always tacitly watched. On the lamp shade she saw delphiniums and marble cupids being painted in against a salmon-pink sky. 'Oh, *how* pretty!' she said.

'It will look better varnished. I think the idea is pretty. This is an order, for a wedding present, but later I hope to do one for Anna, as a surprise – Daphne dear, I'm sure Portia wouldn't mind the music.'

Daphne groaned, but got up and restarted the wireless. Then she kicked off her court shoes and lighted a cigarette. 'You know,' she said, 'I feel spring in my bones today.'

'I know, dear; isn't it nice?'

'Not in my bones.' Daphne looked with a certain interest at Portia. 'Well,' she said, 'so they didn't take *you* abroad.'

'They couldn't, you see, dear,' said Mrs Heccomb quickly. 'They are going to stay with people who have a villa. And also, Portia comes from abroad.'

'Oh! And what do *you* think of our English policemen, then?'

'I don't think I –'

'Daphne, don't always joke, dear. Be a good girl and tell Doris to clear tea.'

Daphne put her head back and bellowed, *'Doris!'* and Doris gave her a look as she nimbled in with the tray. Portia realized later that the tomb-like hush of Smoot's library, where she had to sit all day, dealing out hated books, was not only antipathetic but even dangerous to Daphne. So, once home, she kept fit by making a loud noise. Daphne never simply touched objects, she slapped down her hand on them; she made up her mouth with the gesture of someone cutting their throat. Even when the wireless was not on full blast, Daphne often shouted as though it were. So, when Daphne's homecoming step was heard on the esplanade, Mrs Heccomb had learned to draw a shutter over her nerves. So much of her own working life had been spent in intercepting noise that might annoy others, in saying 'Quietly, please, dear,' to young people, that she may even have got a sort of holiday pleasure from letting Daphne rip. The degree of blare and glare she permitted Daphne may even have been Mrs Heccomb's own tribute to the life force it had for so long been her business to check. So much did she identify noise with Daphne's presence that if the wireless stopped or there were a pause in the shouting, Mrs Heccomb would get up from her painting and either close a window or poke the fire – any lack felt by any one of her senses always made her imagine she felt cold. She had given up hoping Daphne might grow like Anna. But it was firmly fixed in her mind now that she would not wish Portia to return to London and Anna having picked up any of Daphne's ways.

When tea had been cleared, and the lace cloth folded by Doris and put away in the bookcase drawer, Mrs Heccomb uncorked a bottle of varnish and with a tense air applied the first coat. This done, she returned to the world and said: 'Doris seems to be coming on quite well.'

'She ought to,' said Daphne. 'She's got a boy.'

'Already? Oh dear! *Has* she?'

'Yes, they were on the top of the bus I was on. He's got a spot on his neck. First I looked at the spot, then I looked at the boy, then who should I see but Doris grinning away beside him.'

'I do hope he's a nice boy. . . .'

'Well, I tell you, he's got a spot on his neck . . . No, but I say, really, Mumsie, I do wish you'd fly out at Dickie about that bell. It looks awful, hanging out at the root like that, besides not ringing. Why don't we have an electric, anyway?'

'Your father always thought they went out of order, dear.'

'Well, you ought to fly out at Dickie, you ought really. What did he say he'd mend that bell for if he wasn't going to mend it? No one asked him to say he would mend that bell.'

'It was very good of him, dear. I might remind him at supper.'

'He won't be in for supper. He's got a date. He said.'

'Oh yes, so he did. What am I thinking about?'

'Don't ask me,' said Daphne kindly. 'However, don't you worry: I'll eat the old sausage. What is it, by the way?'

'Egg pie. I thought that would be light.'

'*Light?*' said Daphne appalled.

'For Portia after the journey. If you want more, dear, we can open the galantine.'

'Oh well,' said Daphne resignedly.

Portia sat at one end of the sofa, looking through a copy of *Woman and Beauty*. Mrs Heccomb was so much occupied with the lamp shade, Daphne by simply sitting and glooming there, that she wished she could have brought Major Brutt's puzzle – she could have been getting on with that. But you cannot pack a jigsaw that is three-quarters done. As it was, sitting under an alabaster pendant that poured a choked orange light on her head, she felt stupefied by this entirely new world. The thump of the broadcast band with the sea's vibration below it, the smell of varnish, hyacinths, Turkey carpet, drawn out by the heat of the roaring fire came at her overpoweringly. She was not yet adjusted to all this. How far she had travelled – not only in space.

Wondering if this could ever make her suffer, she thought of Windsor Terrace. *I am not there.* She began to go round, in little circles, things that at least her senses had loved – her bed, with the lamp turned on on winter mornings, the rug in Thomas's study, the chest carved with angels out there on the landing, the waxen oilcloth down there in Matchett's room. Only in a house where one has learnt to be lonely does one have this solicitude for *things*. One's relation to them, the daily seeing or touching, begins to become love, and to lay one open to pain. Looking back at a repetition of empty days, one sees that monuments have sprung up. Habit is not mere subjugation, it is a tender tie: when one remembers habit it seems to have been happiness. So, she and Irene had almost always felt sad when they looked round a hotel room before going away from it for always. They could not but feel that they had betrayed something. In unfamiliar places, they unconsciously looked for familiarity. It is not our exalted feelings, it is our sentiments that build the necessary home. The need to attach themselves makes wandering people strike roots in a day: whenever we unconsciously feel, we live.

Upstairs in Waikiki, the bedroom ceilings sloped because of the roof. Mrs Heccomb, saying good night to Portia, had screwed a steel-framed window six inches open, the curtain flopped in the light of a lamp on the esplanade. Portia put her hand up once or twice to touch the slope of ceiling over her bed. Mrs Heccomb had said she hoped she would not be lonely. 'I sleep just next door: you need only tap on the wall. We are all very near together in this house. Do you like hearing the sea?'

'It sounds very near.'

'It's high tide. But it won't come any nearer.'

'Won't it?'

'No, I promise, dear, that it won't. You're not afraid of the sea?'

'Oh, no.'

'And you've got a picture of Anna,' Mrs Heccomb had added, with a beatific nod at the mantelpiece. That had already been looked at – a pastel drawing of Anna, Anna aged about twelve, holding a kitten, her long soft hair tied up in two satin bows. The tender incompetence of the drawing had given the face, so narrow between the hair, a spiritual look. The kitten's face was a wedge of dark on the breast. 'So you won't be lonely,' said Mrs Heccomb, and, having so happily concluded, had turned out the light and gone. . . . The curtain started fretting the window sill; the sea filled the darkness with its approaching sighing, a little hoarse with shingle. High tide? The sea had come as near as it could.

Portia dreamed she was sharing a book with a little girl. The tips of Anna's long fair hair brushed on the page: they sat up high in a window, waiting till something happened. The worst of all would be if the bell rang, and their best hope was to read to a certain point in the book. But Portia found she no longer knew how to read – she did not dare tell Anna, who kept turning pages over. She knew they must both read – so the fall of

Anna's hair filled her with despair, pity, for what would have to come. The forest (there was a forest under the window) was being varnished all over: it left no way of escape. Then the terrible end, the rushing-in, the roaring and gurgling started – Portia started up from where they were with a cry –

'– *Hush, hush*, dear! Here I am. Nothing has happened. Only Daphne running her bath out.'

'I don't know where I –'

'You're here, dear.'

'Oh!'

'Did you have a dream? Would you like me to stay a little?'

'Oh no, thank you.'

'Then sleep with no dreams, like a good girl. Remember, you can always rap on the wall.'

Mrs Heccomb slipped out, closing the door by inches. Then, out there on the landing, she and Daphne started a whispering-match. Their whispers sounded like whispers down the clinic corridor, or sounds in the forest still left from the dream. 'Goodness,' said Daphne, 'isn't she highly strung?' Then Daphne's feet, in mules, clip-clopped off across the landing: the last of the bath ran out; a door shut.

Perhaps it was Portia's sense, that by having started awake she had not been a good girl, that now kept her in the haunted outer court of the dream. She had not been kind to Anna; she had never been kind. She had lived in that house with her with an opposed heart ... That kitten, for instance – had it died? Anna never spoke of it. Had Anna felt small at day school? When had they cut her hair off? In the electric light, that hair in the portrait had been mimosa yellow. Did Anna also, sometimes, not know what to do next? Because she knew what to do next, because she knew what to laugh at, what to say, did it always follow that she knew where to turn? Inside everyone, is there an anxious person who stands to hesitate in an empty room? Starting up from her pillow Portia thought: And she's gone. She may never come back.

Mrs Heccomb must have stayed up to keep Dickie quiet. His no-nonsense step had grown loud on the esplanade. Through the floor, Mrs Heccomb was to be heard hush-hushing as Dickie crashed open the glass door. Then he rolled an armchair round and kicked the fire: it sounded like a giant loose in the lounge. There was then the muted clatter of a tray being brought: perhaps they were opening the galantine. Mrs Heccomb may have said something about the bell, for Dickie was to be heard replying: 'What is the good of telling me that now?. . .' Portia knew she must meet him in the morning. She had heard he was twenty-three: the same age as Eddie.

When she came down next morning, at eight o'clock, Dickie was in the act of polishing off his breakfast. There was one particular bus to Southstone he must catch. When she came in he half got up, wiping egg from his chin: when they had shaken hands and both muttered something he bumped back again and went on drinking his coffee, not saying anything more. Dickie was not so enormous as he had sounded, though he was fine and stocky: he had a high colour, a tight-fitting skin, stag-like eyes with a look of striking frankness, a large chin, and hair that though sternly larded would never stay down. Dickie, indeed, looked uncompromisingly vigorous. This working morning, he wore a dark suit and hard collar in a manner that made it clear these things were not really his type. The plunging manner in which he bathed and dressed had been, before this, heard all over the house: he had left behind in the bathroom the clean, rather babyish smell of shaving soap. At Windsor Terrace, with its many floors and extended plumbing, the intimate life of Thomas was not noticeable. But here Dickie made himself felt as a powerful organism. With a look past Portia that said that nothing should alter his habits, he now rose, withdrew from the breakfast table, and locked himself in somewhere behind the chenille curtain. About five minutes later he emerged with his hat and a satisfied, civic air, nodded the same good-bye to Portia and Mrs Heccomb (who passed in and out of the lounge with fresh instalments of breakfast as more people came down) and plunged out through the glass door to dispose of the day's work. Mrs Heccomb, looking out through the sun porch to watch Dickie off down the esplanade, said: 'He is like clockwork', with a contented sigh.

Daphne's library was in Seale High Street, only about ten minutes from Waikiki down the tree-planted walk that links the esplanade to the town. She did not have to be on duty till a quarter past nine, and therefore seldom came down to breakfast before her brother had gone, for she slept voraciously. When Daphne was to be heard coming out of the bathroom, Mrs Heccomb used to signal to Doris: the egg or kipper for Daphne would then be dropped in the pan. Breakfast here was a sort of a running service, which did credit to Mrs Heccomb's organization – possibly her forces rather spent themselves on it, for she looked fatalistic for the rest of the day. Daphne always brought down her comb with her and, while waiting for the egg or kipper, would straddle before the overmantel mirror, doing what was right by her many curls. She did not put on lipstick till after breakfast because of the egg, not to speak of the marmalade. Mrs Heccomb, while Daphne saw to her hair, would anxiously keep the coffee and milk hot under the paisley cosy that embraced both jugs. Her own breakfast consisted of rusks in hot milk, which was, as she said to Portia, rather more Continental. Portia sat on through Dickie's exit and Daphne's entrance, eating the breakfast that had come her way, elbows in as closely as possible, hoping not to catch anyone's eye.

But as Daphne took her place she said: 'So sorry my bath gave you a jump.'

'Oh, that was my fault.'

'Perhaps you had eaten something?'

'She was just tired, dear,' Mrs Heccomb said.

'I daresay you're not used to the pipes. I daresay your sister-in-law has Buckingham Palace plumbing?'

'I don't know what ...'

'That is one of Daphne's jokes, dear.'

Daphne pursued: 'I daresay *she's* got a green china bath? Or else one of those sunk ones with a concealed light?'

'No, Daphne dear: Anna never likes things at all extreme.'

But Daphne only snorted and said: 'I daresay *she* has a bath that she floats in just like a lily.'

At the same time, making a plunge at the marmalade, Daphne sucked her cheeks in at once sternly and hardily, with the air of someone who could say a good deal more. It was clear that her manner to Portia could not be less aggressive till she had stopped associating her with Anna. Anyone who came to Waikiki straight from Anna's seemed to Daphne likely to come it over them all. She had encountered Anna only three times – on which occasions Daphne patiently, ruthlessly, had collected everything about Anna that one could not like. She was not, as far as that went, a jealous girl, and she had a grudging regard for the upper class – had she been more in London, she would have been in the front ranks of those womanly crowds who besiege crimson druggets under awnings up steps. She would have been one of those on-looking girls who poke their large unenvious faces across the flying tip of the notable bride's veil, or who without resentment sniff other people's gardenias outside the Opera. Contented, wry, decent girls like Daphne are the bad old order's principal stay. She delighted to honour what she was perfectly happy not to have. At the same time, and underlying this, there could have been a touch of the *tricoteuse* about Daphne, once fully worked up, and this all came out in her constantly angry feeling against Anna.

She did not (rightly) consider Anna properly upper class. All the same, she felt Anna's power in operation; she considered Anna got more than she ought. She thought Anna gave herself airs. She also resented dimly (for she could never word it) Anna's having made Mumsie her parasite. Had Anna had a title this might have been less bitter. She overlooked, rightly and rather grandly, the fact that had it not been for Anna's father, the Heccombs could not have opened so much galantine.

Some people are moulded by their admirations, others by their hostilities. In so far as anything had influenced Daphne's evolution, it had been the wish to behave and speak on all occasions as Anna would not. At this moment, the very idea of Anna made her snap at her toast with a most peculiar expression, catching dribbles of marmalade on her lower lip.

The Waikiki marmalade was highly jellied, sweet, and brilliantly orange; the table was brightly set with cobalt-and-white breakfast china, whose pattern derived from the Chinese. Rush mats as thick as muffins made hot plates wobble on the syn-

thetic oak. Sunlight of a pure seaside quality flooded the breakfast table, and Portia, looking out through the sun porch,
thought how pleasant this was. The Heccombs ate as well as
lived in the lounge, for they mistrusted, rightly, the anthracite
stove in the should-be dining-room. So they only used the dining-room in summer, or for parties at which they had enough
people to generate a sterling natural heat. . . . Gulls dipped over
the lawn in a series of white flashes; Mrs Heccomb watched
Daphne having a mood about Anna with an eye of regret. 'But
one does not put lilies in baths,' she said at last.

'You might do, if you wanted to keep them fresh.'

'Then I should have thought you'd put them in a wash basin,
dear.'

'How should I know?' said Daphne. '*I* don't get lilies, do I?'
She thrust her cup forward for more coffee, and, with an air of
turning to happier subjects, said: '*Did* you fly out at Dickie
about that bell?'

'He didn't seem to think . . .'

'Oh, he didn't, did he?' said Daphne. 'That's just Dickie all
over, if you know what I mean. Why not let you get the man
from Spalding's in the first place? Well, you had better get the
man from Spalding's. I want that bell done by tomorrow night.'

'Why specially, dear?'

'Some people are coming in.'

'But don't they almost always give a rap on the glass?'

Daphne looked hangdog (her variation of coyness). Her eyes
seemed to run together like the eyes of a shark. She said: 'Mr
Bursely talked about dropping in.'

'Mr Who?' Mrs Heccomb said timidly.

'Bursely, Mumsie. B, U, R, S, E, L, Y.'

'I don't think I have ever –'

'No,' Daphne yelled patiently. 'That is just the point. He
hasn't been here before. You don't want him to see that bell.
He's from the School of Musketry.'

'Oh, in the Army?' said Mrs Heccomb, brightening. (Portia
knew so little about the Army, she immediately heard spurs,
even a sabre, clank down the esplanade.) 'Where did you meet
him, dear?'

'At a hop,' said Daphne briefly.

'Then some of you might like to dance tomorrow night, I expect?'

'Well, we might put the carpet back. We can't all just stick around. – Do you dance?' she said, eyeing Portia.

'Well, I have danced with some other girls in hotels ...'

'Well, men won't bite you.' Turning to Mrs Heccomb, Daphne said: 'Get Dickie to get Cecil ... Goodness, I *must* rush!'

She rushed, and soon was gone down the esplanade. Daphne used nothing stronger than 'goodness' or 'dash': all the vigour one wanted was supplied by her manner. In this she was unlike Anna, who at moments of tension let out oaths and obscenities with a helpless, delicate air. Where Anna, for instance, would call a person a bitch, Daphne would call the person an old cat. Daphne's person was sexy, her conversation irreproachably chaste. She would downface any remark by saying, 'You *are* awful', or simply using her eyes ... When she had quite gone, Portia felt deflated, Mrs Heccomb looked dazed. For Portia, Daphne and Dickie seemed a crisis that surely must be unique: she could not believe that they happened every day.

'Remind me to go to Spalding's,' said Mrs Heccomb.

At this moment the sun was behind a film, but the sea shone and the lounge was full of its light. Mrs Heccomb, to air the place after breakfast, folded back a window on to the sun porch, then opened a window in the porch itself. A smell of seaweed stiffening and salting, of rolls of shingle drying after the sea, and gulls' cries came into Waikiki lounge. One's first day by the sea, one's being feels salt, strong, resilient, and hollow – like a seaweed pod not giving under the heel. Portia went and stood in the sun porch, looking out through its lattice at the esplanade. Then she boldly let herself out by the glass door. A knee-high wall with a very high and correct gate cut the Heccomb's lawn off from the public way. Before stepping over the wall (which seemed, in view of the gate's existence, a possible act of disrespect) Portia glanced back at the Waikiki windows. But no one watched her; no one seemed to object. She walked across to the lip of the esplanade.

Seale sea front takes the imperceptible curve of a shallow, very wide bay. Towards the east horizon, the coast rises – or rather, inland hills approach the sea: an imposing bluff is crowned by the most major of Southstone's major hotels. That gilt dome, the flying flags receive at about sunset their full glory, and distantly glitter, a plutocratic heaven, for humbler trippers on the Seale esplanade. On sunless clear mornings, the silhouette of the Splendide seems to be drawn on the sky in blue-grey ink ... On from Seale towards Southstone, the forcible concrete sea wall, with tarmac top, stretches empty for two miles. The fields the sea wall protects drop away from it, unpeopled and salty, on the inland side. The abstract loneliness of the dike ends where the Seale–Southstone road comes out to run by the sea.

West of Seale, you see nothing more than the marsh. The dead flat line of the coast is drawn out into a needle-fine promontory. The dimming gleaming curve is broken only by the martello towers, each smaller, each more nearly melted by light. The silence is broken only by musketry practice on the ranges. Looking west of Seale, you see the world void, the world suspended, forgotten, like a past phase of thought. Light's shining, shifting slants and veils and own interposing shadows make a world of their own ... Along this stretch of the coast, the shingle has given place to water-flat sands: the most furious seas only slide in flatly to meet the martello towers.

Standing midway between these two distances, hands knotted behind her back, Portia looked out to sea: the skyline was drawn taut across the long shallow bow of the bay. Three steamers' smoke hung in curls on the clear air – the polished sea looked like steel: amazing to think that a propeller could cut it. The edge of foam on the beach was tremulous, lacy, but the horizon looked like a blade.

A little later this morning, that blade would have cut off Thomas and Anna. They would drop behind the horizon, leaving behind them, for only a minute longer, a little curl of smoke. By the time they landed at Calais, their lives would have become hypothetical. To look at the sea the day someone is crossing is to accept the finality of the defined line. For the senses bound our feeling world: there is an abrupt break where their power stops – when the door closes, the train disappears round the curve, the plane's droning becomes inaudible, the ship enters the mist or drops over the line of sea. The heart may think it knows better: the senses know that absence blots people out. We have really no absent friends. The friend becomes a traitor by breaking, however unwillingly or sadly, out of our own zone: a hard judgement is passed on him, for all the pleas of the heart. Willing absence (however unwilling) is the negation of love. To remember can be at times no more than a cold duty, for we remember only in the limited way that is bearable. We observe small rites, but we defend ourselves against that terrible memory that is stronger than will. We defend ourselves from the rooms, the scenes, the objects that make for hallucination, that make the senses start up and fasten upon a ghost. We desert those who desert us; we cannot afford to suffer; we must live how we can.

Happily, the senses are not easy to trick – or, at least, to trick often. They fix, and fix us with them, on what is possessable. They are ruthless in their living infidelity. Portia was learning to live without Irene, not because she denied or had forgotten that once unfailing closeness between mother and child, but because she no longer felt her mother's cheek on her own (that Eddie's finger-tip, tracing the crease of a smile, had more idly but far more lately touched), or smelled the sachet-smell from Irene's dresses, or woke in those hired north rooms where they used to wake.

With regard to Eddie himself, at present, the hard law of present-or-absent was suspended. In the first great phase of love, which with very young people lasts a long time, the beloved is not outside one, so neither comes nor goes. In this dumb, exalted, and exalting confusion, what actually happens plays very little part. In fact the spirit stays so tuned up that the beloved's real presence could be too much, unbearable: one wants to say to him: 'Go, that you may be here.' The most fully lived hours, at this time, are those of memory or of anticipation, when the heart expands to the full without any check. Portia now referred to Eddie everything that could happen: she saw him in everything that she saw. His being in London, her being here, no more than contracted seventy miles of England into their private intense zone. Also, they could write letters.

But the absence, the utter dissolution, in space of Thomas and Anna should have been against nature: they were her Everyday. That Portia was not more sorry, that she would not miss them, faced her this morning like the steel expanse of the sea. Thomas and Anna, by opening their door to her (by having been by blood obliged to open their door) became Irene's successors in all natural things. He, she, Portia, three Quaynes, had lived, packed close in one house through the winter cold, accepting, not merely choosing each other. They had all three worked at their parts of the same necessary pattern. They had passed on the same stairs, grasped the same door handles, listened to the strokes of the same clocks. Behind the doors at Windsor Terrace, they had heard each other's voices, like the continuous murmur inside the whorls of a shell. She had breathed smoke from their lungs in every room she went into, and seen their names on letters each time she went through the hall. When she went out, she was asked how her brother and sister were. To the outside world, she smelled of Thomas and Anna.

But something that should have been going on had not gone on: something had not happened. They had sat round a painted, not a burning, fire, at which you tried in vain to warm your hands ... She tried to make a picture of Thomas and Anna leaning over the rail of the ship, both looking the same way. The picture was just real enough, for the moment, to make her want to expunge from their faces a certain betraying look. For they looked like refugees, not people travelling for pleasure. Thomas – who had said he always wore a cap on a ship – wore the cap pulled down, while Anna held her fur collar plaintively to her chin. Their nearness – for they stood with their elbows touching – was part of their driven look: they were one in flight. But already their faces were far less substantial than the faces of Daphne and Dickie Heccomb ... Then Portia remembered they would not be aboard yet: in fact, they would hardly have left London. And the moment they *were* aboard, Anna would lie down: she was a bad sailor; she never looked at the sea.

3

DEAR Miss Portia: You will be sorry to hear that Phyllis has interfered with your puzzle, which I had put newspaper over like you said. She had orders not to, but overlooked that. Owing to me being busy packing Mrs Thomas, Phyllis was sent to see to your room, she did not know what was under the newspaper so gave the table a nudge. She upset some sky and part of the officers, but I have put the pieces in a box by your bed. She was upset when I told her you set store by it. I think it well to tell you, lest you should be disappointed when you get back. Phyllis will not be let go in your room again, where she has no business really.

Mr and Mrs Thomas were got off in good time for their train to Italy, and today I am getting the curtains to the cleaners. I was glad to know from Mrs Heccomb's telegram that you reached Seale. I have no doubt Mr and Mrs Thomas were glad also. I hope you are taking care of that wind along the front, which is very treacherous at this time of year. Mrs Heccomb spoke of the cold there last time she was up, she seemed pleased to get Mrs Thomas's former nutria coat. You did ought to wear a cardigan between your coat and your jumper, I packed you two but likely you will forget.

I hear Major Brutt called this afternoon and was disappointed to find the family gone. It seems he mistook the day, owing to what he thought Mrs Thomas had said. He asked for you and was told you were at the sea. You would not know the house with the curtains gone, not what you have been used to. Also Mr Thomas's books are out to be electric cleaned, preparatory to washing the shelves down. Your friend Mr Eddie came to the door after a muffler he says he left, and particularly remarked on the smell of soap. He also took from the drawing-room some French book he says he loaned to Mrs Thomas. I had to unsheet the drawing-room for him to find this, the room having been covered ready for the sweep.

I trust that you will do well at the seaside. I once visited Seale along with my married sister who lives at Dover. It is said to be a nice residential place. No doubt the time will fly till you come back. I must now close. Yours respectfully,

R. MATCHETT

P.S. Should you wish anything sent, no doubt you would write. A picture postcard would be sufficient.

Q. and M. S',
Friday

Darling Portia: Thanks for your letter written before starting. It is awful to realize you are away, in fact I hoped I might not, but I do. I rashly went round to Windsor Terrace to get back that red scarf, and it was as if you had all died of the plague and Matchett was disinfecting it after you. The house reeked of awful soap. Matchett had got all Thomas's books in a heap, and seemed to be dancing on them. She gave me a singularly dirty look. I felt your corpses must be laid out in the drawing-room, which was all sheets. That old crocodile took me up under protest and stood snapping her jaws while I dug out *Les Plaisirs et les jours*, which I'm anxious to get back before Anna loses it. It felt odd, while I was in the drawing-room, to know I wouldn't hear you scuttering on the stairs. Everything really had a charnel echo and I said to myself, 'She died young'.

I say, darling, how much do you think Matchett knows about you and me? It was a foul bleak day and I could have cried.

Now remember how awful I often feel and write me long letters. If you write too much about Dickie I shall come down and shoot him, I am a jealous man. Is he as awful as Anna says, and is Daphne? I really do want you to tell me everything, you are horrid to say that I don't read your letters. Shall I come down one week-end, even not to shoot Dickie? It might be frightfully funny if I did. I suppose they could have me to stay, don't you? But of course that all depends how things pan out; at present I am having an awful time.

This office is going to bits without Thomas, which would be gratifying for Thomas to know. I can't tell you how awful they all are. I always did know all these people were crooks. They intrigue in really a poisonous way, and nothing is getting done. However, that gives me more time to write to you. You see I'm not using the office paper: I look after Thomas's interests while he's gone.

Oh, darling Portia, it's awful not to see you. Please do feel awful too. I saw a pair of Indian silver baby's bangles in Holborn. I think I'll send them to you for your silly wrists.

Do you remember Saturday?

I think it is just like them, packing you off like that to the seaside when everything could be so nice now. Anna locks you up like jam. I hope it will sleet and freeze all the time she is in that vulgar Italian villa. I really should laugh if I went to Seale. Do you hear the sea when you are in bed?

I must stop. I do feel homeless and sad. I have got to go out now for drinks with some people, but that isn't at all the same thing. Wouldn't it be nice if you were poking our fire and expecting me home at any minute?

Good-bye, Good night, you darling. Think of me last thing.

EDDIE

The Karachi Hotel,
Cromwell Road,
s.w.

Dear Miss Portia: I was sorry to miss you all when I called at 2 Windsor Terrace. I had hoped to wish your brother and sister-in-law luck on their trip, and hoped to reply personally to that very sweet little message you sent me through Mrs Quayne, reporting your progress made with a certain puzzle. I also meant to have asked if you would care to have another puzzle, as that must be nearly done. To do the same puzzle twice would be pretty poor fun. If you would allow me to send you another puzzle, you could always send on the first to a sick friend. I am told they are popular in nursing homes, but as I enjoy excellent health I have never checked up on this. That kind of puzzle was not much in vogue during the War.

The weather has turned quite nasty, you are 'well out of London' as the saying goes. Your brother's hospitable house was, when I called, dismantled for spring cleaning. What a dire business that is! I hope you have struck some pleasant part of the coast? I expect you may find it pretty blowy down there. I have been kept pretty busy these last days with interviews in connexion with an appointment. From what I hear, things look quite like shaping up.

Some good friends of mine in this hotel, whose acquaintance I made here, have just moved on, and I find they leave quite a gap. One is often lucky in striking congenial people in these hotels. But of course people rather come and go.

Well, if you feel like trying your skill with yet another puzzle, will you be so good as to send me a little line? Just possibly you might care to have the puzzle to do at the seaside, where the elements do not always treat one as they should. If I were to know your address, I could have the puzzle posted direct to you. Meanwhile, your excellent parlourmaid will no doubt forward this. Very sincerely yours,   ERIC E. J. BRUTT

Portia had never had such a morning's post as this: it seemed to be one advantage of having left London. These three letters came on Saturday morning; she re-read them at a green-tiled table at the Corona Café, waiting for Mrs Heccomb. By this, her second morning, she was already into the Waikiki routine. Mrs Heccomb always shopped from ten-thirty to midday, with a break for coffee at the Corona Café. If she was not 'in town' by ten-thirty, she fretted. With her hive-shaped basket under her elbow, Portia in her wake, she punted happily, slowly up and down the High Street, crossing at random, quite often going back on her tracks. Women who shop by telephone do not know what the pleasures of buying are. Rich women live at such a distance from life that very often they never see their money – the Queen, they say, for instance, never carries a purse. But Mrs Heccomb's unstitched morocco purse, with the tarnished silver corners, was always in evidence. She paid cash almost every-where, partly because she had found that something happens to bills, making them always larger than you think, partly because her roving disposition made her hate to be tied to one set of shops. She liked to be *known* in as many shops as possible, to receive a personal smile when she came in. And she had by this time managed things so well that she was known in every Seale shop of standing. Where she had not actually bought things, she had repeatedly priced them. She did admit herself tied to one butcher, one dairy because they *sent*: Mrs Heccomb did not care for carrying meat, and the milk supply for a household must be automatic. Even to these two shops she was not wholly faithful: she had been known to pick up a kidney here and there, some new shade of butter, a crock of cream.

To Portia, who had never seen a purse open so often (when you live in hotels there is almost nothing to buy) Mrs Heccomb's expenditure seemed princely – though there was often change out of a florin. When Mrs Heccomb had too many pennies, she would build them up, at the next counter she came to, into pillars of twelve or six, and push them across cautiously. Where she paid in coppers only, she felt she had got a bargain: money goes further when you do not break into silver, and any provident person baulks at changing a note. Everything was bought in small quantities, exactly as it was wanted day by day. Today, for instance, she made the following purchases:

> One cake of Vinolia for the bathroom,
> Half a dozen Relief nibs,
> One pot of salmon and shrimp paste (small size),
> One pan scrubber of crumpled metal gauze,
> One bottle of Bisurated Magnesia tablets (small size),
> One bottle of gravy browning,
> One skein of 'natural' wool (for Dickie's vests),
> One electric light bulb,
> One lettuce,
> One length of striped canvas to reseat a deck chair,
> One set of whalebones to repair corsets,
> Two pair of lambs' kidneys,
> Half a dozen small screws,
> A copy of the *Church Times*.

She also made, from a list of Daphne's, and out of a special ten shilling note, a separate set of purchases for the party tonight. Portia bought a compendium – lightly ruled violet paper, purple lined envelopes – and nine pennyworth of three-halfpenny stamps. Infected by the sea air with extravagance, she also bought a jade green box to keep a toothbrush in, and a length of red ribbon for a snood for tonight.

Now Mrs Heccomb had gone to the house agent's for her annual consultation about the summer let. Probably no other householder in Seale began to discuss the summer let so early. The fact was that Daphne and Dickie objected each year more strongly to turning out of Waikiki for the three best months. But their father had built the house for summer letting, and his widow adhered to this with a touch of piety. In July, August, September she took her painting things with her and moved on a round of visits to relatives: meanwhile, Daphne and Dickie were put out to board with friends. In view of the objections they always raised, she liked to get the let clinched well in advance, then to let them know of it as a *fait accompli*. But she was made sad, when she went to the house agent's, by the sense of conspiring against Daphne and Dickie.

So she did not take Portia with her to witness this dark act, but sent her to the Corona to book a table. The Corona was very full at this hour; the fashionable part was upstairs, looking down on the High Street. Only outsiders drank their coffee downstairs. And how bright it was up here, with the smell of hot roasting coffee, the whicker of wicker chairs. A stove threw out roaring heat: sun streamed through the windows, curdling the smoke of a few bold cigarettes. Ladies waiting for ladies looked through back numbers of the *Tatler* and *Sketch*. Dogs on leads wound themselves round the table legs. Paper tulips in vases, biscuits in coloured paper on the tile-topped tables struck bright notes. The waitresses knew everyone. It was so much gayer than London – also, there was abandonment about this morning feast: to be abandoned you must be respectable.

Several times Portia had looked up from her letters to watch one more lady's hat come up past the banisters. But for a long time no hat was Mrs Heccomb's. When Mrs Heccomb did finally come, she shot out of nowhere like a Jack-in-the-box. The three envelopes were still all over the table. Mrs Heccomb threw them a glance whose keenness was automatic, though the keenness was quickly veiled by tact. Not for nothing had she been for years a duenna. Eddie's writing was, to the simple eye, disarming, but Major Brutt's was unflinchingly masculine. Matchett's letter could be put down at once as a letter that was likely to be from Matchett. Mrs Heccomb had not yet seen these handwritings: it was Daphne who galloped out to meet the morning post.

'Well, dear, I'm glad you have not been lonely. Mr Bunstable kept me. Now I shall order coffee. Look, eat a chocolate biscuit while we wait.'

Still slightly flustered by her own arrival, Mrs Heccomb balanced her basket on an empty chair and signalled to a waitress. She looked pink. On top of this she wore, like an extra hat, a distinct air of caution and indecision. 'It is so nice to get letters,' she said.

'Oh yes. This morning I had three.'

'I expect, travelling so much, you and your mother made many nice friends?'

'No, you see we travelled rather *too* much.'

'And now you have made friends with Anna's friends, I expect?'

'Some of them. Not all.'

Mrs Heccomb looked less anxious by several degrees. 'Anna', she said, 'is a wonderful judge of people. Even as a young girl she was always particular, and now such distinguished people come to her house, don't they? One would always be right in liking anyone Anna liked. She has a wonderful way of gathering people round her: it's so nice for you, dear, to have come to a happy house like that. I am sure it must be a great pleasure to her to see you get on so nicely with the people she knows. She would be so wonderfully sympathetic. I expect you love to show her the letters you get, don't you?'

'I only get many letters when I am at the sea.'

Momentarily, Mrs Heccomb looked nonplussed. Then her shoulder was given a sharp tap by a lady leaning across from one of the other tables. A playful, reproachful conversation ensued between them. Portia, herself considerably puzzled, poured cream on to her coffee out of a doll's jug. Soon she was made known to Mrs Heccomb's lady, and stood up politely to shake hands. She stuck the letters back in the pocket of her tweed coat.

When they had left the café and were in the High Street, Mrs Heccomb, pausing outside Smoots', showed with a rather rueful upward gesture where Daphne worked. Portia pictured Daphne behind that window like a furious Lady of Shalott. 'Is she fond of reading?' she said.

'Well, no, but that's not so much what they want. They want a girl who *is* someone, if you know what I mean. A girl who – well, I don't quite know how to express it – a girl who did not come from a nice home would not do at all, *here*. You know, choosing books is such a personal thing; Seale is a small place and the people are so nice. Personality counts for so much here. The Corona Café is run by ladies, you know.'

'Oh.'

'And of course everyone knows Daphne. It is wonderful how she has settled down to the work. I'm afraid her father would not have thought it ideal. But one cannot always foresee the future, can one?'

'No.'

'Almost everyone changes their books there. You must go and see her one morning: she would be delighted. Oh dear, look; it's twelve! We shall have to hurry home.'

They dashed back to the sea down the asphalt walk, then waited about an hour in the lounge at Waikiki while Doris dealt with lunch. Mrs Heccomb turned her lamp shade round and round and said the varnish on it was drying. After lunch she said she'd be quiet just for a minute, then took a nap on the sofa with her back to the sea.

Portia looked several times at Mrs Heccomb napping, then took her shoes off and crept up to explore the bedroom floor of Waikiki, to see which Eddie's room could be. Mrs Heccomb's room, in which she dared not linger, contained a large double bed with a hollow in the middle, and a number of young girls' photographs. Daphne's room smelled of Coty powder (Chypre), an army of evening shoes was drawn up under the bureau, and a Dismal Desmond dog sat on the bed. Snapshots of confident people of both sexes were stuck round the mirror. Dickie's room looked north towards the town, and had that physical smell north rooms so soon acquire. It contained boot jacks, boxing gloves, a stack of copies of *Esquire*, three small silver trophies on ebony stands gleaming underneath framed groups. Doris's room was so palpably Doris's that Portia quickly shut the door again. But she did also discover another room – it was wedge-shaped, like the end of a piece of cheese. Its dormer window looked north. In here were stacks of old cardboard boxes and a dressmaker's bust of quite royal arrogance: the walls were hung with photographs of such tropics as Dr Heccomb had visited. Here also, promisingly, were a stretcher bed, a square of mirror, and a bamboo table. Portia took one more look round, then crept downstairs again. By the time Mrs Heccomb woke, she was half way through a letter.

She was writing: 'There is a room, and I think you would like everything. There are two directions for us to walk in. I will not broach about this till tomorrow, which will be Sunday –'

Mrs Heccomb woke with a little snatch at her hair, as though she heard something in it. 'Busy, dear?' she said. 'We shall have to go out in about an hour. We are going out to tea up the hill – there are two daughters, though both a little older than you.' She tucked in her blouse at the back of her belt again, and for some time moved contentedly round the lounge, altering the position of one or two objects, as though she had had some new idea while asleep. A draught creeping through the sun porch rattled the curtain rings: Waikiki gave one of its shiplike creaks, and waves began to thump with greater force on the beach.

As Mrs Heccomb and Portia, both in chamois gloves, walked sedately up the hill out to tea, the daffodil buds in gardens knocked to and fro. Seale gave one of its spring afternoon dramas of wind and sun, and clouds bowled over the marsh that one saw from here. Down there, the curve of the bay crepitated in changing silver light.

'I expect you often go out to tea with Anna?'

'Well, Anna doesn't often go out to tea.'

On the way home, Mrs Heccomb took Portia to Evensong, which was intoned in the Lady Chapel. Then they went round to the vestry for some surplices, which Mrs Heccomb took home to mend. She could not aspire to do the altar flowers, as she could not afford beautiful flowers, so this was her labour of love for the church. 'The little boys are very rough,' she said, 'the gathers nearly always go at the neck.' It took some time to go through the surplices, and longer still to pin them up in brown paper – Mrs Heccomb, with other ladies with access to the vestry, kept a hoard of brown paper, for their own uses, behind a semi-sacred cupboard of pitched pine. The Vicar did not know of the existence of this. Whenever Mrs Heccomb opened a parcel, she saved the paper to take up to the church, so there was never brown paper at Waikiki ... When they did get back to Waikiki with the surplices, Daphne was punting chairs about the lounge.

Daphne's hair had been re-set, and looked like gilded iron. The door through to the dining-room stood open, so that the heat of the lounge fire might take some of the chill off the dining-room: the breath that came out from there was rather cold, certainly. They all went in there to have a look round, and Daphne blew the dust off a centre-piece of Cape gooseberries with an exasperatedly calm air.

'The bell rings beautifully now, dear.'

'Yes, the bell's all right, but when I tried ringing it Doris shot out and had a sort of fit.'

'Perhaps it's still rather loud.'

'But what I mean is, she must learn not to do that. She can't find the potted meat, either.'

'Oh, I'm so sorry, dear; it's hanging up in my basket.'

'Well, really, Mumsie ... As it is, you see, she hasn't even started the sandwiches. I suppose you've been at that church?' said Daphne, pouncing.

'Well, we just –'

'Well, I do think church might keep. It's Saturday, after all.'

Supper was cold that night, and was eaten early in order to give Doris plenty of time to clear. So they were to dress afterwards. Dickie was rather cold about this evening party, as he had wished to watch an ice hockey match. He had spent his Saturday afternoon in Southstone playing ordinary hockey in the mud. 'I don't see why they want to come,' he said.

'Well after all, Clara's coming.'

'What does she want to come for? This is the first I've heard of it.'

'Well I really must say – I *must* say, really! You asked her yourself, Dickie: you did! You said why not drop in Saturday, and of course she jumped at it. I daresay she's cutting some other date.'

'Well, I don't know what dates all your friends have, but I know I never asked Clara. *Would* I ask Clara when the Montreal Eagles are here?'

'Which eagles, dear?' said Mrs Heccomb.

'They're at the Icedrome tonight – as Daphne has known for weeks.'

'Well, I don't care where your beastly old eagles are. All I know is that you did ask Clara. And you needn't go on as if *I* knew what dates Clara had. I should have thought that was your business, not mine.'

'Oh, would you really?' said Dickie, giving his sister a brassy stare. 'And what grounds, may I ask, have you for saying that?'

'Well, she's only round when you're here,' said Daphne, weakening slightly.

'Where the girl may choose to be is her own business, I take it.'

'Then don't you go making out she's a friend of mine.'

'Oh, all right, all right, all right, you didn't ask her, I did. *I* didn't want to see the Montreal Eagles, oh *no*. Must Cecil come?'

'I just slipped in and asked him,' said Mrs Heccomb. 'I thought you two might forget, and he would have been so hurt.'

Dickie said: 'I don't see why we have got to have Cecil.'

'I do,' said Daphne. 'Mumsie and I thought he would do for Portia.'

'Oh, Daphne, that was your idea, you know.'

For the first time, Dickie looked full at Portia with his commanding stag's eyes. 'You will find Cecil a bit cissie,' he said.

'Oh, Dickie, he's not.'

'Oh, I like Cecil all right, but I can't stand those cissie pullovers.'

'Well, you wear pullovers.'

'I don't wear cissie pullovers.'

'Oh, by the way, Dickie, you ought to see Doris bounce when she hears that bell.'

'Oh, so it rings now, does it?'

'No thanks to you, either.'

'Dickie's so busy, dear – Look, we ought to go up and dress now. And Doris is in there wanting to clear.'

'Then for goodness' sake why doesn't she? Make her open the windows – we don't want the whole place smelling of veal and ham.'

The three ladies went upstairs, Mrs Heccomb taking her last cup of coffee with her. Dickie, after an interval for reflection, could be heard going up to change his appearance, too. Now, all over the bedroom floor of Waikiki, chests of drawers were banged open, taps were run. A black night wind was up, and Waikiki breasted it steadily, straining like a liner: every fixture rattled. This all went to heighten a pre-party tensity of the nerves. Portia wormed her way into her black velvet, which, from hanging only behind a curtain, had taken on a briny dampness inside: the velvet clung to her skin above her chemise top. She combed back her hair and put on the red snood – so tight that it drew the ends of her eyebrows up. With eyes too much dilated to see, she looked past herself in the mirror.

She was first downstairs and, squatting on the tiled kerb in front of the fire, heard the chimney roar. With arms raised from the elbows, like an Egyptian, she turned and toasted her body, feeling the clammy velvet slowly unstick from between her shoulder blades.

This was to be her first party. Tonight, the ceiling rose higher, the lounge extended tense and mysterious. Columns of translucent tawny shadow stood between the orange shades of the lamps. The gramophone stood open, a record on it, the arm with the needle bent back like an arm ready to strike. Doris not seeing Portia, Doris elate and ghostly in a large winged cap passed through the lounge with trays. Out there at sea they might take this house for another lighted ship – and soon this magnetic room would be drawing people down the dark esplanade. Portia saw her partners with no faces: whoever she danced with, it would always be Eddie.

Dickie came down in a dark blue pin-striped suit, and asked if she'd like to help him roll the carpet back. They had got as far as rolling back the settee when a sort of bat-like fumbling was heard at the glass door, and Dickie stopped with a grunt to let in Cecil.

'I say,' Cecil said, 'I'm afraid I've come rather early.'

'Well, you have rather in one way. However, give a hand with the carpet. As usual, everything has been left to me – Oh, by the way, this is Mr Cecil Bowers, Miss Portia Quayne ... By the way, Cecil,' said Dickie, rather more sternly, 'the bell does ring now.'

'Oh? Sorry. It didn't use to.'

'Well, make a note that it does.'

'Dickie, who's *that*?' Daphne wailed over the banisters.

'Only Cecil. He's rolling up the carpet.'

When Cecil had finished rolling up the carpet he straightened his tie and went off to wash his hands. Portia found no special fault with his appearance, though it was certainly not as manly as Dickie's. When he came back, he was beginning to say to her: 'I understand that you have just come from London,' when Daphne appeared and made him carry a tray.

'Now, Cecil,' she said, 'there's no time to stand there chatting.' Her manner made it quite clear that if Cecil *were* for Portia, he would come on to her as one of Daphne's discards. Daphne wore a *crêpe de Chine* dress, cut clinging into the thighs and draped lusciously elsewhere: on it poppies, roses, nasturtiums flowered away, only slightly blurred by the folds. In her high-heeled emerald shoes, she stepped higher than ever. When the bell rang, seeming to tweak at the whole house, and Dickie went to let some more people in, Daphne sent Cecil and Portia into the dining-room to stick the flags on the sandwiches and to count the glasses for cider-cup.

They could only find what was inside the sandwiches by turning up the corners to have a look. Even so, they could not be sure which kind of fish paste was which: Cecil, having made sure they were alone in the room, tasted a crumb of each with his finger-tip. 'Not quite in order,' he said, 'but *que voulez vous?*'

'No one will know,' said Portia, standing behind him.

The complicity set up between her and Cecil made them sit down on two chairs, when they had planted the flags, and look at each other with interest. There was a hum in the lounge, and no one was missing them. 'These do's of Daphne's and Dickie's are very jolly,' said Cecil.

'Do they often have them?'

'Quite frequently. They are always on Saturdays. They always seem to go with rather a swing. But I daresay this may seem quiet after London?'

'It doesn't really. Do you often go to London?'

'Well, I do – when I don't slip over to France.'

'Oh, do you slip over to France?'

'Yes, I must say I often do. You may think me mad, too: everyone here does. Everyone here behaves as though France did not exist. "What is that you see over there?" I sometimes say to them, when it's a clear day. They say, "Oh, that's France." But it makes no impression on them. I often go to Boulogne on a day trip.'

'All by yourself?'

'Well, I have been by myself, and also I often go with a really wonderfully sporting aunt of mine. And once or twice I have been with another fellow.'

'And what do you do?'

'Oh, I principally walk about. In spite of being so easy to get at, Boulogne is really wonderfully French, you know. I doubt if Paris itself could be much Frencher. No, I haven't yet been to Paris: what I always feel is, supposing it rather disappointed me ... "Oh, hullo," all those others always say to me, when I haven't shown up at the Pav or the Icedrome or the Palais, "you've been abroad again!" What conclusions they come to I've no idea,' said Cecil consciously, looking down his nose. 'I don't know if you've noticed,' he went on, 'but so few people care if they don't enlarge their ideas. But I always like to enlarge mine.'

'Oh, so do I.' She looked timidly at Cecil, then said: 'Lately, my ideas have enlarged a lot.'

'I thought they must have,' said Cecil. 'You gave me just that impression. That is why I am talking like this to you.'

'Some of my ideas get enlarged almost before I have them.'

'Yes, that was just what I felt. Usually, I am a bit reserved . . . Do you get on well with Dickie?'

'Well, when you came he and I were just going to roll the carpet up.'

'I hope I was not tactless.'

'Oh no.'

'Dickie's extremely popular,' Cecil said with a mixture of gloom and pride. 'I should say he was a born leader of men. I expect you find Daphne awfully fascinating?'

'Well, she is out most of the day.'

'Daphne', said Cecil, a shade reproachfully, 'is one of the most popular girls I have ever met. I don't suppose one will get near her the whole evening.'

'Oh dear! Couldn't you try?'

'To tell you the truth,' said Cecil, 'I am not doing so badly where I am.'

At this interesting point Mrs Heccomb, in a claret lace dress that could not have come from Anna, looked anxiously into the dining-room. 'Oh, here you are, dear,' she said. 'I was wondering. Good evening, Cecil, I'm so glad you could come. I think they are thinking of dancing quite soon now.'

Portia and Cecil rose and trailed to the door. In the lounge, an uncertain silence told them that the party's first impetus had lapsed. About a dozen people leaned round the walls, sat rather stonily on the settee-back, or crouched on the roll of carpet. They were all looking passively at Daphne, willing though not keen to fall in with her next plan. Mrs Heccomb may have been right when she said they were thinking of dancing – if they *were* thinking, no doubt it was about that. Daphne gave them one or two hostile looks – this was what she called sticking about. She turned, and with Mr Bursely beside her, stickily fingering records, began to hover over the gramophone.

But there was a deadlock here, for she would not start the gramophone till they had got up, and they would not get up till she had started the gramophone. Dickie stood by the mantel-piece with Clara, clearly feeling that he had done enough. His manner rather said: 'Now if we had gone to the Eagles, this would not have happened.' Clara was a smallish girl with crimped platinum hair, a long nose, a short neck, and the sub-servient expression of a good white mouse. Round her neck she wore a frill of white organdie roses, which made her head look as though it were on a tray. Her manner of looking up made Dickie look still more virile. Any conversation they did seem to be having seemed to be due to Clara's tenacity.

Portia's appearing in the doorway with Cecil released some inside spring in Daphne immediately. No doubt she thought of Anna – stung to life, she let off the gramophone, banged the needle down, and foxtrotted on to the parquet with Mr Bursely. Four or five other couples then rose and faced each other to dance. Portia wondered if Cecil would ask her – so far, they had been on such purely mental terms. While she wondered, Dickie stepped from Clara's side, impressively crossed the room, and stood over Portia, impassive. 'Shall we?' he said.

She began to experience the sensation of being firmly trotted backwards and forwards, and at each corner slowly spun like a top. Looking up, she saw Dickie wear the expression many people wear when they drive a car. Dickie controlled her by the pressure of a thumb under her shoulder blade; he supported her wrist between his other thumb and a forefinger – when another couple approached he would double her arm up, like someone shutting a penknife in a hurry. Crucified on his chest against his breathing, she felt her feet brush the floor like any marion-ette's. Increasingly less anxious, she kept her look fixed on the cleft of his chin. She did not flatter herself: this *démarche* of Dickie's could have only one object – by chagrining Clara to annoy Daphne. Across Mr Bursely's shoulder, Daphne threw Dickie a furious, popping look. For Clara was both grateful and well-to-do, and Daphne, by an unspoken arrangement, got her percentage on any fun Clara had.

But Dickie, though inscrutable, was kind: half way through the second record, he said: 'You seem to be getting on quite well.' Too pleased, she left behind one toe, and Dickie immediately trod on it. 'Sorry!' 'Oh, *I'm* sorry!' She had reason to be, so Dickie accepted this. Taking her more in hand, he splayed the whole of one palm against her ribs and continued to make her foxtrot. When the record was over, he took her in state to the fire, where poor Clara had stood. Shrinking but elated queen of the room she looked down it, saw Mrs Heccomb knitting, saw Mr Bursely's hand over the *crêpe de Chine* bow just above Daphne's bottom as they talked in the sun porch with their backs to the room, saw Cecil despondently being civil elsewhere, Clara's head sadly aslant on her white ruff. She hoped no one was bearing her any malice.

'You don't smoke, do you?' Dickie said rather threateningly.

'I'm not really sure how to.'

Dickie, having slowly lighted a cigarette of his own, said: 'I should not let that worry you. Most girls smoke too much.'

'Well, I may never begin.'

'And another thing you had much better not begin is putting stuff on your nails. That sort of thing makes the majority of men sick. One cannot see why girls do it.'

'Perhaps they don't know.'

'Well, I always tell a girl. If one is to know a girl, it is much better to tell her what one thinks. Another thing I don't like is messed-up mouths. When I give a girl tea, I always look at her cup. Then, if she leaves any red muck on the rim, I say, "Hullo, I didn't know that cup had a pink pattern." Then the girl seems quite taken aback.'

'But suppose the cup had really got a pink pattern?'

'In that case, I should say something else. Girls make a mistake in trying to be attractive in ways that simply lose them a man's respect. No man would want to give his children a mother with that sort of stuff all over her face. No wonder the population is going down.'

'My sister-in-law says men are too particular.'

'I cannot see that it is particular to have ideals. I should only care to marry a girl who seemed natural and likely to make a good home. And I think you would find that the majority of fellows, if you asked them, would feel the same. Will you have some lemonade?'

'No, thank you; not yet.'

'Well, if you'll excuse me, I think I must fix myself up for this next dance. You and I might have the sixth from now. I will look for you by the gramophone.'

Portia was going to sit beside Mrs Heccomb when Cecil came up and asked for the next dance. 'You were swept away before I could speak,' he said – but all the same, he looked at her with respect. Cecil's method of dancing was more persuasive, and Portia found she did not get on so well. She took a look at Clara's mouselike hand splayed rather imploringly on a partner's shoulder (Dickie was waltzing with a fine girl in orange) and saw Clara wore no varnish on her nails. Dickie's partner did. After that, she kept twisting round to look at every girl's hands, and this made her collide and bump with Cecil. After three rounds he suggested another talk: clearly he liked her more on the mental plane. They sat down on the settee, in a draught from the sun porch, and Portia began to reproach herself for feeling that Cecil's manner lacked authority. Cecil stopped talking to give a glare. 'Here comes that fellow Bursely from the School of Musketry. He seems to think he can behave all anyhow here. I don't think Dickie really thinks much of him. We must let him see that we are deep in talk.'

But though she obediently fixed her eyes on Cecil, Mr Bursely bumped on to the settee on her other side. 'Am I butting in?' he said, but not anxiously.

'You should know,' muttered Cecil.

Mr Bursely said brightly: 'Didn't catch what you said.'

'I said, I am going to look for a cigarette.'

'Now, what's eating him?' said Mr Bursely. 'As a matter of fact,' he went on, 'you and I *were* introduced, but I don't think you heard: you were looking the other way. I asked Daphne who you were the moment you buzzed in, but she didn't seem to be too keen we should meet. Then I asked the old lady to put us in touch, but she couldn't make herself heard above the up-roar. Quite a little gathering, what?'

'Yes, quite.'

'You having a good time?'

'Yes, *very*, thank you.'

'You look it,' said Mr Bursely. 'The eyes starry and so on. Look here, like to slip out to the so-called bar? Soft drinks only: no licence. Some little bird told me that was the drill here, so I had one or two in the mess before pushing round.' This was more or less evident. Portia said she would rather stay where they were. 'Oh, right-o,' said Mr Bursely: sliding down on the sofa he stuck his feet in their tan shoes a good way out. 'You a stranger in these parts?'

'I only came on Thursday.'

'Getting to know the natives?'

'Yes.'

'I'm not doing badly, either. But of course we mostly cut into Southstone.'

'Who is we?'

'We licentious soldiery. Listen: how young are you?'

'Sixteen.'

'Gosh – I thought you were about ten. Anyone ever told you you're a sweet little kid?'

Portia thought of Eddie. 'Not exactly,' she said.

'Well, I'm telling you now. Your Uncle Peter's telling you. Always remember what Uncle Peter said. Honestly when you first keeked round that door, I wanted to cry and tell you about my wicked life. And I bet you take a lot of chaps that way?'

Not happily, Portia put a finger inside her tight snood. Mr Bursely slewed right round on the sofa, with one arm right along the back. His clean-skinned face, clotted up with emotion, approached Portia's – unwilling, she looked at, not into, his eyes, which were urgent blue poached eggs. Her unnerved look seemed to no more than float on his regardlessness of it.

'Just tell me', said Mr Bursely, 'that you'd be a bit sorry if I was dead.'

'Oh yes. But why should you be?'

'Well, one never knows.'

'No – I suppose not.'

'You *are* a sweet little kid –'

'– Portia,' said Mrs Heccomb, 'this is Mr Parker, a great friend of Dickie's. Mr Parker would like to dance with you.' Portia looked up to find a sort of a rescue party, headed by Mrs Heccomb, standing over the settee. She got up rather limply, and Mr Parker, with an understanding smile, at once danced her away. Bobbing, just out of time, below Mr Parker's shoulder, she looked round to see Daphne, with set and ominous face, take her place on the settee next to Mr Bursely.

4

IN church, during the sermon, Portia asked herself for the first time why what Mr Bursely had said had set up such disconcerting echoes, why she had run away from it in her mind. There was something she did not want to look straight at – was this why, since the party yesterday night, she had not once thought of Eddie? It is frightening to find that the beloved may be unwittingly caricatured by someone who does not know him at all. The devil must have been in Mr Bursely when he asked, and asked with such confidence, if she had not been told she was a sweet little kid. The shock was that she could not, now, remember Eddie's having in effect called her anything else. Stooping down, as she sat beside Mrs Heccomb, to examine the stitching on her brown mocha gloves – which in imitation of Mrs Heccomb she kept on while she sat, wrists crossed on her knee – she wondered whether a feeling could spring straight from the heart, be imperative, without being original. (But if love were original, if it were the unique device of two unique spirits, its importance would not be granted; it could not make a great common law felt. The strongest compulsions we feel throughout life are no more than compulsions to repeat a pattern: the pattern is not of our own device.)

Had Mr Bursely had, behind that opaque face, behind that

expression moulded by insobriety, the impulse that had made Eddie write her that first note? Overlaid, for the rest of the party, by the noise and excitement, was dread that the grace she had with Eddie might reduce to that single maudlin cry. This dread had haunted her tardy sleep, and sucked at her when she woke like the waves sucking the shingle in the terribly quiet morning air.

Everything became threatened.

There are moments when it becomes frightening to realize that you are not, in fact, alone in the world – or at least, alone in the world with one other person. The telephone ringing when you are in a day-dream becomes a cruel attacking voice. That general tender kindness towards the world, especially kindness of a young person, comes from a pitying sense of the world's unreality. The happy passive nature, locked up with itself like a mirror in an airy room, reflects what goes on but demands not to be approached. A pact with life, a pact of immunity, appears to exist – But this pact is not respected for ever – a street accident, an overheard quarrel, a certain note in a voice, a face coming too close, a tree being blown down, someone's unjust fate – the peace tears right across. Life militates against the seclusion we seek. In the chaos that suddenly thrusts in, nothing remains unreal, except possibly love. Then, love only remains as a widened susceptibility: it is felt at the price of feeling all human dangers and pains. The lover becomes the sentient figurehead of the whole human ship, thrust forward by the weight of the race behind him through pitiless elements. Pity the selfishness of lovers: it is brief, a forlorn hope; it is impossible.

Frantic smiles at parties, overtures that have desperation behind them, miasmic reaches of talk with the lost bore, short cuts to approach through staring, squeezing, or kissing – all indicate that one cannot live alone. Not only is there no question of solitude, but in the long run we may not chose our company. The attempt at Windsor Terrace to combat this may have been what made that house so queasy and cold. That mistaken approach to life – of which at intervals they were all conscious, from Thomas Quayne down to the cook – produced the tensions and hitches of an unpromising love affair. Each person at Windsor Terrace lived impaled upon a private obsession, however slight. The telephone, the door bell, the postman's knock were threatening intimations, though still far off. Crossing that springy door mat, the outside person suffered a sea change. In fact, something edited life in the Quayne's house – the action of some sort of brake or deterrent was evident in the behaviour of such people as Eddie. At the same time, no one seemed clear quite *what* was being discarded, or whether anything vital was being let slip away. If Matchett were feared, if she seemed to threaten the house, it was because she seemed most likely to put her thumb on the thing.

The uneditedness of life here at Waikiki made for behaviour that was pushing and frank. Nothing set itself up here but the naïvest propriety – that made Daphne shout but not swear, that kept Dickie so stern and modest, that had kept even Mr Bursely's hand, at yesterday evening's party, some inches above the bow on Daphne's behind. Propriety is no serious check to nature – in fact, nature banks itself up behind it – thus, eyes constantly bulged and skins changed colour with immediate unsubtle impulses. Coming from Windsor Terrace, Portia found at Waikiki the upright rudeness of the primitive state – than which nothing is more rigidly ruled. The tremble felt through the house when a door banged or someone came hurriedly downstairs, the noises made by the plumbing, Mrs Heccomb's prodigality with half-crowns and shillings, the many sensory hints that Doris was human and did not function in a void of her own – all these made Waikiki the fount of spontaneous living. Life here seemed to be at its highest voltage, and Portia stood to marvel at Daphne and Dickie as she might have marvelled at dynamos. At nights, she thought of all that force contained in those single beds in the other rooms.

In terms of this free living, she now saw, or resaw, not only the people she met at Waikiki, but everyone she had known. The few large figures she saw here represented society with an alarming fairness, an adequacy that she could not deny. In them, she was forced to see every motive and passion – for motives and passions are alarmingly few. Any likeness between Mr Bursely and Eddie her love did still hope to reject. All the same, something asked her, or forced her to ask herself, whether, last night on the settee, it had not been Eddie that emerged from the bush?

Portia felt her sixpence for the collection between the palm of her right hand and the palm of her glove. The slight tickling, and the milled pressure of the new coin's edge, when she closed her hand, recalled her to where she was – in Seale church, in a congregation of stalwart elderly men and of women in brown, grey, navy, or violet, with collars of inexpensive fur. The sun, slanting moltenly in at the south windows, laid a dusty nimbus over the furs, and printed cheeks with the colours of stained glass. Turning her head a little, she perceived people with whom she had been to tea. Above the confident congregation the church rose to its kind inscrutable height. Tilting her chin up, she studied the east window and its glittering tale: she had joined the sermon late and just got the gist of it – though it was after Easter, one must not be more callous than one had been in Lent.

Fanned on down the aisle by blasts from the organ, the choir disappeared in the vestry under the tower. Mrs Heccomb, as the procession passed, cast some appraising looks at the surplices. Brasso and the devotion of her fellow ladies had given a blond shine to the processional cross. As the last chords sounded, discreet smiles were exchanged across the aisle, and the congregation jumbled happily out. Mrs Heccomb was a great porch talker, and it was therefore in quite a knot of friends that she and Portia at last started downhill. Daphne and Dickie were not great church-goers: the Sunday after a party they always voted against it. Back at Waikiki the lounge, restored to order, was full of sun; Daphne and Dickie read the Sunday papers in a very strong smell of roasting meat. They had not been down at twenty minutes past ten, when Mrs Heccomb and Portia had started for church. Outside, gulls skimmed in the rather cold air, and Mrs Heccomb quickly shut the glass door.

'Hullo,' said Dickie to Portia. 'And how are *you* this morning?'

'Very well, thank you.'

'Well, at least it is over,' said Dickie, returning to the *Sunday Pictorial*.

Daphne was still wearing her red mules. 'Oh goodness,' she said. 'Cecil is so wet! Coming early like that, then sticking round like that. I don't know how he has the nerve, really ... Oh, and I ought to tell you: Clara's left her pearl bag.'

Mrs Heccomb, rearranging one or two objects, said: 'How wonderfully you have tidied everything up.'

'All but the bookcase,' Dickie said pointedly.

'What do you mean about the bookcase, dear?'

'We shall need a glazier to tidy up *that* bookcase. Daphne's soldier friend put his elbow through it – as you might notice, Mumsie, if you cared to look. There seems to be no suggestion that he should foot the bill.'

'Oh, I don't think we could quite ask him, dear ... It seemed to be a very successful party.'

Daphne, from behind the *Sunday Express*, said: 'It was all right.' She raised her voice. 'Though some people cut their own friends, then are stuffy to other people's. Mr Bursely was shoved against the bookcase by Wallace Parker shoving in that rude way. I'm only thankful he didn't hurt himself. I didn't like him to see us so rough house.'

'If you ask me,' said Dickie, 'I don't suppose he noticed. He'd have stayed stuck in the bookcase if Charlie Hoster hadn't pulled him out. He arrived here pretty lit, and I'm told he nipped down the front and had two or three quick ones at the Imperial Arms. I wonder what he'll smash next time he comes blowing in. I cannot say that that is a fellow I like. But apparently I do not know what is what.'

'Well, Clara liked him all right. That is how she forgot her bag. She stopped on to give him a lift home in her car.'

'So you pointed out. Well, if that bag is Clara's, I don't like it: it seems to me to be covered with ants' eggs.'

'Well, why don't you tell her so?'

'I no doubt shall. I shall no doubt tell her this afternoon. Clara and I are going to play golf.'

'Oh you *are* a mean, Dickie! You never said! Evelyn's expecting us all to badminton.'

'Well, she will simply have to expect me, I'm afraid. Clara's picking me up at half past two. We may buzz back here for tea, or we may go back to her place – By the way, Mumsie, can Doris be sharp with dinner?'

'She's just going to lay, dear. May I move your paper? Daphne, what are you doing after lunch?'

'Well, a lot of us thought we might go for a short walk. Then we're all going round to Evelyn's to badminton. Do you mean you'd like me to take Portia along?'

'That might be nice, dear. You'd like that, wouldn't you, Portia? In that case I may just take a little rest. Last night was so successful that we were rather late.'

The walking party – Daphne, Portia, Evelyn (the fine girl who had worn orange last night), Cecil (who did not seem to have been asked), and two other young men called Charlie and Wallace – deployed slowly along the top of the sea wall in the direction of Southstone. The young men wore plus-fours, pullovers, felt hats precisely dinted in at the top, and ribbed stockings that made their calves look massive. Daphne and Evelyn wore berets, scarves with dogs' heads, and natty check overcoats. Evelyn had brought her dog with her.

The road on top of the wall was as deserted as ever: at the foot of the wall the sea, this afternoon mackerel blue, swelled sleekly between the breakwaters. Here and there a gull on a far-out post would be floated off by the swell, looking rather silly. There was a breakwater smell – a smell of sea-pickled planks, of slimy green boards being sucked by the tides. The immense spring sky arched from the inland woods to the marine horizon. The wall made a high causeway on which the walkers walked between sea and land: here you smelled not only the sea but a land breath – from the market gardens, the woods in clefts of the chalk hills, the gorse budding in its spiny darkness up there on the links where Dickie and Clara were. The crests of two airy tides, the sea's and the land's, breaking against each other above the asphalt, made a nervous elation, so that you spun, inwardly, in the blue-whiteness of the quiet and thrilling day.

Daphne's party walked in a Sundayish dogged manner, using

without sensation their deep lungs. They knew every inch of the sea wall; they looked ahead to Southstone, where the dome of the Splendide was bright gold. The sense of exposure this airy bareness gave them made them, with one another, at once side-long and bold. On the whole, they walked abreast, but as far apart as they could; at times they converged so close that they jogged elbows; if they split up into twos, the twos called across to each other – this was daylight: there was no *tête-à-tête*. At the end of a mile and a half they reached the old lifeboat station, where without a word they all wheeled round to return. The girls fell into a three; the three young men kept pace exactly behind them. They faced west.

With the first touch of evening, the first dazzle, a vague poeticness invaded them. Yawnfuls of ozone stopped the desultory talk. Evelyn took Daphne's arm; Cecil veered out alone to the edge of the esplanade and began to kick a lonely pebble along. A lovely brigantine appeared on the Channel, pink with light.

Portia drew a breath, then suddenly said to Daphne: 'A friend of mine – could he ever come and stay here?'

Brought out with a bang like this, it sounded quite all right.

Daphne veered thoughtfully round, hands in her pockets, chin deep in the folds of her doggy scarf, and Evelyn peered across Daphne, holding on to her arm. '*What* say?' Daphne said. 'A boy friend, do you mean?'

Evelyn said: 'That's what she's been in such a study about.'

'Could he how much?' said Daphne.

'Ever come and stay here?'

'Come and stay here when?'

'For a week-end.'

'Well, if you *have* a boy friend. I don't see why not. Do you see why not, Evelyn?'

'I should have thought it depended.'

'Yes, it depends, naturally. Have you really got a friend, though?'

'Just fancy, her,' added Evelyn. 'Still, *I* don't see why not.'

Daphne said swiftly: 'Friend of your sister-in-law?'

'Oh yes. She, he, they –'

'He'll be a bit ritzy for us, then, won't he? However,' said Daphne looking at Portia derisively, but with a touch of respect, 'if he's really as keen as all that it won't hurt him to lump it. Well, you certainly don't lose any time, do you? Of course, you'll have to square it with Mumsie, of course ... Go *on*: don't be such a little silly. She won't think anything of it; she's used to boys.'

But boys were not Eddie. Portia paused, then said: 'I thought I would ask you, then I thought you might ask her.'

'What's your friend in?' put in Evelyn. 'The Diplomatic?'

'*Who's* in the Diplomatic?' said Charlie, coming alongside.

'Portia's friend who's coming.'

'Well, he is not really: he's in my brother's office.'

'Well, after all,' said Evelyn, adjusting to this. She was the receptionist in Southstone's biggest beauty parlour: her face, whatever Dickie might think of it, continued to bloom in lusciòus and artificial apricot tones. Her father was Mr Bunstable, the important house agent who not only negotiated the Waikiki summer let but had clients throughout the county. Evelyn was thus not only a social light but had a stable position – consequently, she could not be hoped to enter into Daphne's feeling against the Quaynes. Business people were business people. She said kindly: 'Then it's been nice for him, picking up with you.'

'Your sister-in-law', said Daphne with some relish, 'would probably have a fit.'

Evelyn said: 'I don't see why.'

'Say, Cecil,' cried Daphne, whisking round sharply at him, 'must you keep on kicking that old stone?'

'So sorry: I was thinking something out.'

'Well, if you want to think, why come for a walk? Anyone might think this was a funeral – I say, Wallace, I say do listen, Charlie: Portia doesn't think much of any of you boys! She's having her own friend down.'

'Local talent', said Wallace, 'not represented. Well, these ladies from London – what can you expect?'

'Yes, you'd think', said Daphne, 'it should be enough for anyone, watching Cecil kicking that old stone.'

'Oh, it isn't that,' said Portia, looking at them anxiously. 'It's not that, really, I mean.'

'Well, I don't see why she shouldn't,' said Evelyn, closing the matter. She went to the head of some steps to whistle to her dog, which had got down on to the beach and was rolling in something horrid.

The others waited for Evelyn. The act of stopping sent a slight shock through the party, like the shock felt through a train that has pulled up. They were really more like a goods than a passenger train – content as a row of trucks, they stood solidly facing the way they would soon walk. Over still distant Seale, crowned by the church, smoke dissolved in the immature spring sun. The veil etherealized hillside villas with their gardens of trees; behind the balconies and the gables the hill took a tinge of hyacinth blue and looked like the outpost of a region of fantasy. Portia, glancing along the others' faces, was satisfied that Eddie had been forgotten. They did more than not think of Eddie, they thought of nothing.

She had learned to be less alarmed by Daphne's set since she had learned to plumb their abeyances. People are made alarming by one's dread of their unremitting, purposeful continuity. But in Seale, continuity dwelt in action only – interrupt what anybody was doing, and you interrupted what notions they had had. When these young people stopped doing what they were doing, they stopped all through, like clocks. Thus nothing, completely nothing filled this halt on their way to Sunday tea. Conceivably, astral smells of tea-cakes with hot currants, of chocolate biscuits, and warmed leather chairs vibrated towards them from Evelyn's home. They had walked; they would soon be back; they must have done themselves good.

Evelyn's dog came up the steps with a foul smear on its back, was scolded and wagged its rump in a merrily servile way. The dog was ordered to heel, where it did not stay, and the party, still with no word spoken, dropped forward into steady motion again.

At Evelyn's, Portia had time to think about next Sunday (or the Sunday after, was it to be?) for no one said much and she did not play badminton. The Bunstables' large villa had been built in the early twenties in the Old Normandy manner – inside and out it was dark and nubbly with oak. It was a complex of nooks, inside which leaded windows of thick greenish glass diluted the spring sky. The stairs were manorial, the living-rooms sumptuously quaint. Brass or copper disks distorted your face everywhere; there were faience tiles. This Norman influence had blown so obliquely across the Channel that few Seale people knew it as not British, though of some merrier period. The dining-room was so impressively dark that the antiqued lights soon had to be switched on. Evelyn's manner to her mother was disdainful but kindly: her father was out. Cecil, on showing a wish to sit by Portia, was sent to sit next the tea-pot, to talk to Mrs Bunstable. He almost at once dropped a quarter of buttered tea-cake on to one thigh of his plus-fours, and spent most of tea time trying to look *dégagé*, while, with a tea serviette dipped in hot water, he secretly failed to get the butter off.

Tea over, they moved to the glass-roofed badminton court: here the rubber shoes of the whole party hung by their laces from a row of hooks. While the rest put their shoes on, Portia climbed on a high stool close to the radiator. To hitch her heels on an upper rung of the stool made her feel like a bird. She began to imagine Eddie, next Sunday, taking part in all this. Or, when it came to the moment, would they find they would rather stay by the sea – not on the sea wall but out there near the martello towers, watching waves rush up the flat sands in the dusk? No, not for too long – for she and Eddie must on no account miss the Sunday fun. He and she had not yet been together into society. Even his name said on the sea front had made Daphne's friends show several shades more regard for her – though since then they had forgotten why – she felt more kindly embraced by these people already. Supposing she had a wish to be put across, who could do this for her better than Eddie could? How much ice he would cut; how proud she would be of him. The wish to lead out one's lover must be a tribal feeling; the wish to be seen as loved is part of one's self-respect. And, they would be in each other's secret; she would see him just not winking across the room. Alone, one has a rather incomplete outlook –

one is not sure what is funny, what is not. One solid pleasure of
love is to check up together on what has happened. Since they
were together last, she did not think she had laughed – she had
smiled, of course, but chiefly to please people. No, it would be
wrong to stay down by the sea.

Cecil, left out of the first set, edged round the court, and
came to stand by Portia: he propped one foot on the lower rung
of the stool and sent through it the vibration of a sigh. She put
her thoughts away quickly. Away in the lounge, at the far end
of the passage, Evelyn's mother switched the Luxemburg music
on: this fitted the game – the pouncing, slithering players, the
ping of the shots – into a sprightly rhythm, that pleased Portia
but further depressed Cecil. 'I don't care for spring, somehow,'
he said. 'It makes me feel a bit seedy.'

'You don't look seedy, Cecil.'

'I do with all this butter,' said Cecil, plucking unhappily at
his plus-fours. He went on: 'What were you thinking about?'

'I'm not thinking any more.'

'But you were, weren't you? I saw you. If I were a more oncoming sort of fellow I should offer you a penny, and so on.'

'I was wondering what next Sunday would be like.'

'Much the same, I expect. At this time of year, one begins
to want a change.'

'But this is a change for me.'

'Of course it's nice to think it's a change for someone. It will
be a change for your friend too, I expect. Funny, when I first
saw you at Daphne's party, you didn't look as though you had
a friend in the world. That was what drew me to you, I daresay.
I seem to have got you wrong, though. Are you really an
orphan?'

'Yes, I am,' said Portia a shade shortly. 'Are you?'

'No, not at present, but I suppose it's a thing one is bound
to be. The thought of the future rather preys on my mind. I am
quite enough of a lone wolf as it is. I get on well with girls up
to a certain point, but then they seem to find me too enigmatic.
I don't find it easy to let myself go. I don't think most girls ap-
preciate friendship; all they want is to be given a rush.'

'I like friendship very much.'

'Ah,' said Cecil, and looked at her gloomily. 'But if you will excuse my saying so, that may be because you are so young that no fellow has started to rush you yet. Once that starts, it seems to go straight to a girl's head. But you have still got a rather timid manner. Yesterday I felt quite sorry for you.'

She did not know how to reply. Cecil bent down and once more studied his plus-fours. 'Of course,' he said, 'these can go to the cleaners, but that all costs money, you see, and I had been hoping to run over to France.'

'Perhaps your mother could get it off with petrol. Butter is always got off my clothes that way.'

'Oh, is it?' said Cecil. 'I say,' he added, 'I had been rather wondering if you would care to run into Southstone one evening, on the five-thirty bus, and meet me after the office. We could then come in on the second half of the concert at the East Cliff Pavilion, and might get a spot of food there; it is a nice, rather cosmopolitan place. If you would really care –'

'Oh, yes, I should simply love it!'

'Then we might call it a date. We'll fix the date itself later.'

'Oh, that is kind of you. Thank you.'

'Not at all,' said Cecil.

The game was over: Charlie and Daphne had just beaten Wallace and Evelyn. Evelyn came across and pulled Cecil on to the court, saying he must now play instead of her. '*Sure* you wouldn't care to try?' she said to Portia nicely. 'Oh well, I see how you feel. I tell you what, you ought to come round one week-day and have a knock up with Clara. *She* wants practice, you know. Then you could play next time ... My goodness,' exclaimed Evelyn, 'we do want some air in here! The ventilation is awful!'

Kindly pulling Portia along by one elbow, she went to the end of the court and threw open a door. The garden, after the glare of the court lights, was in very dark blue dusk; the door opening made an alarmed bird break out of a thicket. The town lights blinked through bare moving branches: down there they heard the crepitating sea. Evelyn and Portia, standing in the doorway, filled their lungs with the dark sweet salt spring air.

DARLING Portia: What a marvellous idea! Of course I should love to come, but shall I be able to get away? But if they expect me I really must have a try. No, I don't mind if I sleep in their lumber room. I suppose I shall hear Dickie snore through the wall. We are still making fine hay with Thomas out of the office, and if Mr Rattisbone doesn't have one of his phases I do think that I should be able to nip off. Another thing is, though, that I seem to have filled up my next three week-ends. Next week-end, I think, on the whole, should be the easiest for me to get out of – if I make enemies, you must stand by me. If I do come, I will come on that morning train you said. I shall be able to let you know on Friday. I'm so sorry to leave it as late as that.

I do hope all your dashing friends will like me. I shall be so shy. Well, I must stop, you sweet: I've had three late nights and I do feel like death. Directly you go away I start to go to the bad, which shows how important you are to me. But I simply have to be out. You know how I hate my room.

I had just a line from Anna. She sounds quite pleased with everything. Well, I'll let you know. I *do* hope I can come. All my best love.   EDDIE

This rather tormenting letter came on Wednesday morning – by which time Mrs Heccomb was already busy beautifying the lumber room. She had fallen in quite serenely with the idea of this visit, for Eddie had, somehow, been represented to her as an old family friend of Anna's and Thomas's, coming down to see how Portia was getting on. This seemed to her most fitting. What she could not get herself happily reconciled to was, that any friend of the Quaynes should sleep in her lumber room. But Daphne and Dickie refused to make any offer, and they kept a close eye on her every evening to see that she did not move out of her own room. The more briskly Daphne asserted that the lumber room would not kill Eddie, the more Mrs Heccomb's forehead wrinkled up with concern. She could only buy more matting, and move in her Sheraton looking-glass. She also moved in her *prie-dieu* to act as a bedside table, and improvised a red paper frill for the light. She borrowed an eiderdown from Cecil's mother. Portia watched these preparations with growing misgivings; they made her dread more and more that Eddie might not come. She felt a great threatening hill of possible disappointment rising daily over the household's head – for even Daphne was not indifferent, and Dickie had taken note that they must expect a guest. In vain, she implored Mrs Heccomb to remember that Eddie's plans for the week-end hung on a thread.

She was also alarmed when she found what a stalwart preconception of Eddie Mrs Heccomb had – she clearly saw him as a Major Brutt. Daphne knew otherwise: at any mention of Eddie a piglike knowing look would come into Daphne's eyes. Daphne's own affairs were not going too well, for Mr Bursely, in spite of the good beginning, had not been seen since Saturday – Daphne now took a low view of Wallace and Charlie with their civilian ways.

Major Brutt's second puzzle had come on Wedesday morning, by the same post as Eddie's letter, and Portia worked at the puzzle at a table in the sun porch, with a diligence that helped to steady her nerves. It soon promised to represent a magnificent air display. The week was very sunny – her eyes dazzled as she fitted piece into piece, and a gull's shadow flashing over the puzzle would make her suddenly look up. The planes massing against an ultramarine sky began each to take a different symbolic form, and as she assembled the spectators she came to look for a threat or promise in each upturned face. One evening Dickie offered to help her : the table was moved in to under a lamp, and Dickie completed an ambulance she had dreaded to tackle.

She got a postcard from Anna, a short letter from Thomas, a long letter from Lilian, whose sorrows seemed far away.

She went into town every morning with Mrs Heccomb. Mrs Heccomb pressed her to drop in on Daphne at Smoot's. The first call was alarming – in the upstairs library heating drew out a gluey smell from the books; Daphne's nostrils wore a permanent crinkle. In all senses, literature was in bad odour here. The sun slanted its stuffy motes straight on to Daphne's cross curled head; in the dusk at the back of the library Daphne's colleague crouched at a table, reading. Contempt for reading as an occupation was implicit in the way Daphne knitted, stopped knitting to buff her nails, and knitted again, impatiently hiking by the long strand towards her her ball of coral wool. The twitch of the coral ball did not disturb the apathy of the library cat – this furious mouser had been introduced when mice began to get at the *belles lettres*, but he only worked by night. No subscribers were in the library when Portia came in, and Daphne, already leaning back from her desk, looked up with a quite equable scowl.

'Oh, hullo!' she said. 'What do *you* want?'

'Mrs Heccomb thought you might like me to drop in.'

'Oh, by all means do,' said Daphne. Moving her tongue across from one cheek to the other, she went on knitting. Portia, one finger on Daphne's desk, looked round and said: 'What a large number of books.'

'And that isn't all, either. However, do sit down.'

'I do wonder who reads them.'

'Oh, that's quite simple,' said Daphne. 'You'd soon see. Does your sister-in-law read?'

'She says she would like to if she had more time.'

'It's extraordinary how much time people do have. I mean, it really does make you think. I daresay she has a guaranteed subscription? People with those give an awful lot of fuss – they come popping back for a book before one has ordered it. I suppose they feel they are getting their money's worth. What I always say is . . .'

Miss Scott, from the back of the room, gave a warning cough, which meant subscribers were coming in. Two ladies approached the table, said, 'Good morning' placatingly and returned their books. Daphne rolled up her knitting and gave them a look.

'Such a lovely morning. . . .'

'Yes,' said Daphne repressively

'And how is your mother?'

'Oh, she's getting along.'

The lady who had not spoken was already dithering round

a table of new novels. Her friend threw the novels rather a longing look, then turned strongmindedly to the cabinet of *belles lettres*. Raising her nose so as to bring her pince-nez to the correct angle, she took out a succession of books, scanned their title pages, looked through all the pictures, and almost always replaced them with a frustrated sigh. Did she not know that Daphne hated people to stick around messing the books about? 'I suppose there *is* something here I should really like?' she said. 'It's so hard to tell from the outsides.'

'Miss Scott,' said Daphne plaintively, 'can't you help Mrs Adams?'

Mrs Adams, mortified, said: 'I *ought* to make out a list.'

'Well, people do find it helps.'

Mrs Adams did not half like being turned over to Miss Scott, who gave her a collection of well-known essays she was ashamed to refuse. She looked wistfully at her friend, who came back with a gay-looking novel and a happy face. 'You really oughtn't to miss these; they were beautifully written,' said Miss Scott, giving poor Mrs Adams a shrewish look – in her subservient way, she was learning to be as great a bully as Daphne.

Daphne flicked the subscribers' cards out of the box and sat with pencil poised, preparing to make disdainful marks on them. It was clear that Daphne added, and knew that she added, *cachet* to Smoot's by her air of barely condoning the traffic that went on there. Her palpable wish never to read placed at a disadvantage those who had become dependent on this habit, and it was a disadvantage they seemed to enjoy. Miss Scott, though so much more useful, cut no ice: she (unlike Daphne) was not a lady, and she not only read but was paid to read, which was worse. Also, she had not Daphne's dashing appearance: most of the Seale subscribers were elderly, and age and even the mildest form of intellect both tend to make people physical snobs. There may be libraries in which Daphne would not have done so well. But for this clientele of discarded people her bloom and her nonchalance served, somehow, to place her above literature. These were readers who could expect no more from life, and just dared to look in books to see how much they had missed. The old are often masochists, and their slackening hearts twitched at her bold cold smile. Perhaps there was an interchange of cruelty, for Smoot's subscribers had, after all, the power to keep this fine girl chained. A bald patch in the carpet under her desk would have showed, had they cared to look, with what restless fury she dug in her heels. On a sunny day they would tell her it seemed hard she should not be out of doors, then they doddered off with their books in the salty sun down the street.

Portia's respect for Daphne went up with every moment as she watched her flick at the cards in the filing box. Looking up round the shelves she found the authors arranged in quite faultless alphabetical order, and this in itself seemed the work of a master mind. Also, though Daphne loathed print she had rather a feeling for dressy bindings: the books in her keeping had a well-groomed air ... When Mrs Adams had taken her friend away, Miss Scott returned to her reading with a peculiar smile, while Daphne rose and paced once or twice to the window, with both hands moulding her skirt over her hips. Then she bumped back with a snort and went on with her knitting.

'Heard anything more from your boy friend?'

'Not yet. ...'

'Oh well. No doubt he'll come.'

Late that same Thursday, by arrangement, Portia took the bus into Southstone to meet Cecil. Mrs Heccomb's entire confidence in Cecil deprived the expedition of any glamour. Portia, arriving a little too early, waited outside the block of buildings from which Cecil at last emerged, blowing his nose. They walked through draughty streets of private hotels to the East Cliff Pavilion. This vast glassy building, several floors deep, had been clamped skilfully to the face of the cliff, and was entered from the top like a catacomb. Tiers of glazed balconies overhung the sea, which had diluted into a mauvish haze by the time the concert finished. Portia had not a good ear, but she went up in Cecil's estimation by spotting a tune from *Madame Butterfly*. In fact, the orchestra played a good deal of music to which she and Irene had illicitly listened, skulking outside palace hotels abroad. At half past six, attendants drew the curtains over the now extinct view. When the concert was over, Cecil and Portia quitted their plush *fauteuils* for a glass-topped table, at which they ate poached eggs on haddock and banana splits. Though exceedingly brilliantly lit, the hall with its lines of tables was almost empty, and lofty silence filled it. No doubt it would be gay at some other time. Portia listened with an unfixed eye to Cecil's thoughtful conversation: by this time tomorrow, she would know if Eddie were coming or not. They caught the quarter to nine bus back to Seale, and at the gate of Waikiki, saying good night, Cecil gave her hand a platonic squeeze.

The time between Eddie's Friday morning letter and his arrival seemed to contract to nothing. In so far as time did exist, it held some dismay. The suspense of the week, though unnerving, had had its own tune or pattern: now she knew he was coming the tune stopped. For people who live on expectations, to face up to their realization is something of an ordeal. Expectations are the most perilous form of dream, and when dreams do realize themselves it is in the waking world: the difference is subtly but often painfully felt. What she *should* have begun to enjoy, from Friday morning, was anticipation – but she found anticipation no longer that pure pleasure it once was. Even a year ago, the promised pleasure could not come soon enough: it was agony to consume intervening time. *Now*, she found she could wish Saturday were not on her so soon – she unconsciously held it off with one hand. This lack of avidity and composure, this need to recover both in a vigil of proper length, showed her already less of a child, and she was shocked by this loss or change in her nature, as she might have been by a change in her own body.

On Saturday morning, she was awake for a minute before she dared open her eyes. Then she saw her curtains white with Saturday's light – relentlessly, the too great day was poured out, on the sea, on her window sill. Then she thought there might be a second letter from Eddie, to say he was not coming after all. But there was no letter.

Later, the day became not dark but muted; haze bound the line of the coast; the sun did not quite shine. There had been no more talk, when it had come to the point, of Eddie's catching

the morning train: he would come by the train by which Portia
had come. Mrs Heccomb wanted to order the taxi to meet him,
but Portia felt Eddie would be overpowered by this, besides not
being glad to pay for the taxi – so it was arranged that the
carrier should bring down his bag. Portia walked up the station
hill to meet him. She heard the train whistle away back in the
woods; then it whistled again, then slowly came round the curve.
When Eddie had got out they walked to the parapet and looked
over at the view. Then they started downhill together. This was
not like the afternoon when she had arrived herself, for a week
more of spring had already sweetened the air.

Eddie had been surprised by the view from the parapet: he
had had no idea Seale was so far from the sea.

'Oh yes, it is quite a way,' she said happily.

'But I thought it was once a port.'

'It was, but the sea ran back.'

'Did it really, darling: just fancy!' Catching at Portia's wrist,
Eddie swung it twice in a gay methodical way, as, with the god-
like step of people walking downhill, they went down the station
incline. All at once he dropped her wrist and began to feel in his
pockets. 'Oh God,' he said, 'I forgot to post that letter.'

'Oh – an important letter?'

'It had to get there tonight. It was to someone I put off by
telegram.'

'I really do thank you for coming, Eddie!'

Eddie smiled in a brilliant but rather automatic and worried
way. 'I invented all sorts of things. It *had* to get there tonight.
You don't know how touchy people are.'

'Couldn't we post it now?'

'The postmark ... However, everyone hates me already. Anyway, London seems beautifully far away. Where's the next post
box, darling?'

At the idea of this desperate simplification, Eddie's face
cleared. He no longer frowned at the letter but, crossing the
road, plunged it cheerfully into the corner letter box. Portia,
watching him from across the road, had a moment in which to
realize he would be back beside her; in fact, they were together
again. Eddie came back and said: 'Oh, you've tied your hair-

ribbon in a bow at the top. And you are still wearing your woolly gloves.' Taking her hand in his, he scrunched the fingers inside her glove together. 'Sweet,' he said. 'Like a nest of little weak mice.'

They lagged along, all down the turning road. Eddie read aloud the names on the white gates of all the villas – these gates were streaked with green drips from trees; the houses behind them looked out through evergreens. The sea was, for the moment, out of view: a powerful inland silence, tinted grey by the hour, filled the station road. Seale was out of sight behind the line of the hill: its smoke went up behind garden conifers. Later, they heard a stream in a sort of gulch. All this combined to make Eddie exclaim: 'Darling, I do call this an unreal place!'

'Wait till we get back to tea.'

'But where on earth is Waikiki?'

'Oh, Eddie, I told you – it's by the sea.'

'Is Mrs Heccomb really very excited?'

'Yes, very excited – though I must say, it does not take much to excite her. But even Dickie said this morning at breakfast that he supposed he would bump into you tonight.'

'And Daphne – is she excited?'

'I'm sure she really is. But she's afraid you're ritzy. You must show her you're not.'

'I'm so glad I came,' said Eddie, quickening his step.

At Waikiki, Mrs Heccomb's deportment was not, for the first minute, equal to the occasion. She looked twice at Eddie and said: 'Oh . . .' Then she rallied and said how pleased to see him she was. Holding her hand out, she nervously circumscribed the tea table, still fixing her eyes on the silhouette of Eddie as though trying to focus an apparition. When they all sat down to tea, her own back was to the light and she had Eddie in less deceptive view. Each time he spoke, her eyes went to his forehead, to the point where his hair sprang back in its fine spirited waves. In pauses that could but occur in the talk, Portia could almost hear Mrs Heccomb's ideas, like chairs before a party, being rolled about and rapidly rearranged. The tea was bountiful, but so completely distracted was Mrs Heccomb that Portia had to circulate the cakes. It occurred to her to wonder who would pay for them, and whether she had done wrong, on account of Eddie, in tempting Waikiki to this extra expense.

She wondered, even, whether Mrs Heccomb might not pause to wonder. Having lived in hotels where one's bills wait weekly at the foot of the stairs, and no 'extra' is ever overlooked, she had had it borne in on her that wherever anyone is they are costing somebody something, and that the cost must be met. She understood that by living at Windsor Terrace, eating what she ate, sleeping between sheets that had to be washed, by even so much as breathing the warmed air, she became a charge on Thomas and Anna. *Their* keeping on paying up, whatever they felt, had to be glossed over by family feeling – and she had learned to have, with regard to them, that callousness one has towards relatives. Now she could only hope they were paying largely enough for her own board at Waikiki to meet the cost of the cake Eddie might eat. But uncertainty made her limit her own tea.

Eddie had the advantage, throughout tea, of not being familiar with Mrs Heccomb. All he thought was that she was exceedingly shy. He therefore set out to be frank, easy, and simple, which were three things he could seem to be on his head. He could not be expected to know that his appearance, and that the something around him that might be called his aura, struck into her heart its first misgiving for years – a misgiving not about Portia but about Anna. He could not know that he started up in her mind a misgiving she had repressed about Anna and Pidgeon – a misgiving her own marriage had made her gladly forget. A conviction (dating from her last year at Richmond) that no man with *bounce* could be up to any good set up an unhappy twitch in one fold of her left cheek. Apprehensions that someone might be common were the worst she had had to combat since she ruled at Waikiki. No doubt it must be in order, this young man being Portia's friend, since Portia said that he was a friend of Anna's. But what was he doing *being* a friend of Anna's? ... Portia, watching the cheek twitch, wondered what could be up.

Eddie felt he was doing wonderfully well. He liked Mrs Heccomb, and was anxious to please. Not a scrap of policy underlay his manner. Perfectly guilelessly, he understood Mrs Heccomb to be just a little dazzled by him. Indeed, he looked well here – from the moment of coming in, he had dropped into a happy relationship with the things in the room: the blue chenille curtain to the left of his head, the dresser he tilted his chair against, the finished lamp shade that he had seen and praised. He seemed so natural here, so much in the heart of things, that Portia wondered how the Waikiki lounge could have fully existed before he came. There in the sun porch stayed the unfinished puzzle, into which, before he came, she had fitted her hopes and fears. After tea, she took a retrospective look at the puzzle, as though it were a thing left from another age. Eddie stood gaily talking, gaily balancing on the fire kerb. He attracted a look from Doris as she slithered in to clear away the tea.

'It's nice to get back to a proper fire,' he said. 'I have only gas in my flat.'

Mrs Heccomb took the cloth from Doris to fold: it had a crochet border eight inches deep. 'I suppose you have central heating in Mr Quayne's office?'

'Oh yes,' Eddie said. 'It is all completely slap up.'

'Yes, I have heard it is very fine.'

'Anna, of course, has the loveliest log fire in *her* drawing-room. You go and see her quite often, I expect?'

'Yes, I go to Windsor Terrace when I am in London,' said Mrs Heccomb, though still not forthcomingly. 'They are extremely hospitable,' she said – discounting a right to the house as any one person's privilege. She turned on the light over her painting table, sat down, and began to go through her brushes. Portia, watching dusk close round the porch, said: 'I think perhaps I might show Eddie the sea.'

'Oh, you won't see much of the sea, dear, *now*, I'm afraid.'

'Still, we might just look.'

So they went out. Portia went down the path pulling on her overcoat, but Eddie only wound his scarf round his neck. The tide was creeping in; the horizon was just visible in the dark grey air. The shallow curve of the bay held a shingly murmur that was just not silence and imperceptibly ended where silence was. There was no wind, just a sensation round one's collar and at the roots of one's hair. Eddie and Portia stood on the esplanade, watching the sky and water slowly blot themselves out. Eddie stood aloofly, like someone who after hours allows himself to be freely alone again. There was never much connexion between his affability and his spirit – which now, in a sombre way, came out to stand at its own door. Only Portia had this forbidding intimacy with him – she was the only person to whom he need not pretend that she had not ceased existing when, for him, she had ceased to exist. The tender or bold play of half-love with grown-up people becomes very exacting: it tired Eddie. It was only Portia that he could pack off – like that, at the turn of a moment – with tired simplicity. She did, therefore, enjoy one kind of privilege: he allowed her at least to stay in body beside him when he was virtually not there, gone. No presence could be less insistent than hers. He treated her like an element (air, for instance) or a condition (darkness): these touch one with their equality and lightness where one could endure no human touch. He could look right through her, without a flicker of seeing, without being made shamefully conscious of the vacuum there must be in his eyes.

Portia, waiting for Eddie as she had often waited, turned her fists round slowly in her pockets, regretting that he should have been called away just now. The autumnal moment, such as occurs in all seasons, the darkening sea with its little commas of foam offered no limits to the loneliness she could feel, even when she was feeling quite resigned. All at once, a light from mid Channel darted over the sea, picking out its troughs and its polished waves. The lighthouse had begun its all-night flashing. The tip of this finger of light was drawn across Eddie's face – and a minute later, the lamps sprang alight all down the esplanade. She saw, when she turned round, tamarisk shadows cast on lodging-house walls.

'What a blaze!' said Eddie, starting alight also. 'Now this really *is* like the seaside. Have they got a pier?'

'Well, no. But there's one at Southstone.'

'Come down on the beach.'

As they scrunched along, Eddie said: 'Then you've been happy here?'

'You see, it's more like what I was accustomed to. At Anna's, I never know what is going to happen next – and here, though I may not know, I do not mind so much. In a way, at Anna's nothing does happen – though of course I might not know if it did. But here I do see how everyone feels.'

'I wonder if I like that?' said Eddie. 'I suspect how people feel, and that seems to me bad enough. I wonder if the truth would be worse or better. The truth of course I mean, about other people. I know only too well how *I* feel.'

'So do I.'

'Know how I feel?'

'Yes, Eddie.'

'You make me feel rather guilty.'

'Why?'

'Well, you haven't the slightest notion how I behave *sometimes*, and it isn't till I behave that I know quite how I feel. You see, my life depends entirely on what happens.'

'Then you don't know how you may be going to feel?'

'No, I've no idea, darling. It's perfectly unforeseeable. That is the worst of it. I'm a person you ought to be frightened of.'

'But you are the only person who doesn't frighten me.'

'Wait a moment – damn. I've got a stone in my shoe.'

'I have, too, as a matter of fact.'

'Why didn't you say so, silly? Why suffer away?'

They sat down on a roll of beach and each took a shoe off. The light from the lighthouse swept round to where they sat and Portia said: 'I say, you've got a hole in your sock.'

'Yes. That lighthouse is like the eye of God.'

'But are you frightening, do you really think?'

'You ask such snubbing questions. You mean I make a fuss. I suppose, that I'm I at all is just a romantic fallacy. It may be vulgar to feel that I'm anyone, but at least I'm sure that I'm not anyone else. Of course we have all got certain things in common, but a good deal that we have in common is dreadful. When I so much hate so much I see in myself, how do you expect me to tolerate other people? Shall we move on, darling? I love sitting here like this, but these pebbles hurt my behind.'

'Yes, they hurt mine rather, as a matter of fact.'

'I do hate it when you are a dear little soul – It's sweet to be here with you, but I don't feel really happy.'

'Have you not had a nice week in London, then?'

'Oh, well – Thomas gives me five pounds a week.'

'Good gracious.'

'Yes, that is what brains cost by the pound ... I nearly got another stone in my shoe: I think we'd better get back to the promenade. Who lives all along there?'

'Those are just lodging houses. Three of them are to let.'

They climbed back on to the esplanade, faced round and started back to Waikiki. 'All the same,' said Portia, 'don't you think Mrs Heccomb is very nice?'

On a gust of at once excellent spirits Eddie swept in upon Daphne and Dickie, who with the wireless on were standing about the hearth. They looked at him doubtfully. He exchanged a manly handshake with Dickie, and with Daphne a bold look. Then Mrs Heccomb came downstairs, and Daphne at once adopted her policy of addressing striking remarks only to her. Above the wireless going full blast, Mrs Heccomb and Daphne agreed that supper ought to be early, as some of the party wished to go to a movie.

Daphne bawled: 'And Clara's going to meet us there.'

Dickie did not react.

'I say, Clara's coming along to meet us.'

Dickie looked up coldly from the *Evening Standard* to say: 'This is the first I have heard of that.'

'Well, don't be so silly. Clara'll probably pay.'

Dickie grunted and stooped down to scratch his ankle as though an itch *were* a really urgent matter. For a minute Daphne's eyes, dull with consideration, seemed to be drawn right into her face. Then she said to Portia: 'You and your friend coming?' and shot her most nonchalant look into the mantelpiece mirror behind Eddie's ear. '*Shall* we, Eddie?' said Portia, kneeling up on the sofa. At once Eddie dropped into her eyes the profoundest of those quick glances of his. A peaceful malicious smile illuminated his features as he continued not to look Daphne's way. 'If we really are invited,' he yelled back above the music, 'it would be quite divine.'

'Do you really want us, Daphne?'

'Oh, it's all the same to *me*. I mean, *just* as you like.'

So directly after supper they set out. They stopped at Wallace's house to pick up Wallace, then marched, five abreast, down the asphalt walk to the town. It was dark under the trees and the lights twinkled ahead. A breath mounted from the canal as they trooped over the footbridge with a clatter: through an evergreen grove the Grotto Cinema glittered its constellation of gold, red, blue. Clara, with her most sacrificial expression, waited by a palm in the foyer, wearing a mink coat. There was polite confusion at the box-office window, where Dickie, Wallace and, less convincingly, Eddie all made gestures of preparing to stand treat. Then Clara bobbed up from under Dickie's elbow and paid for them all, as they had expected her to do. They filed down the dark aisle to seat themselves in this order – Clara, Dickie, Portia, Eddie, Daphne, Wallace. A comic was on the screen.

During most of the programme, Dickie was more oncoming with Portia than he was with Clara – that is to say, he put one elbow on Portia's arm of his *fauteuil*, but did not put the other on Clara's arm. He breathed heavily. Clara, during a brief hitch in the comic, said she hoped Dickie had had nice hockey. When poor Clara dropped her bead bag, money and all, she was left to recover it. Portia sat with eyes fixed on the screen – once or twice, as Eddie changed his position, she felt his knee touch hers. When this made her glance his way, she saw light from the comic flickering on his eyeballs. He sat with his shoulders forward, in some sort of close complicity with himself. Beyond Eddie, Daphne's profile was tilted up correctly, and beyond Daphne comatose Wallace yawned.

Then the news ran through, then the big drama began. This keyed them all up, even the boys. Something distracted Portia's mind from the screen – a cautiousness the far side of Eddie's knee. She held her breath – and failed to hear Eddie breathe. Why did not Eddie breathe? Whatever could be the matter? She felt some tense extra presence, here in their row of six.

Wanting to know, she turned to look full at Eddie – who at once countered her look with a bold blank smile glittering from the screen. The smile was diverted to her from someone else. On her side, one of his hands, a cigarette between the two longest fingers, hung down slack: she only saw one hand. Hitching herself up on her seat, she looked at the screen, beseechingly, vowing not to wonder, never to look away.

The screen became threatening with figures, which seemed to make a storm: she heard Clara let out a polite gasp. Proof against whatever more was to happen, Dickie heaved till he got his cigarette case out. Not ceasing to give the screen impervious attention, he selected a cigarette, closed his lips on it, and re-settled his jaw. Then he started to make his lighter kick. When he had used the flame, he kindly looked down the row to see if anyone wanted a light too.

The jumping light from Dickie's lighter showed the canyon below their row of knees. It caught the chromium clasp of Daphne's handbag, and Wallace's wrist-watch at the end of the row. It rounded the taut blond silk of Daphne's calf and glittered on some tinfoil dropped on the floor. Those who wanted to smoke were smoking: no one wanted a light. But Dickie, still with the flame jumping, still held the lighter out in a watching pause – a pause so marked that Portia, as though Dickie had sharply pushed her head round, looked to see where he looked. The light, with malicious accuracy, ran round a rim of cuff, a steel bangle, and made a thumb-nail flash. Not deep enough in the cleft between their *fauteuils* Eddie and Daphne were, with emphasis, holding hands. Eddie's fingers kept up a kneading movement: her thumb alertly twitched at the joint.

6

THE empty lodging-house rustled with sea noises, as though years of echoes of waves and sea sucking shingle lived in its chimneys, its half-open cupboards. The stairs creaked as Portia and Eddie went up, and the banisters, pulled loose in their sockets, shook under their hands. Warped by sea damp, the doors were all stuck ajar, and ends of torn wallpaper could be heard fluttering in draughts in the rooms. The front-room ceilings glared with sea reflections; the back windows stared north over salt fields. Mr Bunstable's junior partner Mr Sheldon had inadvertently left the key of this house at Waikiki the other night, when he had come in to cards. The key bore the label 5 Winslow Terrace: Dickie had found it, Eddie had had it from Dickie, and now Eddie and Portia let themselves in. There is nothing like exploring an empty house.

It was Sunday morning, just before eleven: the church bells from uphill came through the shut windows into the rooms. But Mrs Heccomb had gone to church alone. Dickie had gone off to see a man about something; Daphne had stayed reading the *Sunday Pictorial* in a *chaise longue* in the sun porch – though there was no sun. She had set her hair a new way, in a bang over her forehead, and she had not so much as batted an eyelid as Eddie, steering Portia by one elbow, walked away from Waikiki down the esplanade.

The front top bedrooms here were like convent cells, with outside shutters hooked back. Their walls were mouldy blue like a dead sky, and looking at the criss-cross cracks in the ceiling one thought of holiday people waking up. A stale charred smell came from the grates – Waikiki seemed miles away. These rooms, many flights up, were a dead end: the emptiness, the feeling of dissolution came upstairs behind one, blocking the way down. Portia felt she had climbed to the very top of a tree pursued by something that could follow. She remembered the threatening height of this house at the back, and how it had frightened her that first afternoon when she was in the taxi with Mrs Heccomb. Today when they turned the key and pushed open the stuck door boldly, they had heard papers rustle in the hall. But it was not only here that she dreaded to be with Eddie.

He lighted a cigarette and leaned on the mantelpiece. He seemed to measure the small room with his eye, swinging the key from his finger on its loop of string. Portia went to the window, and looked out. 'All these windows here have got double glass,' she said.

'A fat lot of good that would do if the house blew down.'

'Do you think it might really? ... The bells have stopped.'

'Yes, you ought to be in church.'

'I went last Sunday – but it doesn't really matter.'

'Then why go last Sunday, you little crook?'

Portia did not reply.

'I say, darling, you are funny this morning. Why are you being so funny with me?'

'Am I?'

'You know you are: don't be so silly. Why?'

Her back turned, she mutely pulled at the window clasp. But Eddie whistled twice, so that she had to face him. By now, he had twirled the string round his finger so tight that the flesh, with its varnish of nicotine, stood out in ridges between. His eyes held behind their brightness a warning tense look, as though the end of the world were coming. Instinctively putting up one hand to her cheek, she looked at his teeth showing between his lips. He said: 'Well!'

'Why did you hold Daphne's hand?'

'When do you mean?'

'At the cinema.'

'Oh, that. Because, you see, I have to get off with people.'

'Why?'

'Because I cannot get on with them, and that makes me so mad. Yes, I noticed you gave me rather a funny look.'

'You mean, that time you smiled at me? Were you holding her hand then?'

Eddie thought. 'Yes, I would have been, I expect. Were you worried? I thought you cut off rather early to bed. But I thought you always knew I was like that. I like touching, you know.'

'But I have never been there.'

'No, I suppose you haven't.' He looked down and unwound the string from his finger. 'No, you haven't, have you?' he said much more affably.

'Was that what you meant on the beach when you said you never knew how you might behave?'

'And you shot back and wrote it down, I suppose? I thought I had told you not to write down anything about me?'

'No, Eddie, it's not in my diary. You only said it yesterday, after tea.'

'Anyhow, what you mean is not what I'd call behaving – it's not even as important as that. It didn't mean anything new.'

'But it did to me.'

'Well, I can't help that,' he said, smiling reasonably. 'I can't help the way you are.'

'I knew something was happening before Dickie moved his lighter. I knew from the way you smiled.'

'For such a little girl, you know, you're neurotic.'

'I'm not such a little girl. You once spoke of marrying me.'

'Only because you *were* such a little girl.'

'That it didn't matter?'

'No, and I also thought you were the one person who didn't take other people's completely distorted views. But now you're like any girl at the seaside, always watching and judging, trying to piece me together into something that isn't there. You make me –'

'Yes, but why *did* you hold Daphne's hand?'

'I just felt matey.'

'But ... I mean ... You knew me better.'

Eddie's metallic mood broke up, or completely changed. He went across the room to the wall cupboard that he had fixed his eyes on, and carefully latched it. Then he looked round the room as though he had stayed here, and were about to remove his last belongings. He picked up his dead match and dropped it into the grate. Then he said vaguely: 'Come on; let's go down.'

'But did you hear what I said?'

'Of course I did. You're always so sweet, darling.'

Going downstairs brought them one floor nearer the mild sound of the sea. Eddie stepped into the drawing-room for another look round. The margin of floor round where there had been a carpet was stained with reddish varnish, and in the wood-work over the bow window was a hook from which a bird-cage must have hung.

Through the window the sea light shone on Eddie's face as he turned quickly and said, in his lightest and gentlest way: 'I can't tell you how bad I feel. It was only my bit of fun. I honestly didn't think you'd bother to notice, darling – or, that if you did, you'd ever think twice of it. You and I know each other, and you know how silly I am. But if it really upset you, of course it was awful of me. You really mustn't be hurt, or I shall wish I was dead. This is just one more of the ways I keep on and on making trouble. I know I oughtn't to say so, when I've just said I was sorry, but really, darling, it was such a small thing. I mean, you ask old Daphne. It's simply the way most people have to get on.'

'No, I couldn't ask Daphne.'

'Then take it from me.'

'But, Eddie, they thought you were my friend. I was so proud because they all thought that.'

'But, darling, if I hadn't wanted to see you would I have come all this way and broken all those dates? *You* know I love you: don't be so silly. All I wanted was to be with you at the seaside, and here we are, and we're having a lovely time. Why spoil it for a thing that means simply nothing?'

'But it does mean something – it means something else.'

'You are the only person I'm ever serious with. I'm never serious with all these other people: that's why I simply do what they seem to want me to do ... You do know I'm serious with you, don't you, Portia?' he said, coming up and staring into her eyes. In his own eyes, shutters flicked back, exposing for half a second, right back in the dark, the Eddie in there.

Never till now, never since this half-second, had Portia been the first to look away. She looked at the ghostly outline of some cabinet on the paper with its bleaching maroon leaves. 'But you said', she said, 'up there' (she nodded at the ceiling) 'that you need not mean what you say because I am a little girl.'

'When I talk through my hat, of course I'm not serious.'

'You should not have talked about marriage through your hat.'

'But darling, I do think you must be mad. Why should you want to marry anybody?'

'Were you talking through your hat on the beach when you said I ought to be afraid of you?'

'How you do remember!'

'It was yesterday evening.'

'Perhaps yesterday evening *I was* feeling like that.'

'But don't *you* remember?'

'Look here, darling, you must really not exasperate me. How can I keep on feeling something I once felt when there are so many things one can feel? People who say they always feel as they did simply fake themselves up. I may be a crook but I'm not a fake – that is an entirely different thing.'

'But I don't see how you can say you are serious if there's no one thing you keep feeling the whole time.'

'Well, then I'm not,' said Eddie, stamping his cigarette out and laughing, though in an exasperated way. 'You will really simply have to get used to me. I must say I thought you were. You had really better not think I'm serious, if the slightest thing is going to make you so upset. What I do remember telling you last evening is that you don't know the half of what I do. I do do what you would absolutely hate. Yes, I see now I was wrong – I did think once that I could tell you, even let you discover, *anything* I had done, and you wouldn't turn a hair. Because I had hoped there would be one person like that, I must have let myself make an absurd, quite impossible image of you ... No, I see now, the fact is, dear darling Portia, you and I have drifted into a thoroughly sickly, not to say mawkish, state. Which is worlds worse for me than a spot of necking with Daphne. And now it comes to this – you start driving me up trees and barking at the bottom like everyone else. Well, come on, let's go down. We've had enough of this house. We'd better lock up and give the key back to Dickie.'

He moved decisively to the drawing-room door.

'Oh stop, Eddie: wait! Has this spoilt everything for you? I would rather be dead than a disappointment to you. *Please* ... You are my whole reason to be alive. I promise, please, I promise! I mean, I promise not to hate anything. It is only that I have to get used to things, and I have not got used to quite everything, yet. I'm only stupid when I don't understand.'

'But you never will. I can see that.'

'But I'm perfectly willing not to. I'll be not stupid without understanding. *Please –*'

She pulled at his near arm wildly with both hands, making no distinction between the sleeve and the flesh. Not wildly but with the resolution of sorrow, her eyes went round his face. He said: 'Look here, shut up: you make me feel such a bully.' Freeing his arm, he caught both her hands in his in a bothered but perfectly kindly way, as though they had been a pair of demented kittens. 'Such a *noise* to make,' he said. 'Can't you let a person lose an illusion without screaming the house down, you little silly, you?'

'But I don't want you to.'

'Very well, then. I haven't.'

'Promise, Eddie. You swear? I don't mean just because it's about me, but you told me you had so few – illusions, I mean. You do promise? You're not just keeping me quiet?'

'No, no – I mean, yes. I promise. What I said was all in my eye. That's the worst of talk. Now shall we get out of here? I should not mind a drink, if they have got such a thing.'

The echoes of their voices followed them down: once more the stairs creaked; once more the banisters wobbled. In the hall, a slit of daylight came through the letter box. They kicked through drifts of circulars, musty catalogues. Their last view of the hall, with its chocolate walls that light from a front room only sneaked along, was one of ungraciousness, of servility. Would people ever come to this house again? And yet it faced the sun, reflected the sea, and had been the scene of happy holidays.

They ran into Dickie at the gate of Waikiki, and Eddie handed him back the key. 'Thanks very much,' Eddie said, 'it's a nice piece of property. Portia and I have been over it carefully. We rather thought of starting a boarding house.'

'Oh, did you?' said Dickie, with a certain *méfiance*. He headed the two guests up the garden path, then clicked the gate behind them. Daphne could still be seen extended in the sun porch, with the Sunday paper over her knee.

'Here we all are,' Eddie said, but Daphne did not react. They grouped round her *chaise longue*, and Eddie with a rather masterful movement flicked the *Sunday Pictorial* from her person and began to read it himself. He read it with overdone attention, whistling to himself at each item of news. Just after twelve struck, he began to look rather anxiously round the Waikiki lounge, in which he saw no signs (for there were none) of sherry or gin and lime. He at last suggested they should go out and look for a drink, but Daphne asked: 'Where?' adding: 'This is not London, you know.'

Dickie said: 'And Portia does not drink.'

'Oh, well, she can come along.'

'We cannot take a girl into a bar.'

'I don't see why not, at the seaside.'

'It may be that to you, but it's rather more to us, I am afraid.'

'Oh naturally, naturally – well, er, Dickie, shall you and I roll along?'

'Well, I don't mind if I –'

Daphne yawned and said: 'Yes, you two boys go along. I mean, don't just stick around.' So the two boys went along.

'What a thirst your friend always has,' said Daphne looking after them. 'He wanted me to cut off with him somewhere last night, after the movies, but of course I told him everywhere would be shut. How do you think those two boys get along?'

'Who?' said Portia, going back to her puzzle.

'Him and Dickie?'

'Oh . . . I don't think I'd thought.'

'Dickie thinks he chatters rather too much, but of course Dickie would think that. Is what's-his-name, I mean Eddie, a popular boy?'

'I don't know who you mean with.'

'Do girls fall for him much?'

'I don't know many girls.'

'But your sister-in-law likes him, didn't you say? Not that *she's* a girl, of course. I must say, that gives one a funny idea of her. I mean to say, he's awfully fresh. I suppose that's the way he always goes on?'

'What way?'

'The way he goes on here.'

Portia walked round her puzzle and stared at it upside down. Pushing a piece with her finger, she mumbled vaguely: ' I suppose he always goes on about the same.'

'You don't seem to know much about him, do you? I thought you said he and you were such friends.'

Portia said something unintelligible.

'Well, look here, don't you trust that boy too far. I don't know, I'm sure, if I ought to say anything, but you're such a kid and it does seem rather a shame. You shouldn't let yourself be so potty about him, really. I don't mean to say there's any harm in the boy, but he's the sort of boy who must have his bit of fun. I don't want to be mean on him, but honestly – Well, you take it from me – Of course he's no end flattered, having you stuck on him, anybody would be; you're such a nice little thing. And a boy in a way likes to have a girl round after him – look at Dickie and Clara. I wouldn't see any harm in your going round with an idealistic sort of a boy like Cecil, but honestly Eddie's not idealistic at all. I don't mean to say he'd try anything on with you; he wouldn't want to: he'd see you were just a kid. But if you get so potty about him without seeing what he's like, you'll get an awful knock. You take it from me. What I mean to say is, you ought to see he's simply playing you up – coming down here like that, and everything. He's the sort of boy who can't help playing a person up; he'd play a kitten up if we had a kitten here. You've no idea, really.'

'Do you mean about him holding your hand? He does that because he feels matey, he says.'

Daphne's reaction time was not quick: it took her about two seconds to go rigid all over on the *chaise longue*. Then her eyes ran together, her features thickened: there was a pause in which slowly diluted Portia's appalling remark. In that pause, the civilization of Waikiki seemed to rock on its base. When Daphne spoke again her voice had a rasping note, as though the moral sound box had cracked.

'Now look here,' she said, 'I simply dropped you a word because I felt in a sort of way sorry for you. But there's no reason for you to be vulgar. I must say, I was really surprised when you said you had got a boy friend. What I thought was, he must be rather a sap. But as you were so keen to have him, I was all for his coming, and, as you know, I fixed Mumsie about that. I don't wish to blow my own trumpet, I never have, but one thing I will say is that I'm not a cat, and I'd never put in my oar with a girl friend's boy friend. But the moment you brought that boy here, I could see in a moment anybody could have him. It's written all over him. He can't even pass the salt without using his eyes. Even so, I must say I thought it was a bit funny when –'

'When he held your hand? Yes, I did just at first. But I thought perhaps you didn't.'

'Now Portia, you look here – if you can't talk like a lady, you just take that puzzle away and finish it somewhere else. Blocking up the whole place with the thing! I had no idea at all you were so *common*, and nor had Mumsie the least idea, I'm sure, or she wouldn't have ever obliged your sister-in-law by having you to stop here, convenient or not. This all simply goes to show the way you're brought up at home, and I am really surprised at them, I must say. You just take that awful puzzle up to your room and finish it there, if you're really so anxious to. You get on my nerves, always picking about with it. And this is *our* sun porch, if I may say so.'

'I will if you like. But I'm not doing my puzzle.'

'Well, don't just fidget about: it drives anyone crazy.' Daphne's voice and her colour had kept steadily rising: now she cleared her throat. There was a further pause, with that remarkable tension that precedes the hum when a kettle comes to the boil. 'The matter with you is', she went on, gathering energy, 'you've had your head thoroughly turned here. Being taken notice of. Cecil sorry because you are an orphan, and Dickie fussing you up to get a rise out of Clara. I've been letting you go about with our set because I thought it would be a bit of experience for you, when you're always so mousy and shy. I took poor Mumsie's word that you were a nice little thing. But as I say, this does only go to show. I'm sure I have no idea how your sister-in-law and all her set behave, but I'm afraid down here we are rather particular.'

'But if it seemed so very funny to you, why were you patting Eddie's hand with your thumb?'

'People creeping and spying', said Daphne, utterly tense, 'and then talking vulgarly are two things that I simply cannot stick. It may be funny of me, no doubt it is, but I just never could and I never can. Angry with you. I should never lower myself. It's not my fault that you've got the mind of a baby – and an awful baby, if you'll excuse my saying so. If you don't know how to behave –'

'I don't know why to behave ... Then Eddie told me this morning that people have to get off when they can't get on.'

'Oh! So you've had quite a talk!'

'Well, I asked him, you see.'

'The fact is you are a jealous little cat.'

'I'm not any more *now*, Daphne, really.'

'Still, you felt you could do with a bit of that – Oh yes, *I* saw you, shoving up against him.'

'That was the only side I had any ròom. Dickie was right on the other arm of my chair.'

'You leave my brother out of it!' Daphne screamed. 'My goodness, who do you think *you* are?'

Portia, her hand behind her, murmured something uncertain.

'*Pardon? What* did you say?'

'I said, I didn't know ... But I don't see, Daphne, why you're so shocked with Eddie. If what you and he were doing was *not* fun, why should I be jealous? And if you hadn't liked it, you could always have struggled.'

Daphne gave up. 'You're completely bats,' she said. 'You'd better go and lie down. You don't even understand a single thing. Standing about there, not looking like anything. You know, really, if you'll excuse my saying so, a person might almost take you for a natural. Have you got *no* ideas?'

'I've no idea,' said Portia in a dazed way. 'For instance, my relations who are still alive have no idea why I was born. I mean, why my father and mother –'

Daphne bulged. She said: 'You'd really *better* shut up.'

'All right. Would you like me to go upstairs? I'm very sorry, Daphne,' said Portia – from the far side of the puzzle, her downcast eyes meanwhile travelling from Daphne's toe-caps, up the plump firm calves stretched out on the *chaise longue* to the hem of the 'snug' wool dress – 'very sorry to have annoyed you, when you have always been so nice to me. I wouldn't have said about you and Eddie, only I thought that was what you were talking about. Also, Eddie did say that if I didn't understand about people feeling matey, I'd much better ask you.'

'Well, of all the *nerve*! The thing is, you and your friend are both equally bats.'

'Please don't tell him you think so. He is so happy here.'

'I've no doubt he is – Well, you'd better run on up. Here's Doris just coming to lay.'

'Would you rather I stayed upstairs for some time?'

'No, stupid, what about dinner? But do try and not look as though you'd swallowed a mouse.'

Portia pushed round the chenille curtain and went up. Standing looking out of her bedroom window, she mechanically ran a comb through her hair. She felt something in the joints of her knees, which shook. The Sunday smell of the joint Doris was basting crept underneath the crack of her door. She watched Mrs Heccomb, with umbrella and prayer book, come happily down the esplanade with a friend – a lunch-hour breeze must have come up, for something fluttered the wisps of their grey hair; and at the same time the hems of her short curtains twitched on the window sill. The two ladies stopped at Waikiki gate to talk with emphasis. Then the friend went on; Mrs Heccomb waved her red morocco prayer book at the window, as she came up the path, jubilantly, even triumphantly as though she brought back with her an extra stock of grace. While Portia stood at the window there were still no signs of Eddie and Dickie, but later she heard their voices on the esplanade.

The set of temple bells had not yet been struck for dinner, so Portia sat down near her chest of drawers and looked hard at the pastel-portrait of Anna. She did not know what she looked for in the pastel – confirmation that the most unlikely people suffer, or that everybody who suffers is the same age?

But that little suffering Anna – so much out of drawing that she looked like a cripple between her cascades of hair – that urgent soul astray in the bad portrait, only came alive by electric light. Even by day, though, the unlike likeness disturbs one more than it should: *what* is it unlike? Or is it unlike at all – is it the face discovered? The portrait, however feeble, transfixes something passive that stays behind the knowing and living look. No drawing from life just fails: it establishes something more; it admits the unadmitted. All Mrs Heccomb had brought to her loving task, besides pastels, had been feeling. She was, to put it politely, a negative artist. But such artists seem to receive a sort of cloudy guidance. Any face, house, landscape seen in a picture, however bad, remains subtly but strongly modified in so-called real life – and the worse the picture, the stronger this is. Mrs Heccomb's experiment in pastels had altered Anna for ever. By daylight, the thing was a human map, scored over with strawy marks of the chalks. But when electric light struck those shadeless triangles – hair, the face, the kitten, those looking eyes – the thing took on a misguided authority. As this face had entered Portia's first dreams here, it continued to enter her waking mind. She saw the kitten hugged to the breast in a contraction of unknowing sorrow.

What help she did not find in the picture she found in its oak frame and the mantelpiece underneath. After inside upheavals, it is important to fix on imperturbable *things*. Their imperturbableness, their air that nothing has happened renews our guarantee. Pictures would not be hung plumb over the centres of fireplaces or wallpapers pasted on with such precision that their seams make no break in the pattern if life were really not possible to adjudicate for. These things are what we mean when we speak of civilization: they remind us how exceedingly seldom the unseemly or unforeseeable rears its head. In this sense, the destruction of buildings and furniture is more palpably dreadful to the spirit than the destruction of human life. Appalling as the talk with Daphne had been, it had not been so finally fatal, when you looked back at it, as an earthquake or a dropped bomb. Had the gas stove blown up when Portia lit it, blowing this nice room into smithereens, it would have been worse than Portia's being called spying and common. Though what she had said had apparently been dreadful, it had done less harm than a bombardment from the sea. Only outside disaster is irreparable. At least, there would be dinner at any minute; at least she could wash her hands in Vinolia soap.

Before the last chime of the temple bells, Mrs Heccomb had raised the cover and was carving the joint. She did not know that the boys had been to a pub; she understood that they had been for a turn. When Portia slipped into her place between Daphne and Dickie, she was at once requested to pass the broccoli. Upon Waikiki Sunday dinner, the curtain always went up with a rush: they ate as though taking part in an eating marathon. Eddie seemed to be concentrating on Dickie – evidently the drinks had gone off well. Now and then he threw Daphne a jolly look. As he passed up his plate for a second helping of mutton, he said to Portia, 'You look very clean.'

'Portia always looks clean,' said Mrs Heccomb proudly.

'She looks so clean. She must just have been washing. She's still no lady; she uses soap on her face.'

Dickie said: 'No girl's face is the worse for soap.'

'They all think so. They clean with grease out of pots.'

'No doubt. But the question is, do they clean?'

'Oh, have you got enlarged pores on your mind? Those are one of the worries I leave behind in the office. They are one of our greatest assets; in fact I have just been doing a piece about them. I began: "Why do so many Englishmen kiss with their eyes shut?" but somebody else made me take that out.'

'I must say, I don't wonder.'

'Still, I'm told Englishmen do. Of course I take that on hearsay: I've got no way to check up.'

There were signs, all round the table, of Eddie's having once more gone too far, and Portia wished he would take more care. However, by the time the plum tart came in, the talk had begun to take a happier turn. They examined night starvation, imperfectly white washing, obesity, self-distrust, and lustreless hair. Eddie had the good taste not to bring up his two great professional topics – halitosis and flabby busts. Doris had found the nine-pennyworth of cream too stiff to turn out of the carton, so brought it in as it was, which made Mrs Heccomb flush. Daphne said: 'Goodness, it's like butter,' and Eddie spooned a chunk of it out for her. By this time, she looked at him with a piglike but not unfriendly eye. When they had had cream crackers and gorgonzola they rose to settle heavily on the settee. Eddie said: 'Another gambit of ours is fullness after meals.'

Evelyn Bunstable was said to be dropping in, to give Portia's boy friend the once over. However, at about a quarter to three, just when Daphne had asked if they all meant to stick about, something better and far more important happened: Mr Bursely reappeared. Dickie heard him first, looked out of the window, and said: 'Why, who *have* we here.' Mrs Heccomb, coming back from the stairs on her way up to lie down, went quite a long way out into the sun porch, then said: 'It's that Mr Bursely, I think.'

Wearing a hat like Ronald Colman's, Mr Bursely came up the path with the rather knock-kneed walk of extreme social consciousness, and Eddie, who had heard all about him, said: 'You can't beat the military swagger.' Daphne squinted hard at her knitting; Eddie leant over Portia and pinched her gaily in the nape of her neck. He whispered: 'Darling, how excited I am!' Mr Bursely was let into the lounge. 'I'm afraid I've given you rather a miss,' he said. 'But it's been a thickish week, and I got all dated up.' Having hitched his trousers up at the knee, he plumped down on the settee beside Eddie. Portia looked from one to the other face.

Mr Bursely said to Portia: 'How's the child of the house?'

'Very well, thank you.'

Mr Bursely gave her a sort of look, then discreetly passed Daphne his next remark. 'I left my car just along. I thought you and I might go for a slight blow.'

'Oh, I'm fixed up *now*, I'm afraid.'

'Well, unfix yourself, why don't you? Come on, be a good girl, or I shall think you're ever so sick with me. Too bad I can't take you all, but you know what small cars are. I call mine the Beetle; she buzzes along. She –'

'– Actually,' said Dickie, 'I'm playing golf.'

'Clara didn't say so.'

'Because I'm playing with Evelyn.'

'Well, look here, why don't we all forgather somewhere in

Southstone? What about the E.C.P. Why not all forgather there?'

'Oh, all right.'

'Right-o. Well, make it sixish. Bring the whole gang along.'

'Portia and I', Eddie said, 'will just go for a walk.'

'Well, bring young Portia along to the E.C.P.'

'Someone ought to tell Clara. . . .'

'Right-o, then sixish,' Mr Bursely said.

7

THEY walked inland, uphill, to the woods behind the station – the ridge of the woods she had seen from the top of the sea wall. That Sunday, when she had been looking forward to Eddie, woods had played no part in the landscape she saw in her heart.

But here they were this Sunday, getting into the woods over a wattle fence, between gaps in the vigilant notices that said *Private*. Thickets of hazel gauzed over the distances inside; boles of trees rose rounded out of the thickets into the spring air. Light, washing the stretching branches, sifted into the thickets, making a small green flame of every early leaf. Unfluting in the armpit warmth of the valley, leaves were still timid, humid : in the uphill woods spring still only touched the boughs in a green mist that ran into the sky. Scales from buds got caught on Portia's hair. Small primroses, still buttoned into the earth, looked up from ruches of veiny leaves – and in sun-blond spaces at the foot of the oaks, dog violets burned their blue on air no one had breathed. The woods' secretive vitality filled the crease of the valley and lapped through the trees up the bold hill.

There were tunnels but no paths : doubling under the hazels they every few minutes stood up to stretch. '*Shall* we be prosecuted, do you think?'

'Boards are only put up to make woods disagreeable.'

Portia, unlacing twigs in front of her face, said: 'I only imagined us walking by the sea.'

'I've had *quite* enough seaside – one way and another.'

'But you are enjoying it, Eddie, I do hope?'

'Your hair's full of flies – don't touch; they look very sweet.'

Eddie stopped, sat, then lay down in a space at the foot of an oak. Slowly flapping one unhinged arm from the elbow, he knocked the place beside him with the back of his hand till she sat down too. Then, making a double chin, he slowly began to shred up leaves with his thumb-nails, now and then stopping to glance up at the sky – as though someone there had said something he ought to have heard. Portia, her hands clasped round her knees, stared straight down a tunnel of hazel twigs. After some time he said: 'What an awful house that was! Or rather, what awful things we said.'

'In that empty house?'

'Of course. How glad we were to get back to Waikiki. I'm frightened there, but it feels to me rather fine. The mutton bled, did you see? – No, I mean that house this morning. Did I hurt you, darling? Whatever I said, I swear I didn't mean. What did I say?'

'You said you hadn't meant some other things you had said.'

'Well, nor did I, I expect – Or were they things you set store by?'

'And you said there were things you didn't like about us,' said Portia, keeping her face away.

'That's not true, across my heart. I think we are perfect, darling. But I'd much rather you *knew* when I didn't mean what I said, then we shouldn't have to go back and put that right.'

'But what can I go by?'

'Yourself.'

'But Daphne thinks I am bats. She told me not to be potty, before lunch.'

'Don't sit right *up*: I can't look at you properly.'

Portia lay down and turned her cheek on the grass till her eyes obediently met his at a level. His light, curious look glanced into hers – then she dropped one hand across her eyes and lay rigid, crisping her fingers up. 'She says I'm potty about you. She says I haven't got any ideas.'

'Bitch,' Eddie said. 'They all try and pervert you, but no one but me could really do it, darling. I suppose one day you will have ideas of your own, but I really do dread your having any. Being just as you are now makes you the only person I love. But I can see that makes me a cheat. Never *be* potty about me: I can't do anything for you. Or, at least, I won't: I don't want you to change. We don't want to eat each other.'

'Oh no, Eddie – But what do you mean?'

'Well, like Anna and Thomas. And it can be much worse.'

'What do you mean?' she said apprehensively, raising her hand an inch over her eyes.

'What happens the whole time. And that's what they call love.'

'You say you never love anyone.'

'How would I be such a fool? I see through all that hanky-panky. But you always make me happy – except you didn't this morning. You must never show any sign of change.'

'Yes, that's all very well, but I feel everyone waiting; everyone gets impatient; I cannot stay as I am. They will all expect something in a year or two more. At present people like Matchett and Mrs Heccomb are kind to me, and Major Brutt goes on sending me puzzles, but that can't keep on happening – suppose they're not always there? I can see there is something about me Daphne despises. And I was frightened by what you said this morning – is there something unnatural about us? Do you feel safe with me because I am bats? What did Daphne mean about ideas I hadn't got?'

'Her own, I should think. But –'

'But what ideas do you never want me to have?'

'Oh, those are still worse.'

'You fill me with such despair,' she said, lying without moving.

Eddie reached across and idly pulled her hand away from her eyes. Keeping her hand down in the grass between them, he gently bent open her fingers one by one, then felt over her palm with his finger-tip, as though he found something in Braille on it. Portia looked at the sky through the branches over their heads, then sighed impalpably, shutting her eyes again. Eddie said: 'You don't know how much I love you.'

'Then, you threaten you won't – that you won't if I grow up. Suppose I was twenty-six?'

'A dreary old thing like that?'

'Oh don't laugh: you make me despair more.'

'I have to laugh – I don't like the things you say. Don't you know how dreadful the things you say are?'

'I don't understand,' she said, very much frightened. 'Why?'

'You accuse me of being a vicious person,' said Eddie, lying racked by her on the grass.

'Oh, I do *not*!'

'I should have known this would happen. It always does happen; it's happening now.'

Terrified by his voice and face of iron, Portia cried, *'Oh no!'* Annihilating the space of grass between them she flung an arm across him, her weight on his body, and despairingly kissed his cheek, his mouth, his chin. 'You are perfect,' she said, sobbing. 'You are my perfect Eddie. Open your eyes. I can't bear you to look like that!'

Eddie opened his eyes, from which her own shadow completely cut the light from the sky. At the same time frantic and impervious, his eyes looked terribly up at her. To stop her looking at him he pulled her head down, so that their two faces blotted each other out, and returned on her mouth what seemed so much her own kiss that she even tasted the salt of her own tears. Then he began to push her away gently. 'Go away,' he said, 'for God's sake go away and be quiet.'

'Then don't think. I can't bear it when you do that.'

Rolling away from her, Eddie huntedly got to his feet and began to go round the thicket: she heard the tips of the hazels whipping against his coat. He paused at the mouth of every tunnel, as though each were a shut door, to stand grinding his heels into the soundless moss. Portia, lying in her form in the grass, looked at the crushed place where he had lain by her – then, turning her head the other way, detected two or three violets, which, reaching out, she picked. She held them over her head and looked at the light through them. Watching her from his distance, spying upon the movement, he said: 'Why do you pick those? To comfort yourself?'

'I don't know. . . .'

'One cannot leave things alone.'

She could do nothing but look up at the violets, which now shook in her raised hand. In every pause of Eddie's movements a sea-like rustling could be heard all through the woody distance, a tidal movement under the earth. 'Wretched violets,' said Eddie. 'Why pick them for nothing? You'd better put them in my buttonhole.' He came and knelt impatiently down beside her; she knelt up, fumbling with the stalks of the flowers, her face a little below his. She drew the stalks through till the violets looked at her from against the tweed of his coat. She looked no higher till he caught both her wrists.

'I don't know how you feel,' he said, 'I daren't ask myself; I've never wanted to know. *Don't* look at me like that! And don't tremble like that – it's more than I can bear. Something awful will happen. I cannot feel what you feel: I'm shut up in myself. All I know is, you've been so sweet. It's no use holding on to me, I shall only drown you. Portia, you don't know what you are doing.'

'I do know.'

'Darling, I don't want you; I've got no place for you; I only want what you give. I don't want the whole of anyone. I haven't wanted to hurt you: I haven't wanted to touch you in any way. When I try and show you the truth I fill you with such despair. Life is so much more impossible than you think. Don't you see we're all full of horrible power, working against each other however much we may love? You agonize me by being so agonized. Oh cry out loud, if you must: cry, cry – don't just let those terrible meek tears roll down your face like that. What you want is the whole of me – isn't it, *isn't it?* – and the whole of me isn't there for anybody. In that full sense you want me I don't exist. What's started this terrible trouble in you, that you can't be happy with the truth of me that you had – however small it was, whatever might be beyond it? Ever since that evening when you gave me my hat, I've been as true to you as I've got it in me to be. Don't force me to where untruth starts. You say nothing would make you hate me. But once make me hate myself and you'd make me hate you.'

'But you do hate yourself. I wanted to comfort you.'

'But you have. Ever since you gave me my hat.'

'Why may we not kiss?'

'It's so desolating.'

'But you and me –' she began. She stopped, then pressing her face into his coat, under the violets, twisting her wrists in his unsure grip, she said some inaudible things, and at last moaned: 'I can't bear it when you talk.' When she got her wrists free, she once more locked her arms round him, she started rocking her body with such passionless violence that, as they both knelt, he rocked in her arms. 'You stay alone in yourself, you stay alone in yourself!'

Eddie, white as a stone, said: *'You must let go of me.'*

Sitting back on her heels, Portia instinctively looked up at the oak, to see whether it were still vertical. She pressed together her hands, which, torn roughly from Eddie, had been chafed in the palms by the rough tweed of his coat. Her last tears blistered her face; beginning to lose momentum they stuck in smarting patches: she felt in her coat pockets and said: 'I have got no handkerchief.'

Eddie drew from his own pocket a yard of silk handkerchief: while he still held one corner she blew her nose on another, then diligently blotted her tears up. Like a solicitous ghost whose touch cannot be felt, Eddie, with his two forefingers, tucked her damp hair back further behind her ears. Then he gave her one sad kiss, relevant to their two eternities, not to a word that had been said now. But her fear of having assailed, injured, betrayed him was so strong that she drew back from the kiss. Her knees received from the earth a sort of chilly trembling; the walls of the thicket, shot with those light leaves, flickered beyond her eyes like woods passed in a train.

When they settled back on the grass, with about a yard between them, Eddie pulled out his twenty packet of Players. The cigarettes looked battered. 'Look what you've done, too!' he said. But he lit one: threads of smoke began to swim from his nostrils; the match he blew out sputtered cold in the moss. When he had finished the cigarette he made a grave in the moss and buried the stump alive – but before this, several healing minutes had passed. 'Well, darling,' he said, in his natural light intonation, 'you must have had Anna tell you Eddie is so neurotic.'

'*Is* that a thing she says?'

'You ought to know: you've been with her half a year.'

'I don't always listen.'

'You ought to: sometimes she's so right ... Look, let's see ourselves in the distance, then we shall think, how happy they are! We're young; this is spring; this is a wood. In some sort of way or other we love each other, and our lives are before us – God pity us! Do you hear the birds?'

'I don't hear very many.'

'No, there are not very many. But you must hear them – play the game my way. What do you smell?'

'Burnt moss, and all the rest of the woods.'

'And what burnt the moss?'

'Oh, Eddie ... your cigarette.'

'Yes, my cigarette I smoked in the woods beside you – you darling girl. No no, you mustn't sigh. Look at us sitting under this old oak. Please strike me a match: I am going to smoke again, but you mustn't, you are still too young to. I have ideals, like Dickie. We don't take you into bars, and we love you to give us pious morbid thoughts. These violets ought to be in your hair – oh, Primavera, Primavera, why do they make you wear the beastly reefer coat? Give me your hand –'

'– No.'

'Then look at your own hand. You and I are enough to break anyone's heart – how can we not break our own? We are as drowned in this wood as though we were in the sea. So of course we are happy: how can we not be happy? Remember this when I've caught my train tonight.'

'*Tonight?* Oh, but I thought –'

'I've got to be in the office on time tomorrow. So what a good thing we are happy now.'

'But –'

'There's not any but.'

'Mrs Heccomb will be so disappointed.'

'Yes, I can't sleep in her lovely box-room again. We shan't wake tomorrow under the same roof.'

'I can't believe that you will have come and gone.'

'Check up with Daphne: she will tell you for certain.'

'Oh, please, Eddie, don't –'

'Why must I not? We must keep up something, you know.'

'Don't say we're happy with that awful smile.'

'I never mean how I'm smiling.'

'Can we walk somewhere else?'

Following uphill dog paths, parting hazels, crossing thickets upright, they reached the ridge of the woods. From here, they could see out. The sun, striking down the slope of trees, glittered over the film of green-white buds: a gummy smell was drawn out in the warm afternoon haze. To the south, the chalk-blue sea, to the north, the bare smooth down: they saw, too, the gleam of the railway line. In spirit, the two of them rose to the top of life like bubbles. Eddie drew her arm through his; Portia leaned her head on his shoulder and stood in the sun by him with her eyes shut.

On the top of the bus, riding into Southstone, Eddie pulled shreds of moss and a few iridescent bud scales from Portia's hair. He ran a comb through his hair, then passed her the comb. His collar was crumpled; their shoes were muddy; they were both of them hatless; Portia wore no gloves. For the Pavilion they would not be smart enough. But as the Southstone bus rolled along the sea front, they both felt very gay; they enjoyed this ride in the large light lurching glass box. Eddie chain-smoked; Portia put down the window near her and leaned out with her elbow over the top. Sea air blew on her forehead; she borrowed his comb again. As the bus changed gear at the foot of Southstone hill they looked at a clock and saw it was only five – but that gave them time for tea before the others should come.

'I tried to ask Daphne what made one feel matey.'

'Well, you *were* a fish: whatever made you do that?'

'Do you know, I once thought, at a party, that Mr Bursely was rather like you?'

'Bursely? – Oh yes, the chappie. Well I really *must* say . . . I wonder where he and Daphne buzzed to, don't you?'

'They might even go to Dover.'

They were still sitting over their tea at the Pavilion when Dickie, Evelyn, Clara, and Cecil filed in. Evelyn wore a canary-coloured two piece, Clara a teddy-bear coat tied in a bow at her chin. Dickie and Cecil were pin-striped all over – evidently everybody had changed. By this time, the Pavilion hung like an unlit lantern in the pinkish air; the orchestra was playing something from *Samson and Delilah*. Evelyn took her first look at Eddie, and asked if he liked hiking. Cecil, showing incuriosity, looked rather low. Clara kept her eyes on Dickie and said nothing: now and then she looked anxiously into her suède bag. As this was believed to be Mr Bursely's party, nothing could start until he came. Dickie folded open a glass and chromium door and said the girls might like to look at the view.

From the balcony they looked down at the Lower Road, at the tops of the pines and the roof of the skating rink. Eddie leaned so far out over the railing that Portia feared he might be going to show them (as he had shown her) how far he could spit. All that happened, however, was that the violets fell through space from his buttonhole. 'Now you've lost your flowers,' said Evelyn brightly.

'Suppose I'd felt giddy?' Eddie said, with a look.

'Oh, would you be such a sap?'

'Your marvellous yellow coat might make me come over queer.'

'I never,' said Evelyn, not knowing how to take this. 'I say, Dickie, your friend's got a bad head. Don't you think we all ought to go in?'

Dickie looked at his watch, still more sternly than he had looked at it in the time before. 'I can't understand,' he said. 'I told Bursely I would have you girls along here by six. I took it that that was understood – it is now between twenty and twenty-five past. I hope he's not having trouble.'

'Oh well, that's up to Daphne, isn't it?' said Evelyn, saucy, putting stuff on her mouth. Dickie paused till she put away the lipstick, then said coldly: 'I mean, with the car.'

'Oh, it's quite an easy car: I've driven it, so has Clara. I dare-say Daphne's driving this afternoon. Look at Clara shivering. Do you feel cold, dear?'

'Slightly.'

Indoors, among the mirrors and pillars, they found Mr Bursely and Daphne, cosy over a drink. Reproaches and rather snooty laughs were exchanged, then Mr Bursely, summoning the waiter, did what was right by everyone. Clara and Portia were given orangeade, with hygienic straws twisted up in paper; Daphne had another bronx, Evelyn a side-car. The men drank whisky – with the exception of Eddie, who asked for a double gin with a dash of angostura: this he insisted in dashing in himself, and so much fuss had seldom been made before. Daphne looked flushed and pleased. She had taken her hat off: while she talked she re-set her curls with one hand or the other, or glanced down confidentially at the dagger in her green velvet choker scarf. Mr Bursely and she – sitting side by side, saying not much – looked extremely conscious of one another.

Sucking quietly, leaning back from the party, isolated at the end of her long straw, Portia looked on. Now and then her eyes went to the clock – in three hours, Eddie would be gone. She watched him getting excited, saying the next were on him. She watched his hand go to his pocket – would he have enough money? He showed Evelyn what was in his pocket-book; he rolled back his cuff to show the hairs on his wrist. He asked Mr Bursely whether he was tattooed. He picked up the straw that Clara had done sucking, and tickled her neck with it as she burrowed into her bag. 'Oh, I say, Clara,' he said, 'you have never spoken to me.' She looked at him like an askance mouse. He dashed too much angostura into his second gin, then had to send for another gin to drown it. Propping an elbow on Cecil's shoulder, he said how much he wished they could go to France together. He printed his name with Evelyn's lipstick on the piece of paper off Clara's straw. 'Don't forget me,' he said. 'I'm certain you will forget me. Look, I'm putting my telephone number too.'

Dickie said: 'We are making rather a row.'

But Mr Bursely was also out of control. He and Eddie had made one of those genuine contacts that are only possible after drinks. With watery, dream-like admiration they kept catching each other's eye. There was no doubt, Eddie worked Mr Bursely up – first Mr Bursely gave an imitation of Donald Duck, then, making a snatch at Daphne's green celluloid comb, he endeavoured to second the orchestra on it. When the music stopped, he tried a tune of his own. He said: 'I'm a shepherd tootling to my sheep.' 'Sheep yourself,' said Daphne, upsetting her third bronx. 'Give me that back! Stop monkeying with my comb!' 'Look here,' Dickie said, 'you can't make that row here.' 'There's no can't about it,' said Mr Bursely, 'we are.'

Portia heard a rush behind her; the curtains were being drawn; swathes of yellow silk rushed across the dark mauve dusk. Cecil went on with his whisky and said nothing. 'Look here,' said Dickie to Mr Bursely and Eddie, 'if you two don't shut up, I am taking the girls home.'

'No, no, don't do that: we can't do without women.'

Dickie said: 'Better shut up, or you'll find yourself chucked out. This is not the Casino de Paris ... I shall take the girls home, then.'

'Right you are, Mussolini. Or let me.'

'Not all the girls, you can't,' said Mr Bursely, shutting one eye and looking through Daphne's comb.

'Can't I?' giggled Eddie, whacking Cecil's shoulder. 'You just ask Cecil: he knows France.'

'I must say,' said Evelyn sedately, 'I do think you boys are awful.'

'Well, you tell Cecil. Cecil's all in a dream.'

'Cecil's a gentleman wherever he is,' said Daphne, tenderly fingering Cecil's glass. 'Cecil's a really nice boy, if you know what I mean. I've known Cecil since we were both kids. Haven't we known each other since we were kids, Cecil? ... I *asked* you to stop monkeying with my comb. That's *my* comb you've got. Give that comb back here!'

'No, I'm tootling on it: I'm tootling to my sheep.'

Dickie uncrossed his legs and leant back from the table. 'Cecil,' he said, 'we had better get the girls home.'

Cecil carefully smiled, then put his hand to his forehead. Then he rose and left the table abruptly. He was seen to steer his way between several other tables and vanish with the flash of a swing door. Clara said: 'Now there are only seven of us.'

'What a gap he leaves,' said Eddie. 'He was our only thinker. I dread feeling; I know Clara dreads feeling; I see that in her face. You do dread feeling, don't you, Clara? Oh God, look at the time. How am I to catch a train when I don't know where a train is? I say, Daphne, where do I find a train?'

'The sooner the better.'

'I didn't ask when, I know when, I said where? Oh dear, you *are* a hard girl – I say, Evelyn, will you drive me to London? Let us rush through the night.'

But Evelyn, buttoning her yellow coat, only said: 'Well, Dickie, I'm off. I don't know what father would say – No thanks, Mr – er – *I* don't want your telephone number.'

'Oh God,' Eddie said, 'then you are casting me off?'

Then he turned full on Portia, across the table, his frantic swimming eyes. He said loudly: 'Darling, what shall I do? I am behaving so badly. What *shall* I do?' Then he dropped his eyes, giggled, and struck a match and burnt the long spill with his name on it in lipstick. 'There I go,' he said: the ash dropped on the table and Eddie blew some about and ground the rest with his thumb. 'I'd go,' he said, 'but I don't know where there's a train.'

'We'll ask,' Portia said. She got up and stood waiting.

'Well, good-bye, everybody, I've got to get back to London. Good-bye, good-bye: thanks ever so much.'

But: 'It's no use your saying good-bye,' said Dickie contemptuously. 'You must get back to Waikiki to get your things – if you can remember where *that* is? You also said that your train was at ten o'clock; it is now five minutes past eight. It is therefore no use your saying good-bye here. *Hi, look here*, you all: are you all going? Someone must wait for Cecil.'

Eddie went white and said: 'Well, you organize Cecil, blast

you: let Portia organize me. That's the way we get drunks home.'

The three other girls, at these words, scurried ahead like rabbits. Portia turned away to the yellow curtains: she got two apart and wrenched open the glass doors. A gash of dark air fell into the room; several people shivered and looked round. She stepped on to the balcony hanging over the black sea, lit by the windows' muffled yellow light. In a minute, Eddie came after her: he looked round the dark and said: 'Where are you? Are you still here?'

'Here I am.'

'That's right: don't go over the edge.'

Eddie leaned on the frame of another window, folded his arms, and broke out into sobbing: against the windows she saw his shoulders shake. Someone sobbing like that must not be gone near.

8

THE DIARY

Monday

THIS morning Mrs Heccomb did not say anything, as though yesterday had been all my dream. I have gone on with the puzzle, it has been knocked, so part that I did is undone and I could not begin again where I left off. Perhaps it *is* in the way in the sun porch? Daphne did not say anything more either. It is raining, but more dark than it rains.

Tuesday

When I woke, it rained as much as it could, it has stopped now and the esplanade looks shiny. Mrs Heccomb and I went into Toyne's this morning, to buy clips to stop things blowing away, and coming out of Toyne's she looked as though she was going to say something but she did not, perhaps she was not going to. On wet days the street smells much more of salt. This afternoon we went to tea with some people to talk about the church fête and they said what a pity I should not be there. It will be in June, by June I wonder what will have happened?

Wednesday

It is queer to be in a place when someone has gone. It is not two other places, the place that they were there in, and the place that was there before they came. I can't get used to this third place or to staying behind.

Mrs Heccomb has a new piano pupil in Southstone, and took me in there when she went to give the lesson. I waited for her on a seat on the cliff. I saw the flags on the East Cliff Pavilion, but did not go near that.

Thursday

Daphne says Cecil is hurt with me. And she says Eddie burnt a hole in the eiderdown Cecil's mother lent for his bed, which has made an awkward position with Cecil's mother. Daphne says it cannot be helped but she does think I ought to know.

Friday

I got a letter from Eddie, so did Mrs Heccomb, he says to her he will always have memories of here. She showed me the letter and said wasn't it nice, but still did not say any more about Eddie. She looked once as if she was going to but she did not, perhaps she was not really going to.

Cecil came this evening and said he had had an internal chill. I do not think he is really hurt with me.

Saturday

Last week this was the day Eddie was coming.

Dickie is kindly taking me into Southstone to watch that ice hockey, Clara is coming too and we shall go in her car. Daphne and Evelyn are going to dance at the Splendide with Mr Bursely and a man he will bring. Cecil says he has still rather a chill.

Sunday

I went to church with Mrs Heccomb this morning, it was raining hard on the church roof. You can hardly see inland because of all the rain. It must be wet in those woods and everywhere. Today I am going to tea with Cecil's mother.

Monday

I got a letter from Major Brutt thanking me for my letter thanking him for the puzzle. He wonders when we will all be back.

I think they have all forgotten everything that has happened.

Clara has been so kind, she asked me to come with her to Evelyn's house to practise badminton, and we did, but did not get on very well. After that I went back to tea with Clara. Her father is rich, he is in tea. Her house is hot inside and has big game rugs, and on the landings there are flowers with their pots put inside big brass pots. Clara took me up to her bedroom with her, she has Dickie's photograph by her bed, with Yours Dickie written by him on it. She said it was often dull for me and her, because of all the others always working all day, and Clara sometimes thinks she will take something up. She gave me a chiffon handkerchief she has never used, and two necklaces off her own tray. I shall show these at once to Dickie to show how kind Clara is.

Tuesday

I had a letter from Eddie, he says he is well and he asks how they all are. And I have had a letter from Thomas, with a postscript by Anna on one page. Anna said it did make her laugh to think of Eddie at Waikiki. I did not say he'd been here, perhaps Mrs Heccomb did. She says not to write if I'm having such a good time, as they will be back soon and will hear all news then.

Wednesday

Mrs Heccomb suddenly said she was upset about me. I was glad when Cecil took me for a walk on the beach.

Thursday

Mrs Heccomb said she did hope she hadn't said too much, she said she had had a quite sleepless night. I said oh no, she hadn't, because of Cecil. I said I hoped I had not done anything, she said oh no it was not that, only she did wonder. I said wonder what, and she said she did wonder what she ought to have done. I said done when, and she said that was just it, she was not sure when she should have done it, she meant, if she *had* done anything. She said she did hope I knew she was so fond of me and I said I was so glad.

Friday

There are still places I cannot walk past, though we only walked here those two days. When I walk I look for places we did not go. Today I stood on a canal bridge, another canal bridge that we never stood on. I watched two swans, they sailed under the bridge. They say the swans are nesting, but these two kept their heads turned away from each other. Today it is not raining but quite dark, black is all through the air though the green looks such bright green. All the days that go by only make me seem to be getting further and further away from the day I last saw Eddie, not nearer and nearer the day I shall see him again.

Saturday

A fortnight since Eddie came. My last Saturday here.

Dickie came back at three from the Hockey Lunch. He says they have been winding up for the year. I was in the sun porch doing my puzzle, and he asked why I looked like that when he came in. I said it was my last Saturday here. So he asked if I'd like to walk round while he played golf. So when Clara came in her car to call for him they put me into the back part of the car and we drove up to the links. Clara tries with her golf because of Dickie, but Dickie plays a sort of game by himself. You see the woods from the links, right across a valley, but it is lovely up there, there is so much gorse. At the end Dickie said we would have tea, so we went and had tea in the club house. It is handsome in there, there is a huge fire and we had tea right in the bow-window. I did enjoy myself. I think my being there made Clara feel rather more like Dickie's wife, she insisted on getting some more jam. At the end of our tea, Clara got her bag out, but Dickie said, Here, I say, and he paid for the tea. It is only in front of Daphne he is unkind to Clara.

We had been so long that Clara said good gracious, she had to hurry, a judge was coming to dinner at her home. So Dickie said she had better buzz straight back, so she did, and he and I walked home. He said, was I sorry I was going away? I said I was (I am) and he turned round and gave a look at the top of my head and said, so were they all. He said I had become quite one of them. That made me ask, did he like Eddie too. He said, of course he's an amusing chap. I said I was so glad he thought Eddie was funny. He said, he is something of a Lothario, isn't he? I said Eddie was not really, and he said, well, he loses his head a bit, if you know what I mean. I said I did not quite, and he said, well to my mind it is largely a matter of character. He said he judged people by their characters. I said *was* that always a quite good way of judging, as people's characters get so different at times, as it depends so much what happens to them. He said no, I was wrong, that what happened to people depended on their characters. I know Dickie sounds right, but I don't feel he is. By that time we were out on the esplanade and there was a sunset right into our eyes. I said didn't the sea look like glass, and he said yes he supposed it did. I said I did like Clara, and he said oh she's all right but she loses her head. I said then did he mean Clara was like Eddie, and he said he did not. Then we got to Waikiki.

Sunday

My last Sunday. It's very very fine, hot. The leaves are out on the chestnuts, though not big leaves, and the other trees have a quite frilly look. After church Mrs Heccomb and I were asked into someone's garden to have a look at the hyacinths. They are just like all sorts of coloured china. In the garden Mrs Heccomb said to the lady, Next Sunday, alas, we shall not have Portia with us. I thought, next Sunday, I might even see Eddie and yet I still thought, oh I do want to stay here. Now the summer is coming they will do all sorts of things I have not seen them doing yet. In London I do not know what anybody is doing, there are no things I can watch people do. Though things have hurt me since I was left behind here, I would rather stay with the things here than go back to where I do not know what will happen.

On the way back from the hyacinth garden, Mrs Heccomb said what a great pity it was that I had not been for a row on the canal. She says that is where they row in summer. I said, but don't they row in the sea, and she said no, that is so public, the canal is shadier. She said how would it be if she asked Cecil to row her and me there this afternoon. So we went round by Cecil's house, he was out but his mother said she would certainly ask him to row us.

So this afternoon we did. Cecil rowed, and he showed me how to steer, and Mrs Heccomb held up a parasol. It was mauve silk, and once or twice when I was not steering I caught weed in my hands. The weed is strong, and it also caught on the oars. So none of us said much while Cecil was rowing, Mrs Heccomb thought and I looked down in the water or up at the trees. The sun shone almost loudly. A swan came along and Mrs Heccomb said it would be nesting and might likely be cross, so she folded up her parasol to hit at it, and Cecil said, I had better ship my oars. But the swan did not take any notice of us. Later we passed its nest, with the other one sitting there.

All the others were playing tennis somewhere. When I first got here, Mrs Heccomb was wearing her fur coat. Now though it is all pale green it is summer. Things change very fast at this time of year, something happens every day. All winter nothing happened at all.

Tonight Mrs Heccomb is singing in an oratorio. Daphne and Dickie and Clara and Evelyn and Wallace and Charlie and Cecil are all downstairs playing rummy because she is out. But

Mrs Heccomb made me go to bed early, because I caught a headache on the canal.

Monday

Mrs Heccomb is tired after the oratorio, and Daphne and Dickie do not like fine Mondays. Now I shall go out and lie on the beach.

Tuesday

I have not yet had the letter Eddie said he would write, but that must be because I am coming back. This is a new place this week, this is a place in summer. The esplanade smells all over of hot tar. But they all say that of course this will not last.

Wednesday

Tomorrow I shall be going. Because this is my last whole day, Mrs Heccomb and Cecil's mother are going to take me to see a ruin. We are to pack our tea and go in a motor bus.

Clara is going to drive me in her car to the Junction to-morrow, to save the having to change. Clara says she feels really upset. Because this will be my last evening, Dickie and Clara and Cecil are going to take me to the Southstone rink, so's I can watch them skate.

I cannot say anything about going away. I cannot say anything even in this diary. Perhaps it is better not to say anything ever. I must try not to say anything more to Eddie, when I have said things it has always been a mistake. Now we must start to take the bus for the ruin.

Thursday

I am back here, in London. They won't be back till tomorrow.

Part Three

THE DEVIL

I

THOMAS and Anna would not be back from abroad till Friday afternoon.

Everything was ready for them to come back and live. That Friday morning, 2 Windsor Terrace was lanced through by dazzling spokes of sun, which moved unseen, hotly, over the waxed floors. Vacantly overlooking the bright lake, chestnuts in leaf, the house offered that ideal mould for living into which life so seldom pours itself. The clocks, set and wound, ticked the hours away in immaculate emptiness. Portia – softly opening door after door, looking all round rooms with her reflecting dark eyes, glancing at each clock, eyeing each telephone – did not count as a presence.

The spring cleaning had been thorough. Each washed and polished object stood roundly in the unseeing air. The marbles glittered like white sugar; the ivory paint was smoother than ivory. Blue spirit had removed the winter film from the mirrors: now their jet-sharp reflections hurt the eye; they seemed to contain reality. The veneers of cabinets blazed with chestnut light. Upstairs and downstairs, everything smelt of polish; a clean soapy smell came out from behind books. Crisp from the laundry, the inner net curtains stirred over windows reluctantly left open to let in the April air with its faint surcharge of soot. Yes, already, with every breath that passed through the house, pollution was beginning.

The heating was turned off. Up the staircase stood a shaft of neutral air, which, upon any door or window being opened, received a tremor of spring. This morning, the back rooms were still sunless and rather cold. The basement was still colder; it smelled of scrubbing; the light filtered down to it in a ghostly way. City darkness, a busy darkness, collected in this working part of the house. For four weeks, Portia had not been underground.

'Gracious, Matchett, you have got everywhere clean!'

'Oh – so that's where you've been?'

'Yes, I've looked at everywhere. It really *is* clean – not that it isn't always.'

'More likely you'd notice it, coming back. I know those seaside houses – all claptrap and must.'

'I must say,' said Portia, sitting on Matchett's table, 'today makes me wish only you and I lived here.'

'Oh, you ought to be ashamed! And mind, too, you don't get a place like this without you have a Mr and Mrs Thomas. And then where would you be, I should like to know? No, I'm ready for them, and it's proper they should come back. Now don't give me a look like that – what is the matter with you? I'm sure Mr Thomas, for one, would be disappointed if he was to know you wished you were still at that seaside.'

'But I never did say that!'

'Oh, it isn't only what's *said*.'

'Matchett, you do fly off when all I just said was –'

'All right, all right, all right.' Matchett tapped at her teeth with a knitting needle and marvelled at Portia slowly. 'My goodness,' she said, 'they have taught you to speak up. Anyone wouldn't know you.'

'But you go on at me because I have been away. After all, I didn't go, I was sent.'

Sitting up on the table in Matchett's basement parlour, Portia stretched her legs out and looked at her toes, as though the change Matchett detected (was there a change really?) might have begun there. Matchett, knitting a bedsock, sat on one of the chairs beside the unlit gas stove, feet up on the rung of another chair – she had unbuttoned the straps across her insteps, which were puffy today. It was twelve noon: the hands of the clock seemed to exclaim at the significant hour. Twelve noon – but everything was too ready, nothing more was to come till an afternoon train steamed into Victoria and a taxi toppling with raw-hide luggage crossed London from s.w. to n.w.i. Therefore, there had happened this phenomenal stop. In the kitchen, the cook and Phyllis tittered to one another, no doubt drinking tea. In here, the two chairs now and then creaked with Matchett's monolithic repose.

She had had her way like a fury. Tensed on the knitting needles (for she could not even relax without some expense of energy) her fingers were bleached and their skin puckered, like the skin of old apples, from unremitting immersion in hot water, soda, soap. Her nails were pallid, fibrous, their tips split. Light crept down the sooty rockery, through the bars of the window, to find no colour in Matchett: her dark blue dress blotted the light up. She looked built back into the half darkness behind her apron's harsh glaze. In her helmet of stern hair, a few new white threads shone – but behind the opaqueness of her features control permitted no sag of tiredness. There was more than control here: she wore the look of someone who has augustly fulfilled herself. Floor by floor over the basement towered her speckless house, and a reckoning consciousness of it showed like eyes through the eyelids she lowered over her knitting.

Portia, looking through the bars of the window, said: 'It was a pity you couldn't wash the rockery.'

'Well, we did spray the ivy, but that doesn't go far, and those tom cats are always after the ferns.'

'I did imagine you busy – but not *so* busy, Matchett.'

'I don't see you had call to imagine anybody, not with all you were up to with them there.' (This, though worded sharply, was not said sharply: all the time Matchett spoke she was knitting; there was something pacific about the click-click-click.) 'You don't want to be in two places, not at your age. You be at the seaside when you're at the seaside. You keep your imaginings till you need them. Come a spring like this one we've been having, out of sight out of mind should be good enough. Oh, it has been a lovely spring for the airing – down at Mrs Quayne's, I'd have had my mattresses out.'

'But I thought about you. Didn't you think of me?'

'Now when do you suppose I'd have had a minute? If you

had have been here, you'd have been under my feet one worse than Mr and Mrs Thomas if they hadn't gone away. No, and don't you say to me that you went round moping, either: you had your fill of company where you were, and I've no doubt there were plenty of goings on. Not that you've got much to tell; you keep it all to yourself. However, that's always your way.'

'You didn't ask me; you were still so busy. This is the first time you've listened. And now I don't know where to begin.'

'Oh, well, take your time: you've got the rest of the summer,' said Matchett, glancing at the clock. 'I must say, they've sent you back with a colour. I can't see that this change has done you harm. Nor the shake-up either: you were getting too quiet. I never saw such a quiet girl, for your age. Not that that Mrs Heccomb, poor thing, could teach anyone to say no. All I've ever heard her say to Mrs Thomas was yes. But the rest of them down there sound a rough lot. Did you have enough stockings?'

'Yes, thank you. But I'm afraid I cut the knees out of one pair. I was running, and I fell smack on the esplanade.'

'And what made you run, may I ask?'

'Oh, the sea air.'

'Oh, it did, did it?' said Matchett. 'It made you run.' Without a pause in her knitting, she half lifted her eyelids, enough to let her look stay tilted, through space, at nothing particular. How far apart in space these two existences, hers and Portia's, had been for the last weeks; how far apart they still were. You never quite know when you may hope to repair the damage done by going away. Removing one foot cumbrously from the rung of the chair, Matchett hooked with it at the ball of pink knitting wool which had been rolling away. Portia got off the table, picked the ball of wool up, and handed it back to Matchett. She said boldly: 'Is that bedsock for you?'

Matchett's half nod was remote, extremely unwilling. No one *knew* that she slept, that she went to bed: at nights she just disappeared. Portia knew she had trespassed; she said quickly: 'Daphne knitted. She used to knit at the library. Mrs Heccomb could knit, but she used to paint lamp shades more.'

'And what did you do?'

'Oh, I went on with my puzzle.'

'That wasn't much of a treat.'

'But it was a new puzzle, and I only did that when I wasn't doing anything. You know how it is –'

'No, I don't, and I'm not asking, and I don't want mysteries made.'

'There's no mystery, except what I've forgotten.'

'You don't have to say; I'm not asking you. What you do's all one on a holiday. Now it's all over, get it out of your head – I see you've worn the elbows out of that blazer. I told Mrs Thomas that wouldn't be wearing stuff. Did you use your velvet, or was I wrong to pack it?'

'No, I wore my velvet. I –'

'Oh, they dress for their dinner, then?'

'No, I wore it for their party. It was a dance.'

'I did ought to have packed your organdie, then. But I didn't want it to crush, and sea air limpens the pleats out. I daresay your velvet did.'

'Yes, Matchett: it was admired.'

'Well, it's better than they'd see: it's got a nice cut.'

'You know, Matchett, I did enjoy myself.'

Matchett gave another sideways look at the clock, as though admonishing time to hurry for its own sake. Her air became more non-committal than ever; she appeared to be hypnotized by the speed of her knitting, and, at the same time, for her own private pleasure, to be humming an inaudible tune. After about a minute, she receipted Portia's remark with an upward jerk of the chin. But the remark had, by that time, already wilted in the below stairs dusk of this room – like, on the mantelpiece, the bunch of wild daffodils, some friend's present, thrust so sternly into a glass jar. These, too, must have been a gift that Matchett no more than suffered.

'You're glad, aren't you?' Portia more faintly said.

'The things you do ask. . . .'

'I suppose it may have been just the sea air.'

'And I daresay the sea air suited Mr Eddie?'

Unarmoured against this darting remark, Portia shifted on the table. 'Oh, Eddie?' she said. 'He was only there for two days.'

'Still, two days are two days, at the seaside. Yes, I understood him to say he felt fine there. At least, those were his words.'

'*When* were they his words? What do you mean?'

'Now don't you jump down my throat in such a hurry as that.' Running the strand of pink wool over a rasped finger, Matchett reflectingly hummed a few more unheard bars. 'Five-thirty yesterday, that would have been, I suppose. When I was coming downstairs in my hat and coat, just off to meet your train with no time to spare, my lord starts ringing away on the telephone – oh, fit to bring the whole house down, it was. Thinking it might be important, I went and answered. *Then* I thought I should never get him away – chattering on and on like that. However, no doubt that's what Mr Thomas's office telephone's for. No wonder they've got to have three lines. "Excuse me, sir," I said, "but I am just on my way to meet a train." '

'Did he know it was my train?'

'He didn't ask, and I didn't specify. "I am just off to meet a train," I said. But did that stop him? Trains can wait while some people have to talk. "Oh, I won't keep you," he said – then ran on to something else.'

'But what did he run on to?'

'He seemed quite put out to hear Mrs Thomas was not back yet, and that neither were you. "Oh dear, oh dear," he said, "I must have muddled the days." Then he said, to be sure to tell Mrs Thomas, and to tell you, that he would be out of London from the following morning (today morning, that was) but would hope to ring up after the weekend. Then he said he thought I'd be glad to hear that you had looked well at the seaside. "You'd be so pleased, Matchett," he said, "she's really got quite a colour." I thanked him and asked if there would be anything more. He said just to give his love to Mrs Thomas, and you. He said he thought that would be all.'

'So then you rang off?'

'No, he did. It was his tea time, no doubt.'

'Did he say he'd ring up again?'

'No, he left what he had to say.'

'Did you say I was on my way back?'

'No, why should I? He didn't ask.'

'When did he *think* I'd be back?'

'Oh, I couldn't tell you, I'm sure.'

'What made him be going away on a *Friday* morning?'

'I couldn't tell you that, either. Office business, no doubt.'

'It seems to me very odd.'

'A good deal in that office seems to me very odd. However, it's not for me to say.'

'But, Matchett – just one thing more: did he realize I'd be back that very night?'

'What he realized or didn't realize I couldn't tell you. All I know is, he kept chattering on.'

'He does chatter, I know. But you don't think –'

'Listen: I don't think: I haven't the time to, really. What I don't think I don't think – you ought to know that. I don't make mysteries, either. I suppose, if he hadn't thought to say, *you'd* never have thought to tell me he'd been there at Mrs Heccomb's? Now, you get off my table, there's a good girl, while I plug in the iron: I've got some pressing to do.'

Portia said, in a hardly alive voice: 'I thought you said you had finished everything.'

'Finished? You show me one thing that is ever finished, let alone everything. No, I'll stop when they've got me screwed into my coffin, but that won't be because I've got anything finished . . . I'll tell you one thing you might do for me: run up, like a good girl, and shut Mrs Thomas's bedroom window. That room should be aired now, and I won't have any more smuts in. Then you leave me quiet while I get on with my pressing. Why don't you go in the park? It must be pretty out there.'

Portia shut Anna's windows, and gave one blank look at herself in Anna's cheval glass. Before shutting the windows she heard the wooing pigeons, and heard cars slip down the glossy road. Through the fresh net curtains, she saw trees in the sun. She could not make up her mind to go out of doors, for she felt alone. If one is to walk alone, it should be with pleasant thoughts. About this time, Mrs Heccomb, alone today, would be getting back to Waikiki after the morning shopping . . . She lagged downstairs to the hall: here, on the marble-topped table, two stacks of letters awaited Thomas and Anna. For the third time, Portia went carefully through these – it was still possible that something for Miss P. Quayne could have got slipped in among them. This proved not to be so – it had been not so before ... She went through the letters again, this time for interest purely. Some of Anna's friends' writings were cautious, some were dashing. How many of these letters were impulses, how many were steps in some careful plan? She could guess at some of the writings; she had seen these people already, stalking each other. For instance, here was St Quentin's well-cut grey envelope. Now what had *he* got to add to what was already said?

Personal letters for Thomas were not many, but to balance Anna's pile back was quite an affair of art. Portia tried to imagine getting out of a taxi to find one's own name written so many times. This should make one's name mean – oh, most decidedly – more.

With a stage groan, Anna said: 'Now will you look at those letters!'

She did not, at first, attempt to pick them up: she read one or two messages on the telephone pad, and looked at a florist's gilt box on the chair – there was no room on the laden table for it. She said to Thomas: 'Someone has sent me flowers,' but he had already gone into the study. So Anna, smiling at Portia, said nicely to her: 'One can't attempt to open everything, can one? ... How well you're looking: quite brown, almost fat.' She looked up the stairs and said: 'Well, we certainly are clean. You got back yesterday evening, didn't you?'

'Yes, yesterday.'

'And you enjoyed yourself frightfully?'

'Oh yes, I did, Anna.'

'You said so, but we did hope you did. Have you seen Matchett?'

'Oh, yes.'

'Yes, you naturally would have: I was forgetting you got back yesterday ... Well, I must look round,' said Anna picking up the letters. 'How odd I do feel. Will you open those flowers and tell me who they're from?'

'The box looks nice. I expect the flowers are lovely.'

'Yes, I'm sure they are. But I wonder who they are from.'

Anna took her letters up, and went up to have a bath. Five minutes later, Portia came to tap on the bathroom door. Anna was not yet quite into the bath; she opened the door, showing a strip of herself and letting out a cloud of scented steam. 'Oh hullo?' she said. 'Well?'

'They are carnations.'

'What colour?'

'Sort of quite bright pink.'

'Oh God – Who are they from?'

'Major Brutt. He says on the card that they are to welcome you home.'

'This would happen,' Anna said. 'They must have cost him the earth; he probably didn't have lunch and this makes me hysterical. I do wish we had never run into him: we've done nothing but put ideas into his head. You had better take them down and show them to Thomas. Or else give them to Matchett; they might do for her room. I know this is dreadful, but I feel so unreal ... Then you might write Major Brutt a note. Say I have gone to bed. I am sure he would much rather have a note from you. Oh, how was Eddie? I see he rang up.'

'Matchett answered.'

'Oh! I thought you probably would. Well, Portia, let's have a talk later.' Anna shut the door and got into her bath.

Portia took the carnations down to Thomas. 'Anna says these are the wrong colour,' she said. Thomas was back again in his armchair, as though he had not left it, one foot on a knee. Though only a dimmed-down reflection of afternoon came into the study, he had one hand near his eyes, as though there were a strong glare. He looked without interest at the carnations. 'Oh, are they the wrong colour?' he said.

'Anna says they are.'

'Who did you say they were from?'

'Major Brutt.'

'Oh yes, oh yes. Do you think he's found a job?' He looked more closely at the carnations, which Portia held like an unhappy bride. 'There are hundreds of them,' he said. 'I suppose he has found something. I hope he has: we cannot do anything ... Well, Portia, how are you? Did you really have a good time? – Forgive me sitting like this, but I seem to have got a headache – How did you like Seale?'

'Very much indeed.'

'That's excellent: I'm really awfully glad.'

'I wrote and said I did, Thomas.'

'Anna wondered whether you did really. I should think it was nice. I've never been there, of course.'

'No, they said you hadn't.'

'No. It's a pity, really. Well, it's nice to see you again. Is everything going well?'

'Yes, thank you. I'm enjoying the spring.'

'Yes, it is nice,' said Thomas, 'It feels to me cold, of course ... Would you care to go for a turn in the park, later?'

'That would be lovely. When?'

'Well, I think later, don't you? ... Where did you say Anna was?'

'She's just having her bath. She asked me to write something to Major Brutt. I wonder, Thomas, if I might write at your desk?'

'Oh yes, by all means do.'

Having discharged himself of this good feeling, Thomas unostentatiously left the study while Portia opened the blotter to write to Major Brutt. He got himself a drink, carried the drink upstairs, and took a look round the drawing-room on his way. Not a thing had been tweaked from its flat, unfeeling position – palpably Anna had not been in here yet. So then he carried his drink into Anna's room, and sat on the big bed till she should come from her bath. His heavy vague reflections weighted him into a stone figure – Anna jumped when she came round the door at him, her wrapper open, the bunch of steam-blotched opened letters in her hand. Superfluously, she said: 'How you made me jump!'

'I wondered if there were letters. . . .'

'There are letters, of course. But nothing at all funny. However, darling, here they all are.' She dropped the letters on to the bed beside him, and went across to the mirror, where she took off the net cap that kept the waves in her hair. Making a harsh face at her reflection, she began to rub in complexion milk with both hands. Tapping about among the pots and bottles, she had found everything in its known place – the familiarity of all these actions made something at once close in on her: the mood of her London dressing-table. With her back to Thomas, who sat raking through letters, she said: 'Well, here we are back.'

'What did you say?'

'I said, we are back again.'

Thomas looked all round the room, then at the dressing-table. He said: 'How quickly Matchett's unpacked.'

'Only the dressing-case. After that, I turned her out and told her to come back and finish later. I could see from her face she was going to say something.'

Thomas left the letters and sat leaning forward. 'Perhaps she really had got something to say.'

'Well, Thomas, but what a moment – really! Did you hear me say just now that here we were, back?'

'I did, yes. What do you want me to say?'

'I wish you would say something. Our life goes by without any comment.'

'What you want is some sort of a troubadour.'

Anna wiped complexion milk off her fingers on to a tissue, smartly re-tied the sash of her wrapper, walked across, and gave Thomas's head a light friendly unfriendly cuff. She said: 'You are like one of those sitting images that get moved about but still always just sit. I like to feel some way about what happens. We're *home*, Thomas: have some ideas about home –' More lightly, less kindly, she hit at his head again.

'Shut up: don't knock me about. I've got a headache.'

'Oh dear, oh dear! Try a bath.'

'I will later. But just now, don't hit my head ... I thought Portia gave us a welcome.'

'Poor child, oh poor child, yes. She stood about like an angel. It was we who were not adequate. I wasn't very, was I?'

'No, I don't think you were.'

'But you think you were? You bolted into the study. What's in your mind, I suppose, is, why should you rise to occasions when I don't? Let's face it – who ever is adequate? We all create situations each other can't live up to, then break our hearts at them because they don't. One doesn't have to be in love to be silly – in fact I think one is sillier when one's not in love, because then one makes a thing about everything. At least, that is how it is with me. Major Brutt sending those carnations has made me hysterical. Did you see them? They were cochineal pink.'

'I don't create situations, I don't think.'

'Yes, you do; you're creating one by having a headache. Besides you are making creases in my quilt.'

'I'm sorry,' said Thomas rising. 'I'll go down.'

'Now you are making another situation. What I really want to do is to dress and not have to talk, but I can't have you walk out into the night. And Matchett is simply waiting to pop back and rustle about and spring something on me. I know I am disappointing you, darling. I'm sure you would be happier in the study.'

'Portia's down there, writing to Major Brutt.'

'And if you go down, you'll feel you will have to say, "Well, Portia, how are you getting on with your letter to Major Brutt?"'

'No, I shouldn't see the least necessity to.'

'Well, Portia would look up until you did. Now, Major Brutt having sent me those carnations is just the sort of thing that Portia really enjoys,' said Anna, sitting down by the dressing-table, unrolling and putting on a pair of silk stockings. 'Yes, it often does seem to me that you and I are not natural. But I also say to myself, well, who is natural, then?'

Having put his glass down on the carpet, Thomas boldly swung his legs up on to the bed and stretched out on the immaculate quilt. 'I don't think that bath has done you much good,' he said. 'Or is this the way you talk most of the time? We so seldom talk; we're so seldom together.'

'I must be tired; I do feel rather unreal. As I keep saying, all I want is to dress.'

'Well, do dress. Why can't you just dress and why can't I just lie? We don't have to keep on saying anything. However much of a monster you may be, I feel more natural with you than I feel with more natural people – if there are such things. Must you put on those beastly green suède shoes?'

'Yes, because the others aren't unpacked. How hot the afternoon sun is,' said Anna, drawing the curtains behind the dressing-table. 'All the time we were *there*, I kept imagining England coolish and grey, and now we land into this inferno of glare.'

'I expect the weather will break. You don't much like anything, do you?'

'No, nothing,' said Anna, smiling her nice fat malign smile. She finished dressing in the gloom of the curtains, through whose yellows and pinks the afternoon sun beat. The vibration of traffic came through the shut window, through the stiff chintz folds. She gave one more look at Thomas and said: 'I suppose you do know that that ruins my quilt?'

'It can go to the cleaners.'

'The point is, it has just come back from there ... How do you think Portia is?'

Thomas, who had just lighted a cigarette (the worst thing for a headache) said: 'She says she's enjoying the spring.'

'Now whatever makes her do that? Little girls of her age don't just enjoy weather. Someone must have been fussing her up.'

'She may not have been enjoying the spring really, but just felt she must say something polite. I suppose it's possible she enjoyed Seale – in which case, we might have left her there longer.'

'No, if she's to be with us she's got to be with us, darling. Besides, her lessons begin on Monday. If she's not enjoying the spring (and I can't make out if your impression was that she wasn't or that she was) there must be something wrong with her, and you had better find out what it is. You know she will never talk to me. If someone's let her down that would be Eddie, of course.'

Thomas reached down to knock ash off into his empty glass. 'Anyhow, it's high time the lid was put on that. I don't know why we have let it go so far.'

'Oh, it's stationary: it's been like that for months. Evidently you don't know what Eddie is. He doesn't have to go far with anybody to fail them: he can let anyone down at any stage. And what do you expect me to say or do? There are limits to what one can say to people and it isn't really a question of doing anything. Anyhow, she's your sister. As for speaking to Eddie, you must know how touchy he is with me. And she and I feel so shy, and shyness makes one so brutal ... No, poor little Eddie's not a ravening lion.'

'No, he's not a *lion*.'

'Don't be malicious, Thomas.'

Glad, however, to find herself dressed again, Anna gave herself a sort of contented shake inside her green dress, like a bird shaking itself back into its preened feathers. She looked for her case and lighted a cigarette, then came over to sit on the bed by Thomas. Rolling his head round, he at once pulled her head down to pillow level. 'All the same,' said Anna, after the kiss, sitting up and moulding back with her fingers the one smooth curl along the nape of her neck, 'I do think you'll have to get off that quilt.' While she went back to the dressing-table to screw the caps back on to her pots and bottles Thomas rose and, meticulous and gloomy, tried to smooth the creases out of the satin. 'After tea', he announced, 'Portia and I are going for a turn in the park.'

'But do. Why not?'

'If you were half as heartless as you make out, you would be an appallingly boring woman.'

After tea, Thomas and Portia dodged two lines of traffic, successfully crossed the road, and went into the park. They crossed the bridge to the far side of the lake. Here stood the tulips just ready to flower: still grey and pointed, but brilliantly veined with the crimsons, mauves, yellows they were to be. Late afternoon sunshine streamed into the faces of people sitting in deck chairs, along the lake or on the bright grass – shading their eyes or bending their heads down or letting the sun beat on their closed lids, these people sat like reddening stones.

The water was animated: light ran off blades of oars or struck through the coloured or white sails that shivered passing the islands. Bending rowers crossed the mirroring view. The etherealization of the early morning had lifted from the long narrow wooded islands, upon which nobody was allowed to land, and which showed swans' nests at the edge of their mystery. Light struck into the islands' unvisited hearts; the silvery willow branches just shifted apart to let light glitter through. Reflections of trees, of sails, made the water coloured and deep, and water birds lanced it with long ripples.

People approaching each other, beside the lake or on the oblique walks, looked into each other's faces boldly, as though they felt they should know each other. Thin hems of women's dresses fluttered under their coats. Children shuttled about, or made conspiracies that broke up in shouts. But this vivid evening, no grown-up people walked fast: the park was full of straying fancies and leisure.

Thomas and Portia turned their alike profiles in the direction from which the breeze came. Portia thought how inland the air smelled. Looking unmoved up at the turquoise sky above the trees burning thinly yellow-green, Thomas said he felt the weather would change.

'I hope not before these tulips are out. These are the tulips father told me about.'

'Tulips – what do you mean? When did he see them?'

'The day he walked past your house.'

'Did he walk past our house? When?'

'One day, once. He said it had been painted; it looked like marble, he said. He was very glad you lived there.'

Thomas's face went slowly set and heavy, as though he felt the weight of his father's solitary years as well as his own. He looked at Portia, at their father's eyebrows marking, here, a more delicate line. His look made it clear he would not speak. Across the lake, only the parapet and the upper windows of Windsor Terrace showed over the trees: the silhouette of the stucco, now not newly painted, looked shabby and frail. 'We paint every four years,' he said.

In the traffic, half way across the road, Portia suddenly looked up at the drawing-room window, and waved. 'Look out!'

Thomas said sharply, gripping her elbow – a car swerved past them like a great fish. 'What's the matter?'

'There was Anna, up there. She's gone now.'

'If you don't take better care in the traffic, I don't think you ought to go out alone.'

2

HAVING been seen at the window, having been waved to, made Anna step back instinctively. She knew how foolish a person looking out of a window appears from the outside of a house – as though waiting for something that does not happen, as though wanting something from the outside world. A face at a window for no reason is a face that should have a thumb in its mouth: there is something only-childish about it. Or, if the face is not foolish it is threatening – blotted white by the darkness inside the room it suggests a malignant indoor power. Would Portia and Thomas think she had been spying on them?

Also, she had been seen holding a letter – not a letter that she had got today. It was to escape from thoughts out of the letter that she had gone to the window to look out. Now she went back to her *escritoire* which, in a shadowed corner of this large light room, was not suitable to write more than notes at. In the pigeonholes she kept her engagement pad, her account books; the drawers under the flap were useful because they locked. At present, a drawer stood open, showing packets of letters; and more letters, creased from folding, exhaling an old smell, lay about among slipped-off rubber bands. Hearing Thomas's latch-key, the hall door opening, Portia's confident voice, Anna swept the letters into the drawer quickly, then knelt down to lock everything up. But this sad little triumph of being ready in time came to nothing, for the two Quaynes went straight into the study; they did not come upstairs.

They did not come up to join her, though they knew where she was. Looking at the desk key on the palm of her hand,

Anna felt much more cut off from the letters: one kind of lone-liness hammers another in. Directly the two had gone out after tea, she had gone to this drawer with the clearly realized inten-tion of comparing the falseness of Pidgeon with the falseness of Eddie. There are phases in feeling that make the oddest be-haviour quite relevant. She had said what was quite true, at least of herself, when she had told St Quentin, last January, that ex-perience means nothing till it repeats itself. Everything in her life, she could see now, had taken the same turn – as for love, she often puzzled and puzzled, without ever allowing herself to be fully sad, as to what could be wrong with the formula. It does not work, she thought. At times there were the moments when she asked herself if she could have been in the wrong: she would almost rather think that. What she *thought* she regretted was her lack of guard, her wayward extravagance – but had she all the time been more guarded than she imagined, had she been deceitful, had she been seen through? For what had always hap-pened she could still not account. There seemed to be some way she did not know of by which people managed to understand each other.

All I said to Thomas was, to get off my quilt. After that he takes her for a walk in the park.

Ease and intelligence seemed to her to lead to a barren end. Thoughtfully, she put the key of the locked drawer into the inner pocket of her handbag, then snapped the bag shut. Any-body as superficially wounded, but at the same time as deeply nonplussed as Anna seems to themselves to be a forlorn hope. *This* is what one gets for being so nicely nonchalant, for saving people's faces, for not losing one's hair. She could not think why she fussed so much with this key, for the drawer held no secrets: Thomas knew everything. It was true, she had never shown him these letters; though he knew *what* had happened he did not know how, why. Supposing she were to throw this pack of letters at Portia, saying: 'This is what it all comes to, you little fool!'

At this point, Anna lighted a cigarette, sat down by her bag on the yellow sofa, and asked herself why she liked Portia so little. The *idea* of her never leaves me quiet, and by coming into this room she drives me on to the ice. Everything she does to me is unconscious: if it were conscious it would not hurt. She makes me feel like a tap that won't turn on. She crowds me into an unreal position, till even St Quentin asks why do I over-act? She has put me into a relation with Thomas that is no more than our taunting, feverish jokes. My only honest way left is to be harsh to them both, which I honestly am. This afternoon, directly she heard our taxi, she had to snatch open the door and wait for us, all eyes. I cannot even stand in my own window without her stopping to wave, among those cars. She might have been run over, which would have been shocking.

But, after all, death runs in that family. What is she, after all? The child of an aberration, the child of a panic, the child of an old chap's pitiful sexuality. Conceived among lost hairpins and snapshots of doggies in a Notting Hill Gate flatlet. At the same time she has inherited everything: she marches about this house like the Race itself. They rally as if she were the Young Pretender. Oh, I know Matchett's conspiratorial mouth. And it's too monstrous of Eddie; really it's so silly. As far as all *that's* concerned – well, Heaven help her: I don't see why I should.

Well, she'll never find any answer here, thought Anna, lying with her feet up on the sofa, unrestfully clasping her hands behind her head, asking herself what that brother and sister found to say to each other down there. It's no use her looking everywhere like that. Who are we to have her questions brought here?

Pulling the telephone towards her, Anna dialled St Quentin's number. She heard the bell ringing for some time – quite clearly St Quentin was out.

On Monday morning, Thomas went back to the office, Portia went back to her classes in Cavendish Square. Mild grey spring rain set in and shivered on the trees. Thomas, who liked to be right about small things, liked having foretold this change in the weather. The first week the tulips were out, no sun shone on them; they stood in their mauves, corals, and crimsons, fleshily damp, with no one by to see. No, this May afternoon was not like that May afternoon when old Mr Quayne had crept about in the park. Portia did not see Eddie till the end of that week, when she came in on Saturday afternoon to find him at tea with Anna. He seemed very much pleased, greatly surprised to see her, jumped up, smiled all over, took her hand, and exclaimed to Anna: 'Doesn't she look well, still!' He made her sit down where he had been sitting, while he sat on the arm of the chair. Meanwhile, Anna, with just the hint of a flicker, rang for another cup. Portia was in the wrong: she was not expected; she had said she would have tea with Lilian that afternoon. 'Do you know,' went on Eddie, 'it must be months since we have all three met?'

St Quentin, the previous Wednesday, had been more enthusiastic. Portia had met him walking briskly, aimlessly along Wigmore Street – black Homburg hat cocked forward, gloves tightly clasped in both hands behind his back. Half stopping now and then, and turning his whole body, he gave the luxury objects in dark polished windows glances of a distracted intensity. His behaviour was, somehow, not plausible: Portia felt uncertain, as she approached him, whether St Quentin really did not see her, or did see her and wished to show that he did not. She hesitated – ought she to cross the street? – but then made on down the pavement, swinging her dispatch case, like a too light little boat before a too strong wind: she could find no reason to stop. Something about her reflection in a window caught St Quentin's eye, and he turned round.

'Oh, hullo,' he said rapidly, 'hullo! So you're back, too: how nice! What are *you* doing?'

'Going home from lessons.'

'How lucky you are – I am not doing anything. That's to say, I am putting in time. Do you go down Mandeville Place? Shall we walk down Mandeville Place?'

So they turned the corner together. Portia shifted her dispatch case from one hand to the other and said: 'How is your new book?'

Instead of replying, St Quentin looked up at the windows. 'We'd better not talk too loud: this is full of nursing homes.

You know how the sick listen . . . Have you had a nice time?'
he continued, pitching his voice low.

'Yes, very,' she said almost down to a whisper. She had an
inner view of white high beds, fever charts, waxy flowers.

'I'm afraid I can't remember where you were.'

'At Seale. The seaside.'

'Delightful. How you must miss it. I wish I could go away. In
fact I think I shall; there is no reason why I shouldn't, but I'm
in such a neurotic state. Do tell me about something. How is
your diary?'

He saw Portia's face flash his way; she at once threw him a
look like a trapped, horrified bird's. They pulled up to let someone, stepping out of a taxi, cross the pavement and carry a sheaf
of flowers up the stark steps of a nursing home. When they
walked on again, St Quentin was once more up to anything,
while Portia looked ahead steadily, stonily, down the overcast
canyon of the street that was threatening in this sudden gloom
of spring. He said: 'That was just a shot in the dark. I feel certain you should keep a diary. I'm sure you have thoughts about
life.'

'No, I don't think much,' she said.

'My dear girl, that is hardly necessary. What I'm certain you
do have are reactions. And I wonder what those are, whenever I
look at you.'

'I don't know what they are. I mean, what are reactions?'

'Well, I could explain, but must I? You do have feelings, of
course?'

'Yes. Don't you?'

St Quentin bit at his upper lip moodily, making his moustache dip. 'No, not often; I mean, not really. They're not so
much fun for me. Now what can have made me think you kept
a diary? Now that I come to look at you, I don't think you'd be
so rash.'

'If I kept one, it would be a dead secret. Why should that be
rash?'

'It is madness to write things down.'

'But you write those books you write almost all day don't
you?'

'But what's in them never happened – It might have, but never did. And though what is felt in them is just possible – in fact, it's much more possible, in an unnerving way, than most people will admit – it's fairly improbable. So, you see, it's my game from the start. But I should never write what had happened down. One's nature is to forget, and one ought to go by that. Memory is quite unbearable enough, but even so it leaves out quite a lot. It wouldn't let one down as gently, even, as that if it weren't more than half a fake – we remember to suit ourselves. No, really, er, Portia, believe me: if one didn't let oneself swallow some few lies, I don't know how one would ever carry the past. Thank God, except at its one moment there's never any such thing as a bare fact. Ten minutes later, half an hour later, one's begun to gloze the fact over with a deposit of some sort. The hours I spent with thee dear love are like a string of pearls to me. But a diary (if one did keep it up to date) would come much too near the mark. One ought to secrete for some time before one begins to look back at anything. Look how reconciled to everything reminiscences are ... Also, suppose somebody read it?'

This made Portia miss one step, shift her grip on her case. She glanced at St Quentin's rather sharklike profile, glanced away, and stayed silent – so tensely silent that he peered round for another look at her.

'I should lock it up,' he said. 'I should trust no one an inch.'

'But I lost the key.'

'Oh, you did? Look here, do let's get this straight: weren't we talking about a hypothetical diary?'

'Mine's just a diary,' she said helplessly.

St Quentin coughed, with just a touch of remorse. 'I'm so sorry,' he said. 'I've been too smart again. But that does me no good, in the long run.'

'I'd rather not have it known. It is simply a thing of mine.'

'No, that's where you're wrong. Nothing like that stops with oneself. You do a most dangerous thing. All the time, you go making connexions – and that can be a vice.'

'I don't know what you mean.'

'You're working on us, making us into something. Which is not fair – we are not on our guard with you. For instance, now I know you keep this book, I shall always feel involved in some sort of plan. You precipitate things. I daresay', said St Quentin kindly, 'that what you write is quite silly, but all the same, you are taking a liberty. You set traps for us. You ruin our free will.'

'I write what has happened. I don't invent.'

'You put constructions on things. You are a most dangerous girl.'

'No one knows what I do.'

'Oh, but believe me, we feel it. You must see how rattled we are now.'

'I don't know what you *were* like.'

'Neither did we: we got on quite well then. What is unfair is, that you hide. God's spy, and so on. Another offence is, you have a loving nature; you are the loving nature *in vacuo*. You must not mind my saying all this. After all, you and I don't live in the same house; we seldom meet and you seldom affect me. All the same –'

'Are you teasing me now, or were you teasing me before? You must have been teasing one or the other time. First you said you felt sure I kept a diary, then you told me I mustn't, then you asked where it was, then you pretended to be surprised when you knew there was one, after that you called me an unkind spy, now you say I love everyone too much. I see now you knew about my diary . . . *I suppose Anna found it and told you*? Did she?'

St Quentin glanced at Portia from the tail of his eye. 'I don't come out of this well,' he said.

'But did she?'

'I am perfectly able to tell a lie, but my trouble is that I have no loyalty. Yes, Anna did, as a matter of fact. Now what a fuss this will make. Now, can I trust your discretion? You see that nobody can rely on mine.'

Pushing her hat brim further back from her forehead, Portia turned and sized St Quentin up boldly. She believed he had a malignant conscience; she did not feel he was really indiscreet. 'You mean,' she said, 'not tell Anna you told me?'

'I would as soon you didn't,' said St Quentin humbly. 'Avoid scenes; in future keep an eye on your little desk.'

'She told you I had a little desk?'

'I supposed you would have one.'

'Has she often —?'

St Quentin rolled his eyes up. 'Not so far as I know. Don't be at all worried. Just find some new place to keep your book. What I have always found is, anything one keeps hidden should now and then be hidden somewhere else.'

'Thank you,' said Portia, dazed. 'It is very kind of you.' She was incapable of anything past this: her feet kept walking her on inexorably. The conversation had ended in an abyss – impossible to pretend that it had not. Like all shocked people, she did not see where she was – they were well down Marylebone High Street, among the shoppers – from the depth of her eyes she threw wary, unhuman looks at faces that swam towards her, faces looking her way. She was aware of St Quentin's presence only as the cause of her wish to run down a side street. They had been walking fast, in this dreadful dream, for some time, when he cried loudly: 'These *lacunae* in people!'

'What did you say?'

'You don't *ask* what made me do that – you don't even ask yourself.'

She said, 'You were very kind.'

'The most unlikely things one does, the most utterly out of character, arouse no curiosity, even in one's friends. One can suffer a convulsion of one's entire nature, and, unless it makes some noise, no one notices. It's not just that we are incurious; we completely lack any sense of each other's existences. Even you, with that loving nature you have – In a small way I have just ratted on Anna, I have done something she'd never forgive me for, and you, Portia, you don't even ask why. Consciously, and as far as I can see quite gratuitously, I have started what may make a frightful breach. In me, this is utterly out of character: I'm not a mischievous man; I haven't got time; I'm not interested enough. You're not even listening, are you?'

'I'm sorry, I –'

'I've no doubt you're upset. So you and I might be at different

251

ends of the world. Stop thinking about your diary and your Anna and listen to me – and don't flinch at me, Portia, as though I were an electric drill. You ought to want some key to why people do what they do. You think us all wicked –'

'I don't, I –'

'It's not so simple as that. What makes you think us wicked is simply our little way of keeping ourselves going. We must live, though you may not see the necessity. In the long run, we may not work out well. We attempt, however, to be more civil and kindly than we feel. The fact is, we have no great wish for each other – no spontaneous wish for each other, that is to say. This lack of *gout* makes us have to behave with a certain amount of policy. Because I quite like Anna, I overlook much in her, and because she quite likes me she overlooks much in me. We laugh at each other's jokes and we save each other's faces – When I give her away to you, I break an accepted rule. This is not often done. It takes people in a lasting state of hysteria, like your friend Eddie, for instance, or people who feel they have some higher authority (as I've no doubt Eddie feels he has) to break every rule every time. To keep any rule would be an event for him : when he breaks one more rule it is hardly interesting – at least, not to me. I simply cannot account for his fascination for Anna –'

'Does he fascinate Anna?'

'Oh, palpably, don't you think? I suppose the deduction is that she really must have a conventional mind. And, of course he has some pretty ways – No, with me there has to be quite a brainstorm before I break any rule, before speaking the truth. Love, drink, anger – something crumbles the whole scene : at once one is in a fantastic universe. Its unseemliness and its glory are indescribable, really. One becomes a Colossus . . . I still don't know, all the same, what made that happen just now. It must be this close spring weather. It's religious weather, I think.'

'You think she's told Eddie about my diary, then?'

'My dear, don't ask me what they talk about – Why turn down here?'

'I always go through this graveyard.'

'The futility of explaining – this is telling you nothing. Some day, you may hear from somebody else that I was an important man, then you'll rack your brains to remember what I once said. Where shall you live next?'

'I don't know. With my aunt.'

'Oh, you won't hear of me *there*.'

'I think I am to go and be with my aunt, when I'm not with Thomas and Anna any more.'

'Well, with your aunt you may have time to be sorry. No, I am being unfair to you. I should never talk like this if you weren't such a little stone.'

'It is what you've told me.'

'Naturally, naturally. Do you like to walk through the grave-yard? And why has it got a bandstand in the middle? As you're quite near home, do something about your face.'

'I don't have any powder.'

'I'm not really sorry that this has happened: it was bound to happen sooner or later – No, I don't mean powder: I just mean your expression. One thing one must learn is, how to confront people that at that particular moment one cannot bear to meet.'

'Anna's out to tea.'

'If we had not said all this, I'd get you to have tea with me in a shop. But anyhow, I'm due somewhere at a quarter to five. I think I ought to go back now. I suppose you're sorry we met?'

'I suppose it's better to know.'

'No, truly it is not. In fact I've done something to you I could not bear to have done to myself. And the terrible thing is, I am feeling the better for it. Well, good-bye,' said St Quentin, stopping on the asphalt path in the graveyard, among the tombs and the willows, taking off his hat.

'Good-bye, Mr Miller. Thank you.'

'Oh, I shouldn't say that.'

That had been on Wednesday. This Saturday, Portia soon moved out of Eddie's chair, which he slipped gladly back to, to take her accustomed place on the stool near the fire. A pallid flare and a rustling rose from the logs; the windows framed panoramas of wet trees; the room looked high and faint in rainy afternoon light. Between Portia and Anna extended the still life of the tea-tray. On her knees, pressed together, Portia kept balanced the plate on which a rock-cake slid. Beginning to nibble at the rock-cake, she sat watching Anna at tea with Eddie, as she had watched her at tea with other intimate guests.

By coming in, however, she had brought whatever there was to a nonplussed pause. The fact that they let her see such a pause happen made her the accessory she hardly wanted to be. Eddie propped an elbow on the wing of his chair, leaned a temple on a palm, and looked into the fire. His eyes flickered up and down with the point of flickering flame. Desultorily, and for his private pleasure, he began to make mouths like a fish – curling his lower lip out, sucking it in again. Anna, using her thumb-nail, slit open a new box of cigarettes, then packed her tortoise-shell case with them. Portia finished her cake, approached the tray, and helped herself to another – taking his eyes from the fire for one moment, Eddie accorded her one irresponsible smile. 'When do we go for another walk?' he said.

Anna said: 'Are you ready for more tea?'

'A fortnight ago,' said Portia, for no reason, going back for her cup, 'I was having tea at Seale golf club with Dickie Heccomb and Clara – a girl there that he sometimes plays golf with.'

Anna ducked in her chin and smiled vaguely and nodded. Absently, she said, 'Was that fun?'

'Yes, the gorse was out.'

'Yes, Seale must have been fun.'

'There's a picture of you there, in my room.'

'A photograph?'

'No, a picture holding a kitten.'

Anna put her hand to her head. 'Kitten?' she said. 'What do you mean, Portia?'

'A black kitten.'

Anna thought back. 'Oh, that black kitten. Poor little thing, it died . . . You mean, when I was a child?'

'Yes, you had long hair.'

'A chalk drawing. Oh, is that in her spare room? But who is Clara? Tell me about her.'

Portia did not know how to begin – she glanced at Eddie. He came to himself and said with the greatest ease: 'Clara? Clara's position was uncertain. She was hardly in the set. All the same, she haunts me – perhaps because of that. She spends ever so much money hoping to marry Dickie – Dickie Heccomb, you know. Besides money, she keeps inside her handbag a sort of mouse's nest that she dives into whenever things get too difficult. Doesn't she, Portia? We saw Clara do that.'

Anna said: 'I wish I could.'

'Oh, you would never need to, Anna darling ... Well, we made Clara pop into her handbag that night at the E.C.P. When we all behaved so badly. I was the worst, of course. It was really dreadful, Anna: Portia and I had been for a nice walk in some woods, then I ruined the day by getting tight and rowdy. I had made a fine impression when I first got to Waikiki, but I'm afraid that spoiled it.' Eddie gave Portia an equivocal sidelong look, then turned his head and went on talking to Anna. 'Clara's position was really trying, you see: she had eyes only for Dickie, and Dickie had eyes only for Portia here.'

She made a dumbfounded movement. 'Oh, Eddie, he *hadn't*!'

'Well, there were goings-on – they were perfectly one-sided, but there were goings-on as far as Dickie does go. I heard him breathing over you at the movies. He breathed so much that he even breathed over me.'

'Eddie,' Anna said, 'you really are very common.' She looked remotely, sternly down at her finger-nails, but after a minute could not help saying: 'Did you all go to the movies? When?'

'That first evening I got there,' Eddie said fluently. 'Six of us. All the set. I must say, I really was shocked by Dickie: not only is he an old Fascist, but he does not know how to behave at all. At the seaside, they really do go the pace.'

'How dreadful for you,' said Anna. 'And so, what did you do?'

'It was in the dark, so I could not show how I felt. Besides, his sister was holding my hand. They really are a fast lot – I do think, Anna, you ought to be more careful where you send Portia off to another time.'

This did not go down well. 'Portia knows how to behave,' said Anna frigidly. 'Which makes more difference than you would ever think.' She gave Portia what could have been a

kindly look had there been the least intention behind it. To
Eddie she said, with enraged softness: 'For anybody as clever
as you are, you are really not good at describing things. To
begin with, I don't think you ever know what is happening:
you are too busy wondering what you can make of it.'

Eddie pouted and said: 'Very well, ask Portia, then.'

But Portia looked down and said nothing.

'Anyhow,' Eddie said, 'it has been an effort to talk, when I
don't feel in the mood to. But one has got to be so amusing here.
I'm sorry you don't like what I say, but I have been more or
less talking in my sleep.'

'If you are so sleepy, you had better go home.'

'I can't see why the idea of sleep should offend you as much
as it seems to, Anna. It is the natural thing on a rainy spring
afternoon, when one's not compelled to be doing anything else,
especially in a nice quiet room like this. We ought all to sleep,
instead of talking away.'

'Portia has not said much,' said Anna, looking across the fire.

At the very sound, on Eddie's lips, of the word, desire to sleep
had spread open inside Portia like a fan. She saw reflections of
rain on the silver things on the tray. She felt blotted out from
the room, as little present in it as these two others truly felt her
to be. She moved a little nearer the fireplace, so as to lean her
cheek on the marble upright, with as little consciousness of her
movement as though she had been alone in some other place.
Behind shut eyes she relaxed; she refreshed herself. The rug
under her feet slid and wrinkled a little on the polished floor;
the room, with its image of cruelty, swam, shredded, and slowly
lost its colour, like a paper pattern in water.

Since the talk with St Quentin, the idea of betrayal had been
in her, upon her, sleeping and waking, as might be one's own
guilt, making her not confront any face with candour, making
her dread Eddie. Being able to shut her eyes while he was in
this room with her, to feel impassive marble against her cheek,
made her feel in the arms of immunity – the immunity of sleep,
of anaesthesia, of endless solitude, the immunity of the journey
across Switzerland two days after her mother died. She saw that
tree she saw when the train stopped for no reason; she saw in

her nerves, equally near and distant, the wet trees out there in the park. She heard the Seale sea, then heard the silent distances of the coast.

There was a pause in the drawing-room. Then Anna said: 'I wish I could just do that; I wish I were sixteen.'

Eddie said: 'She looks sweet, doesn't she?' At some later time, he came softly across to touch Portia's cheek with his finger, to which Anna, though still there, did not say anything.

3

'REALLY, Anna, things *have* gone too far!' Eddie, out of the blue, burst out on the telephone. 'Portia has just rung me up to say you've been reading her diary. And I could say nothing – someone was in the office.'

'Are you on the office telephone now?'

'Yes, but it's lunch time.'

'Yes, I know it is lunch time. Major Brutt and two other people are here. You are ruthlessly inconsiderate.'

'How was I to know? I thought you might think this urgent. I do. Are they in the room?'

'Naturally.'

'Well, good-bye. *Bon appétit*,' added Eddie, in a loud bitter tone. He hung up just before Anna, who returned to the table. The three guests, having heard in her voice that note of lover-like crossness, tried not to look askance: they were all three rather naïve. Mr and Mrs Peppingham, from Shropshire, had this Monday been asked to lunch because they were known to have a neighbour in Shropshire who was known to be looking for an agent, and it seemed just possible Major Brutt might do. But during lunch it became clearer and clearer that he was only impressing the Peppinghams as being the sort of thoroughly decent fellow who never, for some reason, gets on in the world. Tough luck, but there you are. He was showing a sort of amiable cussedness; he ignored every hoop that Anna held out for him.

The Peppinghams clearly thought that though no doubt he had done well in the War, he had not, on the whole, been unlucky in having *had* the War to do well in. It became useless for Anna to draw him out, to repeat that he had grown rubber, that he had had – for he had had, hadn't he? – the management of a quite large estate. In Malay, of course, but the great thing was – wasn't it? – to know how to manage men.

'Yes, that is certainly so,' agreed Mr Peppingham, safely.

Mrs Peppingham said: 'With all these social changes, I sometimes fear that's a lost art – managing men, I mean. I always feel that people work twice as well if they feel they've got someone to look up to.' She flushed up the side of her neck with moral conviction and said firmly: 'I'm quite sure that is true.' Anna thought: These days, there's something dreadful about talk; people's convictions keep bobbing to the surface, making them flush. I'm sure it was better when people connected everything of that sort with religion, and did not talk about religion at meals. She said: 'I expect one thinks about that in the country more. That is the worst of London: one never thinks.'

'My dear lady,' said Mr Peppingham, 'thinking or not thinking, there are some things that you cannot fail to notice. Destroy tradition, and you destroy the sense of responsibility.'

'Surely, for instance, in your husband's office –' Mrs Peppingham said.

'I never go to the office. I don't think Thomas inspires hero worship, if that's what you mean. No, I don't think he'd know what to do with that.'

'Oh, I don't mean hero worship. I'm afraid that only leads to dictators, doesn't it? No, what I mean', said Mrs Peppingham, touching her pearls with a shy but firm smile and flushing slightly again, 'is *instinctive* respect. That means so much to the people working for us.'

'Do you think one really inspires that?'

'One tries to,' said Mrs Peppingham, not looking very pleased.

'It seems so sad to have to try to. I should so much rather just pay people, and leave it at that.'

Phyllis inhibited Mrs Peppingham from any further talk about class by firmly handing the orange *soufflé* round. PAS

AVANT LES DOMESTIQUES might have been carved on the Peppinghams' dining-room mantelpiece, under HONI SOIT QUI MAL Y PENSE. Mrs Peppingham helped herself and, with a glance at Phyllis's cuff, was silent. Anna, plunging the spoon and fork into the *soufflé* with that frank greed one shows in one's own house when there is enough of everything, said: 'Besides, I thought you said that it was instinctive. Whose instincts do you mean?'

'Respect's a broad human instinct,' said Mr Peppingham, letting one eye wander to meet the *soufflé*.

'Oh yes. But do you think it is still?'

The two Peppinghams' eyes, for less than a second, met. They share the same ideals, thought Anna. Do I and Thomas? Perhaps, but what ever are they? I do wish Major Brutt would say something or contradict me: the Peppinghams will start thinking *he* is a Red. What a misleading reputation my house has – the Peppinghams must have come here for Interesting Talk, because they feel they don't get enough of that in Shropshire. The yearnings of the County are appalling. They forget Major Brutt has come here to get a job; they probably are offended at meeting only him. If I had asked an author, which they must have expected, things could not be more hopeless than they are now, and it might have put the Peppinghams into a better mood – besides showing Major Brutt up as the practical man. I thought that my *beaux yeux* should be enough to send Major Brutt and the Peppinghams into each other's arms. But these Peppinghams are not nice enough to be flattered. No, they are full of designing hardness; all they think is that I'm making use of them. Which I would do if I could, but they are impossible. They despise Major Brutt for being nicer than they are and for not having made good in their line. If he would only flush and argue, instead of just sitting. Oh dear, oh dear, I shall never sell him at all.

'You disapprove of my ideas, don't you?' she threw out to Major Brutt with a frantic summoning smile.

But he only crumbled his bread and quietly ate the crumbs. 'Oh, I don't think I'd venture to. Not wholesale. I don't doubt for a moment there's a great deal in what you say.' Looking kindly at her with his straight grey eyes, he added: 'One reason I should like to settle down is that then I might begin to think things out for myself. Not knowing exactly what may turn up is inclined to make one a bit unsettled, and often when I've intended to have a think – for after all, I've got a bit of time on my hands – I find I am not in form, so I don't get much thinking done. Meanwhile, it's a treat to listen to a discussion, though I don't feel qualified to shove my oar in.'

'My only quarrel with this charming lady', said Mr Peppingham (who was becoming odious), 'is that she will not tell us what her ideas *are*.'

Anna (now throwing up the sponge completely) replied: 'I could if I knew what we were talking *about*.'

Mr Peppingham, tolerant, turned to dig in the cheese. Anna wanted to reach along the table, grip Major Brutt's hand and say: No good. I've drawn you another blank. I've failed to sell you and, to be perfectly honest, you really don't do much to sell yourself. No good, no good, no good – we can't do any more here. Back with you to *The Times* advertisement columns, and the off-chance of running into a man who has just run into a man who could put you on to a thing. You ran into us. Well, that hasn't got you far. Better luck next time, old boy. *Je n'en peux plus*.

In fact, he constituted – today, by so mildly accepting, with his coffee, that there would be nothing more doing about this Shropshire thing, and at all times by the trustfulness of his frequentation of the Quaynes as a family – the same standing, or, better still, undermining reproach as Portia. He was not near enough their hearth, or long enough at it, to take back to Kensington with him any suspicion that the warmth he had found could be illusory. His unfulfilled wishes continued to flock and settle where the Quaynes were, and no doubt he thought of them in the lounge of his hotel, or walking along the Cromwell Road. No doubt he stayed himself on the idea of them when one more thing fell through, when something else came to nothing, when one more of his hopeful letters was unanswered, when yet another iron went stone cold, when he faced that the money was running out. He gave signs that he constantly thought of them. Does it make one more nearly good and happy to be thought good and happy? The policy of pity might keep Anna from ever pointblank disappointing him. He was the appendix to the finished story of Robert. Useless, useless to wish they had never met – they had been bound to, apparently. In a sort of sense, Major Brutt had been legated to her by Robert. Or, was it that she felt she found in him the last of Robert's hurting, hurting because never completely bitter, jokes – one of those hurting exposures of her limitations, to obtain which he seemed able to hire fate?

Major Brutt outstayed the Peppinghams – thus giving her no chance to sing his merits in private, to say that whoever got him would be lucky, or to repeat that he was a D.S.O. Ready to say good-bye after a few minutes, he stood up and looked round the drawing-room.

'Those were lovely carnations you sent me the other day. I got Portia to send you a line because I was tired, and because I hoped I should see you soon. You know how one feels when one gets back. But that makes it all the nicer to find flowers.'

He beamed. 'Oh, good,' he said. 'If they cheered you up –'

Some obscure wish to bestir herself, to be human, made her say:

'You did not, I suppose, hear any more of Pidgeon since we've been away?'

'Now it's funny your asking that –'

'Funny?' said Anna.

'Not that I heard *from* him – that's the devil, you know, about not having a fixed address. People soon give up buzzing letters along. Of course, I've got an address, at this hotel, but when I write from there it never looks permanent. People take it you'll have moved on – at least, so I find. But if I'd had an address I might not have heard from Pidgeon. He never was one to write.'

'No, he never was – But what were you going to say?'

'Oh yes. Now that really was very funny. It's the sort of thing that's always happening to me. About a fortnight ago, I missed Pidgeon by about three minutes – literally, by just about that. A most extraordinary thing – I mean, only missing him by about an inch when I didn't know he was in the country at all.'

'Tell me about it.'

'Well, I happened to go into a fellow's club – with the fellow, I mean – and run into another fellow (I hadn't seen him for years, either) who'd been talking to Pidgeon about three minutes ago. Talking to Pidgeon in that very club. "By Jove," I said, "that's funny. Is he in the club still?" But the other fellow said not. He said he'd gone. I said, which way did he go? – having some idea that I might make after him – but the other fellow of course had no idea. It seemed to me an amazing coincidence and I made up my mind I must tell you about it. If I had got there three minutes earlier ... It's simply chance, after all. You can't foresee anything. Look, for instance, how I ran into you. In a book, that would sound quite improbable.'

'Well, it was improbable, really. *I* never run into people.'

Major Brutt drove his hands down slowly into his pockets, considering something rather uncertainly. He said: 'And of course, that week you were abroad.'

'Which week?'

'The week I just missed Pidgeon.'

'Oh yes, I was abroad. You – you heard no more? He's not in London still?'

'That I can't tell; I wish I could. It's the very devil. He might be anywhere. But this other fellow seemed to get the idea that Pidgeon was just off somewhere – "on the wing", as we always used to say. He's generally just off somewhere. He never liked London much.'

'No, he never liked London much.'

'And yet, do you know, though I cursed missing him, it seemed better than nothing. When he's once turned up, he may turn up again.'

'Yes, I do hope he'll turn up – But not where I ever am.'

Fatalistically, she faced having got this out at last. She looked at herself in the glass with enormous calm. Major Brutt, meanwhile, turning his shoulder against the mantelpiece, investigated a boat-shaped glass of roses, whose scent had disturbed him for some time. Reverently, with the tip of a finger, he jabbed at the softness of the crimson petals, then bent over to sniff exhaustively. This rather stagy, for him rather conscious, action showed he knew he stood where she might not wish him to stand – outside a shut door, a forgotten messenger for whom there might be an answer and might not. Perplexity, reverence, readiness to be sad or reliable showed in every line of his attitude. He would be glad to move, if she gave him the word. It was not his habit to take notice of flowers, or of any small object in a room, and by giving the roses such undue attention, he placed himself in an uneasy relation to them. He jabbed once more and said: 'Do these come from the country?'

'Yes. And your nice carnations have just died.'

Or was it likely he could be missing a cue, that Anna might have created this special moment in which it was his business to ask bluntly: Look here, just what *did* happen? Where's the whole thing gone to? Why are you not Mrs Pidgeon? You are still you, and he still sounds like himself. You both being you was once all right with you both. You are still you – what has gone wrong since?

He looked at her – and the delicate situation made his eye as nearly shifty as it could ever be. He looked, and found her not looking at him. Instead, she took a handkerchief from her bag and blew the tip of her nose in a rapid, businesslike way. If she ever did seem to deliberate, it was while she put away the handkerchief. She said: 'I should not be such a monster if Pidgeon had not put the idea into my head.'

'My dear girl –'

'Yes, I must be; everyone thinks I am. That horrid little Eddie rang me up at lunch to tell me I was unkind to Portia.'

'Good heavens?'

'You don't really like Eddie, do you?'

'Well, he's not much my sort. But look here, I mean to say –'

'Robert thought nothing of me,' said Anna laughing. 'Did you not know that? He thought nothing of me at all. Nothing really happened; I did not break his heart. Under the circumstances – you see now what they were, don't you? – we could hardly marry, as you must surely see.'

He mumbled: 'I expect it all turned out for the best.'

'Of course,' said Anna, smiling again.

He said quickly: 'Of course,' looking round the handsome room.

'But how I do skip from one thing to another,' she went on, with the greatest ease in the world. 'The past is never really the thing that matters – I just thought I'd clear that up about Robert and me. No, if I do seem a little rattled today, it is from being rung up in the middle of lunch and told by a stray young man that Portia is not happy. What am I to do? You know how quiet she is; things must have gone really rather a long way for her to complain to an outside person like that. Though, of course, Eddie is very inquisitive.'

'If I may be allowed to say so,' said Major Brutt, 'it sounds to me the most unheard of, infernal cheek on his part. And that is to put it mildly. I must say I really never –'

'He always is cheeky, the little bastard,' she said, reflectively tapping the mantelpiece. 'But it is Portia that I'm worried about. It all sounds so unlike her. Major Brutt, you know us fairly well as a family: do you think Portia's happy?'

'Allowing, poor kid, for having just lost her mother, it never struck me she could be anything else. She seemed to fit in as though she'd been born here. As girls go, she has quite the ideal life.'

'Or is that the nice way you see things? We do give her more freedom than most girls of sixteen, but she seemed old enough for it: she took care of her mother. But I see now that a girl has to be older before she can choose her friends – especially young men.'

'You mean, there's been a bit too much of *that* little chap?'

'It looks rather like that now. Of course, I blame myself rather. He has always been a good deal at this house – he's lonely, and we've tried to be nice to him. Except for that, I do think during the winter Portia got on very happily here. She seemed to be settling down. Then, as you know, she went away to the seaside, and I'm afraid some trouble may have begun there. My old governess is an angel, but I'm afraid her step-children are not up to much, and they may have upset Portia. She has not been quite the same since she came home. Even our old housemaid notices it. She isn't nearly so shy, but at the same time she is less spontaneous. No, I suppose we were wrong in ever making that break – in going away, I mean – while she was settling down with us. That came too soon; it unsettled her; it *was* silly. But Thomas really needed a holiday; he's had a fairly hard winter in the office.'

'She's such a dear girl. She *is* a sweet little kid.'

'If you were me, then, you'd just tell Eddie to go to the devil?'

'Well, more or less – Yes, I certainly would.'

'And just have a word with Portia?'

'I'm sure *you* could manage that.'

'Do you know, Major Brutt, I'm most stupidly shy?'

'I feel certain', he said with vigour, 'she'd be most upset if she thought she's upset you. I'd be ready to swear she hasn't the least idea.'

'She hasn't any idea how Eddie talks,' Anna said with a sharpness she simply couldn't control. 'Major Brutt, this has been a wretched afternoon for you: first those dreadful people at lunch, and now my family worries. But it cheers me up to feel you feel Portia's happy. You must come back soon and we'll have a much nicer time. You will come again soon?'

'There's nothing I'd like better. Of course, as you know, my plans are rather unsettled still. I shall have to take up whatever may come along, and the Lord only knows where that might involve being sent.'

'Not right away, I do hope. I am so glad, at any rate, that you're not going to Shropshire. Thomas and I were mad to consider that idea; I see now that it would not have done at all. Well, thank you for listening: you have been an angel. It's fatal', she concluded, holding her hand out, 'to be such a good friend to a selfish woman like me.' With her hand in his, being wrung, she went on smiling, then not only smiled but laughed, looking out of the window as though she saw something funny in the park.

Upon which he took his leave. She, not giving herself a moment, sat down to dash off that little letter to Eddie.

Dear Eddie: Of course I could not say so at lunch but I should, if I were you, be rather more careful about using the office telephone. It must be hard to know when is the once too often, but I'm afraid the once too often may have been passed. The fact is, I hear that Thomas and Mr Merrett are going to have a drive about all these personal calls that get put through and taken. The girl at the switchboard must have ratted, or something. You must not think this unkind of Thomas and Mr Merrett; they seem to feel it is a matter of principle. Even though you are getting on so well at the office, I should be a little careful, just for a week or two. I feel it is more considerate to tell you: you know I do want you to get on well.

However much your friends may have to say to you, I should ask them to wait till you get back to your room. And if I were you I should ring them up from there. I'm afraid this may send up your telephone bill, but that seems a thing that simply cannot be helped.   Yours,

                                                                ANNA

When Anna had written this, she glanced at the clock. If she were to send this to post now, it could only reach Eddie tomorrow morning. But if it went round by special messenger, he would find it when he came in, late. That is the hour when letters make most impression. So Anna rang up for a special messenger.

At half past four, that same Monday afternoon, Lilian and Portia came up Miss Paullie's area steps into Cavendish Square. Lilian had taken some time washing her wrists, for her new bangles, though showy, left marks on them. So these two were the last of a long straggle of girls. After the silence of the classroom, the square seemed to be drumming with hot sound; the high irregular buildings with their polished windows stood glaring in afternoon light. The trees in the middle tossed in a draught that went creeping round the square, turning the pale undersides of their leaves up. Coming out from lessons, the girls stepped into an impermeable stone world that the melting season could not penetrate – though seeing the branches in metallic sunlight they felt some forgotten spring had once left its mark there.

Lilian cast a look at those voluptuous plaits that hung over her shoulders, down her bosom. Then she said: 'Where are you going now?'

'I told you: I am meeting someone at six.'

'That's what I mean – six is not now, you silly. I mean, are you going home for tea, or what?'

Very nervous, Portia said: 'I'm not going home.'

'Then look, we might have tea in a shop. I think some tea might be good for your nerves.'

'You really are being very kind, Lilian.'

'Of course, I can see you are upset. I know myself what that is, only too well.'

'But I've only got sixpence.'

'Oh, I've got three shillings. After what I've been through myself,' said Lilian, guiding Portia down the side of the square, 'I don't think you ever ought to be shy of me. And you can keep my handkerchief till this evening, in case you need it again when you meet whoever it is, but please let me have it back tomorrow; don't let them wash it, because it is one with associations.'

'You are being kind.'

'I go right off my food when I am upset; if I try to eat I simply vomit at once. I thought at lunch, you're lucky not to be like that, because of course it attracts attention. It was a pity you had attracted attention by being caught using Miss Paullie's telephone. I must say, I should never dare do that. She was perfectly beastly, I suppose?'

'She was scornful of me,' said Portia: her lip trembled again. 'She has always thought I was awful since last term, when she found me reading that letter I once got. She makes me feel it's the way I was brought up.'

'She is just at the age when women go queer, you know. *Where* did you say you had got to meet your friend?'

'Near the Strand.'

'Oh, quite near your brother's office?' said Lilian, giving Portia a look from her large near-in gelatinous dark grey eyes. 'I do think, Portia, you ought to be careful: an untrustworthy man can simply ruin one's life.'

'If there wasn't *something* one could trust a person about, surely one wouldn't start to like them at all?'

'I don't see the point of our being such bosom friends if you don't confess to me that this is really Eddie.'

'Yes, but I'm not upset because of him; I'm upset about something that's gone on.'

'Something at home?'

'Yes.'

'Do you mean your sister-in-law? I always did think she was a dangerous woman, though I did not like to tell you so at the time. Look, don't tell me about this in Regent Street, because people are looking at us already. We will go to that A.B.C. opposite the Polytechnic; we are less likely to be recognized there. I think it's safer than Fuller's. Try and be calm, Portia.'

Actually, it was Lilian who commanded attention by looking sternly into every face. Beside her goddess-like friend, Portia walked with her head down, butting against the draughty air of the street. When they came to the crossing, Lilian gripped Portia's bare arm in a gloved hand: through the kid glove a sedative animal feeling went up to Portia's elbow and made the joint untense. She pulled back to notice a wedding carpet up the steps of All Souls', Langham Place — like a girl who has finished the convulsions of drowning she floated, dead, to the sunny surface again. She bobbed in Lilian's wake between the buses with the gaseous lightness of a little corpse.

'Though you are able to eat,' said Lilian, propping her elbows on the marble-topped table and pulling off her gloves by the finger-tips (Lilian never uncovered any part of her person without a degree of consciousness: there was a little drama when she untied a scarf or took off her hat), 'though you are able to eat, I should not try anything rich.' She caught a waitress's eye and ordered what she thought right. 'Look what a far-off table I got,' she said. 'You need not be afraid of saying anything now. I say, why don't you take off your hat, instead of keeping on pushing it back?'

'Oh Lilian, I haven't really got much to tell you, you know.'

'Don't be so humble, my dear; you told me there was a plot.'

'All I meant was, they have been laughing at me.'

'What made them laugh?'

'They have been telling each other.'

'Do you mean Eddie, too?'

Portia only gave Lilian an on-the-run look. Obedient slowly, she took off the ingenuous little hat that Anna thought suitable for her years, and put the hat placatingly down between them. 'The other day,' she said, 'that day we couldn't walk home together, I ran into Mr St Quentin Miller – I don't think I told you? – and he very nearly gave me tea in a shop.'

Lilian poured out, reproachful. 'It does no good', she said, 'to keep on going off like that. You are only pleased you nearly had tea with St Quentin because he is an author. But you don't love him, do you?'

'Eddie *has* been an author, if it comes to that.'

'I don't suppose St Quentin's half so mean as Eddie, laughing at you with your sister-in-law.'

'*Oh*, I didn't say that! I never did!'

'Then what's the reason you're so mad with her? You said you didn't want to go home.'

'She's read my diary.'

'But good gracious, Portia. I *never* knew you ever –'

'You see, I never did tell a soul.'

'You are a dark horse, I must say. But then, how did *she* know?'

'I never did tell a soul.'

'You swear you never did?'

'Well, I never did tell a single soul but Eddie. . . .'

Lilian shrugged her shoulders, raised her eyebrows, and poured more hot water into the teapot with an expression Portia dared not read.

'We-ell,' she said, 'well, good gracious, what *more* do you want? There you are – that's just what I mean, you see! Of course I call that a plot.'

'I didn't mean him. I don't mean a plot like that.'

'Look, eat some of that plain cake; you ought to eat if you can. Besides, I'm afraid people will look at us. You know, I don't think you're fit to go all the way down the Strand. If you didn't eat any cake, we could afford a taxi. I shall go with you, Portia: I don't mind, really. I think he ought to see you have got a friend.'

'Oh, he *is* a friend. He is my friend all the time.'

'And I shall wait, too,' Lilian went on, 'in case you should be too much upset.'

'You are being so kind – but I'd rather go alone.'

There is no doubt that sorrow brings one down in the world. The aristocratic privilege of silence belongs, you soon find out, to only the happy state – or, at least, to the state when pain keeps within bounds. With its accession to full power, feeling becomes subversive and violent: the proud part of the nature is battered down. Then, those people who flock to the scenes of accidents, who love most of all to dwell on deaths or childbirths or on the sick-bed from which restraint has gone smell what is in the air and are on the spot at once, pressing close with a sort of charnel good will. You may first learn you are doomed by seeing those vultures in the sky. Yet perhaps they are not vultures; they are Elijah's ravens. They bring with them the sense that the most individual sorrow has a stupefying universality. In them, human nature makes felt its clumsy wisdom, its efficacy, its infallible ready reckoning, its low level from which there is no further drop. Accidents become human property : only a muffish dread of living, a dread of the universal in our natures, makes us make these claims for 'the privacy of grief'. In naïver, humbler, nobler societies, the sufferer becomes public property; the scene of any disaster soon loses its isolated flush. The proper comment on grief, the comment that returns it to poetry, comes not in the right word, the faultless perceptive silence, but from the chorus of vulgar unsought friends – friends who are strangers to the taste and the mind.

In fact, there is no consoler, no confidant that half the instinct does not want to reject. The spilling over, the burst of tears and words, the ejaculation of the private personal grief accomplishes itself, like a convulsion, in circumstances that one would never choose. Confidants *in extremis* – with their genius for being present, their power to bring the clearing convulsions on – are, exceedingly often if not always, idle, morbid, trivial, or adolescent people, or people who feel a vacuum they are eager to fill. Not to these would one show, in happier moments, some secret spring of one's nature, the pride of love, the ambition, the sustaining hope: one could share with them no delicate pleasure in living: they are people who make discussion impossible. Their brutalities, their intrusions, and ineptitudes are, at the same time, possible when one could not endure the tender touch. The finer the nature, and the higher the level at which it seeks to live, the lower, in grief, it not only sinks but dives: it goes to weep with beggars and mountebanks, for these make the shame of being unhappy less.

So that, that unendurable Monday afternoon (two days after Portia had seen Eddie with Anna, nearly a week after St Quentin's revelation – long enough for the sense of two allied betrayals to push up to full growth, like a double tree) nobody could have come in better than Lilian. The telephone crisis, before lunch at Miss Paullie's, had been the moment for Lilian to weigh in. To be discovered by Lilian weeping in the cloakroom had at once brought Portia inside that subtropical zone of feeling: nobody can be kinder than the narcissist while you react to life in his own terms. To be consoled, to be understood by Lilian was like extending to weep in a ferny grot, whose muggy air and clammy frond-touches relax, demoralize, and pervade you. The size of everything alters: when you look up with wet eyes trees look no more threatened than the ferns. Factitious feeling and true feeling come to about the same thing, when it comes to pain. Lilian's arabesques of the heart, the unkindness of the actor, made her eye Portia with doomful benevolence – and though she at this moment withdrew the cake plate, she started to count her money and reckon up the cost of the taxi fare.

'Well, as you feel,' she said. 'If you're crazy to go alone. But don't let the taxi stop where you're really *going*. You know, you might be blackmailed, you never know.'

'I am only going to Covent Garden.'

'My dear – why ever not tell me that before?'

4

EDDIE did not think Covent Garden a good place to meet, but he had had no time to think of anywhere else – his telephone talk with Portia had been cut off at her end while he was still saying they might surely do better. He had to be thankful that there had, at least, been time to put the lid on her first idea: she had proposed to meet him in the entrance foyer of Quayne and Merrett's. And this – for she was such a good, discreet little girl, trained to awe of Thomas's office – had been enough to show her desperate sense of emergency. She would arrive distraught. No, this would never have done.

Particularly, it would not have done this week. For Eddie's relations with the firm of Quayne and Merrett were (apart from the telephone trouble, of which, still unconscious, he was to hear from Anna) at the present moment, uncertain enough. He had annoyed many people by flitting about the office as though he were some denizen of a brighter clime. There had been those long weekends. More, the absence of Thomas, the apparent susceptibility of Merrett to one's personal charm had beguiled Eddie into excesses of savage skittishness: he had bounced his weight about; he had been more nonchalant in the production of copy, at once more coy and insolent in his manners than (as it had been borne in on him lately) was acceptable here. He had lately got three chits of a damping nature, with Merrett's initials, and the threat of an interview that did not promise to take the usual course. There had been an unseemly scene in a near-by bar, with a more than low young man recruited by Mr Merrett, when Eddie had been warned, with a certain amount of gusto, that one could not go to all lengths as Mrs Quayne's fancy boy. This had been a time when a young man in the tradition should have knocked the speaker's teeth down his throat: Eddie's attempt to look at once disarming, touchy, tickled, and not taken aback had just not come off, and his automatic giggle had done nothing to clear the air. Mr Quayne's kid sister sitting in the foyer would, without doubt, have been the finish of him.

Covent Garden just after six o'clock, with its shuttered arcades, was not gay. Across the façades, like a theatre set shabby in daylight, and across the barren glaring spaces, films of shade were steadily coldly drawn, as though there were some nervous tide in the sky. Here and there, bits of paper did not blow about but sluggishly twitched. The place gave out a look of hollow desuetude, as though its desertion would last for ever. London is full of such deserts, of such moments, at which the mirage of one's own keyed-up existence suddenly fails. Covent Garden acted as a dissolvent on Eddie: he walked round like a cat.

Then he saw Portia, waiting at the one corner he did not think they had said. Her patient grip on her small case, her head turning, the thin, chilly stretch of her arms between short sleeves and short gloves struck straight where his heart should be – but the shaft bent inside him: to see her only made him breezily cross.

'Well, you have come a way,' he said. 'I do feel so flattered, darling.'

'I came in a taxi.'

'Did you? Listen, whatever happened? You seemed to have some sort of fit on the line, just when I was thinking about some much better place to meet.'

'I don't mind here; it's all right!'

'But you did rattle me, ringing off like that.'

'I was using the telephone in Miss Paullie's study, and she came in and caught me. We're not allowed to telephone from that place; we may only ask to send messages.'

'So then you got hell, I suppose. Who would be young!'

'I'm not so young as all that.'

'Well, *in statu pupillari*. Where now?'

'Can't we simply walk about?'

'Oh, all right, if you like. But that isn't much fun, is it?'

'How can this be fun?'

'No, it's not very promising,' said Eddie, starting to walk rather faster than she could. 'But now, look here, darling, I'm ever so sorry for you but really you must not work yourself up like this. I think it's *dingy* of Anna to read your diary, but I always told you not to leave it about. And what a good thing, now, that I made you promise not to write about us. You didn't, of course?' he added, flicking a look at her.

She said, all in a gasp: 'I see now why you asked me not.'

A perceptible twitch passed over Eddie's features. 'What on earth are you getting at *now*?' he said.

'Please don't be angry, please don't be angry with me – Eddie, you told Anna about my diary?'

'Why in God's name should I?'

'For some sort of a joke. Some part of the joke that you always have with her.'

'Well, my poor dear excellent lamb, as a matter of interest – no, I didn't . . . As a matter of fact . . .'

She looked dumbly at him.

'As a matter of fact,' he went on, '*she* told *me*.'

'But I told you, Eddie.'

'Well, she had told me first. She's been at that book for some time. She really is an awful bounder, you know.'

'So when I told you, you knew.'

'Yes. I did. But really, darling, you make too much of things, like keeping this diary. It's ever so honest and it's beautifully clever, and it's sweet, just like you, but is it extraordinary? Diaries are things almost all girls keep.'

'Then, why did you pretend it meant something to you?'

'I loved to have you tell me about it. I am always so moved when you tell me things.'

'And all this time you've let me go on with it. I did write down *some* things about you, of course.'

'Oh God,' said Eddie, stopping. 'I did think I could trust you.'

'Why are you ashamed of having been nice to me?'

'After all, that's all between you and me. I can't have Anna messing about with it.'

'You don't mind, then, about all the rest of my life? As a matter of fact, there's not much rest of my life. But my diary's me. How could I leave you out?'

'All right, go on: make me hate myself . . . By the way, how did you find this out?'

'St Quentin told me.'

'*There's* a crook if you like.'

'I don't see why. He was kind.'

'More likely, he was feeling bored with Anna. She goes on with the same joke far too long ... Now for God's sake, darling – you really *must not* cry here.'

'I only am because my feet do hurt.'

'Didn't I say they would? Round and round this hellish pavement. Look, shut up – you really *can't*, you know.'

'Lilian always thinks people are looking. Now you are just like Lilian.'

'I must get a taxi.'

On the crest of a sob, she said: 'I've only got sixpence. Have you got any money?'

Portia stood like a stone while Eddie went for a taxi, came back with one, gave the address of his flat. Once they were in the taxi, with Henrietta Street reeling jerking past, he miserably took her in his arms, pushing his face with cold and desperate persistence into the place where her hair fell away from her ear. 'Don't,' he said, 'please don't, darling: things are quite bad enough.'

'I can't, I can't, I can't.'

'Well, weep if it helps. Only don't reproach me so terribly.'

'You told her about our walk in the wood.'

'I was only talking, you know.'

'But that wood was where I kissed you.'

'I can't live up to those things. I'm not really fit to have things happen, darling. For you and me there ought to be a new world. Why should we be at the start of our two lives when everything round us is losing its virtue? How can we grow up when there's nothing left to inherit, when what we must feed on is so stale and corrupt? No, don't look up: just stay buried in me.'

'*You're* not buried; you're looking at things. Where are we?'

'Near Leicester Square Station. Just turning right.'

Turning round in his arms to look up jealously, Portia saw the cold daylight reflected in Eddie's dilated eyes. Fighting an arm free, she covered his eyes with one hand and said: 'But why can't we alter everything?'

'There are too few of us.'

'No, you don't really want to. You've always only been playing.'

'Do you think I have fun?'

'You have some sort of dreadful fun. You don't want me to interfere. You like despising more than you like loving. You pretend you're frightened of Anna: you're frightened of me.' Eddie pulled her hand from his eyes and held it away firmly, but she said: 'You're like this now, but you won't let me stay with you.'

'But how could you? You are so childish, darling.'

'You say that because I speak the truth. Something awful is always with you when I'm not. No, don't hold me; let me sit up. Where are we now?'

'I wanted to kiss you – Gower Street.'

Sitting up in her own corner of the taxi, Portia knocked her crushed hat into shape on her knee. Flattening the ribbon bow with her fingers, she moved her head away a little and said: 'No, don't kiss me now.'

'Why not now?'

'Because I don't want you to.'

'You mean', he said, 'that I didn't once when you did?'

She began to put on her hat with an immune little smile, as though all that had been too long ago. The tears shed in that series of small convulsions – felt by him but quite silent – had done no more than mat her lashes together. Eddie noted this while he examined her face intently, while he with one anxious finger straightened her hat. 'You're always crying now,' he said. 'It's really awful, you know ... We're just getting there. Listen, Portia, how much time have you? When do they expect you home?'

'That doesn't matter.'

'Darling, don't be sappy – if you're not back, someone will have a fit. Is there really any good in your coming into my place? Why don't I see you home, instead?'

'It's *not* "home"! Why can't I come in?' Knotting her hands in their prim, short gloves together she screwed her head away and said in a muffled voice: 'Or have you invited somebody else?' The taxi drew up.

'All right, all right then: get out. You must have been reading novels.'

The business with the taxi fare and the latch-key, the business of snatching letters from the hall rack, then of hustling Portia quietly upstairs preoccupied Eddie till he had turned a second Yale key and thrown open the door of his own room. But his nerves were at such a pitch of untoward alertness that he half expected to find some fateful figure standing by his window, or with its back to the grate. In the state he was in, his enemies seemed to have supernatural powers: they could filter through keyholes, stream through hard wood doors. The scene with Portia had been quite slight so far, but the skies had begun to fall – like pieces of black plaster they had started, still fairly gently, flaking down on his head. However, there was no one. The room, unaired and chilly, smelled of this morning's breakfast, last night's smoke. He put the two letters (one was 'By Hand', with no stamp) down on the centre table, threw open a window, knelt to light the gas fire.

With the crane-like steps of an overwrought person, Portia kept going round and round the room, looking hard at everything – the two armchairs with crushed springs, the greyish mirror, the divan with its scratchy butcher-blue spread, pillows untidily clipped into butcher-blue slips, the foreign books overcrowded, thrust with brutality into the deal shelves. She had been here before; she had twice come to see Eddie. But she gave the impression of being someone who, having lost their way in a book or mistaken its whole import, has to go back and start from the beginning again.

Only a subtler mind, with stores of notes to refer to, could have learned much from Eddie's interior. If this interior showed any affection, it was in keeping the bleakness of college rooms – the unadult taste, the lack of tactile feeling bred by large stark objects, tables, and cupboards, that one does not possess. The concave seats of the chairs, the lumpy divan suggested that comfort was a rather brutal affair. Eddie's work of presenting himself to the world did not, in fact, stop when he came back here, for he often had company – but he chose by all kinds of negligence to imply that it did. Whatever manias might possess him in solitude, making some haunted landscape in which cupboards and tables looked like cliffs or opaque bottomless pools, the effect (at least to a woman) coming in here was, that this was how this fundamentally plain and rather old-fashioned fellow lived when *en pantoufles*. On the smoky buff walls and unpolished woodwork neurosis, of course, could not write a trace. To be received by Eddie in such frowsty surroundings could be taken as either confiding or insolent. If he *had* stuffed a bunch of flowers (never very nice flowers) into his one art vase, the concession always seemed touching. This was not all that was touching: the smells of carpet and ash, of dust inside the books, and of stagnant tea had a sort of unhopeful acquiescence about them. This was not all phony – Eddie did need to be mothered; he was not aesthetic; he had a contempt for natty contrivances, and he did sincerely associate pretty living with being richer than he could hope to be. To the hideous hired furniture and the stuffiness he did (with a kind of arrogance) acquiesce. Thus he kept the right, which he used, to look round his friends' room – at the taste, the freshness, the ingenuity – with a cold marvelling alien ironic eye. Had he had a good deal of money, his interior probably would have had the classy red Gallic darkness of a man-about-town's in a Bourget novel – draperies, cut-glass lamps, teetering bronzes, mirrors, a pianola, a seductive day-bed, and waxy *demi-monde* flowers in *jardinières*. Like the taste of many people whose extraction is humble, what taste he had lagged some decades back in time, and had an exciting, anti-moral colour. His animal suspiciousness, his bleakness, the underlying morality of his class, his expectation of some appalling contretemps which should make him have to decamp from everything suddenly were not catered for in his few expensive dreams – for there is a narrowness about fantasy: it figures only the *voulu* part of the self. Happily he had to keep what taste he had to himself. For as things were, this room of his became a *tour de force* – not simply the living here (which he more or less had to do) but the getting away with it, even making it pay. He was able to make this room (which was not even an attic) a special factor, even the key factor, in his relations with fastidious people ... There were some dying red daisies in the vase, which showed he had had someone to tea last week.

'Your flowers are dead, Eddie.'

'Are they? Throw them away.'

Portia, lifting the daisies from the vase, looked with a sort of unmeaning repulsion at their slimy rotting stalks. 'High time, too,' said Eddie. 'Perhaps that was the stink – In the waste-paper basket darling, under the table, there.' He took up the vase and prepared to make off with it to the lavatory. But there was a dripping sound as Portia went on holding up the daisies. She said: 'Eddie. . . .'

He jumped.

'Why don't you open that letter from Anna?'

'Oh God! Is there one?'

'I mean the one you've just brought up. It hasn't got any stamp.'

Eddie stood with the vase and gave a tortured giggle.

'Hasn't it?' he said. 'How extraordinary! She must have sent round by special messenger. I thought that looked like her writing. . . .'

'Surely you must know it,' said Portia coldly. She put down the daisies and watched them make a viscous pool on the cloth, then she took up the letter. 'Or, I will.'

'Shut up. Leave that alone!'

'Why? Why should I? What are you frightened of?'

'Apart from anything else, that's a letter to me. Don't be such a little rat!'

'Well, go on, read it. Why are you so frightened? What are the private things you and she say?'

'I really couldn't tell you: you're too young.'

'Eddie. . . .'

'Well, leave me alone, damn you!'

'I don't care if I'm damned. What do you and she say?'

'Well, quite often we have talks about you.'

'But you used to talk a lot before *you* got to know me, didn't you? Before you had said you loved me, or anything. I remember hearing you talking in the drawing-room, when I used to go up or down stairs, before I minded at all. Are you her lover?'

'You don't know what you're saying.'

'I know it's something you're not with me. I wouldn't mind

279

what you did, but I cannot bear the things I think now that you say.'

'Then why keep asking?'

'Because I keep hoping you might tell me you were really saying something not that.'

'Well, I am Anna's lover.'

'Oh ... Are you?'

'Don't you believe me?'

'I've got no way of telling.'

'I thought it didn't seem to make much impression. Why make such a fuss if you don't know what you do want? As a matter of fact, I'm not: she's far too cautious and smart, and I don't think she's got any passion at all. She likes to be far more trouble.'

'Then why do you – I mean, why –?'

'The trouble with you has been, from the very start, that you've been too anxious to get me taped.'

'Have I? But *you* said we loved each other.'

'You used to be much gentler, much more sweet. Yes, you used to be, as I once told you, the one person I could naturally love. But you're all different, lately, since Seale.'

'Matchett says so too – Eddie, will you turn out the fire?'

'What's the matter – do you feel funny? What's made you feel funny? Why don't you sit down, then?' He came hurriedly round the table pinning her with a hard look, as though he dared her to crumple, to drop down out of sight. Then he put one stony hand on her shoulder and pushed her down into an armchair. His high-pitched insensibility was not being acted – he sat on the arm of the chair, as he so often used to do, stared boldly into the air above her head, and giggled, as though the scene were as natural as it could ever be. 'If you pass out here, darling, you'll lose me my job,' he said. He took off her hat for her and put it down on the floor. 'There, that's better. I do wish to God you smoked,' he said. 'Do you still not want the fire? And why should you pass out?'

'You said everything was over,' Portia said, looking straight up into his eyes. They stayed locked in this incredulous look till Eddie flinched: he said: 'Have I been unkind?'

'I've got no way of telling.'

'I wish you had.' Frowning, pulling his lip down in the familiar way, that made this the ghost of all their happier talks, he said: 'Because I don't know, do you know? I may be some kind of monster; I've really got no idea ... The things I have to say seem never to have had to be said before. Is my life really so ghastly and so extraordinary? I've got no way to check up. I do wish you were older; I wish you knew more.'

'You're the only person I ever –'

'That's what's the devil; that's just what I mean. You don't know what to expect.'

Not taking her anxious eyes from his face – eyes as desperately concentrated as though she were trying to understand a lesson – she said: 'But after all, Eddie, anything that happens has never happened before. What I mean is, you and I are the first people who have ever been us.'

'All the same, most people get to know the ropes – you can see they do. All the other women I've ever known but you, Portia, seem to know what to expect, and that gives me something to go on. I don't care how wrong they are: it somehow gets one along. But you've kept springing thing after thing on me, from the moment you asked why I held that tart of a girl's hand. You expect every bloody thing to be either right or wrong, and be done with the whole of oneself. For all I know, you may be right. But it's simply intolerable. It makes me feel I'm simply going insane. I've started to live in one way, because that's been the only way I can live. I can see you get hurt, but however am I to know whether that's not your own fault for being the way you are? Or, that you don't really get hurt more than other people but simply make more fuss? You apply the same hopeless judgements to simply everything – for instance, because I said I loved you, you expect me to be as sweet to you as your mother. You're damned lucky to have someone even as innocent as I am. I've never fooled you, have I?'

'You've talked to Anna.'

'That's something different entirely. Have I ever not spoken the truth to you?'

'I don't know.'

'Well, have I? If I weren't innocent to the point of deformity, would you get me worked up into such a state? Any other man would have chucked you under the chin, and played you up, and afterwards laughed at you for a silly little fool.'

'You have laughed at me. You've laughed at me with them.'

'Well, when I'm with Anna you do seem pretty funny. I should think, in fact I'm certain that you'd seem funny to anybody but me. You've got a completely lunatic set of values, and a sort of unfailing lunatic instinct that makes you pick on another lunatic – another person who doesn't know where he is. You know I'm not a cad, and I know you're not batty. But, my God, we've got to live in the world.'

'You said you didn't like it. You said it was wicked.'

'That's another thing that you do: you pin me down to everything.'

'Then why do you say you always tell me the truth?'

'I used to tell you the truth because I felt safe with you. Now –'

'Now you don't love me any more?'

'You don't know what you mean by love. We used to have such fun, because I used to think that we understood each other. I still think you're sweet, though you do give me the horrors. I feel you trying to put me into some sort of trap. I'd never dream of going to bed with you, the idea would be absurd. All the same, I let you say these quite unspeakable things, which no one has the right to say to anyone else. And I suppose I say them to you too. Do I?'

'I don't know what is unspeakable.'

'No, that's quite clear. You've got some sense missing. The fact is, you're driving me mad.' Eddie, who had been chainsmoking, got up and walked away from the armchair. He dropped his cigarette behind the gas fire, stopped to stare at the fire, then automatically knelt down and turned it out. 'Apart from everything else, it's time you went home,' he said. 'It's going on for half past seven.'

'You mean you would be happier without me?'

'*Happy!*' said Eddie, throwing up his hands.

'I must make some people happy – I make Major Brutt happy,

I make Matchett happy, when I don't have secrets; I made Mrs Heccomb rather happy, she said ... Do you mean, though, that *now*, you feel you could be as happy without me as you used to be with me when you thought I was different?'

Eddie, with his face entirely stiff, picked up the forgotten dead daisies from the table, doubled their stalks up, and put them precisely into the waste-paper basket. He looked all round the room, as though to see what else there was out of place; then his eyes, without changing, without a human flicker, with all their darkness of immutable trouble, returned to Portia's figure, where they stopped. 'I certainly do feel that at the moment,' he said.

Portia at once leaned down to reach her hat from the floor. The titter of the silly chromium clock, and a telephone ringing on and on in some room downstairs filled up the pause while she put on her hat. To do this, she had to put down Anna's letter, which, unconsciously, she had been holding all this time: she got up and put it down on the table – where Eddie's unseeing eyes became fixed on it. 'Oh,' she said, 'I haven't got any money. Can you lend me five shillings?'

'You won't want all that just to get back from here.'

'I'd rather have five shillings. I'll send you a postal order for it tomorrow.'

'Yes, do do that, darling, will you? I suppose you can always get money from Thomas. I've run rather short.'

When she had put her gloves on, she slipped the five shillings in small silver, that he had rather unwillingly collected, down inside the palm of her right glove. Then she held out her hand, with the hard bulge in the palm. 'Well, good-bye, Eddie,' she said, not looking at him. She was like someone who, at the end of a too long visit, conscious of having outstayed their welcome, does not know how to take their leave with grace. This unbearable social shyness of Eddie, her eagerness to be a long way away from here, made her eyes shift round different parts of the carpet, under their dropped lids.

'Of course I'll see you down. You can't wander about the stairs alone – this house is lousy with people.'

Her silence said: 'What more could they do to me?' She

waited: he put the same stone hand on her shoulder, and they went through the door and down three flights like this. She noted things she had not seen coming up – the scrolls, like tips of waves, on the staircase wallpaper, the characters of scratches on the olive dado, the chaotic outlook from a landing window, a typed warning on a bathroom door. For infinitesimal moments in her descent she paused, under Eddie's hand, to give these things looks as though it helped to fix her mind on them. She felt the silent tenseness of other people, of all those lives of which she had not been conscious, behind the shut doors; the exhausted breath of the apartment house, staled by so many lungs, charged with dust from so many feet, came up the darkening shaft of the stairs – for there were no windows down there near the hall.

Down there, Eddie glanced once more at the letter-rack, in case the next post should have come in. He swung open the hall door boldly and said he had better find a taxi for her. 'No, no, no, don't: I'll find one easily ... Good-bye,' she said again, with a still more guilty shyness. Before he could answer – while he still, in some reach of the purely physical memory, could feel her shoulder shrinking under his hand – she was down the steps and running off down the street. Her childish long-legged running, at once awkward (because this was in a street) and wild, took her away at a speed which made him at once appalled and glad. Her hands swung with her movements; they carried nothing – and the oddness of that, the sense that some-thing was missing, bothered him as he went back upstairs.

Here he found, of course, that she had left the dispatch case, with all her lessons in it, behind. And this quite small worry – for how on earth, without comment, was he to get it back? this looked like further trouble for the unlucky pupil at Cavendish Square – pressed just enough on his mind to make him turn for distraction to the more pressing, dangerous worry of Anna. He got bottles out of a cupboard, made a drink for himself, gave one of those defiant laughs with which one sometimes buoys up one's solitude, drank half the drink, put it down, and opened the letter.

He read Anna's note about the office telephone.

5

THE Karachi Hotel consists of two Kensington houses, of great height, of a style at once portentous and brittle, knocked into one – or, rather, not knocked, the structure might hardly stand it, but connected by arches at key points. Of the two giant front doors under the portico, one has been glazed and sealed up; the other up to midnight, yields to pressure on a round brass knob. The hotel's name, in tarnished gilt capitals, is wired out from the top of the portico. One former dining-room has been exposed to the hall and provides the hotel lounge; the other is still the dining-room, it is large enough. One of the first-floor drawing-rooms is a drawing-room still. The public rooms are lofty and large in a diluted way: inside them there is extensive vacuity, nothing so nobly positive as space. The fireplaces with their flights of brackets, the doors with their poor mouldings, the nude-looking windows exist in deserts of wall: after dark the high-up electric lights die high in the air above unsmiling arm-chairs. If these houses give little by becoming hotels, they lose little; even when they were homes, no intimate life can have flowered inside these walls or become endeared to them. They were the homes of a class doomed from the start, without natural privilege, without grace. Their builders must have built to enclose fog, which having seeped in never quite goes away. Dyspepsia, uneasy wishes, ostentation, and chilblains can, only, have governed the lives of families here.

In the Karachi Hotel, all upstairs rooms except the drawing-room, have been partitioned up to make two or three more: the place is a warren. The thinness of these bedroom partitions makes love or talk indiscreet. The floors creak, the beds creak; drawers only pull out of chests with violent convulsions; mirrors swing round and hit you one in the eye. Most privacy, though least air, is to be had in the attics, which were too small to be divided up. One of these attics Major Brutt occupied.

At the end of Monday (for this was the end of the day unless you were gay or busy) dinner was being served. The guests could now dine in daylight – or rather, by its unearthly reflections on the façades of houses across the road. In the dining-room, each table had been embellished some days ago, with three sprays of mauve sweet peas. Quite a number of tables, tonight, were empty, and the few couples and trios dotted about did not say much – weighed down, perhaps, by the height of the echoing gloom, or by the sense of eating in an exposed place. Only Major Brutt's silence seemed not uneasy, for he, as usual, dined alone. The one or two families he had found congenial had, as usual, just gone: these tonight were nearly all newcomers. Once or twice he glanced at some other table, wondering whom he might get to know next. He was learning, in his humble way, to be conscious of his faint interestingness as a solitary man. On the whole, however, he looked at his plate, or at the air just above it; he tried hard not to let recollections of lunch at Anna's make him discontented with dinner here – for, really, they did one wonderfully well. He had just finished his plate of rhubarb and custard when the head waitress came and mumbled over his ear.

He said: 'But I don't understand – "Young lady –?" '

'Asking for you, sir. She is in the lounge.'

'But I am not expecting a young lady.'

'In the lounge, sir. She said she would wait.'

'Then you mean she's there now?'

The waitress gave him a nod and a sort of slighting look. Her good opinion of him was being undone in a moment: she thought him at once ungallant and sly. Major Brutt, unaware, sat and turned the position over – this *might* be a joke, but who would play a joke on him? He was not sprightly enough to have sprightly friends. Shyness or obstinacy made him pour himself out another glass of water and drink it before he left the table – rhubarb leaves an acid taste in the teeth. He wiped his mouth, folded his table napkin, and left the dining-room with a heavy, cautious tread – conscious of people pausing in what they were hardly saying, of diners' glum eyes following him.

One's view into the lounge, coming through from the other house, is cut across by the row of shabby pillars that separate the lounge from the entrance hall. At first, in those dregs of daylight, he saw nobody there. Glad there was no one to see him standing and looking, he challenged the unmeaning crowd of armchairs. Then he saw Portia behind a chair in the distance, prepared to retreat further if the wrong person came. He said: 'Hullo, hul-*lo* – what are *you* doing here?'

She only looked at him like a wild creature, just old enough to know it must dread humans – as though he had cornered her in this place. Yes, she was terrified here, like a bird astray in a room, a bird already stunned by dashing itself against mirrors and panes.

He pushed on quickly her way through the armchairs, saying, more urgently, less easily, lower – 'My dear child, are you lost? Have you lost your way?'

'No. I came.'

'Well, I'm delighted. But this is a long way from where *you* live. At this time of night –'

'Oh – is it night?'

'Well, no: I've just finished my dinner. But isn't this just the time when you ought to be having yours?'

'I don't know what time it is.'

Her voice rang round the lounge which, whatever despair it may have muffled, cannot have ever rung with such a homeless note. Major Brutt threw a look round instinctively: the porter was off duty; nobody was arriving; they had not begun to come out from dinner yet – there would be the cheese, then the coffee, always served at table. He went round the chair that barricaded her from him and kept them in their two different worlds of uncertainty: he felt Portia measuring his coming nearer with the deliberation of a desperate thing – then, like a bird at still another window, she flung herself at him. Her hands pressed, flattened, on the fronts of his coat; he felt her fingers digging into the stuff. She said something inaudible. Grasping her cold elbows he gently, strongly held her a little back. 'Steady, steady, steady – Now, what did you say?'

'I've got nowhere to be.'

'Come, that's nonsense, you know ... Just stay steady and try and tell me what's the matter. Have you had a fright, or what?'

'Yes.'

'That's too bad. Look here, don't tell me if you would rather not. Just stay still here for a bit and have some coffee or something, then I'll take you home.'

'I'm not going back.'

'Oh, come . . .'

'No, I'm not going back there.'

'Look, try sitting down.'

'No, no. They all make me do that. I don't want to just sit down: I want to stay.'

'Well, *I* shall sit down. Look, I'm sitting down now. I always do sit down.' Having let go of her elbows he reached, when he had sat down, across the arm of his chair, caught her wrist and pulled her round to stand like a pupil by him. 'Look here,' he said, 'Portia, I think the world of you. I don't know when I've met someone I thought so much of. So don't be like a hysterical little kid, because you are not, and it lets me down, you see. Just put whatever's the matter out of your head for a moment and think of me for a minute – I'm sure you will, because you've always been as sweet as anything to me, and I can't tell you what a difference it's made. When you come here and tell me you're running off, you put me in a pretty awful position with your people, who are my very good friends. When a man's a bit on his own, like I've been lately, and is marking time, and feels a bit out of touch, a place like their place, where one can drop in any time and always get a warm welcome, means quite a lot, you know. Seeing you there, so part of it all and happy, has been half the best of it. But I think the world of them, too. You wouldn't mess that up for me, Portia, would you?'

'There's nothing to mess,' she said in a very small voice that was implacable. 'You are the other person that Anna laughs at,' she went on, raising her eyes. 'I don't think you understand: Anna's always laughing at you. She says you are quite pathetic. She laughed at your carnations being the wrong colour, then gave them to me. And Thomas always thinks you must be after something. Whatever you do, even send me a puzzle, he thinks that more, and she laughs more. They groan at each other when you have gone away. You and I are the same.'

Steps in the hall behind him made Major Brutt crane round automatically: they *were* beginning to come out from dinner now. 'You must sit down,' he said to Portia, unexpectedly sharply. 'You don't want all these people staring at you.' He pulled another chair close: she sat down, distantly shaken by the outside force of what she had just said. Major Brutt intently watched four other people take their own favourite seats. Portia watched him watch; his eyes clung to these people; their ignorance of what he had had to hear made his fellow hotel guests the picture of sanity. There are moments when one can comfort oneself by a look at the most callous faces – these have been innocent of at least one crime. When he could not look any more without having to meet their looks, he dropped his eyes and sat not looking at Portia. It was she, for the moment, who felt how striking their silence, their nearness here had become – anxiety, and the sense of being pursued by glances still more closely than she had been all day made her sit stone still, not even moving her hands.

There seemed no reason why Major Brutt should ever raise his eyes from the floor: he had begun, in fact, to stroke the back of his head. She interposed, in a low voice: 'Is there no other place –?'

He frowned slightly.

'Haven't you got a room here?'

'I've been a pretty blundering sort of fellow.'

'Oh, *can't* we go upstairs? Can't we go somewhere else?'

'I don't know what made me think they would have time for me . . . What's that you're saying?'

'Everyone's listening to us.'

But that still did not matter. He watched, with an odd grim sort of acquiescence, three more people come between the pillars, sit down. Then older ladies in semi-evening dresses cruised through the hall and upstairs: they were the drawing-room contingent. Major Brutt's grey eyes returned to Portia's dark ones. 'No, there's nowhere else,' he said. He waited: a conversation broke out at the other end of the lounge. He pitched his voice underneath this. 'You'll just have to talk more quietly. And mind what you say – you've no business to talk like that.'

She whispered: 'But you and I are the same.'

'Besides, anyhow,' he went on frowning at her, '*that* doesn't alter – nothing alters – anything. You've got no right to upset them: can't you see that's a low game? I'm going to take you right back – now, pronto, at once.'

'Oh no,' she said, with startling authority. 'You don't know what has happened.'

They sat almost knee to knee, at right angles to each other, their two armchairs touching. Their peril, the urgent need to stop him from this mistake, made the lounge, the rest of the world not matter – ruthless as a goddess, she put a small sure hand on the arm of his chair. So he wavered more when he said: 'My dear child, whatever's happened, you'd so much better go home and have it out.'

'Major Brutt, even if you hated them you couldn't possibly want me to do anything worse. It would never stop at all. Having things out would never stop, I mean. Besides, Thomas is my brother. I can't tell you down here ... Do you like this hotel?'

He readjusted to this in two or three seconds, hummed slowly at her, said: 'It suits me all right. Why?'

'If you left tomorrow, what they thought would not matter: you could tell them I was your niece who had got a pain and had got to lie down, then we could talk in your room.'

'That would still not do, I'm afraid.'

But she interposed: 'Oh, *quickly*! I'm starting to cry.' She was: her dilated dark eyes began dissolving; with her knuckles she pressed her chin up to keep her mouth steady; her other fist was pressed into her stomach, as though here were the seat of uncontrollable pain. She moved her knuckles, to mumble: 'There've been people all day ... I just want half an hour, just twenty minutes ... Then, if you say I must ...'

He shot up, knocking a table, making an ash-bowl rattle, saying loudly: 'Come, we'll look for some coffee.' They went through the dining-room arch to the other stairs – there was no lift – then she darted up ahead of him like a rabbit. He followed, stepping heavily, ostentatiously, whistling nonchalantly a little flat, fumbling round all the time for his room key, passing palms on landings with that erect walk of the sleep-walker – his usual walk. Her day had been all stairs – all the same, her look became wilder, more unbelieving as, whenever she turned her head, he kept signalling: 'Up up.' This house seemed to have no top – till she came to the attic floor. At Windsor Terrace, that floor close to the skylight was mysterious with the servants' bodily life; it was the scene of Matchett's unmentioned sleep. Under this hotel skylight he came abreast with her: whistling louder, he unlocked his own door. Till now, she had not seen him approach anything with the authority that comes from possession. After that second, she was looking doubtfully over a lumpy olive sateen eiderdown at a dolls' house window dark from a parapet.

'I fit pretty tight,' he said. 'But, you see, they give me cut price terms.'

His anxious nonchalance, and his caution – for he went out again to knock on the other doors, to be certain there was nobody on this landing – made her not speak as she passed the end of the bed to sit, facing the window, on the edge of his eiderdown. He said: 'Well, here we are,' with an air of solemn alarm – he had just fully realized their position. His chair back grated against the chest of drawers: on the mat there was just room for his feet. 'Now,' he said, 'go on. What made you cry just now?'

'All those people everywhere, the whole time.'

'I mean, what brought you here? What is this you say you are running from?'

'Them all. What they make happen –'

He interrupted, austerely: 'I thought there was something special; I thought something had happened.'

'It has.'

'When?'

'It always has the whole time; I see it has never stopped. They were cruel to my father and mother, but the thing must have started even before that. Matchett says –'

'You ought not to listen to servants' talk.'

'Why? When she's the person who sees what really happens? They did not think my father and mother wicked; they simply despised them and used to laugh. That made all three of us funny, I see now. I see now that my father wanted me to belong somewhere, because he did not: that was why they have had to have me in London. I hope he does not know that it has turned out like this. I suppose he and my mother did not know they were funny: they went on feeling upset because they thought they had once done an extraordinary thing (their getting married had been extraordinary) but they still thought life was quite simple for people who did not do extraordinary things. My father often used to explain to me that people did not live the way we did: he said ours was not the right way – though we were all quite happy. He was quite certain ordinary life went on – yes, that was why I was sent to Thomas and Anna. But I see now that it does not: if he and I met again I should have to tell him that there is no ordinary life.'

'Aren't you young to judge?'

'I don't see why. I thought when people were young that they were allowed to expect life to be ordinary. It did seem more like that at the seaside, but as soon as Eddie came it all got queer, and I saw even the Heccombs did not believe in it. If they did, why were they so frightened by Eddie? Eddie used to say it was he and I who were mad, but he used to seem to think we were right, too. But today he said we were wrong: he said I gave him the horrors and told me to go away.'

'That's it, is it? You two have had a quarrel?'

'He's shown me all my mistakes – but I have not known what to do. He says I've gone on taping him too much. I never could stop asking him why he did some things: you see, I thought we wanted to know each other.'

'We all take these knocks – this is your first, I daresay. Look here, my dear child, do you want a handkerchief?'

'I have one somewhere.' Automatic, compliant, she pulled a crushed one out of a buttoned pocket, held it up to please him, then, in a hand that went on sketching vague motions, held it crunched up tight. 'How can you say "first"?' she said. 'This can't happen again.'

'Oh, one forgets, you know. One can always patch oneself up.'

'No. Is this being grown up?'

'Nonsense. This is no time to say so, and you'll bite my head off, but you'll do better without that young man. Oh, I know I've got no business to chip bits off him, but –'

'But it isn't just Eddie,' she said, looking amazed. 'The thing was, he was the person I knew. Because of him, I felt safer with all the others. I did not think things could really be so bad. There was Matchett, but she got cold with me about Eddie; she liked me more when she and I were alone: now she and I are not the same as we were. I did not mean to be wrong, but she was always so angry; she wanted me to be angry. But Eddie and I weren't angry: we soothed each other. But I find now, he was with them the whole time, and they knew. I can't go back there now I know.'

'One's feelings get hurt; one cannot avoid that. One really can't make a war out of that, you know. A girl like you, Portia, a really good girl, ought not to get her back to the wall. When people seem to give you a bad deal, you've got to ask what sort of deal they may have once got themselves. But you are still young enough –'

'I don't see what age has to do with it.'

He swivelled round on his chair, as wretchedly as a schoolboy, to look, in glum, dumb, nonplussed communication at his own rubbed ebony hairbrushes, his stud-box, his nail-scissors – as though these objects, which had travelled with him, witnessed to his power somehow to get through life, to reach a point when one says, It doesn't really much matter. Unhappy on his bed, in this temporary little stale room, Portia seemed to belong nowhere, not even here. Stripped of that pleasant home that had seemed part of her figure, stripped too, of his own wishes and hopes, she looked at once harsh and beaten, a refugee – frightening, rebuffing all pity that has fear at the root. He tried: 'Or look at it this way –' then spoilt this by a pause. He saw what a fiction was common sense.

However he had meant to finish, she would hardly have listened. She had turned to grasp his bed-end, to bend her forehead down on her tight knuckles. Her body tensely twisted in this position; her legs, like disjointed legs, hung down: her thin lines, her concavities, her unconsciousness made her a picture of premature grief. Happy that few of us are aware of the world until we are already in league with it. Childish fantasy, like the sheath over the bud, not only protects but curbs the terrible budding spirit, protects not only innocence from the world but the world from the power of innocence. Major Brutt said: 'Well, cheer up; we're in the same boat.'

She said, to her knuckles: 'When I thought I'd be older, I thought Eddie'd be the person I would marry. I saw I'd have to be different when that happened, but not more different than I could be. But he says he knew I thought that; it is that that he does not like.'

'When one's in love –'

'Was I? How do you know? Have you been?'

'In my time,' declared Major Brutt, with assertive cheerfulness. 'Though it may seem funny to you, and for one or another reason I never cut much ice. For the time being, of course, that queers everything. But here I am, after all. Aren't I?' he said, leaning forward, creaking the cane chair.

Portia almost gave him a look, then turned her head to lay the other cheek on her knuckles. 'Yes, *you* are,' she said. 'But today he said I must go. So what am I to do now, Major Brutt?'

'Well, it may seem tough, but I still don't see why you can't go home, after all. We've all got to live somewhere, whatever happens. There's breakfast, dinner, so on. After all, they're your people. Blood's thicker –'

'No, it isn't; not mine and Anna's. It, it isn't all right there any more: we feel ashamed with each other. You see, she has read my diary and found something out. She does not like that, but she laughs about it with Eddie: they laugh about him and me.'

This made Major Brutt pause, redden, and once more turn his head to look out of the window behind his chair. He said, to the parapet and the darkening sky: 'You mean, they're quite hand in glove?'

'Oh, he's not just her lover; it's something worse than that ... Are you still Anna's friend?'

'I can't get over the fact that she's been very good to me. I don't think I want to discuss that ... But look, if you feel, if you *did* feel there was anything wrong at home, you should surely stick by your brother?'

'He's ashamed with me, too: he's ashamed because of our father. And he's afraid the whole time that I shall be sorry for him. Whenever I speak he gives me a sort of look as much as to say, "Don't say that!" Oh, he doesn't want me to stick. You don't know him at all ... You think I exaggerate.'

'At the moment –'

'Well, this sort of moment never really stops ... I'm not *going* home, Major Brutt.'

He said, very reasonably: 'Then what do you want to do?'

'Stay here –' She stopped short, as though she felt she had said, too soon, something important enough to need care. Deliberately, with her lips tight shut, she got off the bed to come and stand by him – so that, she standing, he sitting, she could tower up at least a little way. She looked him all over, as though she meant to tug at him, to jerk him awake, and was only not certain where to catch hold of him. Her arms stayed at her sides, but looked rigid, at every moment, with their intention to move in unfeeling desperation. She was not able, or else did not wish, to inform herself with pleading grace; her sexlessness made her deliver a stern summons: he felt her knocking through him like another heart outside his own ribs. 'Stay here with you,' she said. 'You do like me,' she added. 'You write to me; you send me puzzles; you say you think about me. Anna says you are sentimental, but that is what she says when people don't feel nothing. I could do things for you: we could have a home; we would not have to live in a hotel. Tell Thomas you want to keep me and he could send you my money. I could cook; my mother cooked when she lived in Notting Hill Gate. Why could you not marry me? I could cheer you up. I would not get in your way, and we should not be half so lonely. Why should you be dumbfounded, Major Brutt?'

'Because I suppose I am,' was all he could say.

'I told Eddie you were a person I made happy.'

'Good God, yes. But don't you see –'

'Do think it over, please,' she said calmly. 'I'll wait.'

'Its no good beginning to think, my dear.'

'I'd like to wait, all the same.'

'You're shivering,' he said vaguely.

'Yes, I am cold.' With a quite new, matter-of-fact air of possessing his room, she made small arrangements for comfort – peeled off his eiderdown, kicked her shoes off, lay down with her head into his pillow and pulled the eiderdown snugly up to her chin. By this series of acts she seemed at once to shelter, to plant here, and to obliterate herself – most of all that last. Like a sick person, or someone who has decided by not getting up to take no part in a day, she at once seemed to inhabit a different world. Noncommittal, she sometimes shut her eyes, sometimes looked at the ceiling that took the slope of the roof. 'I suppose', she said, after some minutes, 'you don't know what to do.'

Major Brutt said nothing. Portia moved her head on the pillow; her eyes roved placidly round the room, examined things on the washstand. 'All sorts of pads and polishes,' she said. 'Do you clean your own shoes?'

'Yes. I've always been rather fussy. They can't do everything here.'

She looked at the row of shoes, all on their trees. 'No wonder they look so nice: they look like chestnuts ... That's another thing I could do.'

'For some reason, women are never so good at it.'

'Well, I'm certain I could cook. Mother told me about the things she used to make. As I say, there'd be no reason for you and me to always live in hotels.'

The preposterous happy mirage of something one does not even for one moment desire must not be allowed to last. Had nothing in Major Brutt responded to it he would have gone on being gentle, purely sorry for her – As it was, he got up briskly, and not only got up but put back his chair where it came from, flat with some inches of wall, to show that this conversation was closed for good. And the effort this cost him, the final end of something, made his firm action seem more callous than sad. To stop any weakening pause, he kept on moving – picked up his two brushes, absently but competently started to brush his hair. So that Portia, watching him, had all in that moment a view of his untouched masculine privacy, of that grave abstractedness with which each part of his toilet would go on being performed. Unconscious, he could not have made plainer his determination always to live alone. Clapping the brushes together, he put them down with a clatter that made them both start. 'I'm sure you will cook,' he said, 'I'm all in favour of it. But not for some years yet, and not, I'm afraid, for me.'

'I suppose I should not have asked you,' Portia said – not confusedly but in a considering tone.

'I feel pleased,' he admitted. 'In fact, it set me up no end. But you think too much of me, and not enough of what I'm trying to say. And, at the finish of this, what I still ask you to do, is: forget this and go home.' He dared hardly look at the eiderdown, under which he still heard no stir. 'It's not a question of doing the best you can do, it's a question of doing the only thing possible.'

Portia, by folding her arms over it tightly, locked the eiderdown, her last shelter, to her chest. 'That will do no good, Major Brutt. They will not know what to say.'

'Well, let's hear what they do say. Why not give them a chance?' He paused, bit his upper lip under his moustache, and added: 'I'll come with you, of course.'

'I can see you don't really want to. Why?'

'I don't like to spring this on them – your just turning up with me, I mean, when they've had hours to worry. I've got to telephone – Why, you know', he added, 'they'll be calling out the police, the fire brigade.'

'Well, if you so much want to, you may tell them I'm with you. But, please, you are not to tell them I'm going back. That will all have to depend.'

'Oh, it will, will it? On what?'

'On what they do then.'

'Well, let me tell them you're safe.'

Without any further comment, she turned over and put her hand under her cheek. Her detachment made her seem to abandon being a woman – she was like one of those children in an Elizabethan play who are led on, led off, hardly speak, and are known to be bound for some tragic fate which will be told in a line; they do not appear again; their existence, their point of view has had, throughout, an unreality. At the same time, her body looked like some drifting object that has been lodged for a moment, by some trick of the current, under a bank, but must be dislodged again and go on twirling down the implacable stream. He picked up her hat and hung it on the end of the bed: as he did this, she said: 'You'll come back when you've telephoned?'

'You will wait, like a good girl?'

'If you'll come back, I will wait.'

'And I'll tell them that you are here.'

'And you'll tell me what they do then.'

He took one more look round the darkening room with her in it, then went out, shut the door, started down to go to the telephone – his somnambulist's walk a little bit speeded up, as though by some bad dream from which he still must not wake. As he went down flight after flight he saw her face on the pillow, and saw in a sleep-bound way how specious wisdom was. One's sentiments – call them that – one's fidelities are so instinctive that one hardly knows they exist: only when they are betrayed or, worse still, when one betrays them does one realize their power. That betrayal is the end of an inner life, without which the everyday becomes threatening or meaningless. At the back of the spirit a mysterious landscape, whose perspective used to be infinite, suddenly perishes: this is like being cut off from the country for ever, not even meeting its breath down the city street.

Major Brutt had a mind that did not articulate: he felt, simply, things had changed for the worse. His home had come down; he must no longer envisage Windsor Terrace, or go there again. He made himself think of the moment – he hoped that the Quaynes would have some suggestion ready, that something could be arranged about Portia crossing London, that he would not have to go with her to their door. But as he went into the upright telephone coffin, he did not doubt for a moment that he was right to telephone, though they might laugh, they would certainly laugh, again.

6

ST QUENTIN, drawn to the scene of his crime – or, more properly, to its moral source – was drinking sherry at Anna's when the alarm broke. St Quentin had been, up to then, in good spirits, relieved to find how little guilty he felt. Nothing was said on the subject of diaries.

The trouble began on the ground floor of 2 Windsor Terrace and moved up. While St Quentin and Anna were at their sherry, Thomas came home, happened to ask for Portia, was told she was not back. He thought no more of this until Matchett, in person, came to the study door to say Portia was still not in yet, and to ask Thomas what he meant to do. She stood in the doorway, looking steadily at him: these days they did not often confront each other.

'What I mean,' she said, 'twenty to eight is late.'

'She must have made some plan, and then forgotten to tell us. Have you told Mrs Quayne?'

'Mrs Quayne has company, sir.'

'I know,' said Thomas. He almost added: Why else do you think I am down here? He said: 'That's no reason not to ask Mrs Quayne. She may quite likely know where Miss Portia is.'

Matchett gave Thomas a look without any quiver; Thomas frowned down at his fountain pen. 'Well,' he said, 'better ask her, at any rate.'

'Unless you would wish to, sir. . . .'

Under this compulsion, Thomas heaved himself up from his writing-desk. Evidently, Matchett was thinking something – but was Matchett not always thinking something? If you look at life one way, there is always cause for alarm. Thomas went upstairs, to gain the drawing-room landing enough infected by whatever Matchett did think to open the door sharply, then stand on the threshold with a tenseness that unnerved the other two. 'Portia isn't back,' he said. 'I suppose we know where she is?'

St Quentin at once got up, took Anna's glass to the tray, and gave her some more sherry. The business with this enabled him to stay for some time with his back to the Quaynes: he gave himself more sherry, then filled a glass for Thomas. Then he strolled away and, looking out of the window, watched people calmly rowing on the lake. He told himself that if this had been going to happen it would have happened before: the argument therefore was that it could not be happening now. Five days had elapsed since he had lifted his hat to Portia in the graveyard, having just said to her what he had just said. At the same time – he had to face it – you cannot be sure how long a person may not take to react. Shocks are inclined to be cumulative. His heart sank; he loathed his renewed complicity with the child's relations and wanted to leave their house. He heard Thomas agree with the quite disconcerted Anna that it might be well to telephone to Lilian's home.

But Lilian's mother said that Lilian was out with her father: quite certainly, Portia was not with them. 'Oh dear,' Lilian's mother said, with a touch of smugness, 'I'm so sorry. What a worry for you!' Anna at once hung up.

Then Thomas started, on a sustained note that soon became rather bullying: 'You know, Anna, no one but us would let a girl of that age run round London alone.' 'Oh, shut up, darling,' said Anna, 'don't be so upper class. At her age, girls are typists.' 'Well, she is not a typist; she's not likely to learn to be anything, here. Why don't we send Matchett to fetch her, in the afternoons?' 'We don't live quite on that scale: Matchett's rather too busy. One thing Portia can learn here is to look after herself.' 'Yes, in theory all that is excellent. But in the course of learning she might, perhaps, get run over.' 'Portia takes no chances: she's much too scared of the traffic.' 'How can you know what she's like when she's alone? Only the other evening, just outside here, I had to pull her back from right under a car.' 'That was because she suddenly saw me.' Anna with a bold and frightened little inflection, said: 'Well, do we start to ring up the hospitals?'

'Before that,' said Thomas, impervious, 'why not ring up Eddie?'

'Because, for one thing, he is never in. Also, why on earth should I?'

'Well, you quite often do. I grant that Eddie's not bright, but he might have some idea.' Thomas picked up the glass of sherry St Quentin had left poured out, and drank it. Then he said: 'After all, they are quite thick.'

'By all means let's try everything,' Anna said, with the perfect smoothness of ice. She dialled Eddie's number, and for some time waited. She had been right: he was out. She hung up again and said: 'What a help telephones are!'

'What other friends has she got?'

'I can't really think of any,' said Anna frowning. Taking a comb from her bag, she ran the comb through her hair – and this nonchalant action only proclaimed her utter lack of indifference. 'She ought to have friends,' she said. 'But we can do that for her?' Her eye travelled round the room. 'If you were not here, St Quentin, I could telephone you.'

'I'm afraid I should not be much help, even if I were not here ... I'm so sorry I can't think of anything to suggest.'

'Well, do try. You're a novelist, after all. What *do* people do? But, after all, Thomas, it isn't eight o'clock yet: it's not really so late.'

'Late for her,' said Thomas relentlessly. 'Late if there's never any place you do go.'

'Well, she may have gone to a movie. ...'

But Thomas, whose voice had become legal – obdurate, tough, tense – bore this down without considering it. 'Listen, Anna,' he said, 'has anything special happened? Had she been upset about anything?'

The sort of blind dropping over the others' faces made it clear that they were not prepared to say. The air immediately tightened, like the air of a court. Thomas cast a second look at St Quentin, wondering how he came to come in on this. Then, looking back at Anna, he saw that behind her face, with its non-committal half smile and dropped eyelids, Anna clearly believed she was alone. An individual deep guilty knowledge isolated her and St Quentin from each other – she did not even see St Quentin's fishy look; *she* had no idea he had anything on his mind. This split in the opposite party encouraged Thomas, who just allowed Anna to finish saying: 'I didn't see her this morning, as a matter of fact,' before, himself, going on saying: 'Because, of course, in that case she might just be staying out. It's a thing one's inclined to do.'

'Yes, you are,' agreed Anna. 'But Portia's almost unfairly considerate. However, how can one know what people might do?'

St Quentin, amiably putting down his glass, put in: 'She's quite a mystery to you, then?' Ignoring this, Anna said: 'Then, Thomas, you mean she may just be trying it on?'

'We all have our feelings,' he said, looking oddly at Anna.

St Quentin said: 'Possibly Portia really hasn't got much talent for home life.'

'What you both really mean', said Anna, from her end of the sofa, a handsome image, not turning a hair, 'is, that I am not nice to Portia? How little it takes to bring things to the top. No, it's all right, St Quentin: we're not having a scene.'

'My dear Anna, do if you want. The thing is, I don't feel I am being very much use. Unless I can be, hadn't I better go? If I can do anything later, I'll come back. If I go, I'll go back and sit by my telephone.'

'Goodness,' she said tartly, 'it's not such a crisis yet. It won't be even nearly a crisis for half an hour. Meanwhile, it's eight – the whole point is, are we to have dinner? Or don't we want to have dinner? I don't know, really: this sort of thing has never happened before.'

Neither St Quentin nor Thomas seemed to know how they felt, so Anna rang downstairs on the house telephone. 'We'll have dinner now,' she said. 'We won't wait for Miss Portia, she'll be a little late ... I'm sure that is best,' she said, 'there are no half measures. We either have dinner or telephone the police ... The best thing you can do, St Quentin, is, stay and support us – that is, if you're not dining anywhere else?'

'It would not be that,' said St Quentin, quite frankly at bay. 'But the point is, *is* there much point in my being here?'

'The point is, you're an old family friend.'

The evening became more gloomy and overcast. Clouds made a steely premature dusk, and made the trees out in the park metallic. Anna had had the candles lit for dinner, but, because it should still be light, the curtains were not drawn. The big shell of columbines on the table looked theatrical in a livid way: out there on the lake the people went on rowing. Phyllis served dinner to Thomas, Anna, St Quentin: no one looked at the time. Just after the duck came in, the dining-room telephone started ringing. They let it ring for some seconds while they looked at each other.

'I'll answer,' said Anna – but not moving yet.

Thomas said: 'No, I think I'd better go.'

'I could, if you'd both rather,' St Quentin said.

'No, nonsense, said Anna. 'Why shouldn't I? It may not even be anything at all.'

St Quentin steadily ate, his eyes fixed on his plate: Anna kept shifting her grip on the receiver. 'Hullo?' she said. 'Hullo? ... Oh, *hullo*, Major Brutt. ...'

'Well, he says she's there,' she said, sitting down again.

'Yes, I know, but *where*?' said Thomas. '*Where* does he say she is?'

'At his hotel,' said Anna, with no expression. 'That sort of hotel that he stays at, you know.' She held out her glass for some more wine and then said: 'Well, that is that, I suppose?'

'I suppose so,' said Thomas, looking out of the window. St Quentin said: 'Does he say what she's doing there?'

'Just being there. She turned up.'

'Now what, then?' Thomas said. 'I take it he's going to bring her home?'

'No,' said Anna, surprised. 'He wasn't suggesting that. He –'

'Then what *did* he want?'

'To know what we meant to do.'

'So you said?'

'You heard me – I said I'd ring up again.'

'To say – I mean, what are we meaning to do?'

'If I had known, I'd have told him, wouldn't I, Thomas dear?'

'Why on earth not tell him, just bring her straight round? The old bastard's not as busy as that. We could give him a drink or something. Or why not just let him put her into a taxi? What could be simpler?'

'It's not so simple as that.'

'I don't see why not. What are the complications? What in God's name *was* he chattering on about?'

Anna finished her wine, but after that only said: 'Well, it *could* be simpler, if you know what I mean.'

Thomas picked up his table napkin, wiped his mouth, glanced once across at St Quentin, then said: 'What you mean is, she won't come home?'

'She doesn't seem very keen to, just at the minute.'

'Why just at the minute? Do you mean she'll come later?'

'She is waiting to see whether we do the right thing.'

Thomas said nothing. He frowned, looked out of the window, and rapped his thumbs on the table each side of his plate. 'Then you mean, something *is* up?' he finally said.

'Major Brutt seemed to think so.'

'Damn his eyes,' Thomas said. 'Why can't he keep out of this? What is it, Anna? *Have* you any idea?'

'Yes, I must say I have. She thinks I read her diary.'

'Does she keep a diary?'

'Yes, she does. And I do.'

'Oh! Do you?' said Thomas. Having seemed not to think of this for some time, he began to rap with his thumbs again.

'Darling, must you do that? You make all the glasses jump – No, it's not at all odd: it's the sort of thing I do do. Her diary's very good – you see, she has got us taped. Could I not go on with a book all about ourselves? I don't say it has changed the course of my life, but it's given me a rather more disagreeable feeling about being alive – or, at least, about being me.'

'I can't see, all the same, why that should send her right off at the deep end. His hotel's right off in Kensington, isn't it? And why Brutt? Where does he come in?'

'He has sent her puzzles.'

'Still, even that could be something,' said St Quentin. 'Even that, I suppose, could be quite encouraging.'

'I've got housemaid's tricks,' Anna went on, 'and more spare time than a housemaid. All the same, I should like to know how she knew I'd been at her diary. I put it back where it lives; I don't leave finger marks: I should have seen if she'd tied a thread round it. Matchett cannot have told her, because I never touch it unless I know Matchett is out ... That's what puzzles me. I really should like to know.'

'Would you?' St Quentin said. 'Well, that's simple: I told her.' He looked at Anna rather critically, as though *she* had just said some distinctly doubtful thing. The pause, through which Thomas made his steady aloofness felt, was underlined by the swimming entrance of Phyllis, who changed the plates and brought in a strawberry *compote*. St Quentin, left face to face with what he had just said, stayed composedly smiling and looking down. Meanwhile: 'Oh, Phyllis,' said Anna, 'you might tell Matchett Miss Portia has rung up. She has been delayed; we're expecting her back later.'

'Yes, madam. Should cook keep her dinner hot?'

'No,' said Anna. 'She will have had dinner.' When Phyllis had gone, Anna picked her spoon up, looked at the strawberries, then said: 'Oh, did you really, St Quentin?'

'I suppose you want to know why?'

'No, I'd much rather not.'

'How like Portia – she took no interest, either. Of course, Portia had had a shock, too, and though I felt very much moved to tell her about myself, she was in no mood to listen. As I said to her in Marylebone High Street, how completely closed we are to one another ... But what *I* should like to know is, how do you know she knows?'

'Yes, by the way,' said Thomas, coming alive abruptly, 'how do you know she knows?'

'I quite see,' said Anna, slightly raising her voice, 'that whatever anyone else may have done – betray confidences, or run off to Major Brutt – it is *I* who have been to blame, from the very start. Well listen, St Quentin, listen, Thomas: Portia has not said a word about this to me. That would not be her way. No, she simply rang up Eddie, who rang me up to complain how unkind I'd been. That happened today. When did you tell her, St Quentin?'

'Last Wednesday. I so well remember, because –'

'— Very well. Since Wednesday, something else must have happened to bring all this to a head. On Saturday I did think she looked odd. She came in and found Eddie here at tea. Possibly he and she blew off in some way when they were down at Seale. Perhaps Eddie got a fright.'

'Yes, he's sensitive,' said St Quentin. 'Do you mind if I smoke?' Having lighted cigarettes for himself and Anna, he added: 'How I do hate Eddie.'

'Yes, so do I,' said Thomas.

'*Thomas* – you never said so!'

With a gigantic air of starting to ease himself, Thomas said: 'Yes, he is such a little rat. And his work's been so specious. Merrett wants to fire him.'

'You can't do that, Thomas: he'd starve. Why should Eddie starve simply because you don't like him?'

'Why should he not starve simply because you do? That principle seems to me the same throughout, and bad. Worse things happen to better people.'

'Besides,' St Quentin said gently, 'I don't think Eddie would starve. He'd turn up for meals here.'

'No, you can't do that, Thomas,' Anna wildly repeated, pulling her pearls round. 'If he is being slack, simply give him a good fright. But you can't sack him right out of the blue. You've got nothing against him, except being such a donkey.'

'Well, we can't afford donkeys at five pounds a week. When you asked me to put him in, you insisted he was so bright – which I must say he was, for the first week. Why did you say he was bright if you say he is such a donkey, and if he's such a donkey, why is he always here?'

Anna looked at St Quentin but did not look at Thomas. She left her pearls alone, ate a spoonful of *compote*, then said: 'Because he is running after her.'

'And you think that's a good thing?'

'I really could not tell you. After all, she's your sister. It was you who wanted to have her here. No, it's all right, St Quentin, we're not having a scene – If you didn't like it, Thomas, why didn't you say so? It seems to me we have talked about this before.'

'She seemed to know what was what, in her own way.'

'In fact, you wouldn't cope, but you always hoped I might.'

'Look, what did you mean just now about them blowing off at Seale? What business had he down there? Why couldn't he stay in London? Was that old fool Mrs Heccomb running a *rendezvous*?'

Anna went very white. She said: 'How dare you say that? She was my governess.'

'Oh, yes, I know,' said Thomas. 'But was she ever much of a chaperone?'

Anna paused, and looked at the candle-lit flowers. Then she asked St Quentin for one more cigarette, which he with the discreetest speed supplied. Then she returned and said very steadily: 'I'm afraid I don't quite understand you, Thomas. Am I to take it you don't trust Portia, then? It is you, I suppose, who should know if we're right to trust her or not. You knew your father: I really never did. I never saw any reason to spy on her.'

'Except by reading her diary.'

St Quentin, sitting with his back to the window, turned round and had a good look out. He said: 'It's getting pretty dark outside.'

'St Quentin means that he wishes he wasn't here.'

'Actually what I do mean, Anna, is, didn't you say you would telephone Major Brutt?'

'Yes, he'll be waiting, won't he? So, I suppose, will Portia.'

'Very well, then,' said Thomas, leaning back, 'what *are* we going to say?'

'We should have kept to the point.'

'We've kept a good deal too near it.'

'We must say something. He'll think us so very odd.'

'He's got every reason,' said Thomas, 'to think us odd already. You say, he says she'll come home if we do the right thing?'

'Do we know what the right thing is?'

'I suppose that's what we're deciding.'

'We shall know if we don't do it. It will be quite simple: Portia will simply stay there with Major Brutt. Oh, heaven keep me', said Anna, sighing, 'from insulting a young person again!

But it hasn't simply been me – you know, we are all in it. We know what we think we've done, but we still don't know what we did. What did she expect, and what is she expecting now? It's not simply a question of getting her home this evening; it's a question of all three going on living here … Yes, this is a situation. She's created it.'

'No, she's just acknowledged it. An entirely different thing. She has a point of view.'

'Well, so has everybody. From the outside we may seem worthless, but we are not worthless to ourselves. If one thought what everyone felt, one would go mad. It does not do to think of what people feel.'

'I'm afraid', St Quentin said, 'in this case we may have to. That is, if you are anxious to get her home. Her "right thing" is an absolute of some sort, and absolutes only exist in feeling. There they both are, waiting in Kensington. Really you will have to do something soon.'

'Even supposing one wanted to for a moment, how is one to know how anyone else feels?'

'Oh, come,' said St Quentin. 'In this case, none of us are so badly placed. I am a novelist; you, Anna, have read her diary; Thomas is her brother – they can't be *quite* unlike. However much we may hate to, there's no reason, now we have got to face it, why we should not see more or less what her position is – or, I mean more, see things from her position … May I go on, Anna?'

'Yes, do. But really we must decide. What are you doing, Thomas?'

'Drawing the curtains. People are looking in … Are we not to have any coffee?'

'St Quentin, wait till the coffees come.'

The coffee was brought. St Quentin, one elbow each side of his cup of coffee, continued slowly to rub his forehead. At last he said: 'I think you're jealous of her.'

'Does she know that? If not, it can't be called her position.'

'No, she's not properly conscious of enjoying everything you are so jealous of. She may not enjoy it herself. Her extraordinary wish to love –'

'– Oh, I'd never want *that* back –'

'Her extraordinary expectation that whatever offers offers to lead you somewhere. What she expects to get at we shall never know. She wanders around you and Thomas, detecting what there is not and noting clues in her diary. In a way, of course, she has struck unlucky here. If you were much nicer people, living in the country –'

'What proof have you', said Thomas, breaking in for the first time, 'that much nicer people do really exist?'

'Suppose that they did, and you were those much nicer people, you would not be bothered with her – what I mean is, you would not be so concerned. As it is, you are both unnaturally conscious of her: anybody would think she held the clue to the crime … Your mother, for instance, Thomas, must have been a nice person living in the country.'

'So, as a matter of fact, was my father, until he fell in love. All there is to nice easy people, St Quentin, is, that they are fairly impermeable. But not impermeable the whole way through. Yes, I know just the sort of people you've got in mind – you're a novelist and you've always lived in town – but my experience is that they've all got a breaking-point. And my conviction is that a thorough girl like Portia would be bound to come to it in them pretty soon. No, the fact is that nobody can afford to have a girl as thorough as that about.' Thomas refilled his glass with brandy and went on: 'I don't say we might not have kept the surface on things longer if we had lived in some place where we could give her a bicycle. But, even so, could she keep on bicycling round for ever? She'd be bound, sooner or later, to notice something was up. Anna and I live the only way we can, and it quite likely may not stand up to examination. Look at this conversation we're having now, for instance: it seems to me the apogee of bad taste. If we were nice easy people living in the country we should not for a moment tolerate you, St Quentin. In fact, we should detest intimacies, and no doubt we should be right. Oh, no doubt we should be a good deal jollier than we are. But we might not do Portia better in the long run. For one thing, we should make her feel pretty shady.'

'Which she is,' said Anna. 'Throwing herself at Eddie.'

'Well, what did you do, at not much more than her age?'

'Why always bring that up?'

'Why always have it in mind? ... No, she is growing up in such a preposterous world that it's quite natural that that little scab Eddie should seem as natural to her as anyone else. If you, Anna, and I had come up to scratch, she might not –'

'Yes, she always would. She wanted to pity him.'

'Victimized,' said St Quentin. 'She sees the victimized character. She sees one long set of attacks on him. She would never take account of the self-inflicted wrong – the chap who breaks his own arm to avoid going back to school, then says some big bully has done it for him; the chap who lashes himself to his bedroom chair so as not to have to go and cope with the burglar – oh, she'd think he was Prometheus. There's something so showy about desperation, it takes hard wits to see it's a grandiose form of funk. It takes nerve to make a fuss in a big way, and our Eddie certainly has got nerve. But it takes guts not to, and guts he hasn't got. If he had, he'd stop Anna having him on. Oh, he won't stop baying the moon while he's got someone to listen and Portia'll listen as long as anyone bays the moon.'

'How right you must be. All the same, you are so brutal. Does one really get far with brutality?'

'Clearly not,' said St Quentin. 'Look where we all three are. Utterly disabused, and yet we can't decide anything. This evening the pure in heart have simply got us on toast. And look at the fun she has – she lives in a world of heroes. Who are we to be sure they're as phony as we all think? If the world's really a stage, there must be some big parts. All she asks is to walk on at the same time. And how right she is really – failing the big character, better (at least, arguably) the big flop than the small neat man who has more or less come off. Not that there is, really, one neat unhaunted man. I swear that each of us keeps, battened down inside himself, a sort of lunatic giant – impossible socially, but full-scale – and that it's the knockings and batterings we sometimes hear in each other that keeps our intercourse from utter banality. Portia hears these the whole time; in fact she hears nothing else. Can we wonder she looks so goofy most of the time?'

'I suppose not. But how are we to get her home?'

St Quentin said: 'How would Thomas feel if he were his own sister?'

'I should feel I'd been born in a mare's nest. I should want to get out and stay out. At the same time, I should thank God I was a woman and did not have to put up one particular kind of show.'

'Yes,' Anna said, 'but that's only because you feel that being a man has run you in for so much. Your lack of gusto's your particular thing. If you were Portia, let off being a man, you would find something else to string yourself up about. But that's not what St Quentin is getting at. The point is, if you were Portia this evening, what would be the only thing you could bear to have us do?'

'Something quite obvious. Something with no fuss.'

'But my dear Thomas, in our relations with her nothing has ever seemed to be obvious. It's been trial and error right from the start.'

'Well, I should like to be called for and taken away by someone who would not make any high-class fuss. They could be as cross as they liked if they'd cut the analysis.' Thomas stopped and looked sternly at Anna. 'She's not fetched from places nearly enough,' he said. 'When she is fetched, who generally fetches her?'

'Matchett.'

'Matchett?' St Quentin said. 'You mean Matchett your housemaid? Are they on good terms?'

'Yes, they're on very good terms. When I am out for tea I hear they have tea together, and when they think I am out say good night. They say a good deal more – but what, I have no idea. Yes, I have though: they talk about the past.'

'The past?' said Thomas. 'What do you mean? Why?'

'Their great mutual past – your father, naturally.'

'What makes you think that?'

'Their being so knit up. They sometimes look like each other. What other subject – except of course, love – gives people that sort of obsessed look? Talk like that is one climax the whole time. It's a trance; it's a vice; it's a sort of complete world.

Portia may have defaulted lately because of Eddie. But Matchett will never let that drop; it's her *raison d'être*, apart from the furniture. And she is least likely of all to let it drop with Portia about the house. Portia's coming here was a consummation, you see.'

'Consummation my aunt. Has this really been going on? If I'd had any idea, I'd have fired Matchett at once.'

'You know quite well Matchett stays with the furniture. No, you inherited the whole bag of tricks. Matchett thinks the world of your father. Why shouldn't Portia hear about her father from someone who sees him as *someone*, not just as a poor ignominious old man?'

'I don't think you need say that.'

'I've never said it before ... Yes, St Quentin: it's Matchett she talks to chiefly.'

'Matchett – is that the woman with the big stony apron, who backs to the wall when I pass like a caryatid? She's generally on the stairs.'

'Yes, she's generally up and down ... Why not Matchett, after all?'

'It's "why not" now, then, not "why"? Well, how would you feel, Anna?'

'If I were Portia? Contempt for the pack of us, who muddled our own lives then stopped me from living mine. Boredom, oh such boredom, with a sort of secret society about nothing, keeping on making little signs to each other. Utter lack of desire to know what it was about. Wish that someone outside would blow a whistle and make the whole thing stop. Wish to have my own innings. Contempt for married people, keeping on playing up. Contempt for unmarried people, looking cautious and touchy. Frantic, frantic desire to be handled with feeling, and, at the same time, to be let alone. Wish to be asked how I felt, great wish to be taken for granted –'

'This is all quite new, Anna. How much is the diary, how much is you?'

Anna quieted down. She said: 'You said, if I were Portia. Naturally, that's impossible: she and I are hardly the same sex. Though she and I may wish to make a new start, we hardly

shall, I'm afraid. I shall always insult her; she will always per-
secute me ... Well then, it's decided, Thomas – we are to send
Matchett? Really, we might have thought of that before, without dragging all this up.'

'Decidedly we send Matchett. Don't you agree – St Quentin?'
'Oh, by all means –

> We'll send Matchett to fetch her away,
>   Fetch her away, fetch her away,
> We'll send Matchett to fetch her away,
>   On a cold and frosty –'

'St Quentin, for *heaven's sake* – !'
'Sorry, Anna. I felt quite outside myself. So glad this is all
arranged.'

'We've still got to think. What are we to tell Matchett? Which
of us is to ring up Major Brutt?'

'No one,' said Thomas quickly. 'This is a *coup* or nothing.
We don't talk; we do the obvious thing.'

Anna looked at Thomas: her forehead smoothed out slowly.
'Oh, all right,' she said. 'Then I'll tell her to get her hat.'

Matchett said: 'Yes, madam.' She stood waiting till Anna
turned back into the dining-room. Then she started heavily up
the silent staircase: by the time she came to the second landing
she was undoing her apron at the back. She stopped to open the
door of Portia's room and, in the dusk, take a quick look round.
Though the bed was turned down, the nightdress lying across it,
the room seemed to expect nobody back. An empty room gets
this look towards the end of an evening – as though the day had
died alone in here. Matchett, holding the unfastened straps of
her apron together in the small of her back with one hand,
switched on the electric fire. Standing up again, she took one
look out of the window: steel-green under the sky the tree tops
were in their order, the park was not shut yet. Matchett then
went on up, to her own room that no one saw but herself.

When she came down in her hat, her dark overcoat, still holding her black suède-finish gloves, with her morocco handbag
pressed to her ribs, Thomas was in the hall, holding the door
open. He was looking anxiously for her, up the stairs. A taxi

ticked outside so near the step that it seemed to be something in the hall.

'Here's your taxi,' Thomas said.

'Thank you, sir.'

'I'd better give you some money.'

'I carry all I shall need.'

'Then all right. Better get in.'

Matchett got into the taxi; she shut the door after herself. She sat upright, took one impassive look out of each window, then unfolded her gloves and started putting them on. Through the glass, she watched Thomas give some direction to the driver – then the taxi croaked into gear and lumbered off down the terrace.

Matchett not only buttoned her gloves but stroked the last wrinkle out of them. This occupied her to half way up Baker Street. *Then*, she electrically started, paused, one thumb over the other, and said, aloud: 'Well, to think ...' She looked anxiously through the glass at the driver's back. Then she put down her bag beside her, heaved herself forward and began to try to slide open the glass panel – but her gloved fingers only scrabbled on it. The driver twitched his head once or twice. Then the lights went against him; he pulled up, slid open the panel, and looked obligingly in. 'Ma'am?' he said.

'Here, do you know where you're to go to?'

'Where he just said, don't I?'

'Well, so long as you do know. But don't you come asking me. It's not my business. You've got to know your own way.'

'Ho, come,' said the driver, nettled. 'I didn't start this, did I?'

'None of that, young man. You mind your own business, which is to know what address the gentleman said.'

'Ho, so that's what you want to know? Why not ask me out straight?'

'Oh, *I* don't want to know. I just wanted to know you did.'

'Rightie-o, auntie,' said the driver. 'Then you chance it. Isn't life an adventure?'

Matchett sat back, not saying another word. She did not even attempt to shut the panel: the lights changed and they shot forward again. She picked up her bag from the seat, crossed her hands on it, and thereafter sat like an image. She did not even look at a clock, for she could do nothing about time. Crossing the great wasteful glare of Oxford Street, they took a cut through Mayfair. At corners, or when the taxi swerved, she put one hand out and stiffly balanced herself.

Inside her, her spirit balanced in her body, with a succession of harsh efforts, as her body balanced inside the taxi. When at moments she thought, she thought in words.

I don't know, I'm sure.

Mrs Thomas certainly never thought to mention, and I never thought to ask. Whatever came over me? All Mr Thomas said, when he put me in the taxi, was, did I need money outside of what I had. No, Mr Thomas didn't mention, either, taking it Mrs Thomas would be sure to have said. And there, you see, if I'd just left that door open I'd have heard what he said to the man. But I shut the door. Whatever came over me? No, I never thought to notice what he said to the man. And I wouldn't ask *him* right out, not after all that sauce. You don't know what drivers are. Not a nice class.

Oh well, it does seem queer. I ought to say to myself, well, things will get overlooked. What with all that hurry and that. The hotel was all she said, the hotel. But one of those might be anywhere. I can't but worry – oh, I am vexed with myself, not thinking to ask like that. How am I to know the place is the right place? He might stop and put me down anywhere, well knowing that not knowing I wouldn't know. I had no call to let on I didn't know. That did make me look wrong . . . Not one of the drivers off our stand.

And what do I say if they say, Oh no, Major Brutt's not *here*, or Oh no, we know no one of that name. How am I to say, none of that, now: this is the place I was told, this is where I've orders to wait. Oh, they could put me right out, now I don't know the address. Any little buttons could put me wrong. Oh, he might say to me, and as saucy as anything, but you've come to the wrong place.

Let alone they ought to have said, I should have had it in writing.

It was Mrs Thomas being all in a rush. She quite put me

about. If she was to be in a hurry, why did she not send down and give the order before? When Phyllis came down and said, Well, they've heard all right, but she's to be in late, I was only waiting to go and put on my hat. Phyllis said, they *are* talking away in there. They beat all, tonight, she said, it must be that Mr Miller.

If they was to talk less and make up their minds more. I've never seen Mrs Thomas in such a rush. She couldn't hardly wait till she'd got it said. It was as if she didn't half like to ask. Well, I'm used to taking her orders, I'm sure. Take a taxi both ways, she said, we've just sent for the taxi. She kept looking at me, for all she didn't quite look. At the same time, she spoke as if she was there to tell me to do some sort of a conjuring trick. Then how she did run back into that dining-room, yes, and shut the door. They were all in there.

Oh, Hyde Park, is it? . . . Well, I don't know, I'm sure.

I know I said to myself, as I went up for my hat, well now, there's *something* she hasn't said. It was in my mind while I got my hat. Then when I came down and there was Mr Thomas, I looked at him and said to myself, now, there's *something* I ought to ask. If I'd just have taken notice of what he said to the driver. But I was put about with my gloves to put on and all that hurry and that. It didn't come to mind not till we were in Baker Street. Then I said to myself, well, we're off to – and I stopped. Oh, I did feel queer. It all came over me.

Just fancy me just going off like that. Fancy me going off to where I've got no idea. Fancy going off just like an image. Fancy going off when you don't know the address.

Well, he does know, I suppose. I've no reason to think he doesn't. But fancy me depending on a fellow like him. Oh, they should have thought to have told me, one of them or the other. They did ought to have thought. Forgetfulness is one thing. But this isn't natural, really.

It puts me wrong. Why, there's not a thing I can say.

That's them all over. That's where they're different, really. That's where they're not like Mr Quayne.

Not like Mr Quayne. He would always think of a thing. He'd tell you, but he would say why. He wouldn't never put you in that sort of position, not with a taxi man. He wouldn't leave you to be put in the wrong. Oh, he was fair, he was fair in all that he did. For all there were many worse that would point him down.

Yes, and what would he think of *you*, out all over London at this time? No, it wasn't right of you, not to give me a turn like that. What would your father say, I should like to know? To start with, you never said you would not be back for your tea. I'd got a nice tea for you, I was keeping it. It wasn't till half past five that I thought to myself, oh well! She's with that Lilian, I thought, but she did ought to have said. So then I expected you round six. No, you did give me a turn. I couldn't hardly believe the clock. When I did hear the front door, it was nothing but Mr Thomas.

I couldn't believe the clock. It didn't seem like you, really. Not like what you was. Whatever's come over you? Oh, you have got a silly fit, these days. First one thing, then it's another. Stuffing nonsense under your pillow – I could have told you then. You'll do yourself no good. You're not like what you were. And when it's not that Eddie, it's those Heccombs, and this that and the other off at the seaside. You didn't ought to have gone to the seaside; it was there you came back from with that silly fit. You did ought to know better, after all what I told you. No good ever came of secrets – you look at your father. And you didn't ought to have gone to a gentleman's hotel.

South Kensington Station ... Well, I don't know, I'm sure.

Well, and did you get a good supper? Wholesome, was it? You never know at those places; they're out to make what they can. And that Major Brutt's just an innocent: he would never know. Him and his puzzles. However ... No, what I'm on about is, you staying out like this, you coming right off here, you giving me such a turn. No, it's high time you came out of this silly fit. You stay quiet, now, and remember what I said. I've got your fire on; it looks nice in your room now; and I've got those biscuits you like. You'd be all right if you'd only be like you were.

No, I'm not going on at you. No, I'm done now. I've said what I've said. Don't you be upset and silly. You come back with Matchett and be a good girl.

My, the hotels in this street! They're like needles in hay.

Now, what does he think he's up to? Oh, so we're stopping are we? Well, I don't know, I'm sure.

The driver, slowing into the kerb, looked boldly at her through the panel. He pulled up, then pottered round to open the door – but Matchett was out already standing and looking up. The sad gimcrack cliff of the hotel towered above her, with colourless daylight showing over the top. 'Well, ma'am,' said the driver, 'here's our little surprise.' With a movement of implacable dignity she drew herself up and read *The Karachi Hotel*. Her eyes travelled stonily down the portico to the glass door, the dull yellow brass knob, then down the steep steps blowsy from many feet. Not looking round, she said: 'Well, if you've brought me wrong, don't think you'll get your money. You can just drive right back and I'll speak to the gentleman.'

'Yes, and how'm I to know you'll be coming back out of here?'

'If I don't come out of here with a young lady, that'll be because you'll have brought me wrong.'

Matchett straightened her hat with both hands, gripped her bag more firmly, mounted the steps. Below the steps the grey road was all stucco and echoes – an occasional taxi, an occasional bus. Reflections of evening made unlit windows ghostly; lit lights showed drawing-rooms pallid and bare. In the Karachi Hotel drawing-room, someone played the piano uncertainly.

All the same, in the stretched mauve dusk of the street there was an intimation of summer coming – summer, intensifying everything with its heat and glare. In gardens outside London roses would burn on, with all else gone in the dusk. Fatigue but a sort of joy would open in all hearts, for summer is the height and fullness of living. Already the dust smelled strong. In this premature night of clouds the sky was warm, the buildings seemed to expand. The fingers on the piano halted, struck true notes, found their way to a chord.

Through the glass door, Matchett saw lights, chairs, pillars – but there was no buttons, no one. She thought: 'Well, what a place!' Ignoring the bell, because this place was public, she pushed on the brass knob with an air of authority.

MORE ABOUT PENGUINS, PELICANS,
AND PUFFINS

For further information about books available from Penguins please write to Dept EP, Penguin Books Ltd, Harmondsworth, Middlesex UB7 0DA.

In the U.S.A.: For a complete list of books available from Penguins in the United States write to Dept DG, Penguin Books, 299 Murray Hill Parkway, East Rutherford, New Jersey 07073.

In Canada: For a complete list of books available from Penguins in Canada write to Penguin Books Canada Limited, 2801 John Street, Markham, Ontario L3R 1B4.

In Australia: For a complete list of books available from Penguins in Australia write to the Marketing Department, Penguin Books Australia Ltd, P.O. Box 257, Ringwood, Victoria 3134.

In New Zealand: For a complete list of books available from Penguins in New Zealand write to the Marketing Department, Penguin Books (N.Z.) Ltd, Private Bag, Takapuna, Auckland 9.

In India: For a complete list of books available from Penguins in India write to Penguin Overseas Ltd, 706 Eros Apartments, 56 Nehru Place, New Delhi 110019.

Elizabeth Bowen in Penguins

A selection

EVA TROUT

Few writers can match the brilliance of Elizabeth Bowen's prose. And here the formal grace of her style, her flair for mischievous social comedy and the subtlety of her dialogue go into creating one of her most formidable – and moving – heroines.

'Resonant, beautiful and often very funny ... Eva is triumphantly real, a creation of great imaginative tenderness ... Elizabeth Bowen is a splendid artist, intelligent, generous and acutely aware, who has been telling her readers for many years that love is a necessity, and that its loss or absence is the greatest tragedy man knows' – Julian Webb in the *Financial Times*

'Rarely have I come across a novel in which sexual frustration (and sexuality) have been so richly and powerfully conveyed' – Roger Baker in *Books and Bookmen*

THE LITTLE GIRLS

In 1914 they had been eleven years old, three little girls at St Agatha's, a day school on the South Coast. Fifty years later, Dinah, beautiful as ever, advertises in the national newspapers to find the other two – Clare, now established with a successful business, and Sheila, a married woman, glossy, chic and correct.

In this brilliantly orchestrated novel, as subtle and compelling as a mystery story, Elizabeth Bowen asks: can friendship be taken up where it left off? What are the revelations – and the dangers – in summoning up childhood?

'There is that recurring shiver of delight ... for this story is poetic in its awareness, its stimulus, its beauty of writing; and as full of clues, hints and half-revealed secrets as any thriller' – *Scotsman*